HIDEOUT

HIDEOUT

AN ALICE VEGA NOVEL

LOUISA LUNA

DOUBLEDAY

NEW YORK

Copyright © 2022 by Louisa Luna

www.doubleday.com

DOUBLEDAY and the portrayal of an anchor with a dolphin are registered
trademarks of Penguin Random House LLC.

Front-of-jacket photograph © Olivia Bee / Trunk Archive
Jacket design by John A. Fontana

Library of Congress Cataloging-in-Publication Data
Names: Luna, Louisa, author.
Title: Hideout : an Alice Vega novel / Louisa Luna.
Description: First Edition. | New York : Doubleday, [2022] |
Series: An Alice Vega novel
Identifiers: LCCN 2021049253 | ISBN 9780385545532 (hardcover) |
ISBN 9780385545549 (ebook)
Subjects: GSAFD: Suspense fiction. | Mystery fiction.
Classification: LCC PS3612.U53 H53 2022 |
DDC 813/.6—dc23/eng/20211201
LC record available at https://lccn.loc.gov/2021049253

MANUFACTURED IN THE UNITED STATES OF AMERICA
1 3 5 7 9 10 8 6 4 2
First Edition

For my father,
author of the original Hideout,
who told us stories about the player who ran the other way

HIDEOUT

1

ZEB WILLIAMS KICKED THE TURF WITH THE TIP OF HIS CLEAT AND thought about what was underneath. The field used to be real green, but the school switched it to the Brillo Pad when Zeb got to UC Berkeley in '81. He thought that was lousy, since he'd mostly learned the game on grass. But he also had experience with dirt, mud, pavement. He'd gone down on a lot of sidewalks growing up, face smashed into the curb. The Italians would make fun of his bruises but shut right up when they saw how good he was with a ball. Soccer wasn't his thing; basketball sometimes, but what he was really good at was any game when he had to throw and catch across a field. He started playing football at Riordan in the city when the coaches discovered he could also kick. Even cross-country his freshman year. On top of the rest, it turned out he could run, too.

He took a deep breath in through his nose and wished the field was natural so he could smell it a little bit. Right then it would've made him feel like he was in the right place, about to kick an extra point.

"You ready, Two?" said Bear Thomas, the holder, jogging in place while the last seconds of the time-out ticked.

The joke on Bear was always "Hey, Bear, what would you do if your mama named you Bruin?" Or "Duck," or "Trojan." And then, when they really wanted to piss him off: "She should've named you Cardinal after all."

Now, though, no one was joking, and Bear was jacked up; Zeb watched him hit his palm against the side of his helmet, still dancing around in his spot.

Zeb raised his head about an inch but cast his eyes up higher, toward the stands, and suddenly he could hear all the people. Sixty-five thousand, they told him. That's what they were expecting. It always surprised him, the sound that that many people made. Most of the time, it was one continuous noise that hushed and rose to a shriek, over and over, like a fighter jet flying back and forth.

Carmen was up there somewhere. She seemed too refined for cheering. Although, since they started dating, she'd told him it was hard for her to watch the games because she got so nervous about the outcome. Apparently, she'd never cared that much before.

He smiled behind his face mask, thinking about her. He liked her because she was so honest. Other girls only talked about what they thought he wanted to hear: game stats; odds; recruiting news. Or they'd do their best not to care less, too preoccupied by modern dance or politics or whatever they studied. It would not have occurred to Carmen to pretend to be cool. She would be just fine in life.

Which brought him back: what was underneath the turf? He'd heard it was a thin layer of rubber below the Brillo. Below that, gravel. Below that, concrete. Below that, dirt. Below that, below that . . .

The time-out was done. Bear clapped his hands once.

"Go," he said to Zeb, then squatted, waiting for the snap.

Zeb nodded, glancing up at the board. 6–6. 4th quarter. 7 seconds. The Stanford kicker was already in the doghouse for missing his extra point, all the love from the fans dried up the second the ball sailed just past the left goalpost. Could be me, thought Zeb. Could be any of us at any time.

He shook out his hands and his feet and then kept a little bend in his knees, left foot in front of the right, torso leaning forward.

Buck Reinhart snapped the ball, and Bear caught it, set it upright, and held his right arm out like he always did, like he was balancing the ball with the power of his mind.

Zeb waited. On the clock it took less than a second, but time on the field was different. Sometimes he felt like it might be a new year out in the world by the time the game was finally over.

He stepped forward—left, right, left—but instead of kicking with his right, he leaned down all the way and grabbed the ball with one hand, gave Bear a shove with the other. Bear tumbled to the ground in shock.

Zeb looked down at the ball tucked nice and snug in his forearm, then back up at the clock. 4 seconds now. He didn't have much time at all.

He turned around and started to run, headed for Stanford's end zone.

He heard Bear yelling as he chased him; Bear had been a corner in high school, too, so he was fast, but not as fast as Zeb. He could see the Cal defense coming for him off the sidelines: Jimmy Moffat the tackle, Roger Swain the outside linebacker, flags falling at their feet. If they caught him they'd crush him—hitting the turf wasn't like hitting the grass. It would be Jasper Alley in the city all over again, with the Italians piled on top of him, all of them giddy with the game, laughing away how much it hurt.

His teammates weren't laughing. They were screaming his name, at first Roger Swain shouting, "Wrong way, Two, wrong way!" It had happened before, players getting disoriented after a sack and charging for the wrong end of the field, but when Zeb didn't stop or slow down, Roger and the rest seemed to realize this wasn't a mistake.

The sound from the crowd had taken on a sky-high pitch—to Zeb they sounded like the spaceship's laser from *War of the Worlds* when it fried up the priest. Only louder.

Thirty, twenty, ten.

Some of the Stanford band and cheerleaders stood scattered in the end zone, confused, sipping cans of beer, tossing pom-poms into the air carelessly.

Zeb spotted a narrow route between a cheerleader and a guy holding a trombone and accelerated, lighter with each step. That was one thing he could say for the turf—it didn't cling to the cleats like grass and dirt did, gave him a spring when he landed on the balls of his feet.

He barreled into the end zone, the screech of the crowd higher and louder than before, the refs' whistles shrieking. People began to jump down from the stands onto the field, dropping over the wall.

Zeb threw the ball backward over his shoulder, knowing it would be impossible for his teammates to resist catching it, like bridesmaids with a bouquet, even though the game was over now.

He pumped his arms, free of the ball, heading for the passage he'd scoped out, but then the trombone player moved, the hand slide sticking right into Zeb's path.

Zeb crashed into the musician's shoulder and knocked the instrument out of his hand but kept heading for the exit. He caught a whiff of a cheerleader's hairspray—strong, like rubbing alcohol. He heard the clash of his teammates against the band and the cheerleaders, the thumps of them hitting the ground. He didn't look back but imagined them all tangled, some laughing, others peeling themselves off the turf to keep up the chase.

Into the corridor, and instead of making a right to the locker room, he ran straight into the parking lot and slowed down for a few seconds to hop on one foot and then the other, pulling off his cleats and tossing them to the ground. He stripped off his jersey and threw it up in the air as he gained speed, heading for the edge of the lot, still hearing the collective shriek of the crowd. He thought about running to Piedmont Avenue, where he might be able to blend in with the kids, or running a little farther, to Carmen's sorority, to wait for her. He thought about running all the way to the interstate, figured it was about three miles. He thought about running across the Bay Bridge to the city, back to Jasper Alley, where he grew up, and maybe when he got there he'd get to see all the kids he grew up with, and maybe they wouldn't have changed at all, still ten or eleven or twelve years old, still cracking crude jokes and chugging Coke from the bottle, wrapping their old footballs with masking tape to stop the air leaks. Maybe they'd be right on the corner where he left them, and when he finally made it there, they'd see him running toward them and say, "Where ya been, Zeb?"

San Francisco was not Alice Vega's favorite town, on account of the weather. She preferred the heat straight up, never ran the a/c in her own house in the Sacramento Valley except during the most brutal of heat waves; otherwise, it was windows open. At home she typically walked around in yoga shorts and a tank top, but for work, every day, including today, she wore black—pants, shirt, jacket, boots. A Springfield pistol in a shoulder holster over the shirt, under the jacket. She'd worn the straps as tightly as she could stand it for so many years, just shy of cutting off circulation, that there was now an outline on her skin of the holster pocket, a collection of pink lines like an architect's sketch on her ribs, just south of her left breast.

Work brought her to a lot of places she didn't care for. She stood on the front steps of a big yellow house in Pacific Heights and pressed the doorbell, the glass front door wide behind a decorative iron frame. She heard the two-tone echo inside and figured it might be a minute. Lots of stairs. She turned around and looked at the street, empty and quiet for a Saturday. It was noon, fifty-five degrees, and the sun was out but muted, some wisps of fog hanging in the air.

A young tan man came to the door, bald with a black beard and glasses, wearing a mustard shirt and white pants that appeared over-sized and expensive. He opened the door; the glass hummed as it shook on the frame.

"Ms. Vega?" he said, tentative.

"Yes," said Vega. "Mr. Fohl?"

"No, no, I'm Samuel. The Fohls' assistant," he said, embarrassed to correct her. "Come in, please."

Vega stepped into a large hall roughly the size of her whole house. There was a black-and-white-checkered parquet floor, and an ornate carved wooden ceiling. A tiled wall fountain burbled quietly in the corner.

"It's Tiffany," said Samuel, catching Vega's gaze.

Vega nodded, accepting the information as she would a ticket from a parking-lot payment machine.

"This way, please," said Samuel, and led her to an adjoining room.

The ceiling was engraved wood in the new room as well, and there were two wine-red leather couches, not a crease on them, facing each other.

"What will you have to drink?" said Samuel, his hands clasped behind his back. "We have flat and sparkling water, or something stronger if you prefer."

"No, thanks," said Vega.

"Very good," said Samuel. "Anton is wrapping something up. He'll be with you shortly."

He left the room. Vega let her eyes travel along the edges of the windowpane. Outside, there was a bush of papery purple flowers clipped into the shape of a box.

She examined the room now. There was a dark wood sideboard the length of the entire wall opposite her, a white vase holding an arrangement of black lacquered sticks on top of it. Behind that stretched a long rectangular mirror, the top pitched at an angle so it leaned forward, almost as if it were put there to capture the full-body reflection of whoever was sitting on the couch. Vega saw herself in the glass, the crooked black sticks crossing the image of her face.

"Ms. Vega," said the man she'd come to see.

He rushed into the room, swung his arm back leading up to the handshake, as if to gain momentum. Vega stood and extended her hand, and their palms slapped together, so it was really more of a high-five. He held a folded sheet of paper in his other hand.

"Anton Fohl," he said. "I'm so sorry to keep you waiting. I was on one of those calls. . . ."

He trailed off and looked to Vega for approval, she guessed, expecting her to say, "Oh, it's no trouble," or "Please—just to sit in this delightfully appointed room has been pleasure enough," but he had not, of course, ever met Vega and therefore didn't know that she purposefully didn't partake in small talk unless she was trying to glean information from a person, much the way someone would pull and pick the meat from the delicate bones of a steamed fish.

"Please," he continued, gesturing for her to sit.

Vega sat, and Fohl sat on the opposite couch, so they were now about six or seven feet away from each other. Vega had not researched Fohl before meeting. She'd wanted to rely on her first impressions, and then piece the rest together later. Social media was great for that, but it was all through the filter of the screen through the filter of the author's engineering, which was two screens too many for Vega. She trusted her own eyes.

Fohl was handsome, in his fifties, with walnut-colored hair, the gray woven throughout with a white streak above each ear, so precisely placed it seemed to have been dyed that way. His eyes were a saturated blue-green and by far the most noticeable features on his face, save the lone boyish dimple in his left cheek, visible only when he smiled.

"Can we get you something to drink?" said Fohl, glancing at Samuel, who hovered in the doorway.

"No, thanks," said Vega.

"We're good, Samuel, thank you," said Fohl.

Samuel withdrew, and Fohl placed the sheet of paper on the

cushion next to him. He leaned forward and rested his knees on his elbows.

"You must have had quite a drive," he said. "Coming from where? Sacramento?"

"Not that far," said Vega. "A little south of there, though."

Fohl whistled, expressing gentle astonishment.

"Well, thank you for coming all this way to speak face-to-face," he said.

Vega smiled and then stopped, waited for more.

Fohl nodded rhythmically, like a bobble-head dog on a dashboard.

"I, uh," he said, then coughed into his fist. "This is not something I wanted to put in an e-mail. I wanted to speak in person, to meet you, first off, but also this is . . ." He paused and pursed his lips, as if conducting an executive search for the right word, but Vega had a feeling he already knew it. ". . . a different sort of case than you're used to."

He paused again—Vega presumed, to allow her time to digest the disclaimer, but she already had, and she thought that if Fohl knew about half the cases she took that didn't make press coverage, he might rethink his assumptions.

"Don't get me wrong," said Fohl, holding his hands in front of him as if to stop her from getting him wrong any further. "It's still a missing-person case. It's just that it's likely to be the biggest case of your career."

Fohl winced at the magnitude of his own words, but seemed excited by what he was planning to say.

"My wife, Carmen, went to Cal for undergrad—her father and grandfather went there, but my family and I, well, we went to Stanford, so you can imagine how it went the first time she brought me home to meet the parents."

He didn't laugh, but his eyes grew small as he smiled knowingly. When Vega didn't laugh along with him and just continued to stare, Fohl's smile shrank, the dimple flattening on the plane of his cheek. He seemed thrown off his topic but picked it back up after a moment.

"We met, she and I, in the fall of '85. Married three years later. Two beautiful daughters."

Fohl paused.

"Now you're thinking, Who's the missing person?" he said.

Vega still didn't speak but leaned forward and rested her elbows on her knees, mirroring Fohl's position.

Fohl clasped his hands together and let out a heavy breath.

"Before Carmen met me, she dated someone seriously, and he's the one I'd like you to find. And this," he said, holding up his index finger, "this is where it gets complicated." Fohl took another, even heartier breath than the one before. Then he delivered the name quickly: "It's Zeb Williams."

Vega watched as Fohl rubbed his palms on his knees. Fohl's expression was somewhere between a scowl and a grin. Then it turned to confusion.

"Zeb Williams," he repeated, in case Vega had suffered moderate hearing loss within the past few minutes. "The Cal kicker," he added, now with a forgiving sort of look, as if this new information was all Vega would need to jog her memory.

"Okay," said Vega. "When did you last see him?"

Fohl pressed his lips together, anxious.

"Nineteen eighty-four," he said. "November 17, 1984. It was the last time anyone saw him." He scratched his chin, said, "You really don't know who Zeb Williams the football player is?"

"No," Vega said, without hesitation or apology.

Fohl laughed and shook his head. "I'm sorry—it's just that I thought everyone did," he said.

Vega raised her hand, keeping her arm tight against her torso, like she was about to speak under oath.

"I don't," she said.

"Right," said Fohl, still stunned. "I'm just not sure quite where to start now."

His incomprehension seemed genuine, so Vega thought it best to help him out.

"Let's assume that I can find out what everyone knows from the Internet," she said. "Why don't you tell me what everyone doesn't know. Just what you know."

This made sense to Fohl. He nodded vigorously, relieved.

"They, my wife and Zeb, they met in a California natural-history class. Dated for two years," he said, another cough slipping into his fist. "She knew him very well, or thought she did, and was deeply hurt when he disappeared."

"He never contacted her after he left?" Vega asked.

"No," said Fohl.

Vega believed him. Still, there was a thing that didn't fit. A jangly gold lid for a too-small Mason jar.

"And you never met him personally," she said.

"No," said Fohl. "Only from what Carmen's told me, and, you know, what everyone knows from the media."

Vega paused, briefly peering at her reflection split by the black branches.

"This might be easier if I can ask your wife about him directly," she said.

Fohl scratched his knee. "She's not home right now," he said.

Vega let a moment pass before speaking. Then she said, "Happy to wait."

"Well, that's just it," said Fohl. "If I'm being up front with you." Another cough.

"She doesn't know I'm speaking with you right now," he said with a note of humility. "She doesn't know I'm trying to find Zeb." Then he sighed—he was growing wearier with each sentence—and said, his head bowing, "And I suppose you'd like to know why that is."

"Not really," said Vega.

Fohl lifted his head, startled. "Not really," he repeated. "Why not?"

"None of my business," said Vega. "If I take the job, you're the client, not your wife, unless you indicate otherwise."

"That's great," said Fohl, relieved. "I thought, I assumed, you would have to speak to her first."

"No," said Vega. "If there comes a time when I can't move the case forward unless I speak with her, then that will have to change."

"Of course," said Fohl. "Cross that bridge."

"Without her, it may take longer for me to get certain pieces of information, but I'll get them."

"I admire your confidence," said Fohl. "Seeing that many, *many* people have tried to find Zeb Williams and failed. For over thirty years."

Vega checked her reflection in the mirror on the wall, still behind the branches.

"They don't have my resources," she said.

"Which are?" said Fohl, suddenly haughty, as if he hadn't been the one who'd invited her there.

"By resources I mean my experience," said Vega. "And my specific skill set."

"Of course," said Fohl. "That's why I reached out to you. Because of your work on . . ." He lingered, searching for the words. ". . . specialty cases."

"If I were to take the case, you would have to pay the rate I set, and then, when I find him, you would have to pay a little more," she said.

"*When* you find him," said Fohl, clarifying.

"Yes," said Vega. "When."

"That's fine," said Fohl. "I'll pay whatever you think is fair. There is one more thing, a piece of information you should have."

Fohl unfolded the sheet of paper he'd been holding, leaned forward on the couch, and handed the paper to Vega.

It was a printed copy of a photograph, four people at an outdoor cafe: A woman with dark hair and eyes, wearing an apron. She appeared to be in conversation with two older men sitting at a table, one in a white suit, the other holding a cane. At a neighboring table was a younger man, gazing up at the woman.

"Carmen's father hired a private detective after Zeb disappeared. He traced him to a town in Oregon called Ilona. That picture, that's the last record of Zeb, you know, confirmed. There's been a lot of conjecture between then and now."

"Does anyone else have this picture?" asked Vega. "Would I be able to find it online?"

"No, that's from the PI. Carmen's father didn't like loose ends and had an unlimited amount of capital, you see."

Vega examined the photograph: the four people, their faces, their points of focus.

Fohl continued: "Her maiden name is Wirth."

The young man—Zeb Williams, apparently—stared at the dark-haired woman.

"My wife's," said Fohl. "Same family that owns Pacific Airlines."

Vega recognized that Fohl wanted her to acknowledge this, not to impress her but because he thought it was important, how rich his wife and her family were. Vega was not so sure it was important at all and had other ideas.

"Do you know who this is?" she said, pointing to the woman in the picture.

Fohl sat up even straighter, looking pleased. He took his phone out of his pants pocket.

"I do," he said, tapping the screen. "Cara Simms. Cara with a 'C.'"

"That was from him, your father-in-law's private detective?"

"Yeah."

"What about these other men?" said Vega, holding the paper up so Fohl could see it again.

"Nothing about them—all he found out was the name of the town and her name, Cara Simms."

Vega folded the paper back up into a rectangle.

"Do you have his name, the detective?"

"Died in the late nineties, unfortunately," said Fohl. Then he made a sad face that ranked about a five on the genuine scale.

Vega thought about that. She would have to go about this a different way. First, she would have to learn about football.

She stood, said, "I'll need forty-eight hours to think about it before I accept. If I do, I'll have some additional questions for you."

Fohl, taken aback, stood as well.

"Of course . . . Are you sure?"

"Yes. I'll call you the day after tomorrow," she said, shaking his hand firmly.

"Yes," said Fohl, concern grazing his face.

Vega didn't wait for his offer to show her out and headed toward the entryway. Fohl hurried and cut right in front of her as she reached the door. Vega took a small step back to let him in.

"This lock's a little tricky," he said, then turned a small gold bolt under the knob which did not seem tricky at all.

He opened the door, and Vega went outside, down the front steps.

"Thanks very much for making the trip," he said from the doorway.

"You're welcome," she said. "Speak with you in a couple of days."

She turned away from him and walked to her car, heard him say, "Yes," and then the sound of the heavy door rattling closed.

The fog had burned off completely by then, and Vega looked up at the sun before opening the car door and wondered how quickly she could get to SFO and get on a flight to New York, Newark, or Philadelphia. She knew it would probably end up being a red-eye, but it never bothered her to take night flights. She was not big on sleep.

The sun warmed her face. It was a nice bit of relief and surprise, getting the heat like that.

She couldn't really enjoy it, though. She missed someone.

The boiler made a sound like it was digesting prey. A cramp of a sound, which migrated from one side to the other for a count of ten, stopped, and then started again in the opposite direction.

Max Caplan stood side by side with his eighteen-year-old daughter, Nell, as they both stared at the thing uneasily.

"Well, that doesn't sound great," said Nell after a few minutes.

Cap ran his hand through the uncombed hair on the back of his head.

"Nope," he said. "No, it does not."

"Would explain why the heat keeps switching off in the middle of the night," added Nell.

Cap nodded. For the past week or so, he and Nell had woken up with numb noses and toes. He'd first assumed there was an army of determined mice chewing methodically through the insulation (which had happened a few years back), but then, after inspecting every corner of the attic with an LED flashlight and finding things intact, had finally considered the boiler.

"How long do boilers last?" said Nell, nibbling her black-painted fingernail.

"About fifteen years, I think," said Cap. "But that's what I don't get. We just got this one."

"Really?" said Nell. "Because I don't remember it getting here, which would imply it was purchased when I was too little to remember. Say, three years old?"

Cap thought about it. It certainly didn't feel like it had been fifteen years, but he recalled the old boiler, a different brand and make, which had come with the house, and then, when this one had arrived, his wife at the time, Jules, saying, "This goes against everything I stand for as a feminist who believes in upending gender stereotypes, but this new boiler has made me a real woman."

Then it all started to come back. He was still married to Jules when they got this boiler, so it was at least seven or eight years ago; they were still, in fact, happy, which turned the hands of the clock back even further. It could, he supposed, have easily been fifteen years. Before he was fired from the Denville Police Department, before the divorce, before he opened up shop as a private investigator.

Before Vega. BV.

"I guess that makes sense," he conceded. "I just can't believe it's been that long."

"Way back to the aughts, Old Man Caplan," said Nell, patting him on the back. "You going to help me with the bass, or what?"

Cap stared for another minute at the boiler, then inhaled sharply and turned to face his daughter.

"Yep. Then I guess I've got to make some calls."

"At least it's not that cold," said Nell, heading toward the stairs. "It's supposed to get up to fifty today, says my phone."

"Good thing global warming doesn't exist," said Cap, following her.

They came up to the ground floor of the house, a few degrees warmer than it had been in the basement. Nell walked toward her five-piece drum set on the floor near the front door.

"Neither does climate change, I hear," she said, taking a powder-blue puffer coat from a peg on the wall.

Cap smiled at his daughter. She was good. She was better than she had been. She'd been seeing a therapist biweekly now for almost a year and a half to work through the trauma of being held hostage during the first case Cap had worked with Alice Vega. And it was finally paying off. Nell had had a productive and fulfilling autumn, put her energy into playing music in a band with her friends and writing so eloquently about her harrowing experience that, along with her stellar GPA, varsity soccer, and volunteer history, she had secured early admission to an Ivy League school.

And, unlike in years past, Cap actually wasn't worried about paying his share. There would, of course, be loans, but work had been steady for him for some time now, since he had accepted a full-time position as chief investigator for Vera Quinn, Denville's resident public-interest lawyer.

Now, looking at his daughter, Cap realized he wasn't overwhelmed with guilt over having placed her in danger. She wasn't too thin, and was only a moderate amount of sullen. Just in the past couple of months, she seemed to have regained a bit of her old spark. He watched her as she zipped up her coat and checked her pockets for wallet, keys, phone. She squatted a little to pick up her snare and toms by their stands, and Cap saw the natural chestnut roots of her hair coming in behind the dyed black.

"Dad, what's wrong?" she said, noticing him not moving.

Cap felt overwhelmed, wasn't confident about speaking without choking on his words.

"Are you having an emotional moment?" she said kindly.

Cap nodded.

"Is it okay if we continue that tomorrow, and you help me with the bass right now?" she asked, just as kindly.

Cap laughed.

"Yeah, I'll hit 'pause.'"

Nell smiled and picked up the snare and toms and opened the front door. Cap bent over and grabbed the bass drum, not heavy but wide, and followed her out.

It was barely cold, the air wet but not crisp, the sky dull gray and looking more fit for rain than snow. Winter should look like winter, he thought bitterly.

Nell popped the trunk on her hatchback, and Cap pushed the bass inside; the back seat was already folded forward. He helped Nell stack the snare and toms and saw the cymbals positioned in the passenger seat so they'd make the least amount of noise possible at stop signs.

"Thanks, Dad," said Nell, shutting the hood.

"You got it, Bug. You staying the night at Carrie's?"

"Yeah, I think so," said Nell. "That okay with you?"

"'Course," he said, breathing through a pang in his stomach.

"I'll be back in the morning," she said. "I have some Euro to read, but we could go for a run if it's not raining?"

The pang left, as quick as it had come. He smiled with relief.

"I'll wait for you, then."

"It's a date," Nell said.

She walked around to the driver's side and got in. Cap started up the stairs to the house as Nell turned on the engine. She powered down the passenger-side window.

"What are you having for dinner?" she called to him over the cymbals.

"Leftovers," Cap shot back, without thinking.

Nell made a face. "Dad, there's, like, nothing in there. Can you order yourself something, please? We can go grocery shopping tomorrow."

Cap nodded, hoped it looked convincing.

"You're promising me you'll order food?" Nell said.

Cap held up three fingers. Scout's honor.

"Okay," she said, suspicious.

She fiddled with her phone, and ambient music blasted from the car's speakers. She powered up the window, the music now muffled. Then she waved once more, reversed fluidly out of the driveway, and was gone.

Cap watched the car turn the corner and hurried into the house. Shut the door, locked the two deadbolts. Checked the windows in the living room, which were locked. Then the downstairs bathroom windows. Then into his office to check the door and windows there.

Then upstairs to his room, the upstairs bathroom, then the small extra bedroom.

Then Nell's room, where she had the window open a crack. Cap shut it, putting an unnecessary amount of weight into pushing the frame down, and then locked it.

He went back downstairs and peered through the blinds in the front window. An unfamiliar burgundy minivan was parked across the street. No one inside. The pang returned to Cap's stomach, and he pressed it with his hand. Was it possible to empathize with a boiler? he thought. But, truthfully, he'd been having stomach pains for some time now, ever since he returned from his last case with Vega in California, five months before. So perhaps the boiler was empathizing with him.

He grabbed the remote from the couch and flipped on the TV,

turned to local news. Soon he would have a beer and call the people about the boiler. But, first, he went back to his office, to the top shelf of the closet, and pulled down the microvault, the small rectangular safe where he stored his Sig handgun. He tapped in the key code and heard the snap of the lock releasing, then opened the top of the case.

Cap picked up the Sig, then the loaded magazine, from their foam imprints, and slid the magazine into the gun.

This is how it was on the nights he was alone. Days were usually better.

Cap walked to the couch and sat, turned up the TV, placed his handgun on the table in front of him, and waited for the hours to pass.

On the red-eye, Vega did some reading. First she wanted the outline, and then she'd fill in the color, only searching for information about Zeb Williams before 1984. She read about how he grew up in the North Beach neighborhood of San Francisco, raised by his grandmother. Played football in high school, got a scholarship to UC Berkeley.

She looked at team pictures on fan sites, on the high school's alumni page, from old newspaper clippings, but they were all static: Zeb Williams kneeling in the front row or standing in the back, looking as young and dumb as everyone else. There was nothing to be discerned from his face flat on the screen.

Everyone had an opinion, but it all sounded like nonsense to her: this was why he was a great player; this was how he used to kick; it was the shape of his feet; what made him different was that he was so fast; it was because he could take a hit. Vega clicked all the windows closed. The commenters didn't know any more than she did. He was just a flat face on a screen to them, too.

"Please get me anything on Zeb Williams, kicker at Cal Berkeley 1981–1984," Vega emailed the Bastard, her dedicated freelance hacker.

Then she closed her laptop and looked out the window at the brightening sky and saw that the local time was almost 6:00 a.m.

He'd be up soon.

· · ·

Sunday morning, Cap woke up on the couch. Two empty cans on the coffee table, the TV still on but muted. His Sig was on his chest, and he had one hand on it.

He sat up and saw his breath. It was colder in the house than the day before, the boiler further along in its demise. Cap recalled talking to the technician the night before, the guy telling Cap he charged double on the weekends, so Cap had said to forget it, figured he and Nell could bundle up until Monday. Now he questioned the decision, rubbing his palm against the tip of his nose.

He squinted to see the time on the cable box—7:08 a.m.—and was relieved to realize that he'd slept until sunrise. Many nights, he woke at three or four only to lie awake until the birds chirped. Waking up when it was light out gave him a sense of normalcy, of everyday-ness, with which he only identified about half the time. He would take what he could get.

He stood, felt the elderly in his muscles (he hadn't run in two days, but the way his lower back and hips felt, it was like he'd just done a 5K barefoot on the sidewalk), and went to his office to put away the gun. Then he headed upstairs to take a shower.

After he returned to his office, he checked his e-mail and read a message from his boss, Vera, sending him contact information for a new client. He hit the print button, waited for the printer to warm up, and sent Nell a text: "You want to stay at Carrie's 1 more night? New boiler coming tomorrow." He tapped "send" and added, "❄ in here."

Nell sent him a crying-while-laughing face, then "U sure? At mom's tomorrow thru Wed."

Cap smiled at the phone. He knew Nell was perfectly fine spending any and all nights at friends' houses, but also knew that she was sensitive to Cap's and Jules's need to spend time with her, now more than ever, since she'd be off to college soon.

"Yes of course!" Cap wrote, then added another exclamation point to further express his support of the idea.

Just then the printer made a ratcheting sound. Cap set the phone down on his desk and reached to the shelf behind his chair where the printer sat. "Jam Tray 2," read the little screen. Cap made a small sound of disapproval, more out of habit than of actual frustration, pulled the tray out, and flattened the stack of paper inside. Usually, that was all it took. Not a jam; just a wrinkle.

Cap's phone buzzed once more, and he glanced at it, expecting another emoji from Nell.

But it wasn't that. It was a text from Alice Vega.

He felt all the air rush out of him, vacuum-style, as he picked up his phone and stared at the screen.

"Can you speak?" read the text.

Now or in general? Cap thought, allowing a small laugh to creep from his lips. She wanted to have a conversation. He hadn't spoken to her in almost five months, since they'd said goodbye outside the San Diego Police Department. They hadn't hugged. Their eyes had been heavy with exhaustion from the case they'd been working, and also from having been awake the entire night before in Cap's hotel-room bed.

More than that rushed send-off on the street, what stuck out in his mind most was the sun rising that morning, shining a column of light through the gap in the curtains, how he couldn't believe the night was already over as he kissed her face everywhere.

There hadn't been a lot of talking. I'm too old for this, Cap thought a number of times, not necessarily with regards to the physical activity. It had been the intensity that gave him pause, the emotion. He'd never had blood-pressure issues, but felt like his heart couldn't sustain it all—almost dying violent, messy deaths three times in as many days, and then Vega, her body and her voice and her mouth.

And, as physical as it was, it also wasn't—their bodies had been through so much, in so short a time, that kissing her softly in that stream of morning sunlight had had an otherworldly, elevated sort of feeling to it—and his body for once was light, ageless.

But then, when Cap had returned home, he'd crashed back to Earth, a bag of broken bones. He still lived inside the trauma of forced electroshock at the hands of a psycho, the red circle burn on his left temple a reminder every time he glanced in the rearview. He found that the only time he felt right was when he was around Nell, allowing himself to be diverted by her life, by his love and worry for her, or when he was running. Work was okay, but almost too boring to be a proper distraction.

Can he speak? Could he speak, was the question.

Unfortunately, there was no way to hack Vega, even if he did his best to shut out the memory of her face and hands and hair, but there was no use in trying to plan a step ahead of her. She was already there; she'd already planned a dozen moves ahead. It was just the way her head worked. Cap knew better than to call it a gift. It was not a thing that had been bestowed upon her by an unseen neuro-fairy. He'd guessed that some of it was innate—she had a good memory for numbers and names—but the rest of it she'd trained herself to do, during years of not sleeping or eating much and just thinking: thinking like the victim and thinking like the criminal.

"Hi," Cap sent back. Then, "Sure. Free now."

He tapped "send" and stared at the screen for three full minutes. No dots. No ringtone. No buzz.

Go about your business, he thought, which is the advice he would have given Nell. Do your thing. You do you. Don't be pathetic. He would not have said that last one to Nell, but felt totally cool about saying it to himself. He pulled the sheet of paper with the client's information from the printer and reviewed it.

He examined the phone screen once more, just to make sure Vega wasn't texting or calling at that very moment, and then dialed the client's number. He was immediately shooed into voice mail, so began his standard shtick:

"Hi, Mr. Ferad, this is Max Caplan, with Vera Quinn's office. I believe she let you know I'd be calling."

Then the doorbell rang, and he jumped from his chair and walked to the window, still talking: "I just have a few questions to ask you about your case."

He saw a few cars parked on the block: a beat-up Ford truck that belonged to his neighbor, a couple of generic sedans he didn't recognize, and then, down the block a little farther, the burgundy minivan from the day before. Cap pressed his head sideways against the glass, squinting, and stumbled over his last words of the message: "When, uh, you have a moment, please give me a call."

He left his number and tapped the red button to end the call, stuck the phone in his back pocket. He kept squinting, as if his eye might act as the lens of an endoscopic camera to curve around and see who was at the front door, even though he knew the only way to get a complete view was to look through the living-room window to the porch, where the guest would be able to see him as well.

It couldn't be, he thought.

He pulled away from the window and left his office, walked up to the front door, and didn't open it. Waited one more minute.

The doorbell rang again. Cap didn't jump this time but fought off a ripple of nausea. He shook his head—at himself or at her, he wasn't sure.

Then he opened the damn door.

He was thin. His face, narrow, and Vega couldn't make out any shape of his body in the sweatshirt and jeans. Still, it was him, his eyes, dark like the black coffee he drank on a normal morning, unless he was dead tired, when he would add cream and sugar because he needed the protein and the rush. Even his smile looked weaker.

"You're too thin," said Vega.

Cap laughed. "You sound like Nell," he said.

"Nell is observant."

He nodded. "You want to come in, Vega?" he said, holding the door open wide.

Vega went inside.

She took in the living room, her eyes scanning the furniture, the tan couch with a different blanket draped over the top (almost two years before, when she'd been there last, it was a multicolored afghan; now it was dark blue and lightweight and looked like something purchased at an airport for a long flight). She breathed deeply through her nose and smelled beer in the air, also felt cold air hitting her nostrils.

"Sorry about the chill," said Cap, shutting the door, standing behind her. "Boiler's busted. New one's coming tomorrow."

Vega turned around to face him. "Nell here?"

Cap shook his head. "At a friend's."

The way he said it, the way he shook his head, his shoulders hunched forward in a way Vega couldn't recall seeing before—it wasn't just that he had lost weight; he wasn't sleeping, either.

"You're tired," she said.

Cap sniffed out a laugh this time, pinched his nose with his thumb and finger as if it tickled him. Then he sighed. "Yeah, I'm tired, Vega. I don't sleep very well." He pointed at her with his chin. "You come all this way to tell me how shitty I look?"

Now Vega smelled something different in the air between them. It was aggression, and she could always sense it, from men especially, from a city block away. From a man she knew as well as she knew Cap, she could detect it in a syllable, a breath, a nod.

"No, I didn't," she said, and walked toward the kitchen.

She moved around the small table, placed her hand on the back of the chair she'd sat in two years ago, remembered eating spaghetti. She glanced in the small waste bin against the wall, lined with a blue recycling bag, saw two beer cans there.

"You want something to drink?" said Cap, heading to the cupboard over the sink. "I think Nell might have some tea in here."

"No, thanks."

Cap leaned against the counter now and stared at her. "You want to sit down?" he said, the annoyance creeping into his voice.

"I'm good," said Vega.

He laughed again; it wasn't forced, but it sure wasn't joyful.

"Well, what the hell do you want to talk about?" he said, voice rising. "I don't hear from you for five months, and then you show up."

"I haven't heard from you, either," Vega said quietly.

"Correct," said Cap; he pushed off the counter and started to pace. "You really can't tell me you don't know this about yourself, but sometimes you're a little difficult to communicate with, right?"

Vega didn't respond, let him talk it out.

"And I figured, if you wanted to talk to me, you would've talked to me. And you didn't. You let me think whatever I was going to think, let me spin this around in my head over and over."

He made circles in the air with his index finger.

"And then you're ready to talk, so here you are. So—talk, Vega."

He placed his hands on the back of the chair in front of him, lifted it an inch off the ground, and slammed it back down.

"Talk," he said again, firmer.

Vega sat down.

"You're angry," she said.

He gawked at her.

"Excellent work, detective," he said.

Vega ignored his tone and continued: "I don't think you're angry because I haven't called you. I think you're angry because I almost got you killed three times."

Cap seemed taken aback. He raised his shoulders in a middling shrug. "That was the way the case went," he said plainly. "We did the job."

"You wouldn't have worked the job if I hadn't brought you in."

"You didn't cuff me to your steering wheel," he said. "I could have bailed out at any time."

"No, you couldn't have."

"What?" said Cap, the earlier fury replaced by orneriness. "You would have stopped me?"

"No," said Vega. "I mean, you, Caplan, you've never not wrapped up a case in your whole life."

Cap paused. Vega watched him think about it, his face softening for less than a second, then reset to resentment. He sniffed and sneered, having a miniature argument with himself.

"I don't need your approval to be pissed off," he said. "So, if that's why you're here . . ." He trailed off and laughed. "Why are you here?"

Vega didn't speak right away. She could take his anger. She could take anything he had to give her. It didn't even set the tip of her nose out of place.

"I've been offered a case, and I wanted to know what you thought about it," she said.

Cap stared at her, dumbfounded. They were both silent for a moment.

Finally, Cap spoke: "And calling, e-mailing, texting—these methods didn't interest you?"

"No, not really," she said. "I need your opinion on this case, on whether or not I should take it, and I thought it would be easier for me to do that in person. You texted that you were free to speak. Is that still true?"

There was not a whiff of sarcasm in her voice.

Cap was momentarily disarmed.

"Yeah, it's still true," he said, massaging one side of his jaw with his thumb. "You came all this way. Might as well tell me."

Vega folded her hands on the table in a neat little knot. "I've been offered a substantial amount of money to find someone named Zeb Williams."

Cap stopped rubbing his jaw, and his eyes became large, the dark semicircles underneath disappearing.

"The football player," added Vega.

"Yeah, I know," said Cap. "Who wants you to find Zeb Williams?"

"A Silicon Valley guy named Anton Fohl, married to Williams's college sweetheart."

"The airline heiress, right?" Cap said.

"That's right," said Vega. "So who is he again—Zeb Williams?"

Cap laughed once more, but this was a laugh Vega remembered and associated with him, no longer with the shroud of bitterness from before. This was him being shocked by her, but delighted about it.

"Zeb Williams the Cal kicker?" he said, incredulous. "Number two? Wait a sec, here, Vega," he said, running his hands through his hair. "You mean to tell me you *don't* know who he is?"

"Not really."

"You're from California!" Cap shouted, still delighted. "How have you not heard of Wrong Way Williams?"

Vega shrugged a little, flipped her hands palm-up on the table as if to show she had no cards hidden.

"I don't really follow sports," she said.

Now Cap gave her a reproachful look. "Zeb Williams transcends sports," he said. "He was, like, a cultural phenomenon."

Vega shook her head, her mood lifted by seeing Cap so suddenly animated.

"Didn't you look him up?"

"Only the basics. Raised by his grandmother, scholarship to Cal," said Vega. "Disappeared in '84."

"Right, but you know how he disappeared? The conditions of his disappearance?"

"No, I thought you could tell me about it."

"All you have to do is google his name or 'Zeb's Run' or probably even 'The Run'—I can get my laptop," he said, pointing toward his office.

"Or you could just tell me about it," Vega said again.

"Okay," said Cap, a little invigorated by the challenge, his eyes scanning the room, as he pondered where to start. "Okay," he said again, sounding more definitive. "Every year, Cal and Stanford play a game—the Big Game, they call it, it's been going on for a hundred years or something, that's how long they've been rivals."

Vega flashed on Anton Fohl's cheery admission that his Stanford alumni family was less than thrilled he'd married a Cal girl.

"So—it's the fourth quarter. Game's tied. Five or six seconds to go. Cal's just scored a touchdown, so that means it's point-after time," Cap explained. "The extra point would put Cal ahead, right? So—five, six seconds on the clock—Williams is on the three-yard line. Usually, a kicker's pretty clear anywhere within thirty."

Vega gave a small nod.

"Snapper snaps," said Cap, throwing an imaginary ball backward between his legs. Then he jogged backward a couple of feet, playing another role. "Holder catches and sets the ball down right in front of Williams."

Cap crouched, his hand hovering about a foot off the ground. Then he stood upright and took one large step back, away from the kitchen table and the phantom ball. He took a small step forward and another to the left.

"He sets up like he's going to kick, right?" he said.

Vega continued to nod, even though she really had no idea what he was pantomiming. She had seen games on TV; sometimes her mother's second husband, TJ, would put them on; sometimes they'd be on in the background at her father's or brother's house when she visited, which was not often. At bars when she was on a job. Maybe she went to one in high school—she could not recall.

"And the holder has the ball for only a second, second and a half, so Zeb steps up like he's going to kick, and at the very last millisecond of that one-point-five, he doesn't kick."

Cap froze, letting the suspense build, hunched over with his hands on his knees. He gave Vega the side-eye.

"He shoves the holder, who's his teammate, right, and he swipes the ball . . ."

Cap stood with his arm curled into his chest.

". . . and Zeb Williams *runs the opposite way*," he said, drawing the words out, pointing into the living room. "Away from his team, away from where he's supposed to be, where he's supposed to kick the field goal."

Cap did a trot around the kitchen table, then began to circle the couch.

"Now, Williams was a decent kicker," he said. "But what no one counted on was that he'd been a runner before then—cross-country. He had the wind," Cap said, patting his chest.

"So he runs," Cap continued, heading toward the window. "At the forty, at the thirty, the whole Cal team's behind him, fans are going just batshit, jumping down the wall out of the stands." Cap gestured to the wall behind the TV, as if the fans were dropping down right then. "But no one can get near him, and he does it, he runs into the end zone where Stanford is supposed to score. So the ref signals a safety."

Cap reached his arms above his head and made a triangle, palms pressed against each other as if he were praying.

"Which is a punishment, like a penalty score awarded to the other team, so Stanford wins, eight–six. And Williams drops the ball and just keeps running, out of the stadium, knocking people over—reporters, cheerleaders, the trombone player—and people keep chasing him, but they all get clogged up, fans are running onto the field, and somehow Williams gets lost in the crowd."

Cap held out his hands, the magic trick complete.

"Poof."

He paused. Vega stared at him.

"No smart phones, see," Cap added, calmer now. "Later, they find the helmet and the jersey and the cleats in the parking lot. No Williams."

Cap turned his head and gazed out the window now, separating two blinds with his fingers. Vega did not think he was actually looking for Zeb Williams but didn't know what was out there instead.

"Then what?" she said.

Cap released the blinds and glanced back at her.

"No one ever finds him. Plenty of people look for him, call themselves the 2s, after his jersey number. He's like a folk hero, or Elvis or Bigfoot or something—every now and then someone will post a picture online. You wouldn't have to try too hard to find some Zeb Williams conspiracy theorists, you know, people who believe he's been abducted by aliens, something. . . ."

Cap let his thought taper off and walked back from the living room to the kitchen. He sat at the table opposite Vega and leaned back in the chair, crossed his arms. They stared at each other.

"You ever do any cold cases?" he asked her.

Vega leaned forward, her hands still folded in front of her.

"Not really," she said. "Dead skips don't settle bail."

"And he's not a minor in distress, either. So what is it that interests you about this case?" Cap asked.

"The money," said Vega.

"I didn't realize Alice Vega worried about such concerns," he said.

"I'm not worried," said Vega. "Every few cases I bank a lot of money, so I don't have to worry."

"Why does his ex-girlfriend's husband want to find him anyway?" Cap fired back, in full cop-mode.

"I don't know."

"You're just doing this one for the money," Cap said, clarifying.

"That's right."

"You came all this way for my opinion, correct?" said Cap. "On whether or not you should take this case?"

"Not exactly."

"So you lied before, when you said that's why you came here?"

"Yes."

They were silent. Vega's hands were cold, and she squeezed them together on the table, tried to keep the blood flowing.

"Then why did you come?" said Cap.

"I already decided to take the case," she said. "I came here to ask you to work on it with me."

Cap seemed tired again.

"I have a job here now," he said.

"You probably have vacation days," Vega countered.

Cap smiled. It was reserved, but it was still a smile.

"I have a Nell."

"She's a big girl," said Vega. "Turned eighteen in November, right?"

Now Cap laughed. "Yeah, that's right. She's eighteen."

"She going to school next year?"

"She sure is," said Cap. "Early admission to Princeton."

"Princeton," Vega repeated. "That's a big deal, right?"

"It is."

"Close, though. New Jersey's close?"

"About a two-hour drive, so, yeah, close."

"You're proud," Vega observed.

"Always," said Cap.

Cap's expression grew troubled as the thought of Nell appeared to dissolve.

"You don't need me. You could do this job with both hands and a foot tied behind your back. Look," he said, correcting himself. "I'm not convinced Zeb Williams can be found, period, but, hell, if anyone has a chance, it's you."

Vega wanted to blow hot air into her hands but didn't move.

"No shit," she said.

"Sorry?"

"No shit," she repeated, and when he kept staring at her, she continued: "I don't need you to come with me. I would like you to. I think you should. I think it will make you feel better."

Cap ran through it: texting Nell and Jules and Vera, throwing clothes and toiletries and the Sig into a suitcase, getting on a plane with Vega, chasing leads and interviewing witnesses. He knew that, even with a job that sounded as benign as this one did, it would still be with Vega, and she would wake up as Vega and go to sleep as Vega, and find a shit-ton of trouble in between.

Cap shut his eyes and felt an involuntary shudder pass through his shoulders. The fantasy was over. He used to have a habit of running his finger along his ear, the ridge that had been shot off during the first case he worked with Vega, but now sometimes he tapped the electroshock scar instead. What would it be next time? Would he gingerly rub the stump where his hand or foot used to be?

Cap opened his eyes.

"You sure you don't want some tea, Vega? Temp's going down in here, I think."

Vega shook her head. Usually, the problem was not knowing where to start, but right now, this time, she thought about how, when she started, there'd be no way she could finish. About how nothing had been the same for her, either, since they said goodbye in San Diego five months before, about how the scar tissue had mended over the knife wound in her side and looked not unlike a long tangle of fishing wire, about how that same wound might wake her up at odd hours pulsing like an artery, about how, after being awakened by the wound, she would not go back to sleep but inevitably let her thoughts snake and curl around the memory of Cap's teeth on her neck and chin and fingers, as if he were attempting to eat her up whole, like she was a blue-rare steak.

Finally, she blew warm breath into her hands. Cap was right: the temp was going down.

"Dude's long gone. No e-mail, no taxes, no Social," the Bastard had written. But he had sent Vega some more links and files and photos, all of which were available to the public online.

On the plane back to San Francisco, Vega skimmed it all on her laptop. Newspaper articles first. Pictures from the game: fans with faces painted blue and gold, the Cal offensive line, a cluster of bodies in the end zone, Zeb Williams in the dark jersey running and running. Then, afterward: The angry Cal mob; the elated Stanford fans. Weeks afterward, long-haired bikers on Harleys on the open road, activists arrested for protesting Reagan's Star Wars plan, fans at metal clubs on the Strip in Hollywood—all of them holding up two fingers, but not for peace, for Zeb Williams. Number two.

The 2s have posted pictures, too. Potential sightings: northern California, Oregon, Washington, up through Wyoming, over to Minnesota and Wisconsin. There he was on a motorcycle. There he was working in a feed-and-seed shop. Some of them looked real-ish to Vega, not altered or photoshopped.

But none as real as the photocopy that Fohl had given her, with Zeb in profile, gazing up at Cara Simms. Just that sliver of his face in a crummy printed reproduction of a picture was worth more than all the yearbook head-shots.

Vega sent an e-mail to the Bastard with Cara's name in the "subject" line and wrote in the body, "Can you please find her?"

Vega figured it was about an eight-hour drive to the town called Ilona, or a ninety-minute flight to Eugene and then a half-hour drive. When she landed at SFO, she wouldn't even have to leave the airport or the terminal; she could just find the new gate and get right back on a plane.

She closed her laptop and unfolded the paper again to look at the photo, the creases starting to fray. Someone, one of those three people, might still live in the area. At least one of them had to still be alive and might remember some details about Zeb Williams. And if Vega had to bet, she'd put her chip down on the dark-haired woman he couldn't look away from.

2

ILONA WAS ABOUT TWENTY-FIVE MILES SOUTH OF EUGENE, WHERE, Vega discovered, there were quite a few towns with female names: Dorena, Alma, Lorane. And Cara Simms still lived there.

Ilona was about five miles west from the I5, in the direction of the ocean. The Bastard had sent Vega some reading material gathered from tax records and local news: Cara Simms had been the proprietor of a coffee shop called only "Coffee Shop"; her father, Lester Simms, had owned the building and paid taxes on Coffee Shop for eleven years prior to Cara's sale of the property in February of 1985 to someone named Matthew Klimmer, who turned it into a diner.

The year after The Run, Vega thought. Maybe soon after the photo with Zeb Williams had been taken by the PI. The Bastard had turned up a home address as well as W-2's from Cascade High School, where Cara had been working as an English teacher for the past seventeen years. Vega didn't bother to check the school's Web site for what time the first bell rang; she figured that if she arrived on Cara Simms's doorstep by 6:00 a.m. and waited, she could probably catch her before she left for work.

Vega had spent the night in a motel near Eugene Airport. She'd left the window open and woken up to the sound of rain in trees. It was still raining now, the sun not quite up, the sky coated in a woolly gray.

Cara Simms's house was somewhat secluded, on a patch of grassy land that took up about a square acre, surrounded by woods. It was an A-frame, small and wooden and weather-beaten, paint stripped and chipped all over. A light was on upstairs, and one downstairs, too, so Vega figured someone must be awake. There was a single car in the driveway, a silver Honda hatchback. Also, a stained and splintered wooden swing set on the lawn.

Vega parked on the road and walked up the grassy slope toward the entrance. As she approached, she noticed two things: that the hatchback was sticker-new, not a scratch on it, with temporary plates, and also that there was a series of faded red blotches on the porch, directly in front of the front door.

There was a window in the door, a white lace curtain on the inside. Vega peered around the scalloped edges of the curtain but couldn't get a good look—maybe a table, maybe the staircase. Lights definitely on.

Vega knocked softly on the glass, and no one came. So she knocked a little louder; the window rattled in the pane. A woman came to the door and parted the curtains down the middle. Vega recognized her instantly as Cara Simms from the picture. She looked exactly like herself. Older, sure. Her hair not as long and now pulled back, dyed brown but gray at the roots. She wore a sleeveless blouse and jeans. Dark-brown eyes, tan skin, slender. She did not look happy to see Vega at all.

"Yes?" she said through the glass.

"Hi, Ms. Simms. My name is Alice Vega. I'm sorry to bother you so early—"

"What do you want?" said Cara Simms, enunciating every word.

"I'm looking for Zeb Williams."

Cara laughed a small, brittle laugh.

"I thought I'd seen the last of you," she said. "The 2s."

"I'm not a 2," said Vega, unoffended. "I find missing persons. I've been hired by a man named Anton Fohl."

Cara shrugged and shook her head. "Whoever that is, you can tell him he's a little late. I haven't seen Zeb Williams in over thirty years."

"I understand," said Vega. "I'm hoping I might be able to ask you a few questions about him, anyway."

Cara's frown aged her; her eyes were tiny black stones.

"Keep hoping," she said. "It's not going to happen."

Vega expected her to close the curtains and retreat, but she didn't. Instead she unlocked and opened the door.

"Who is this guy that hired you?" she said.

"Anton Fohl," said Vega. "From San Francisco. He's married to a woman named Carmen, maiden name Wirth."

Now Cara laughed heartily, throwing her head back a little. But it wasn't a happy sound.

"His ex wants to find him . . . now?" she said.

"Her husband does," said Vega. "I don't know what she wants."

"Zeb Williams was a guy I slept with a few times," Cara said, without much effort. "And that's it."

She slapped her palm on the door frame.

"You tell your boss and the princess that," she said. "What do they want with me, anyway?"

"This picture," said Vega, reaching into the inside pocket of her jacket and pulling out the printed photo. She pressed it against the screen door. "I wanted to ask you about it."

Cara's eyes raced over the image. Vega thought about how people who are shocked rarely look shocked. They look confused, as if a trick has been played on them.

"I have nothing to say," she said. "Please, leave."

The words were strong, but Vega noticed another thing. Cara's breathing had accelerated.

"You're trespassing on my property," said Cara. "Leave—now."

Her face was not full of rage, though it should have been. Vega got the distinct feeling that Cara was afraid, which would make sense under slightly different circumstances, but right now, at the moment, Vega did not think she herself was particularly scary. If you had never met Vega, you would think she was a petite to average-sized moderately attractive woman in her thirties dressed head to toe in black. She would, in fact, blend in almost anywhere. To her knowledge, she hadn't given Cara Simms a reason to be afraid of her, which meant, Vega figured, Cara Simms was afraid of something else.

"Okay, I will," said Vega, calm.

She began to turn around and cast her eyes down, to the porch. Then she stopped and stared at the red stains. Vega realized they weren't set in a random pattern, that they had been words, but she struggled to make out the exact letters.

Then Vega glanced to the gleaming silver car with the temporary plates again.

"Is everything all right, Ms. Simms?" said Vega.

Cara swallowed. "No, it's not all right. You're still here."

Vega reached into the inside pocket of her jacket again and pulled out a card. She held it up so Cara could see.

"I'm going to leave my card, in case you change your mind."

Vega squatted and placed the card right in the center of the stains, expecting to hear Cara say, "I won't." But she didn't. Vega stood up again and nodded. Cara stared at her and didn't move from the door.

Vega left, walked down the steps of the porch and down the incline, got into her car, and drove away, didn't look back. She guessed that Cara would stand at the door and watch her until her car was out of sight for good, because that was what you did when you were afraid, thought Vega: you peered out of windows, between the curtains, and watched and waited.

Vega imagined Cara opening the door and picking up Vega's card and examining it. Vega imagined her shoving it into her paper-recycling bin and then fishing it out and setting it down on her kitchen counter or nightstand or coffee table and coming home from work and maybe having a drink and saying to herself, Okay, maybe I do have something to say after all.

Vega decided she would stay at one of the roadside motels she'd seen just off the interstate and wait for a call. In the meantime, she would walk around downtown Ilona and see if she couldn't find out what had Cara Simms so scared.

Cap knew he couldn't stop Nell from doing what she wanted to do, but he could still try wielding the best tool he had, the one passed down in his family for generations, the one his mother sharpened every day just in case she might have to use it: guilt.

"You need to practice on a school night?" he said, once again wrangling the bass drum out the front door.

"We don't need to," said Nell, holding her snare drum. "We want to. It's a healthy and constructive way to expend the excess energy of adolescence."

Cap shrugged, unimpressed.

"You said before you were okay with it," said Nell, opening the trunk of the hatchback. "Are you really okay with it?"

Cap pushed the bass drum in. "I guess," he said, pouting a little.

"I'm not sleeping over," she said, sliding the snare on top of the bass. "I'll be back in three hours, tops. We could even eat late, if you want."

"It's a deal," said Cap. "You want Chinese?"

"Indian," said Nell. "Tandoori vegetables and the fried things, the pakoras." She kissed him on the cheek. "Just go, like, watch sports for a while and relax, Dad. You've been working all day."

It was true. He hadn't even taken off his coat or tie yet. He'd been interviewing Mr. Ferad and his co-workers about their former employer, and it was shaping up to be a straightforward case of the boss trying to squeeze more work out of employees than their contracts had specified. Cap predicted that Vera Quinn would make a phone call to the boss by the end of the week with her usual "We'd be happy to let a judge take a look at these contracts, but it might be easier for us just to come to an agreement amongst ourselves, don't you think?"

Done and done.

"Three hours," said Cap. "Not that I'll be watching the clock or anything."

Nell laughed. "Don't do that. Sports. No news," she said. "You don't need to get all depressed."

She got in the car and turned on the music—a chorus of women with an organ in the background.

"Bye, Dad!"

She reversed out of the driveway, a little too fast for Cap's taste, K-turned onto the street, and then was off, to the corner and gone.

Cap went inside, took off his coat, and hung it on a hook by the door. As he headed upstairs to his room to change, he noticed how warm it was on the second floor, where the bedrooms were, the new boiler doing its job.

He took off his tie, shirt, pants. Put on jeans and the Dodgers sweatshirt, and just sat on the bed for a minute. He pinched a bit of material on the sweatshirt and lifted it to his nose, to see if it smelled like Vega at all.

Cap had still not told Nell that Vega had even been there; he didn't quite know why. Maybe it was that he didn't want to hear one of her possible reprimands—"Why didn't you go with her? You totally *do* have vacation days!" or worse—"She came all this way to see you, and you still didn't tell her how you feel about her?!"

They had hugged at the front door. Even now he wasn't sure who'd leaned in first; it had just happened naturally. It was not a long, clinging, possible-precursor-to-an-accidental-kiss sort of hug. It was quick but intense, both of them squeezing; Cap had been worried that Vega's head was at a weird angle on his shoulder and that the muscles in her neck would cramp, so he'd pulled away first.

"Bye, Caplan," she'd said. Her expression looked pained but nothing too bad, like she was reading subtitles in a language she didn't understand.

"Bye, Vega."

Then she'd left. Off to find Zeb Williams.

Now Cap second-guessed himself again. But the longer he sat there on the bed, the more he realized he shouldn't. He was tired. Head-and-body tired. And he couldn't imagine a future when that wouldn't be the case.

Then a yellow note taped to the mirror behind his dresser caught his eye. It had not been there this morning. He stood up and went to it, Nell's handwriting becoming clearer as he approached. He smiled as he read it: "Watch some sports!" Then, beneath the words, a little happy face. Two dots and a curve.

Cap thought he'd get back at her. He flipped the note over, grabbed the pen from the top of his dresser, and wrote, "Reminder: Spend more time with Old Man Caplan before he goes to the Nursing Home!!!" He chuckled, imagining her response, her eye roll and shout from her room, "Hilarious, Dad!"

He walked out of his room and into hers. Nell always left her door open, trusted Cap not to root around in her desk or dresser drawers, which he'd never done, never had to do. He taped the note to the mirror behind her dresser and laughed again, pleased with himself. As he reread the note, something in the mirror's reflection stood out to him. He thought his eyes might be playing a trick, which was possible, he told himself. The muted shine from Nell's green desk lamp was the only light source; most of the room was murky, the January sun down for at least an hour already.

He turned and walked slowly toward Nell's bed, as if the object might scurry away if he moved too fast. He squatted and saw that it was exactly what he'd thought it was on the floor next to the bed: the bass-drum beater, about a foot long, stainless steel, with a head shaped like a doctor's reflex hammer except with a flat face so it would make the most contact with the drum. Cap remembered Nell showing it to him when she bought it, saying it was exactly the type she wanted: "More contact, more rock." Hard to play the bass without the beater.

Cap's mind flooded with the worst—she's doing drugs, getting drunk and driving, messing around with a twenty-five-year-old junior-high graduate who just lost his job at the Sub-Stop in the mall food court.

Then he picked up the beater and scolded himself: She just forgot it. She'll come right back when she realizes. In fact, he thought, if he checked his phone, she'd probably already texted him to ask if she left it under her bed.

Cap left the room, jogged down the stairs and to his coat on the rack, dug his phone out of the pocket and looked at the screen. No texts from Nell or anyone else. He checked his voice mails, missed calls, emails. Nothing. He began writing a text to her: "You forgot your bass beater. It is here." But he paused before he hit the arrow to send. She might still be driving, after all, and he didn't want her to be distracted.

This might have been what he told himself as he deleted the message, watching letter by letter disappear. But that was not the real reason, of course. He wanted to wait until she realized she'd left the beater behind.

He went to the living room and turned on ESPN, as instructed. He sat on the couch with his phone and the beater next to him, his eyes creeping over to the screen of the phone every few seconds, waiting for the text to come through. One hour, then two. Finally, a text from Nell arrived: "Heading home! Did u order food yet??" Smiling-face-with-teeth emoji.

Cap stared at the screen, expecting more to come. It didn't.

"Will do now," he texted back. "See u soon."

Then he went back upstairs and placed the beater exactly where he had found it on the floor next to her bed. And when Nell came through the door at 9:00 p.m., he smiled and waved to her from the couch as if everything was perfectly fine.

. . .

It wasn't much of a town, Vega found out soon enough. She turned off the GPS and drove down roads that were paved and dirt and gravel, backed up when she hit dead ends, pulled over and got out and walked in the woods, all the time the rain never stopping, just thinning out here and there. The trees were tall and seemed to curve when Vega looked up, as if the crowns were pressed against the roof of a snow globe. There were mountains, too: a row of green hills on one side, and a snow-capped on the other, farther away. Sometimes she saw another car on the road, but not too often. She stopped at a fruit stand on the side of the road and bought a pear, paused for a few minutes in the middle of a muddy road to let a family of four turkeys cross.

She found a grid of blocks with stores and businesses, a few people walking and driving. Downtown, she guessed. She drove slowly and then saw a familiar thing—the coffee shop from the PI's picture of Zeb Williams. Except now it appeared to be two separate businesses: a restaurant, the sign on the awning reading "Ilona Diner," and, next to it, a liquor store.

Vega parked, got out, and crossed the street to the diner, unconcerned about finding a crosswalk. She didn't go inside, just stood at the railing bordering the outdoor seating section, where there was no one sitting currently. Vega peered through a diamond-shaped window into the diner, saw two people at the counter, two people at a booth. She placed her hands on the railing and examined the tables, looked at the chair where Zeb Williams had sat. She doubted it was the same chair, but this was the place.

She left the diner, running one finger along the railing until it ended. She passed a few more businesses: a pharmacy, a bar, a store that appeared to sell only sweaters, an antiques shop. Vega paused at the window of the last and stared at the sign: "Collectibles, Games, Sports Paraphernalia." She went inside.

The bell jingled above the door. The space was small, cluttered with an assortment of unrelated items: lamps, rugs, picture frames, suitcases, clocks with broken hands. Figurines with chipped noses, little cars, and matted stuffed animals. Though Vega didn't know anything about this particular industry, she thought everything looked like it could be sold at a garage sale for nickels.

A man emerged from a curtained doorway behind a glass display case in the back of the store. He was in his sixties, with gray hair and glasses, wearing a denim shirt and jeans. He was chewing on something.

"Help you find something?" he said, and covered his mouth with his fist while he finished swallowing.

"The sign said, 'Sports Paraphernalia,'" said Vega, pointing to the door with her thumb behind her, over her shoulder.

"Yeah, we have a few items," said the man. "Any sport you looking for specifically?"

"Football."

"Football," the man repeated, glancing around the room. "Not sure we have much in the way of football at the moment."

He looked down, into the case.

"Oh, here's something for you," he said, tapping on the glass.

Vega approached the counter and looked down. There were some baseball cards on a black velvet board, also some coins.

"Over here," he said, pointing to two ticket stubs in the corner. "A ticket from the '98 Super Bowl and one from the '99. Broncos won both. If you're interested, I could give you both for a hundred fifty dollars."

Vega examined the stubs, then let her eyes wander to the baseball cards.

"What about college football?" she asked.

"You know, I don't think I have anything," said the man. "This stuff comes in waves. One season I'll have all college, the next all pro. Sometimes more baseball, sometimes NBA. Right now I have mostly baseball. If you're interested in any equipment, I just got some really fun pieces."

"Maybe," said Vega, still scrutinizing the cards. "How long has this store been around?"

"Since '92," said the man. "You passing through?"

"Yeah, visiting a friend," said Vega. "Were you in town when Zeb Williams was here?"

The man made a tsk-ing sound with his teeth. "I lived over in Bend at the time," he said.

Vega could sense him bristling, resisting the urge to say another thing.

"Personally, I never understood those people," Vega said quietly, keeping her eyes cast down on the baseball cards. "The 2s."

"Fools," said the man. "I say, hey, live and let live, you know? I don't judge. But you ask me, I think Zeb Williams was the start of college ball going downhill."

Vega let her eyes wander to the wall behind him and saw a long shelf, where there were baseballs frozen in plastic cubes and mitts displayed on wooden spools.

"I hear you," she said. "Quite a thing he did."

"That's just it," said the man. "He pulls that stunt for no reason, just because he could, just because he felt like it. Made the game into a circus. He took away the integrity of it that day. Then it all became about the money anyway."

"Always does," said Vega. Then she pointed at a thin bat, also on the long shelf. "Is that a fungo?"

"It surely is," said the man. "I like a gal knows her baseball terms. Would you like to see it?"

"Sure."

The man turned around, pulled a stepladder off a hook on the wall, and unfolded it. He climbed up to the top step and lifted the small bat off the shelf, came back down, and handed it to Vega with two hands, like it was a sword.

"So this bat was used for training by our own Hillsboro Hops—where'd you say you were from?"

"California," said Vega, tightening her grip around the handle.

"All right, then," said the man, as if this made good sense to him. "The Hops are a Minor League team here. The coach a few years back preferred the aluminum bat to the wood. Don't understand that myself, but maybe my palms just aren't sweaty enough."

He laughed, and Vega did as well—only a little bit, to encourage him.

"What's it weigh, you think?" said Vega.

"Twenty-two ounces or so."

"So you never met him?" she said.

"Who's that—Williams?" said the man. "No, like I said, I was over in Bend."

"That's right," said Vega. "Know anyone who did?"

"Who met him? I think a lot of folks. Not a big town, you know."

Vega held the fungo by the knob with her right hand, at her side. With her left, she pulled the paper picture from her pocket and unfolded it.

"You know any of these people?" she asked, holding it up. "Besides Zeb?"

He leaned forward, squinted.

"Hard to say," he said. "The woman, she looks like Cara Simms, used to own the diner—it was a coffee shop back then. Makes some sense. I heard they were an item."

"Right," she said. "What about the men? Either of them familiar to you?"

"The one in white I know from somewhere," he said, waving a finger at the picture. "Maybe I've seen him around. The other one, no." He looked away then. "So you *are* a fan of his?"

"No," said Vega. "Asking for a friend."

The man nodded, seemed a little vexed but too polite to air it.

Vega tucked the picture into her pocket and took a step back, gripped the handle of the fungo with both hands, and swung it once lightly. Then again, stronger and faster.

"That's a nice swing," said the man. "But these are just for practice hits, right?"

"Right," said Vega. "How much?"

The man thought about it, looked sideways at Vega and the bat.

"How's fifty?" he said, as if he were expecting an argument. "On account of it being a collector's item."

Vega took out her wallet and removed some bills, placed them on top of the case.

"No change," she said.

"You sure?" said the man.

"Yeah," said Vega. "Consider it a donation."

"Most generous of you," he said. "Name's Kent, by the way. Kent Gable."

"Alice Vega."

"Nice to meet you," he said. "Hope you stop by again before you leave town."

"Hope so, Kent."

She had turned to leave when he said, "You know, you might want to ask Red Peller about that picture. He's been here forever."

"Know where I can find him?"

"Peller Hardware, down the road. Can't miss it."

She said thanks and then left, resting the barrel of the bat on her shoulder. It had a strangely comforting feeling to her, like it was supposed to be there.

The day moved into afternoon, and the showers had let up. Vega left the bat in the trunk of her car and walked around town some more.

She went to the Ilona Diner, ate a scrambled egg, and drank a cup of tea, sitting at the counter. The waitress was young and didn't seem too interested in being a waitress. She stood by the register and played around with her phone while Vega ate.

When Vega was done, she stood and followed the pointing-hand sign to the restroom. It was a single room, unisex, with a toilet in a stall and a urinal next to the sink. While Vega washed her hands, she noticed something in the mirror—graffiti on the wall behind her. The words were red: "liberty pure."

She left the restroom and went back to the counter, where the waitress was still tapping away at her phone.

"Excuse me," said Vega.

The girl looked up, struggling hard not to be annoyed. She wore a white tee shirt and white cutoffs with a black apron. Her lips were shiny with a clear gloss.

"Do you want more hot water?" she said, moving toward the coffee brewer. Then she stopped walking and said gravely, "I have to charge you if you want another tea bag."

"I don't need another tea bag," said Vega. "Or water. Just wanted to let you know there's some graffiti in your bathroom. Says 'Liberty Pure.'"

A look came over the girl's face that Vega couldn't quite discern.

"Oh yeah. We know," she said. "That paint's really hard to get off. It, like, stains everything."

Vega nodded.

"So what is that—Liberty Pure?" said Vega. "Are they a band?"

"No, they're, like, you know, a gang," said the waitress, sounding surprised that Vega didn't know.

"Yeah?" said Vega, sitting down on the stool again. "What kind of gang?"

The girl looked a little uncertain now. "You know, a gang," she said again, quieter, barely moving her lips as she spoke the word.

"Okay," said Vega. "They live here? In Ilona?"

"Around," the girl said, blushing suddenly.

Vega wiggled the fingers on her right hand, playing pretend piano; just pull the thread, she thought.

"They give you any trouble?" said Vega. "Besides tagging the bathroom?"

"No," the girl said right away.

She hurried back to the register and grabbed her phone.

"So, look, if you don't want anything else, excuse me, okay?"

The girl disappeared through a swinging blue door into the kitchen. There was someone else in there—the cook, Vega imagined, though she couldn't see anyone on the other side of the pass-through window.

"Okay," said Vega, when the girl was well out of earshot.

Vega put some money on the counter along with her business card, set a salt shaker on top of both, and left.

Vega found Peller Family Hardware two blocks south of the diner.

When she went inside, the smell of sawdust and turpentine hit her nose. The store was bigger than the antiques shop and more organized. Vega walked through an aisle of industrial-strength cleaning supplies, rodent and insect traps. She came to the counter, where there was tall man around sixty. He passed a big cardboard box to a teenage boy with a crew cut and pink semicircles under his eyes.

"Howdy," the older man said to Vega, nice and friendly. "Can we help you?"

"Yeah," said Vega. "You got any paint?"

"Sure do. What kind of paint you looking for?" he asked. Then he said to the boy, "Put that downstairs—aisle three, back shelf."

The boy left through a doorway, and the man focused on Vega again.

"We have outdoor and indoor, but not a big selection," he warned. "We can special-order any color you want, though."

"I'm looking for red spray paint," said Vega.

The man thought about this, seemed troubled.

"You bet. My guy'll have to take a look downstairs. We only keep white and black up here. How many cans you need?"

"As many as you have," said Vega.

"Gotcha," said the man, up to the challenge.

He picked up the receiver of a phone attached to the wall and pressed some buttons.

"Hey, could you bring up cans of red spray paint, however many we got? Should be bottom shelf, aisle five."

The man paused but didn't hang up; he was listening.

"Could you take a look, please? I know I haven't thrown out any expireds."

The man paused again, then said tersely, "Thank you," and hung up. He smiled at Vega, lifted a box from the floor to the counter, and began to slice it open with a box cutter from his back pocket.

"So you doing some car touch-ups?" he asked.

"Maybe," said Vega.

"You might need factory-matched paint," he said, making a note of the box's contents on a pad next to the register. "What color's your vehicle?"

"Hard to describe," said Vega. "But I'll know it when I see it."

The boy came through the doorway carrying half a dozen cans in his arms. He unloaded them onto the counter clumsily; one can rolled off and dropped to the floor with a clang. Vega saw right away that all of them had blue lids, not red.

"Riley," said the man, exasperated. "I said red."

Riley bent down to grab the fallen can and stood back up, stared at the others.

"We're all out of red," he said.

The man huffed.

"Hell we are," he muttered. "Excuse me," he said to Vega and disappeared through the door.

The boy, Riley, was doing his very best not to look Vega in the eye, or at any part of her, really. He lined up the blue spray-paint cans in a neat little row and then peered inside the box the man had left on the counter.

Vega took a step closer. Riley still didn't look at her, removed a fistful of Styrofoam bits from the box, and turned to the garbage can. Vega folded her arms and leaned on the counter, like she was requesting a song at a piano bar. Riley gave her one glance and then averted his gaze.

"Riley, right?" she said.

Riley gave a jerk of his head in affirmation.

"My name's Vega," she said.

Riley grabbed two more handfuls of Styrofoam, dropped them into the trash. Vega just watched him, staring right at his face. Didn't say a word.

"There's a Walmart in Eugene you could go to," he suggested.

"Why would I want to do that?"

"To, you know, get the paint," said the boy, his eyes coasting back and forth along the counter, still far from Vega's line of sight.

"Oh yeah," said Vega. "That's a good idea, Riley. You seem like a pretty smart kid," she said, leaning forward. "Unfortunately, you can't just be smart these days, you have to watch your back, too. Just the kind of world we live in, I guess," she said, wistful. "And I've only been in Ilona a few hours, but it seems like that kind of town."

Riley froze, stopped scooping Styrofoam.

"You from the paper?" he said.

That landed on Vega a certain way. Most people, when they realized she knew something they didn't want her to know, or at least knew she was in the ballpark, would ask if she was a cop, not a reporter.

"Nope," said Vega. "I'm from California."

Just then the man returned, holding a clipboard. "It's the damnedest thing," he said to Vega. "I don't understand how we're out, but we're out."

"Strange," said Vega. "Hey, you're Red, is that right?"

"Yes, ma'am." Friendly surprise. "We met?"

"No, I got your name from Kent, over at the antiques shop. My name's Alice Vega."

They shook hands, and then he said, "I'll place an order today for the cans, probably get them in a couple of days. You could swing back then if you like."

"That's great, thanks, but I actually have an unrelated question for you."

She pulled the picture from her pocket and unfolded it.

"Kent said you might know who these people are," she said, tapping her finger on the image of the man in the white suit and the man with the cane.

Red reared his head back so he could focus, and a puzzled smile emerged.

"That Zeb Williams?" he said.

"It is," said Vega. "Did you know him when he was here?"

"I didn't know who he was until he was gone. Hadn't realized he'd been the kid washing dishes at the coffee shop."

"You happen to remember how long he stayed in town?"

Red blew air out in a quiet whistle.

"Not long. Couple three months, maybe," he suggested, then squinted at the picture again. "That's Cara Simms, there. And that's Dart," he said, pointing to the man in white.

"Dart?" said Vega.

"Yeah, he's lived here since the seventies, used to be an actor on a TV show out in Los Angeles. Quite a character. Now, I'm not sure . . ." said Red, digging around in his brain. "I think I heard a rumor he was in a, what do you call it, a mental sort of a facility at one point? He doesn't get out much anymore, though. I haven't seen him for a few years now."

"He still lives in town?"

"Far as I know, he's still in the trailer camp, near the I-PUD."

"I-PUD?"

"Sorry, Ilona Public Utility Department. When you come down into town from the interstate, instead of a left, you go right, and there's the I-PUD, and I believe he lives in one of the trailers up there. I remember seeing him with Zeb back then. Heard they used to shoot fruit on the old Fenton farm."

"What about the other guy?" said Vega, tapping the image of the man with the cane.

Red squinted at it, shook his head. "Don't recognize that one," he said. Then he shifted his gaze from the picture back to Vega. "You're not the first, you know, come looking for Zeb Williams."

"That's what I hear."

"Good luck with it."

"Thanks for your help," she said to him. Then she shifted her attention to the boy: "Thanks, Riley."

Riley nodded again, staring at the box.

"You know what? On second thought, I'll take a couple cans of that blue. Just in case, right?"

Red smiled, a little confused but happy to make a sale. Vega paid for the paint and turned around, walked down the same aisle she'd taken when she came in, her eyes drawn to the rodent traps. Professional pest management, the boxes boasted. Eliminates on contact, clean disposal. All you had to do was add the bait.

Vega found the local newspaper online. *The South Oregon Gazette*, it was called. Vega sat in her car for a while and read some articles on her phone. She used the search term "Zeb Williams," and nothing came back. Then she tried "Liberty Pure" and got eight hits, all stories from the fall about the local chapter of a white-nationalist group vandalizing homes and businesses with spray paint or, in one case, breaking a window.

The most recent article was dated November 1, and then nothing more about Liberty Pure. Vega clicked on the name of the writer of all eight stories, Beatrice Dauley, and scanned the titles of her stories after November 1. Pumpkin patches closing because of early frost. Alternatives to turkey for Thanksgiving. Where to pick and cut your own Christmas tree.

Vega scrolled to find the contact information at the bottom of the page and saw the address was a PO box. She wrote a quick note to the Bastard and waited. Maybe Beatrice Dauley had other things to share besides holiday tips.

Vega parked on a dirt road and walked up to the house, a double-wide next to a river. There was a long wooden trough perpendicular to the house with green vines and tomatoes growing inside. No cars parked in front.

She stepped up to the small porch and knocked on the front door. A small set of wind chimes hung from the roof of the porch and rang a few high notes. Vega waited a minute, then knocked again. Still no answer. Vega turned around and leaned over the railing of the porch.

The sky was bright, the sun still muted by a blanket of clouds. The air had a sweet wet smell that Vega had come to associate with the trees here. She heard the water in the river shushing, some birds peeping and squeaking.

She waited about an hour. Then a blue van came into view and took a right at Vega's car on the road; it pulled up and stopped about twenty feet from the house, next to the vegetable trough. Vega recognized Beatrice Dauley as the driver, having seen her small square head-shot embedded in the articles online: ashy-blond hair, thick glasses. There were three dogs in the back seat.

Beatrice cut the engine and got out of the car right away, panic and anger spreading over her face.

"Who are you?" she demanded, unable to hide the tremor in her voice.

"My name's Alice Vega," Vega said, stepping down from the porch. "I'm a private investigator. Hoping you have a moment to answer a couple of questions, Ms. Dauley."

The dogs filed out of the car, each one scruffier and scrappier than the last. One of them had three legs. Not exactly the best candidates for guard dogs, Vega thought.

"What is this about?" said Beatrice.

"I find missing persons," said Vega. "I've been hired to find Zeb Williams. I know you've written for the Gazette for a long time and thought you might be able to offer some insight."

Beatrice paused, blinked.

"Zeb Williams," she repeated. "That's going back a ways."

"Yes, ma'am, I realize," said Vega.

"I was in high school when that all happened," said Beatrice. "I don't think I have any information you wouldn't be able to find online."

"You'd be surprised," said Vega. "You may know more than you think you do."

Beatrice thought about it. Vega could tell she was resistant but no longer afraid, which was helpful.

"Do you have any ID I could look at?" Beatrice said. Calm and professional.

"Sure."

Vega took out her wallet, removed her driver's license and PI union license card and handed them both to Beatrice, who straightened her glasses and examined the cards.

She looked at Vega and then again at the cards, checking to make sure the face matched the picture, and handed the cards back to Vega. "I only have a few minutes," she said.

"Anything you can spare."

Beatrice went up the stairs and through the door, held it open for Vega to enter.

The room was long and open—a living room, dining area, and kitchen combined—with light oak-colored cabinets and floors. There were about two dozen boxes stacked along the wall, labeled in black marker: "Kitchen," "Bedroom," "Living Room." The place smelled like wet fur and cigarette smoke.

Two of the dogs, including the three-legged guy, circled Beatrice's legs, sniffing and licking. The third one—a bulky pit or bulldog mix, Vega guessed—settled onto a round plush pet-pillow.

Vega followed Beatrice and the other two dogs into the kitchen area and watched Beatrice toss her purse onto a rectangular island in the middle of the room.

"I have to feed them," said Beatrice, opening a cupboard under the sink. She pulled out two cans of wet food and set them on the island. "You have pets?" she said as she snapped a can opener onto the first can.

The dogs began to yip and jump onto Beatrice's legs. Vega shot a glance over to the big girl on the dog bed, who looked in the direction of the sound but wasn't compelled to do anything about it just yet. Beatrice twisted the lever on the opener.

"No," said Vega.

Beatrice nodded as if this was information she'd already guessed. Then she pulled a box of cigarettes from the breast pocket of her flannel shirt and shook it, pulled a cigarette from the top with her lips, and lit it with a Bic from the same pocket.

"Smoke?" she said.

"Sure."

Beatrice slid the pack to Vega and handed her the lighter.

Beatrice walked to the corner of the kitchen, and the two dogs followed her, tails up. She scooped the food from the can into two silver bowls on the floor, and the dogs got to work. She picked up a third bowl, this one green, and brought it back to the island.

"Zeb Williams?" she said.

"That's right," said Vega.

"You know he hasn't been seen around these parts since the eighties."

"That's what I hear."

"So . . ." said Beatrice, flipping her hand over like a game-show hostess presenting a prize. "What brings you here, then?"

"I came to talk to Cara Simms."

"Cara Simms," Beatrice repeated, blowing out smoke. "Why's that, now?"

"Do you know her?" asked Vega.

"Not personally," said Beatrice, cranking open the second can. "But I've seen her. Know people who know her. Friends of friends."

"You know any reason why she might be a target for harassment?"

Beatrice's eyebrows arched just a bit. Skeptical, thought Vega. Most likely because Beatrice had conducted a few interviews herself and knew what it felt like to ask the questions.

Beatrice pointed her cigarette at Vega and said, "You're here to find Zeb Williams, but it sounds like you're more interested in Cara Simms. Now, why would that be?"

Vega paused, tapped her cigarette on the edge of the ashtray, and said, "She's really my only lead at the moment. Her and an older guy named Dart."

Beatrice thought about this, narrowed her eyes down to slivers.

"How'd you find me, anyway?" she said, suspicious.

Vega took a chance. She had a feeling her discussion with Beatrice Dauley would prove more productive if Vega told her the truth.

"I have a guy," said Vega. "He's good with addresses."

"Too bad he can't find Zeb Williams for you."

"It is too bad."

The two women stared at each other, neither speaking for at least a minute. Men usually started in with the threats just after the thirty-second mark; they just didn't have the patience for a good long stare.

"You're right," Vega conceded. "I am interested in Cara Simms."

"Why?"

"I think her property was vandalized by some kids in a gang called Liberty Pure. I think they probably did something to her car, too, so she had to get a new one." Vega tapped her fingers on the surface of the island, then continued: "I think maybe if I can speak to these boys I can convince them to leave Cara Simms alone, and then maybe she'll be more likely to return the favor, tell me what I need to know."

"What does she do for a living now?" said Beatrice, spooning the contents of the can into the green bowl.

"She teaches English at Cascade High School."

Beatrice laughed through her nose. Then she picked up the green bowl with the food and brought it to the big girl on the pillow. She set it down in front of her head, and the dog's tail whipped against the cushion, though she didn't make a move for the food.

"You didn't come here to ask me about Zeb Williams," said Beatrice, returning to the island. "You read my stuff about Liberty Pure."

"That's right," said Vega. "You wrote a lot of articles about them, and then stopped."

Beatrice flinched, squinting.

"The *Gazette*'s not a big operation," she began. "There's only three of us total. We all work from home. We're not in it for the money, either. I make my living doing freelance copywriting for medical journals."

She shook her head and rolled her eyes.

"I wanted to cover life in our small town in the current climate, as it were. How things have changed, how they've stayed the same, et cetera. So, about a year ago, we, everyone in town, start seeing the graffiti tags for Liberty Pure. I make some calls, neighboring towns—they're popping up there, too.

"I do a little research, find out about the white-nationalist bent, and so I take it right to the sheriff. Guy named Fenton. He says thanks, he'll keep an eye out. Then I start publishing articles."

"Fenton?" said Vega. "Does he own a farm?"

Beatrice shook her head, confused.

"Not Sheriff Fenton, I don't think, but his family might have owned property a while back."

Vega nodded, said, "You started publishing articles."

Beatrice seemed to run out of breath for a second. She took a long drag and shook her head again, the movement so slight it was almost imperceptible.

"Right, I publish some articles. And these kids, these boys, from what I can tell, are just out of high school. Or early twenties. They egg my house, slit the tires on my car. I ignore it. Keep putting out articles. Then . . ."

She took a breath but nothing on her face changed.

"I had another dog. She was eleven, but wasn't sick. She just started throwing up and wouldn't stop."

She looked toward the dog on the pillow, who'd just begun to eat her meal.

"I stopped writing articles. Left the place I was renting and moved here three months ago. Tried to stay under the radar."

"Has it worked?" said Vega.

"So far," said Beatrice, shrugging.

Vega gave her a nod. "Did you report what happened to your dog?"

"To the sheriff? Sure," she said, the bitterness plain. "He said animals eat all kinds of things. Sometimes they get sick."

"You think maybe these kids had Cara Simms as a teacher?" Vega asked.

Beatrice shook free from her moment of grief. She cleared her throat. "Maybe. Maybe they have some acolytes still in high school and she pissed one of them off. Not that they need a reason. Here's the thing— Wait, where are you from?"

"California. Sacramento Valley."

"Okay, you may or may not know this about this area, but it's white. Real white. You would not think that white nationalists or alts would find much to be upset about around here, but they do, because they're also just asshole kids. So whoever they feel is against them, they're going to harass," said Beatrice, clearly having thought it through before. "Cara Simms, maybe she cut one of them off in a parking lot, maybe she gave one of them an F on a book report— who knows? Point is, law enforcement's useless."

"Why is that?" said Vega.

"Couple reasons," said Beatrice. "Sheriff Fenton has a son, Derek, who graduated high school two or three years ago and seems like a likely candidate for a hate group. Kid's best friend is a guy named Neil Klimmer."

"Klimmer," said Vega, remembering. "He bought the coffee shop from Cara Simms."

"His father, Matt, did, but, yes, same family," said Beatrice, impressed. "There's not much to own in Ilona, but Matt Klimmer has the monopoly on most of it—businesses downtown and land on the outskirts.

"I did a little research when I was writing the articles, checked out some Reddit groups, even got a good lead, someone who acted a lot like a recruiter would for that kind of thing. Looking for teenagers to indoctrinate."

A phone rang, and Beatrice grabbed her purse from the island and dug through it.

"Sorry," she said, when she had pulled out her phone and checked the screen. "Nothing." She stuck the phone back in her purse, and continued: "I had this idea I'd pose as a millennial, try to get something out of this guy, see if there's anything bigger beyond the spray paint. And, if I'd gotten that far, see if I could connect him to the kids in Ilona."

She paused and took a short drag; the tobacco was almost down to the filter.

"Then my dog died, and that was it."

She stamped out the cigarette and seemed done with talking.

"You were saying," said Vega. "The second reason the sheriff's useless."

"Right," said Beatrice, remembering. "That would be because he's a rat-fucking racist pig himself, so maybe he doesn't mind a little local white-boy terrorism."

Vega smiled, appreciating the honesty. And the anger. It made her feel right at home.

3

VEGA STOPPED AT HER MOTEL ROOM AND SEARCHED FOR "LIBERTY Pure" on Reddit, which came up empty. Then she did another search for "Liberty," and over five thousand posts came back. Next she cleared the search bar and did a filter search for any posts relating to southern Oregon and freedom of speech, and found a subgroup titled "america4americans." She read post after post, unsure of what exactly she was looking for. The discourse was what she expected: Ping-Pong volleys between the dabblers ("i'm just not interested in the nanny state feeding me by the tit anymore"), the cheerleaders ("Finally someone has the b*llz to post an unbiased view"), and the true believers ("preserve usa for our children"). Back and forth.

Then she checked the notes on her phone for the screen name of the potential recruiter Beatrice Dauley had given her and typed it into the search bar: "crinklecut94." A couple hundred posts. Vega began to skim. In some of them, crinklecut directed specific posters to a meet-up page, along with some white-pride language that almost sounded like a self-help book: "It's about pride, not prejudice—learn how not to be ashamed of yourself." If people in law enforcement or a district attorney's office were gathering information after a crime had been committed, for example, they'd be hard-pressed to point to crinklecut's posts as evidence that he'd been recruiting off the board.

Then she wrote an e-mail to the Bastard: "(1) Any way to ID Reddit users by screen name? Looking for 'crinklecut94.' Also info about same. (2) Other direction: users are Neil Klimmer and Derek Fenton—can you find screen names? Any info on them, too. (3) Can you find list of properties/businesses owned by Matthew Klimmer?"

Then she shut her laptop and left the motel, went downtown to find the sheriff.

Vega had passed the Ilona sheriff's office earlier in the day without realizing it. The building was a crumbling brick two-story with no signage, looked like it belonged in Frontierland, except an amusement park couldn't fake the rise and plunge of the mountains in the distance behind it. There was one white cruiser parked in front, which hadn't been there before—Vega was pretty certain she would have noticed the sheriff logo on the car door if it had been.

Vega parked next to the cruiser. She got out and walked up the two concrete steps to the front door, pushed the horizontal bar under the pane of glass with "Ilona County Sheriff" printed in faded gold lettering, and went inside.

It was a small office, just one main room. Close to the front door was a long folding table with a sign-in sheet on a clipboard and some other papers. Behind the table were six desks in pairs of two, set up head to head. There was one guy who sat at a desk—late twenties, tan short-sleeved uniform.

"Howdy," said the guy at the desk, standing up. "What can I do for you?"

"I'm looking for Sheriff Fenton."

The guy walked away from the desks toward the folding table, not in a hurry.

"Sheriff's tied up," he said. "I'm the deputy here. I can help you."

"I'd like to schedule a meeting with the sheriff," said Vega. "If he's tied up now, I can come back later."

Vega did a brief intake: Name plate on left breast pocket read "Rutledge," small razor cut above the lip, uniform pressed sloppily along the pant seam line. More wrinkles in the clothes than in the face. His hair was short and flat on top and looked to be the only thing about him that wasn't disheveled. Current expression: slightly confused, maybe even a little annoyed.

"He's busy," said Rutledge. "Like I said, I can help you with whatever you need."

"I hope so," said Vega. "Because what I need is to speak with Sheriff Fenton. I'm happy to wait."

Rutledge straightened out the furrows.

"Ma'am, like I said, you can't meet with the sheriff today. So, unless you'd like to let me know how I can help, I'll have to ask you to leave."

"Hmm, okay, then," she said. "There's something I'd like to bring to the sheriff's attention, so maybe I could tell you and you could pass it on?"

"Yes," said Rutledge, with a great deal of relief. "Yes, I can do that."

"My name's Alice Vega," she began, then paused and said, "Do you want to write it down?"

"I can remember it," said Rutledge.

"You sure? It's a lot," said Vega, scrunching up her nose.

"Yes, I'm sure, ma'am," said Rutledge, hemorrhaging patience.

"If you say so," said Vega, drumming her fingertips on the table. "My name is Alice Vega. I'm a private investigator from California, and I'm here on a case. I've been doing some research, walking around your town, asking questions, and so on, and it's become clear to me that you might have some white-nationalists/alt-right types here."

Rutledge's nostrils flared, pupils dilated.

"I know," she said. "It's disturbing stuff. Sometimes these guys can stay under the radar. Anyway, I have a friend in the FBI, and I'm sure he could point you in the right direction within the organization in terms of domestic terrorism. I'd be happy to put Sheriff Fenton in touch with him so you all could prune these weeds before they become problematic."

Vega made scissors with her index and middle finger and brought them together. Snip.

Rutledge's nostrils were even bigger now.

He didn't speak right away, so Vega continued, pulling a card from her inside pocket: "Here's my card. He can give me a call whenever."

Vega started to hand Rutledge the card, and he reached out to take it from her, but then Vega pulled it back at the last second.

"You know what? On second thought," she said, "I think we'd probably save time if I just went ahead and called my friend. Then he can reach out to the sheriff directly. Yeah, that sounds better, right?"

Rutledge licked his lips. Dry mouth, bro?

"Let me just see if I can free up the sheriff for you now for a few minutes," he stammered.

"Oh, I thought he was tied up," said Vega, innocent.

"He was, but he might have finished early," said Rutledge. "The meeting he was in."

"Well, great," said Vega. "My lucky day."

Rutledge smiled and nodded, teeth clenched. Then he turned and hurried past the desks to go through a door in the back of the room.

Vega waited. She glanced at the sign-in sheet, which was blank.

Rutledge burst through the door, a little out of breath. "Sheriff's free for a few, ma'am," he said. "If you could come with me."

Vega walked around the folding table, past the desks, to the door, and followed Rutledge up a flight of stairs that leaned slightly to the right. Vega bet if she set a marble down on the floor it would roll toward the center of the building; the whole place was so old it was slowly sinking into the mud.

Upstairs was a small stuffy office with a box fan in the window. There was Sheriff Fenton, standing behind his desk, moving papers around. He was big—Vega put him over six foot—in his fifties, black tattoos on his arms. A little roll of a belly hung over his belt, but not much; he looked to be in decent shape. He wore a tan uniform, like Rutledge, except Fenton had brown cowboy boots on his feet instead of the black tactical cop shoe.

"Sheriff Jay Fenton," he said, extending his hand. "Thanks, Chip, we're good," he said to Rutledge, who disappeared back down the stairs.

"Alice Vega," said Vega, shaking his hand.

"Have a seat, ma'am," he said, friendly. "Where you in town from?"

"California," she said, sitting.

"Yeah?" said Fenton, sitting as well. "Northern or southern?"

"Northern."

"Nice," he said, tilting back in his chair. He crossed one ankle over the opposite knee, looked relaxed. "Get warm there?"

"Sure."

Fenton rocked back and forth for a few seconds, stared at Vega. "My deputy says you might have some information for me," he said.

"Yeah, I think so."

She didn't add anything right away.

Fenton chuckled. "You going to tell me what that is?"

"Sure," said Vega. "Like I told your deputy, I'm a private investigator here on a case, and, unrelated to that case, I've observed some
things that would indicate the presence of white nationalists in your
town."

"Can I ask what your case is about?" Fenton asked right away.
"Maybe I could be helpful to you in that regard."

"I'm looking for Zeb Williams."

Fenton smiled, then saw Vega was not laughing.

"So you're a 2, that right?"

"No, I have a client."

"Right, your client," he said. "And who might that be?"

"No one you know."

"Huh," said Fenton. Then he made a sound like he was sucking something out from between his two front teeth. "So what's the
nature of your information, then?"

"I know someone in the FBI, and if you like, I'd be more than
happy to connect you to him."

"That's kind of you to offer, Miss Vega."

"I just figured, small town, you probably have limited resources.
Your past reports to federal agencies may have gone unnoticed," said
Vega. "My FBI friend will listen to me. He may be able to place your
report on the top of the pile."

Fenton whistled, impressed—or pretending to be, which Vega
thought far more likely.

"Well, that's something. And it's much appreciated, don't get me
wrong," he said. "We're aware of the situation and have it under control. We don't really require any federal involvement at this time, but
thanks for coming in."

"Okay," said Vega. Then she continued: "It's been my experience
that these things can escalate quickly. Bringing in help on a fed level
might prevent that from happening."

"Yeah, right now I don't think so," said Fenton. "Again, kind of
you to offer, but no, thanks."

Vega ignored him, kept talking. "So, when I say escalation, it
might be helpful to think about it like an escalator," said Vega, hold-

ing her arm at a slant in front of her. "Down here you have graffiti," she said, pointing to her elbow. "Then, here, you have, I don't know, trashing a car, cutting up tires," she added, tapping the middle of her forearm. "Then, up here," she continued, pointing to her fist, "you have violence. Against pets or humans, maybe. All of it can happen pretty quickly."

"I'm not worried about that happening here," said Fenton. "I keep my town orderly, rest assured, Miss Vega."

"So, if people in your town were to lodge complaints with you, you'd investigate all of those?" Vega waited for it to land, but only for a second. "You would never, say, just look the other way, click 'delete,' and empty the trash because those complaints might involve someone close to you?"

Fenton unfolded his legs and leaned forward now.

"No, I would not," he said slowly. Then he ran his eyes up and down her torso. "Private investigator, huh? You must have made yourself pretty useful in some regard to get that kind of attention from a fed."

He'd downshifted into patronizing now, or possibly even vulgar—Vega wasn't sure which, or if it was both. She didn't respond or even move, just waited to see what he would do next.

He rubbed his mouth, maybe worried he'd said too much.

"Thanks, but no, thanks. Kind of you to offer your services," he said, sounding like an automated message.

"I really"—Vega propped her forearms on her knees—"like to make myself useful. I've made a whole career out of it. You know how?"

Fenton knocked on his desk with the knuckle of his middle finger.

"You're gonna tell me right now, aren't you?" he said.

"I have to, because you'll never guess," she said. "The thing is, Sheriff, I'm pretty good with people."

Vega waited in the car down the block from Peller Hardware until it closed. According to the Web site, the store closed at five-thirty, and it was now almost five.

The sun had gone down, fast and early even for January, and the rain had started again, weighty drops that landed on the windshield with plunks. Vega had zipped up her jacket and drummed her fingers on the wheel to keep them from getting numb.

Her phone had buzzed a few times throughout the day, and she'd only scanned the messages, ignored the texts, and missed calls that had come through when she saw they weren't from Cara Simms. Now she was more thorough, reading and deleting, glancing at the rearview every few seconds to make sure the hardware store wasn't closing early.

Scrolling through her texts from midday, she saw one from Cap: "Did you find Zeb yet???"

Vega rubbed her thumb back and forth on the screen and then typed back: "Not yet. Another thing going on."

She waited for the dots, but they didn't come. Now it was 8:00 p.m. on the East Coast; maybe he was having dinner with Nell, or working. Or sitting on the couch being tired and thin.

At 5:10, she looked in the rearview and saw Riley, the boy with the jitters, leave the hardware store. He pulled up the hood of his sweatshirt over his head and buttoned his jean jacket, then began to walk in the opposite direction from Vega.

She got out of the car and jogged after him, icy raindrops hitting her face. One landed on her bottom lip, and she touched it with her tongue and drank it up, keeping her eyes on Riley, who wasn't acting like he knew anyone was behind him.

He approached a white pickup truck and removed keys from his jeans pocket, aimed the keys and made the truck beep. Vega waited until she was about a foot away and said loudly, "Riley."

He jumped and turned, lost his balance a little bit, and leaned against the door of the truck.

"What do you want?" he said, startled.

"What happened to all that red spray paint, Riley?"

"What?" he said, confused. Then he shrugged and said, "Sold out, I guess."

"Sold out," Vega repeated.

She took a step closer to him; though she knew at this distance he could try to make contact—he could give her a hit to the kidneys, a kick, push her away with two hands on her shoulders—she had a feeling he wouldn't. He was more scared than pissed. He was also a little soft in the middle and under his chin, just a couple of inches taller than she, and, if Vega had to guess, had probably been on the losing end of any schoolyard fistfights thus far in his life. She knew she could take him right down to the sidewalk if she had to.

"Red spray paint's probably not too popular, so your boss didn't notice them missing in the first place, but when he checks the inventory, and all the receipts, he's going to see the sales for all those cans, right?"

Riley looked shocked now. The rain split the air between them, got in his eyes, and made him blink. It got in Vega's eyes, too, but she didn't blink, just let the water well up and spill over her bottom lids.

"Unless you did something stupid, like give them away," she said.

That was the tipping point for Riley. He stepped sideways to get out of Vega's invisible hold, stumbled on the curb, and then hurried around the front of the truck to the driver's side.

Vega followed him.

"Get the fuck away from me," he said, his voice cracking. "I'll call the police."

He opened the door of the truck and climbed inside. Vega stayed in the street, a good two feet away from him. He fumbled with his keys and finally started the engine up. He turned to look at Vega, a cloud of steam blooming on the window near his mouth. Then he sped into the street in front of her, ran a stop sign, and turned the corner.

Vega stood in the street in the rain for a minute. She went back to her car, sat in the driver's seat for another few, and checked her phone.

Cap had written back: "Don't get yourself into trouble, V."

Vega ran her thumb over the screen and sent a text back. Just two words, and not the ones Cap wanted to hear, she thought. But at least they were honest.

" 'Too late'?" Cap read aloud, the question mark his, not Vega's.

He sat up very straight on the couch. Nell was at Jules's for the night; the TV was on; the Sig was on the cushion next to him. It had given him a sense of calm to text Vega. He tried to picture her, but realized he had no idea where in the country she was. What time zone, what weather system, what state, city. Was she in her car or in bed or jabbing some guy in the Adam's apple with her elbow? And was he more worried about her or the population at large?

Cap muted the TV. He stared at the words again: "Too late." He tapped her name at the top of the screen and then the little phone icon. "Alice Vega, Calling," the screen read. She picked up on the first ring.

"Caplan," she said, as if she were expecting him.

"What does that mean, 'too late'?" he said. "Too late for what? Where are you anyway?"

"Oregon. Small town called Ilona. Smaller than Denville, even. Comes with its own ethically challenged sheriff."

He could tell he was on the speaker, could hear white noise in the background.

"How long have you been there—a day?"

"Just about, yeah."

"And you've already figured the sheriff's problematic?" Cap said. He stood up from the couch and picked up the Sig in his left hand.

"He didn't seem too interested in hiding it," said Vega.

"You've *met* him already?" said Cap, walking to the kitchen.

"Sure," she said. "I'm pretty sure his son is involved in a white-nationalist gang that harasses the locals, one of whom is Cara Simms, who had a moment with Zeb Williams when he passed through here in the eighties."

"No shit," said Cap. He set the Sig on the kitchen counter and opened the fridge. "So—wait, Vega, that's not the job, though, right? You're supposed to find Zeb Williams."

She paused, then said, "I'm doing both things."

Cap pulled out a can of beer and popped it open.

"It's not like you to get distracted," he said, and took a sip of foam off the top.

"I don't get distracted, Caplan," she said. "But there are enough questions to ask around here for two, so, anytime you want to join me, the offer still stands."

Cap leaned his forehead against the freezer and pressed the phone as close as he could to his ear and cheek. He set the beer down next to the gun.

"You wouldn't have called me if you weren't at least a little interested," she said, her voice softer, the fuzz in the background faint.

"Well, sure," he said. "Like I said, this is Elvis-Bigfoot territory, except it relates to sports. So, yeah, for those of us who deign to be entertained by such things, Zeb Williams is a big deal."

"If you work the case with me, I bet he'll sign a football for you when we find him," said Vega.

Cap laughed. "You got some ironclad confidence there, girl."

"Confidence has nothing to do with it," she said.

"Oh yeah?" said Cap, aware that he was pushing her. "What is it, then?"

He heard her breath, the light reverb of air against the phone; he realized she'd taken him off the speaker.

"Just the truth," she said. "No need to dress it up."

Cap wished he could do a quick rewind, to have her sitting in his kitchen for one more minute.

"I'm worried about you, Vega," was all he could marshal.

"Don't worry about me," she said, sounding very close. "I bet you still have on the same sweatshirt and jeans you were wearing on Sunday."

"Vega," said Cap, pulling his head away from the refrigerator. "If this is your attempt at phone sex, it's not great."

"Fuck off," she said. Then, "Change your clothes and eat something and get some sleep, for a fucking change."

She hung up on him, and Cap looked at the phone and laughed, because he knew, even though she would like it if he believed otherwise, despite her invective, that she was laughing, too.

Vega kicked her legs up into the handstand in the dark. It was just after five, the sun not due to rise until seven-forty. She had only slept about four hours or so, which wasn't unusual for her. What was unusual was the thickness of the sleep, the depth of the dreams, the unnerving feeling that if someone had tried to wake her he wouldn't have been successful.

She'd been up late, reading on her laptop. The Bastard had responded to her initial inquiry:

Attached see list and map of properties owned by Matthew Klimmer.

Can't find screen names for Derek Fenton/Neil Klimmer without devices they're writing from. Possible but will take time. Sending through mailing addresses, car lease payments, utilities, etc. Same prob with IDing crinklecut94. He posts about a lot of IRL meet-ups in the area for "young people who care about freedom."

Vega had replied with an IM: "Any meet-ups happening soon?" The Bastard wrote: "Doesn't work like that. He picks you."

She'd gone back to Reddit, created a profile, typed and retyped screen names, trying to land on the one that might grab crinklecut's attention. She hadn't wanted to come off like one of the kooks, so couldn't throw out a line with something like "lynchmob" or "hitlerbabe." She'd wanted to give the impression of being a little more disciplined, felt that crinklecut would be attracted to that. If he was trying to build an army, he wouldn't want the guys too crazy to make it past basic.

Vega had stared at her screen. She'd stared at the blank bar after "Type your user name here." Vega had typed, "ahundredpercentpure." Then had hit "save changes."

She'd found where crinklecut94 had posted most recently: on a board about the public-school system being rigged toward political correctness. The chat was ongoing, and Vega had glanced at the posts and read crinklecut's last: "never allow the machine to think for you. always think for yourself."

Vega had written as a reply, "unfortunately if you're a teacher they don't let you say what you really think anymore. totally conditioned messaging." She'd tapped "send" and waited for an hour for any response or a comment or an upvote from anyone, then had finally gone to sleep.

She'd woken up suddenly, though, like she'd heard a noise. She'd looked out the motel-room window, opened the front door, and hadn't seen anything except her rental car parked at the concrete stopper in the lot right in front of her room.

Now it was raining heavily; Vega could hear the drops hit the ground outside over the hum of the heating unit under the window.

The image of Cap floated by—he was wearing the old sweatshirt and the jeans he'd had on when she saw him last, leaning against the refrigerator, drinking coffee. Still tired, still thin. Sometimes when she was in the handstand, things took on a certain shine; the numbers doubled and multiplied and equaled a definitive solution. Now it became clear that she had made Cap this way.

She'd known it before; she hadn't said sorry. But she also knew Cap didn't need that from her. The thing that really poked her in the chest was that, right now, she knew, for certain, that he didn't need anything from her at all.

Vega broke out of the handstand and sat on the nubby blue carpet for a minute. The rain splashed on the window in a sporadic way. Vega knew that it was supposed to be a soothing sound, that people bought machines and downloaded apps so they could hear it all the time, but to her it sounded like some kind of medieval war machine, cogs and gears turning and tightening in preparation for something big and bad.

She went to the bathroom and took a short shower, got out, and wrapped a towel around her upper body. When she came out of the bathroom, she saw that her phone on the bedside table was lit up with a text. She hurried to it, still soaking wet, and read the message.

It was not from Cap. It was actually not from anyone she'd expected, but it woke her up just the same; any urge to hesitate fell away with the water dripping off her skin onto the floor in a circle at her feet.

Rachel Bishop was the waitress's name. Vega waited in her car around the corner from the diner and watched her park across the street. Rachel got out of her car, saw Vega right away, and jogged across the street, wearing a green hooded poncho.

Vega leaned over and opened the passenger-side door, and Rachel slid in and shut the door, bringing the smell of rain and hair product with her.

"Hi," she said, pulling the hood back. Then she pulled a gold vape pen from her purse and said, "You mind?"

Vega shook her head.

Rachel powered the window down an inch, stuck the skinny end of the pen into her mouth, and inhaled.

"So you're not a cop," she said, then blew smoke out the window.

Vega shook her head, smelling the mint from the smoke.

"I couldn't tell you about Liberty Pure yesterday, because Waldy, in the kitchen, would've heard me, and he would've told my boss."

She said it with a sense of gravitas, as if Vega knew what all this meant.

"Who's your boss?"

"Matt," she said, sucking on the pen. "He owns the diner, and the liquor store, and, like, some farms."

She paused and exhaled more smoke.

"Matt Klimmer," said Vega, remembering the name.

"Yeah, that's him. I don't know him very well, though. He only comes by the diner on weekends sometimes, to go through the cash box and line up the register and stuff."

"So is Matt one of them—the Liberty Pure?" asked Vega.

"No, I think he's, like, too old maybe? It's his son, Neil." She laughed a little, then said, "He was a total a-hole in high school, but only because he acted smarter than everyone all the time, which he is not. His parents both went to UO, and he couldn't get in. And he didn't even apply to Wilson."

"What's Wilson?" asked Vega.

"It's the community college where everyone goes around here. I'm taking courses there to get my A.A., and then maybe transfer to a four-year."

She paused again, continued to smoke.

Vega prompted: "You wrote in your text you had more to say. Did you just want me to know his, Neil's, name? Or is there something else?"

"Yeah, there's something else . . ." she said, wiping a raindrop from the tip of her nose. "He's, like, best friends with another guy, who used to beat him up in middle school—but then they became friends at some point and total losers together, and that guy is big, he was on the football team, and now he beats people up for Neil. He's like Neil's serf."

"His serf?" Vega said, not sure she heard correctly.

"Yeah, it's like a servant who has to work on a lord's estate."

"I know what a serf is," said Vega. "What's the big guy's name?"

"Derek Fenton."

"Sheriff's son?"

"Yeah. But also . . ."

Rachel looked over her shoulder, suddenly nervous and not so sassy. "He dates my little sister."

"Fenton does?"

"For a few months now," Rachel said, her lips turning down. "She used to bring him by the house, but he's such a turd my dad was like, 'I don't want to see him here anymore.' Apparently, the sheriff got him a job at the energy company, but all they'll let him do is drive the van. And Claire was like, 'Oh, his co-workers are so mean to him,' and I was like, 'Yeah, because he's dumb and lazy.' I didn't say exactly that, but, you know, I was thinking it."

"So did it start to become a problem, besides you and your dad not liking Derek?"

Rachel sighed a short breath. "Before, I really didn't care about Neil or Derek and them, because, whatever, they spray-paint and get drunk. . . ."

Vega held her tongue about Beatrice Dauley's dog for the moment.

"But now Claire's coming home drunk all the time, and she stopped even trying to go to school and is just being, you know . . ." Then she whispered, ". . . a butthole." She inhaled from the pen again and continued, "If it was just us, I don't think I'd care that much, but my parents, our parents, all they've done is work, and my dad, it'll put him into cardiac arrest if Claire doesn't finish high school."

"Does she pick fights with you and your parents?" said Vega.

"Yeah, all the time."

"What about?"

"My parents want her to go to school, because they, like, don't want her to be broke and ruin her life, and she's telling them to mind their business, dumb stuff like that. My mom even got her a job at this plant nursery, because she's friends with the lady who owns it, but Claire got fired in a minute."

"Do you know if your sister has, or had, an English teacher named Cara Simms?"

"I had Miss Simms," said Rachel. "And Claire definitely had her for senior English before she dropped out. She's really tough. But I liked her," Rachel added quickly. "When you're a senior, most teachers don't care if you cut class or what-have-you, but Miss Simms did.

She'd, like, stare at you when you came in the next day," Rachel said, with a faint fondness.

"You ever hear your sister talk about Cara Simms?" asked Vega. "In a negative way, maybe?"

Rachel thought about it. "I can't remember, but it makes sense," she said. Then she paused. "One time, when I was a senior, this kid, Marcus, cut school and missed senior English, and then, the next day, in class, Miss Simms made him stand in front of the class and read a monologue from *Measure for Measure* when the guy's in jail. It was a good burn."

"Would you say your sister's got a bad temper?"

Rachel shrugged. "I mean, she didn't use to, but lately, yeah, she talks a lot of trash to our parents. Told me to eff off when I told her to leave them alone."

"So you think it's conceivable that Cara Simms did something to make her angry, like embarrass her in front of the class."

"Yeah," said Rachel. "It's probably more than conceivable. It's probably, like, a high percentage."

Rachel stopped talking, and Vega had the feeling she was holding back.

"Does Claire talk about anything else when she gets drunk, besides argue with your parents?" Vega asked.

"Yeah," said Rachel, rubbing a raindrop on her slicker in circles. "She's always talking shit about Black people and Mexicans, but that's not her, you know, that's Derek and Neil and those idiots. She's just, like, the microphone."

Rachel glanced at Vega and rubbed her nose with her palm.

"I know the way I'm talking about her makes her sound like a racist and an uninformed sort of person, but she's not. My parents raised us the right way."

Rachel's eyes became glossy, but no tears leaked. Her forehead softened.

"You're worried about her," said Vega.

"Yeah, I'm worried," she said. "That's why, you know, when I saw your card and it said 'private investigator,' and you asked about it, I thought . . . I don't know. Are you investigating them—Liberty Pure?"

"No," said Vega. "I'm here on a missing-persons case. It's unrelated."

"Oh," said Rachel, crestfallen. "Then I guess I just told you all that for no reason."

"I wouldn't say that," said Vega. "Tell you what—I'm planning to stick around town for a few days anyway. Why don't you text me if anything stands out to you?"

"Like what?"

Vega shrugged. "I bet a lot of people come through the diner. At some point, the Liberty Pure guys were in the bathroom, for example. You seem like you notice things, but there's a trick to it."

Vega shifted her body in her seat so that she was facing Rachel, who also turned, to face Vega, intrigued.

"Don't stare. Just observe. Don't think about it, just try to remember it."

"So, like, don't try too hard?"

"Exactly," said Vega. "See, me, I stick out in a small town, because everyone knows everyone. But you fit right in."

"I don't even have to try," said Rachel, starting to get it.

"Yep."

"But what am I looking for?" said Rachel, becoming frustrated.

"We don't know yet. So look at everything. And then text me."

Rachel nodded, but her eyes still held the panic.

"How do I . . ." she began, but then caught herself.

"Know you can trust me?" Vega said, finishing her thought. "You don't. But you did text me this morning, so some part of you trusts me already."

Rachel sneered and shook her head. "There's this sick neighborhood cat that kept eating the compost scraps we put out," she said. "It didn't do that because it trusted us."

"No, it did that because it was desperate," said Vega. "But think about it analytically. I have nothing to gain from this. You can look me up online if you want to."

"I already did," Rachel said.

"Good," said Vega. "You should go to work now."

Rachel nodded and opened the car door.

"Thanks," she said, then pulled the hood of her poncho back up over her head.

Vega started to say something, but Rachel was already out, the door shut behind her. Vega watched her hurry to the sidewalk and head to the corner. The rain had slowed down, and the sun was beginning to lighten the sky.

Vega waited until Rachel turned the corner, almost in an effort to be polite, so that she wouldn't even be in the same vicinity while Vega sent an e-mail to the Bastard asking for everything he could find on Rachel's sister and her friends.

She hit "send," and then a notification lit up the screen: "crinkle-cut94 upvoted your post."

The first place she went was the Klimmers' property. Neil still lived with his parents, Matthew and Lila, in a three-story house with a cherrywood exterior set on an eight-acre lot of field and woods, the closest neighbor a half-mile away. There were two cars in a circular driveway bordered by tall green-leafed plants, with a horse stable in the distance. After cruising past the house, Vega turned around and parked on the side of the road at the intersection that preceded the property line. She sat for about an hour, waiting for someone to go in or come out, but no one did except the mail carrier.

Then she drove to the house that had Derek Fenton's name on the rental lease, along with another guy, named Duane Smith. It was a light-blue-paneled single-level ranch-style. Nothing fancy. One red pickup in the driveway. Overgrown, unmowed lawn. A swinging bench and a folding chair on the porch. A wooden fence to the right of the house, bordering what Vega guessed was a backyard.

She parked across the street from the house and sat there for a half-hour. She thought she saw some movement through one of the windows, but wasn't sure, and wasn't compelled to stick around to find out.

Not yet.

4

VEGA FOLLOWED RED PELLER'S DIRECTIONS FROM A COUPLE OF days before. She drove as if she were heading back to her motel, leaving town, then took a right at the I-PUD, which looked more like a ski cabin than a public-utility building.

After about a quarter-mile, Vega spotted the trailers in a clearing in the woods. Four of them in a square formation, surrounded by trees with branches sticking straight out to the sides like helicopter blades. None of the vehicles were that big—no highway monsters for families going to Mount Rushmore. These were all single-cabin, some in better shape than others, but all in a state of shabby, most raised on bricks with the tires removed.

As Vega pulled over and parked on the side of the road, she saw some round charcoal grills and what appeared to be a burn barrel—a rusty garbage can with a few lines of smoke rising out of it, a trailer on either side.

Vega got out of the car and walked toward the barrel, her boots sinking into the mud with each step. She heard running water but couldn't see the source—a river or a creek nearby. She smelled campfire smoke, and beneath that something rotten and earthy, like a bucket of old mushrooms.

Then she heard music but didn't see any people. It sounded like a show tune from a musical or a forties movie: a woman singing about love with an orchestra of horns in the background.

A TV flickered in the first trailer she passed, but she couldn't see anyone through the greased glass of the window. She followed the sound of the music. It came from a CD player set on top of a produce crate in front of the opposite trailer, which was only about

twenty feet long, with the word "Stargazer" across the side in faded
lettering.

Before Vega got to the small door of the Stargazer, a man
emerged, wearing jeans but no shirt, with blurry tattoos of what
were once photo-realistic faces on his chest and arms. Vega put him
in his fifties, although he might have been in his forties, or even thirties, just tan and burned out. He was carrying a yellow bucket, and
nodded when he saw Vega.

"What's up?" he said, haylike hair falling around his shoulders.

"Hi," said Vega. "I'm looking for Dart."

The man dumped brown water from the bucket onto the ground.
Vega watched the grass suck it up.

"Yeah? Why's that?" he said, not aggressive, more like it was his
accepted responsibility to know.

"Do you know where I can find him?"

The man flipped the hair out of his face. "Mr. Abilene Dart
doesn't like visitors of any kind," he said. "You related to him?"

"No," said Vega. "I need his help."

The man laughed a phlegmy laugh and dropped the bucket on
the ground.

"Well, I'll tell you this—he can't hardly help himself. He's old and
crazy, and he likes his guns."

"Are you friends with him?" asked Vega.

"As friendly as I am with anyone here," said the man, gesturing
to the other trailers. "We're forced to rely on each other for things,
because of our situation up here. But that old fucker, I'm just hoping
he doesn't die and I have to clean up all his shit."

"Which trailer is it?" said Vega.

The man shook his head at her, like she was a lost cause.

"That way," he said, pointing. "His place is set behind us, which
is how he likes it. It's an old Airstream."

"Thanks," said Vega.

"Good luck, and duck," he said, then turned and went back into
his trailer.

Vega walked past the camp and saw the Airstream, aluminum
and shaped like a burrito, leopard-dotted near the bottom. It was
raised about a foot off the ground on cinder blocks, with sand bags
along the perimeter, surrounded by wet grass.

Vega stepped on the rolling step stool in front of the oval-shaped door and knocked.

She could still hear the music from the tattooed man's trailer. That woman sang and sang about love, and how pumped she was that it was coming her way. The song was quieter now, but still just loud enough to drown out the squelch of footsteps behind her.

It was only because of the heat, the draft, the slight shift in the air that Vega knew someone was close.

She turned around fast, and her face was about a foot away from the muzzle of a sawed-off shotgun. The guy holding the gun was Dart.

"You police?" he said.

His voice was a rasp, like his tonsils had been seared.

"No," said Vega, holding both her hands out to the side, keeping her elbows tucked in tightly to her body.

She glanced away from the gun and examined the old man. She recognized his face immediately from the photo; his features were more or less the same, except his hair was pure white now. He was thin; his eyes were cloudy and gray. But still—handsome in a weathered way, tan, tall. He wore cowboy boots, blue jeans, and a flannel shirt. A belt with a big silver buckle. He was old but did not seem shaky in the least, which Vega was glad about.

"Ronny send you?" he said.

"I don't know who that is."

"Who, then?"

He pulled the shotgun back an inch but didn't move his feet, reaffirmed his grip.

Vega guessed he wouldn't shoot. If he were that unstable, he would have already fired.

"I've been hired to find Zeb Williams. I understand you and he were close."

"He and who?" he said. "You don't know my name, girl."

"It's Dart, right?" said Vega. "Abilene Dart?"

Dart wrinkled up his nose, Vega thought perhaps to clear the sweat from his upper lip. "I don't know anything about Zeb Williams," he said.

Vega knew it was possible he was telling the truth. He was old; he may have been institutionalized for some chunk of his life, so maybe had an on-again/off-again relationship with reality. But the way he'd paused made Vega think otherwise. There is a way to do this, she thought. Every person was a lock. Not the kind that had a key, just one twist and then open sesame. A combination lock: at least three numbers, three turns, a series. She'd already hit the first with the names.

"You two used to shoot fruit together. Do you remember?"

Dart lowered the gun a little and took his shoulders out of firing stance as confusion swept over his face. Still pointing in Vega's direction.

"How'd you know that? You a reporter?"

"Private investigator," said Vega. "Not police."

"So that means you work for who?"

"This case, a guy named Fohl. But he's just the person paying me to find Zeb. Most days, I work for myself."

Dart lowered the gun a little more, kept it aimed loosely at Vega's chest. He huffed out a laugh.

"I work for myself, too."

"I bet we have more in common than that," said Vega.

She still held her hands out at her sides, like she was a kid saying "Ta-daa" after a tap routine. She felt some sweat beads gathering under her arms.

"How about we talk about it," she said.

"Talk about it," Dart repeated.

Vega wasn't sure how much was getting through. In such a case, best to lay it out.

"Look, I haven't come to rob you or take you somewhere you don't want to go," she said. "But it will be easier for me to tell you more if you stand down with the firearm."

He thought for a second, then moved his lips around, chewing on the response.

"Why's that exactly, now?" he said.

"Just wouldn't mind it, is all," she said. "Give me a chance to tell you some things I've learned about your town, here."

"My town," he repeated. "Like what?"

"Like it's not made for people like you and me. People who work for themselves."

She watched the corners of his mouth twitch, and then he let out a breath as he lowered the gun fully to his side, muzzle down.

. . .

Inside the trailer, Vega sat on a stained cushioned bench across from a counter with a hot plate on top. At one end of the space was a narrow bed with rumpled sheets, a bathroom at the other end. Although Dart wasn't hunching, he seemed too tall for the room—all the furniture small, clothes and canned food and newspapers cluttered at his feet.

"I got water, beer, milk, chocolate milk," he said, leaning down into a mini-fridge.

"I'm good, thanks."

He stood up straight again, with a carton of milk and a can of chocolate syrup, and shut the fridge door with his knee. He took a clear plastic cup from a cabinet above the counter and began to spoon syrup into it.

"Lot of people think things about me, spread all kinds of stories. For example, I know my name is not really Abilene Dart. I had it legally changed to that in 1979. My given name is Duncan Richards. I know that because I have a birth certificate, and also because my son's name is Duncan Ronald Richards, Jr., aka, quote unquote, 'the Worm Child.'"

He poured milk into the cup. It appeared to be in about a fifty-fifty ratio to the chocolate.

"Here," he said, remembering something.

He left the counter and went to a short gray filing cabinet against the wall. He opened the bottom drawer and removed a thick hardbound photo album, handed it to Vega.

"Those are all real pictures. No doctoring with computers."

Vega flipped through the sticky sheets, unsure of what the pictures were supposed to prove, but Dart seemed determined that she see them. They appeared to be behind-the-scenes photos from the set of Dart's TV show: Dart in the makeup chair; Dart shaking hands with a costar; the whole gang smoking cigarettes and looking bored.

"You know who that is, right?" he said, pointing to the image of a pretty redhead, one of the only pictures in color. She wore a dress with a petticoat and held a pink parasol.

"I don't," said Vega.

"That's Martha Vickers," said Dart. "She was in two episodes, and she was in *The Big Sleep*. You know what she said about Bogart?"

"What?"

"He was a soft touch. Would cry at the drop of a hat."

Dart tapped the spoon on the rim of the glass and took a sip of the drink, which was as dark as coffee. Then, remembering something, he said, "Wait a minute, now."

He rested his cup on the counter and went back to the filing cabinet, opened the top drawer. He took out a cigar box and handed it to Vega.

"Go ahead, open it," he said, pleased.

Vega opened it. There was an Old West sheriff's badge inside. It looked like it had once been silver, but was now a gray matte, the tips of the star's points speckled black.

"That's the original spinning star," he said. "It was all my idea, you know. The writers said it was great. I had to work with the prop guy to make it just right."

Vega nodded and continued to examine the star to show him she was invested in its history.

"You couldn't tell it by watching at home, but there's a button on the back that makes the blades come out. A beautiful thing."

"Looks like it's in good shape," Vega said, handing the box back to him.

"Yes, it is," he said, proud. "Still works, too. After all this time."

"When did you leave Los Angeles?"

"In '72," he answered, shutting the lid. "It was a cesspool of pornography."

"Yeah," said Vega.

"Some guy had the nerve to ask me to make a pornographic Western picture. My agent told me to do it. I said no, thanks—that's not the business I'm in. I left town."

He delivered all of this information in a partially agitated state, but also as if he'd spoken about it many times before, like he was used to being defensive about it.

"And you came here?"

"I spent some time in San Fran, then got up here around '74, '75. Easy place to live."

He seemed ready to say something else, but didn't.

Vega waited a minute, then said, "Easy place to stay, too? You've been here awhile."

"Not all the way through, but, yeah," he said, "it's perfect. No one bothers you. Where else you gonna go?"

Vega didn't have an answer, so she asked, "You remember Zeb Williams?"

"Sure, I do," said Dart. "He was the same age as my son, except not a dullard."

"So he was smart—Zeb, I mean?"

Dart sniffed and shrugged his bony shoulders. "I don't know what kind of grades he got in school, but he was smart with people. He could read faces."

"How'd you know he could do that?" said Vega.

"Because I could do that, too, and I could recognize it," he said, his voice verging on sounding offended. "That's a thing most actors can do. It's all right here," he said, drawing a circle in the air around his face with his finger.

"You remember the first time you noticed he could do that, read faces?" Vega said.

"Oh," said Dart, sighing. He leaned back against the counter and thought. "Sure, the girl, the waitress. Karen?"

"Cara Simms?"

Dart paused, moved his lips around the name without making a sound.

"Cara Simms, yeah," he said. "Her parents were sick, or had just died, something. And he, Zeb, he knew she was sad, just from watching her wipe the tables with a cloth."

Dart took another gulp of the chocolate milk, leaving wet pockets at the corners of his mouth when he took the cup away.

"The two of them, they looked like Steve McQueen and Ali McGraw," he said.

Vega knew they were old movie stars but couldn't picture their faces.

"You remember when Zeb left town?" she asked.

Dart shook his head, said, "Long time ago."

Then he gazed out an oval-shaped window above Vega's head.

"It was cold, like this. Winter."

Vega took the photo from her inside pocket, unfolded it, and held it up to Dart. "Do you know who this guy is, holding the cane?" she asked.

Dart took the paper from her and flipped it over to see if there was anything on the back.

"Where'd this come from?" he said.

"Someone who knew Zeb gave it to me. In California."

"California," Dart echoed, still staring.

"Do you recognize him—the other man?"

"Sure, now I do," said Dart. "Name was Ivan. Lived a few months in an old barn outside of town. Same land where me and the kid used to shoot fruit."

"Did you live there, too?"

"The barn? No, I rented a room at the time from a lady who took in boarders. Let me pay her week to week."

"So you haven't seen him since—Ivan?"

"Nah, but you looking for him or you looking for the kid?" said Dart.

"The kid. Zeb," said Vega. "If Ivan was around, I'd ask him if he'd seen Zeb since then, that's all."

"Yeah, you're out of luck," Dart said, passing the photo back to her. "There were a lot of them for a while—tramps, we used to call them—coming through town. Cara? She gave them free coffee here and there. Before that Klimmer bought everything up, field included."

Dart made a flip-flop gesture with his hand: Go on, get out of here.

"Matt Klimmer?" said Vega.

"That's the one. No more handouts."

Dart held the cup and fixed his eyes on a point in space. He went somewhere else for a minute in his head, and Vega didn't disturb him.

"I remember thinking, That's a fight I'd like to see," Dart said finally. "Zeb and Klimmer."

"Those two ever meet?" said Vega.

"Oh yeah. Zeb didn't care for him. Saw right through him." said Dart. "I saw them once in the middle of the street. The two of them, talking real close together, like this." He pinched his finger and thumb together so there was only a little space between them.

"You know what they were talking about?"

Dart rubbed his chin, then his eyes, like an itch was spreading through his skin. "Nah," he said, shaking the paper. "You could ask Klimmer, though. Not that he does a damn thing to help anyone other than himself, but you could."

"I might do that," said Vega.

Dart continued to study the picture, the paper quivering in his hand.

"Can I have a copy of this picture?" he asked. "I'd like to put it in one of my books."

His eyes were wet as he returned the paper to her.

"I can make you a copy," said Vega. "I have a condition, though."

"No conditions," he said, making an "x" with his hands. "No deal."

It didn't sound to Vega like he was too committed to the refusal.

"Don't you even want to hear it?" she said. "I think you'll like the idea."

"I don't want to go anywhere or see anyone," he said. Then he glanced at what he was wearing. "And I don't want to change my clothes."

"You get two out of those three," said Vega, standing. "But you get to take your favorite firearm."

Dart's mouth turned down in a thoughtful frown as his wiry eyebrows raised, and Vega knew she had him again.

A half-hour later, they were in a field of knee-high grass, the blades bowing from the weight of the rain. A Gothic-style barn, faded red with busted-out windows, sat at an angle in front of a wall of trees.

Dart had driven his own truck and parked it in the middle of the field. Vega was a few minutes behind, because she had to make a stop at the farmers' market stand on the side of the road for pears. She also gave the girl an extra twenty for a couple of wooden crates.

Vega parked her rental next to Dart's car and got out. Vega set up a half-dozen pears on the crates in front of the barn. Then she walked back to Dart, the grass soaking her pant legs below the knee.

"This land belongs to Matt Klimmer, right?" said Vega, remembering the map the Bastard had sent.

"Yeah," said Dart. "He bought it from Fenton's old man." Dart spit out of the side of his mouth.

"Klimmer doesn't seem to be too concerned with trespassers," said Vega, pulling her Springfield out of the holster.

"Nah," said Dart. "He can't do a thing on this land. Too wet for crops. You can't tell by standing on it, but it's lowland down here. Klimmer's ranch is probably up six-, eight-percent grade." Dart squinted at the fruit in the distance. "That fifty feet?"

"Just about," said Vega.

"You're gonna shoot it with that thing?" he said, eyeing the Springfield like it was a water pistol.

"Sure," said Vega. Then she nodded at his shotgun and said, "A double-barrel shorty looks nice, but that target's a stretch for your shotshells."

"We shall see," he said, stuffing a blue earplug into his ear.

Vega pressed an earplug into one of her ears as well.

Dart aimed, still squinting, lifted the rifle with his right hand, and rested it on top of his left forearm for support. Then he pulled the trigger.

The shot was loud and made a hollow echo in the air. One of the crates shattered, the pears flipping into the air before hitting the ground. Dart shook back a step, against the truck.

"Missed the pear," he said. "Sorry about the crate."

Vega shrugged, then stepped forward, held out the Springfield, and looked down the line of her arm. Fifty feet, so the bullet would sink less than an inch in the air, she figured, but this wasn't exact math. She couldn't calculate whether there was a change in the grade of the slope of the field here, or what the effect of the breeze was, and if her stance was off because of the mud. She fired and hit the barn behind the pears, a pane of wood splitting.

"You know how to hold it," said Dart, not patronizing. "Women never used to carry guns. Or they were these little ladylike things that looked like toys. Now they got gun shows just for girls. I saw it advertised a while back."

"I only have it for my line of work," said Vega.

"Private dick, you said?"

"Investigator," said Vega. "Specializing in missing persons."

Dart nodded; now he seemed to absorb what she was telling him on a deeper level than before.

"No farm, no food—why's Klimmer own it, then?" asked Vega, glancing around.

Dart sniffed and shrugged. "Same reason rich folks own anything," he said. "They can, okay?"

Vega nodded, then pointed at the barn. "So that's where Ivan stayed? And other people passing through?"

"Yeah," said Dart, squinting toward the pears, and the barn farther in the distance. "Old Fenton didn't give a hoot. Not like they were shooting drugs in their eyelids, all that stuff." He sighed and rested the shotgun over his left arm again. "Probably some whiskey or beers back and forth."

Then he paused, tilting the shotgun up to the sky while he thought. He looked puzzled, and Vega realized he was remembering something.

"You ever have a drink with Ivan?" she said.

"Yeah," said Dart, a chime of discovery in his voice. "Yeah, I did a few times. I remember once, we were here, me and the kid and Ivan and a fifth of Jack Daniel's. Me and the kid were shooting. I guess we had pumpkins, 'cause, boy, did they come apart. Made a great sound, like chopping wood on a block."

"Zeb a good shot?" asked Vega.

"No, he didn't know what to do with a gun," said Dart. "It was just for fun. Ivan, old Ivan, he was dancing around, like a little jig. He knew my TV show. He said he could do a Slim Pickens impression."

Vega saw the three of them there. She didn't have to try too hard. Three guys with guns, drunk in a field. A lot could occur.

"Was he shooting, too?" asked Vega. "Did Ivan have a gun?"

Dart laughed. "No, Ivan didn't see so good," he said. "Said he was legally blind."

Vega remembered the cane in Ivan's hand in the PI's photo.

Then Dart shook his head. "I haven't thought of that night in years," he said.

"Sometimes it takes coming back to a place," said Vega.

"You're smart," said Dart, pointing a bony finger at her.

He smiled, his upper lip riding high on his gum, his teeth yellowed but ruler-straight.

"Not always," said Vega.

She turned her body toward the targets, stood with her legs shoulder-width apart and knees slightly bent, extended her right hand, gripping the Springfield but not too tightly, clasped her left hand over the right, and fired. A pear exploded into bits in the air.

"Whoo," Dart exclaimed, impressed. "You just sent that one straight to pear heaven to meet his granddaddy."

After Vega said goodbye to Dart, she decided to introduce herself to Matt Klimmer. She pulled into the circular driveway and parked behind a black Camry, got out of the car, and headed toward the front door. The sun was out, the air flowery and fragrant; it reminded Vega of a funeral home. She could see a figure on a trotting brown horse in the distance but couldn't hear it, couldn't hear anything except water dripping off the leaves of the bushes surrounding the driveway.

Before she made it to the welcome mat, the door opened. It was a kid, looked to be about twenty, and Vega guessed it was Neil Klimmer. He was scrawny, with a round, pale face and stringy black hair, dull brown at the roots.

"Who the fuck are you?" he said, accent on the "are," and not the "you," which led Vega to think that the question was actually, Who do you think you are?

"Alice Vega," she said. "Neil, right?"

He stepped out of the house, leaving the door open behind him. Vega stood about a foot away from him. Neither advanced.

"This is private property," he said. "You're trespassing."

"I'm not here to see you," Vega said. "Your dad around?"

His face twitched with indignation. "No," he said.

"That him?" Vega said, nodding to the horse and its rider, both approaching.

"No," Neil said weakly.

Vega glanced at the rider, then back at the boy.

"Basic bitch," he stammered.

"Shitty liar," she said.

Matt Klimmer rode the horse right up to where the field ended and the graveled driveway began.

"Howdy," he called, dismounting. He came through a gap in the bushes toward Vega, pulled off a leather glove, and extended his hand. "Matt Klimmer."

His face looked like Neil's, round, pale, with very light blue eyes and short gray hair. The horse was big and brown with a white diamond between its eyes.

"Alice Vega," she said, shaking his hand. Sweaty, cold.

"So you're the one," he said, friendly. "Looking for Zeb Williams?"

"That's right."

"A little late to the party, you know?" he said, then laughed at his own joke.

"I was hoping I might ask you some questions," she said. "Since you and your family go way back in this town."

"We don't have anything to say to you," said Neil.

"Easy there, Neil," Klimmer said, laughing again. "Why don't you go inside?"

"Dad—" Neil said.

"Go on, now," he said, gentle.

Neil glared once more at Vega and then went inside, slamming the door behind him.

"Like to take a walk with me to the stable?" said Klimmer, nodding to the side. "I have to get this girl set up."

"Sure."

They walked through tall wet grass, Klimmer guiding the horse on his right by the reins. Vega didn't have a lot of experience with horses. She'd never really been around animals that big, hadn't been to a zoo in a lot of years. She could recognize that it was beautiful, but also had an immediate awareness of its weight and strength, and didn't want to get too close.

"Have to apologize for Neil," he said. "He's protective of me and his mother."

Vega smiled politely, even though Klimmer was staring straight ahead, uninterested in how she was receiving the information.

"He's one of these kids, always done well in school, near the top of the class even, but can't settle on one thing. Gets bored easily. I told him, when the right career comes along, he'll know. I'm just glad he still wants to golf with his old man twice a week, even in the cold, right?"

He laughed. Vega quickly understood he said "Right?" a lot, but not because he expected his conversation partner to agree or disagree. It was like he was explaining things to himself.

"He spends a lot of time on social media, but that's how this generation networks. With us, it just used to be shaking people's hands."

They came to the stable, and Klimmer unlatched a wooden half-door and led the horse inside. Vega followed them past a few other stalls, empty except for two at the back of the stable, where there was a horse that was solid brown with a diamond, and a palomino, both calm like statues. It smelled like a pet store, hay and wood chips with a tang of urine. It was warmer in the stable than Vega expected, and then she looked up and saw why: in each stall hung a two-foot-long infrared heater, the panels glowing orange.

Klimmer brought the horse into an open stall and gently turned it around so its head faced out. He unbuckled the saddle and hung it on two large hooks attached to the stable wall. Next to the hooks was a beige rotary phone. Vega stared at it.

"From a million years ago," said Klimmer, catching her gaze. "My dad had it installed so he could work and still spend time with the horses."

"Do you still use it?" said Vega.

"Oh no," said Klimmer, chuckling. "I keep it here because I like to think of my dad. Always working."

"What did your dad do?"

"He was part owner of Western View Logging—hear of it?"

Vega shook her head.

"Probably the biggest logging company in the Pacific Northwest in its time," he said, glancing at Vega to check on how impressed she was.

"He owned it?"

"A third. He had two partners, but, between you and me, he did most of the work." Then he winked at her. Our little secret.

"You ever think about taking over for him?"

"At Western?" Klimmer said, surprised to consider it. "No, he, well, he became ill, and I sold his shares in the company, and then he died."

Vega had more questions to ask about Klimmer's father but sensed this was a time when she should say how sorry she was.

"I'm sorry to hear that."

"Thank you," he said, smiling like a saint in a painting. He began to loosen the bridle from the horse's head and neck and said, "You ever keep horses?"

"No," said Vega. And then a thing hit her—how Cap would answer. So she added, "Might've had a pony ride at a state fair once."

Klimmer smirked. Vega guessed he felt a little sorry for her.

"They develop personalities when they're young. Then, as they get older, you can still see who they are, but the light dims. Just like us."

Klimmer pulled the bit from the horse's mouth and hung it on a hook on a wooden beam. The horse stepped up and down.

"So," said Klimmer, taking a thick brush from another hook. "You're looking for Zeb Williams."

"That's right."

"You're not a 2, though."

"How'd you know?"

"Word gets around," he said. He began to brush the horse's head, the space between its ears and then between its eyes. The horse closed its eyes. "And, if we're being honest, you don't look much like an aging sports fanatic."

Vega held her hands out at her sides, palms up, and said, "All true."

"Someone hired you to find him after all these years," he said, not seeming to expect a response of any kind. "Hard to imagine I'll know anything, but happy to help."

His hospitality was solely relegated to the words he spoke and a small smile on his lips—no crinkles in the forehead or light in the eyes.

"Appreciate it," said Vega. "You've lived in Ilona your whole life, is that right?"

"That's right. I went to UO for college, then came back home."

"I hear you own some farmland. Commercial properties you rent to tenants. The diner downtown and the liquor store next door," recited Vega.

"True," said Klimmer, running the brush along the horse's neck. The horse stopped moving its feet.

"You bought that space from Cara Simms."

"I did," he said, then smiled again, and this time the rest of his face moved. "How do you figure Zeb Williams relates to my business history?"

Vega hesitated before answering; the only sound was the scratch of the brush against the horse's hair. The horse was calm, tail swishing to a ballad beat. Then she said, "The best way to figure out what happened to him is to try to get a complete picture of where he was last seen, which is here."

Klimmer started to brush the horse's mane.

"Ilona. And you own a lot of Ilona," she added.

"It might seem strange, but lots of the small towns around here are owned by primarily one person or business. I find it actually makes things run smoother for everyone. If we have a mudslide issue, I can call my guy at the Geo Commission and he'll take care of it," said Klimmer. "Plumbing problems, electricity—folks at the I-PUD can reach out to my friends at the state level. . . ."

"Pile of manure in the middle of the road?" Vega suggested.

Klimmer paused again in his brushing and grinned.

"Well, I know a guy who can take care of that, too. Now," he said, starting to brush again. "About Zeb Williams, from what I recall, I only met him once or twice when he was here. I'd just come back from school. He was an unassuming kind of guy—a lot of folks didn't even know who he was."

"Did you?" said Vega.

"Well, sure," said Klimmer, keeping his eyes on the horse. "I followed college ball, so I knew exactly who he was the second I saw him. Don't get a lot of celebrities around here."

"From what I've heard," said Vega, "people who knew who he was either loved him or hated him, because of what he did in the Big Game. Which side were you?"

"Not sure I was on one," said Klimmer. "Look, if it had been a Bears–Ducks game, that would have been a different story, right?" he added congenially.

"Do you remember how you met initially?"

Klimmer thought about it, gazing above the horse's back.

"Probably when he was working at the coffee shop. Cara might have introduced us."

"Were you and Cara friendly?"

"Sure," Klimmer said, laughing, his eyes dancing from the brush to Vega, to the stable door behind her. "We both grew up here, you know? Went to the same schools when we were kids." Then he coughed and said, "So she probably introduced me to Zeb, but we just said hello, how are you."

Klimmer stopped talking then, and stepped to his left, to brush the hair on the horse's flank. He appeared to be concentrating, though Vega couldn't be sure if the horse or the memory had his attention.

"And then?" she said.

"Then . . ." He held the brush up, as if to show her the dust on the bristles. "Then—nothing. He left town after a couple of months. I think I said ten words to him total." He resumed brushing, with shorter and quicker strokes.

Vega looked at the horse's head. It was glossy, the hair short. In the bare-bulb light of the stable, she could see the color was copper, like a coin.

Vega set her hand down gently on the horse's head and stroked the bridge of its nose, back and forth. The horse didn't seem to mind; its eyelids sank faster.

"So you don't recall having a disagreement with him about anything?" said Vega.

Klimmer's lips went into a frown as he shook his head once. "Oh, I don't think so. Maybe he gave me the wrong order once?" he suggested, as if Vega had asked him to make his best guess.

"Maybe," said Vega. "I spoke with someone who said that he saw you and Zeb arguing in the middle of the street outside the coffee shop."

Klimmer stopped brushing the horse and squinted. Then he smiled.

"I gotta tell you, I just don't remember that," he said. "It was a long time ago, and I didn't have any connection to the guy."

He began brushing the horse again, this time a little rougher. Its tail shook, the hair fanning up and out like water from a fountain.

Vega looked back to Klimmer. What would it take to make his tail shake?

"Yeah, it was a long time ago," said Vega. "But, just looking at dates, Zeb left town at some point in winter of '85, and Cara Simms sold you her coffee shop in February. And Zeb worked there before he left," Vega said, kicking the toe of her boot in the straw on the floor. "So that's a few connections right there."

Klimmer glanced at Vega and stopped brushing. Vega craned her head forward; she could feel the heat rising up from the horse's skin.

Klimmer went back to brushing. He shrugged.

"Wish I could tell you more," he said. "Just curious—who was it said they saw me arguing with Williams in the middle of the street?"

Vega thought of Dart, saw him flipping the sticky pages of his photo album. She rubbed her thumbnail against her bottom lip, tried to make it look like she was trying to remember.

"You know, I've just talked to so many people since I got here, I'm not sure."

"Gotcha," said Klimmer. "Well, he or she is mistaken. But I'm impressed by his or her memory, that's for sure."

Klimmer walked around the horse and started running the brush along the curve of its back, near the tail. He was brusque about it, swiping back and forth like he was washing a car.

He forced a laugh and then walked up to the horse's head, his face about a foot from Vega's. He watched Vega petting the horse for a second, and then he grabbed the horse by the root of its mane and yanked the head back. Vega pulled her hand away. The horse opened its eyes completely so Vega could see the whites. It bared its teeth and huffed out air. Vega could smell its earthy breath.

"See what I mean?" said Klimmer. "About the personality?"

Cap stared out the living-room window and watched a cone of snow-flakes as small as sawdust twirl in the streetlight's beam.

Nell was at Jules's place again, which meant he was in for another long night. Every time he glanced at the cable box, he hoped that time would have passed, but it had been ten o'clock for about an hour now.

Eventually, he went back to the couch, the gun, and the beer. He unmuted the sound on the TV and switched from local news to ESPN. College Bowl highlights—sacks, rushes, passes. Some respectable runs. All going the right way.

Cap got up and grabbed his laptop from his office, returned to the couch, and searched for Zeb's run; he clicked on the first video-link hit.

As he watched the clip, he couldn't control his smile. Because it was nuts! And also enraging. Cap didn't have any investment in either team, but he was able to muster the shock of the Cal fans on behalf of sports enthusiasts everywhere.

But also a strange joy, because there was such a glorious realization that such a thing could happen.

He watched the clip again and focused on Zeb's teammates this time. Linebackers, running backs—they just couldn't catch him. Not even with the fury in their hearts, thought Cap.

The holder—he had an unusual name, right? Cap searched and found it: Bear Thomas, Binghamton Realty. Cap clicked on the portrait. This was him, so much older. More than a good price for your home; we give you peace of mind.

East Coast, thought Cap, surprised. Without thinking too much about it, he clicked through to a map and plugged in his home address as the starting point, set the destination as Binghamton Realty.

Two hours, forty-one minutes. Traffic is light.

He shut the laptop and tossed it on the couch cushion, next to the Sig. He grabbed the remote and turned the sound up, switched back to news, then to home reno, then to a reality competition show, and sat back down.

Less than a three-hour drive, he thought. He could leave at seven, be back by two, make work calls on the way.

He flipped open the laptop and went back to the Binghamton Realty site. Click to make an appointment with Bear.

Cap clicked. Ten a.m. tomorrow.

"Okay," he said aloud.

Then he yawned and realized he was tired. He turned off the TV, put away his laptop and his gun, and went upstairs to bed; for the first time in a while, he didn't wake up before the birds.

Vega waited in her car for Cara Simms, across the road from the house. It was a little after five in the evening, and Vega figured Cara would be home from work soon.

It had rained on and off all day but seemed on pause now. The sun was just down, but the damp breeze had turned to freezing wind.

Soon the silver hatchback came into view. Vega felt no need to hide; there was no point in concealing either her presence or her purpose for being there. It was really just a matter of when Cara saw her, and how resistant she would or would not be to hearing what Vega had to say.

As soon as Vega was able to see Cara's face through the windshield, Cara recognized her and looked pained, scared, and furious all at once. She accelerated and pulled up so that her and Vega's cars were side by side, their driver's-side windows next to each other. There was a boy sitting in the passenger seat—Vega put him at eleven or twelve years old.

Cara powered her window down, and so did Vega, and Cara started speaking right away: "I told you before I'd call the police."

"That doesn't seem to mean much around here," said Vega. Cara didn't have an immediate response, so Vega kept going: "You may not have guessed this about me, Ms. Simms, because we just met, but I rub some people the wrong way. Sheriff Fenton is one of them."

Something opened up on Cara's face. Surprise and recognition.

"Do you think we might speak for just a few minutes?" Vega said, glancing at the kid, who was playing with his phone. "I understand it's his son that might be responsible for vandalizing your property. Him and his friends. I'm guessing they might have done something to your car, too, the one you had before this one," said Vega, nodding toward the hatchback.

"I thought you were here to ask questions about Zeb Williams," said Cara, also controlling her volume, not particularly argumentative.

"I was," said Vega, facing forward for a second. "I am. I'm also asking questions about other people."

"Like the sheriff's son?"

"Yes," said Vega. "Neil Klimmer, too."

Cara looked in her rearview and over her shoulder, then at the boy next to her. She turned back to Vega.

"You can park behind me" was all she said.

Vega followed her into the driveway, cut the engine, and got out; she leaned against the car while she watched the boy leave from the passenger side of Cara's car, hunched under the weight of a giant red backpack. He glanced over at Vega and seemed neither bothered nor impressed by her. Then he produced a key from a chain around his neck, unlocked the front door, and went inside.

Cara got out of the car next, a messenger bag strapped across her chest and a smaller purse in her hand. She opened the door to the back seat and leaned inside, came back out with two full canvas grocery bags.

"Need a hand?" said Vega.

"No, thanks," said Cara, not meeting Vega's eye.

She'll listen, but you don't have long, Vega thought.

Cara inched up the porch steps with both bags, and Vega gave her some space, staying a few feet behind. Then Cara went through the front door and kicked a rubber doorstop underneath to keep it open. Vega went inside.

To the right was the kitchen, where the light was on. Cara set her bags on a round table in the middle of the room.

The boy was sitting at the table, eating crackers from a reusable food container and writing in an open three-ring binder.

"Ethan, say hi to Miss Vega," Cara instructed as Vega came into the kitchen.

"Hi," said Ethan.

"Hi," said Vega.

Ethan went back to his homework, and Cara began unpacking her groceries. Vega stood near the doorway. She watched them as if they were in a play and she was in the audience. Ethan scribbled in his binder and shoveled as many tiny orange crackers into his mouth as could fit between his thumb and index finger.

Cara went about her business, putting away groceries, but slid her gaze over to Vega every few seconds, then spent the rest of the seconds pretending she was not watching her. She finished emptying one bag, folded it up, placed it on the table, and brushed her fingers over it, as if trying to iron the material. She made no move to unpack the other bag.

Then she placed her hands on the back of the chair in front of her and said to the boy, "Eeth, can you work in your room for a while?"

The boy looked up, offended. He opened his mouth to argue, but Cara cut him off.

"You can have an extra half-hour with Switch or Roblox."

Ethan became at least twice the amount of awake as he had been, jumped out of the chair, and ran from the room, leaving the crackers and the homework.

"I'm not sure what I can do for you," said Cara. "I told you the other day—Zeb Williams was a guy I knew for a couple of months. He didn't want a thing from me except to bus tables at the coffee shop and sleep on my couch." Cara shrugged, the muscles in her face rigid. "Then the 2s tracked him down—you know, his fans. And he left. Said he'd come back, but he didn't. I didn't think he would."

She took in a long breath through her nose.

"I didn't know who he was, didn't know a thing about football, didn't care. I was twenty-two, and my dad had just died. My mom, she wanted to sell the shop as soon as he was in the ground, but I wanted to hold on to it. Sentimental," she said, a feather of derision landing on the word. "She took my sister, who was still a teenager, and moved up to Eugene, but I wanted to stay here. In the house where I grew up." Cara looked around the kitchen.

"But Zeb came, and then he went. I never heard from him again."

Cara lifted her hand and flipped it. A mini-shrug.

"He didn't announce when he was leaving and didn't tell me where he was going. I didn't ask."

Vega leaned against the door frame and didn't speak, waiting for more.

"He was pretty good in bed," said Cara, and then she laughed. "I'm not sure what else I can tell you."

"Did you ever see Zeb argue with Matt Klimmer?" asked Vega.

This took Cara by surprise. She froze where she stood.

"What?" she said. "Zeb and Matt? No. Where did you hear that?"

"Guy named Dart."

"Dart?" said Cara. "The old man? He's still in town?"

"Yeah. In a trailer by the I-PUD. You know him well?"

Cara traced her fingers over the canvas bag as she stared at the table, thinking.

"I haven't seen him in a long time. I don't think he'd remember me, necessarily. A couple years after Zeb, he had a son who came to town and moved him out. I thought he went to an institution, something like that."

"You have an idea why Zeb and Matt might have been arguing?" said Vega.

"I don't know. This is a hundred years ago, realize." Cara folded the bag again, so now it was the size of a dinner napkin. She pressed it with the heels of her hands.

"You sold the coffee shop to Matt Klimmer, right?" said Vega.

"Yeah. But that's no secret," she said.

"Was it a good deal?"

"I needed the cash, so any deal was a good deal," said Cara. "I was paying off my father's hospital bills, and I sent the rest to my mom. She was right in the end—the money that place brought in wasn't worth the trouble. But it was a fair deal, if that's what you're asking."

"Were you on good terms with the family, the Klimmers?"

Finally, Cara's brow loosened. She looked tired but calm.

"Jack, Matt's father, was friends with my folks, especially Dad. They knew each other growing up. Jack was always decent with my father, even though Jack always had a ton more money."

"So Jack Klimmer was decent because he didn't act as rich as he was?"

Cara thought about it. "Yes, actually. That's right."

"What about Matt?"

"This is a small town, surrounded by other small towns. Three elementary schools, two middle, and one high school. I've known Matt since kindergarten. But nothing strange about that," said Cara.

Vega thought she seemed pretty determined to tell her how normal everything was.

"Were you and he friendly?" asked Vega.

Cara breathed in through her mouth like she was gearing up to say something, but then pressed her lips together.

"*Are* you and he friendly?" Vega added. "On account of the small-town thing, you must see him from time to time."

"I see him. We are friendly. We're not friends," Cara said.

Vega could swear that last statement had the pulse of a warning. She just wasn't sure if it was meant for her or someone else.

"Matt Klimmer was a rotten little kid," she said. "He'd trap frogs and tie their legs in knots, stuff like that. He wasn't like his father at all. I was never close with him, and we were in different social circles as we got older."

"Any reason you can think of, why Zeb and Matt Klimmer would get into it?" said Vega.

"No," Cara said, firmer now.

Then she sighed, pinched the bridge of her nose.

"Is there anything else?"

"Yeah," said Vega, pushing off the door frame and walking to the table so she stood directly across from Cara. "You have a student named Claire Bishop?"

Cara blinked in confusion. "Why?"

"You ever come down on her for cutting class?"

Now Cara brought her hand to her lips and chin. "Yes, but . . . ?"

"How did I know? Why don't you tell me what happened first, and then I'll tell you."

Cara looked at Vega with a hint of wariness. She did not seem at all convinced that Vega wouldn't try to use the information against her. She pressed her lips together.

"Kids aren't allowed to cut my class, even the seniors," said Cara, no pride in her voice. Just the facts. "Everyone knows this about me. Either a parent or guardian calls you in as sick, or I mark it as an unexcused absence, and then usually"—she paused, then exhaled—"I exact a penalty in the classroom."

She couldn't hide the crinkle at the corner of her lips.

"It's silly stuff. I make them read a monologue in front of the class or do a puppet show with pencils. Usually, everyone ends up having a laugh about it, even the offenders." She thought for a moment, then added, "Sometimes kids will purposefully cut class just so they can have the spotlight. Those are the theater kids."

Then she smiled—it was quick and full, and then it was over.

"What about Claire?" said Vega.

"She cut my class three days in a row—this was right before she stopped coming to school altogether, about two weeks ago. So . . . extra cuts, extra penalty," said Cara, tilting her head in one direction and then another, tipping a scale. "So I made her do the balcony scene from Romeo and Juliet and play both parts." Cara smirked. "It was funny. The kids liked it."

"Did Claire like it?"

"I don't care," said Cara. "I like my students, but I'm the boss, not their buddy. Respect is more important to me than adulation."

"Was she a good student, aside from the skipping?"

"Decent," Cara said. "Up to a few weeks ago. A lot of the seniors check out after the holidays—I'm used to that. Claire had another look that, unfortunately, I am also used to."

"What's that?"

Cara sighed. "That of a kid who's doing a lot of drinking and drugs on weeknights. It's frustrating. Some kids can dabble. Some kids just get in the hole and don't come out. Claire seems like one of those. Her sister, on the other hand," said Cara, with some affection, "she was a smart cookie."

Cara got tangled somewhere in the memory of Rachel and seemed distracted. But then she fixed her eyes on Vega. "So what is it *you* know, Ms. Vega?" she said.

"Claire Bishop dates Derek Fenton, the sheriff's son," said Vega. She watched Cara lean back as if a gust of wind had blown through the room. "Derek Fenton is tight with Neil Klimmer."

"Yeah," said Cara, somewhat bitter. "Just like their dads in high school. Only difference is, Jay Fenton was always smarter than Matt, even used to write his papers."

"But the Klimmers were always richer than the Fentons, right?"

Cara thought about it.

"There was a time Jay's family owned some farmland, but after Matt sold his dad's part of the logging business, he bought everything he could get his hands on, including the Fenton land."

"What about Derek and Neil?" said Vega.

"What about them?" said Cara, dismissive. Then she answered her own question: "Moderately bright, but after a while they both were tuned out, cut a lot of school. Neil liked to push people's buttons, and Derek seemed go along with it."

"How so?"

Cara cast her eyes somewhere on the ceiling, remembering.

"Neil didn't seem like the type to go on a lot of dates—I realize I'm judging from appearances, but he seemed real awkward around girls, and then, one day, he wasn't."

"He became a player?" said Vega.

Cara laughed. "No, oh my God, no, he went in the other direction, started interrupting girls in class, using a lot of inappropriate language. I reported him for detention a lot. Most of the boys just laughed along with it, including Derek." Cara shook her head, added, "*A lot* of detention that year."

"Were their fathers the same way?"

"I guess it's a little different with Sheriff Jay and Matt. Matt's not dumb, but Jay was always smarter. No one ever saw it, because he was also a jock. I don't know what kind of place you're from, but sometimes that's too much for people to take in a small town, being more than one type." Cara paused and thought. "That's too bad, for Claire, getting caught up with Neil and Derek."

"I'm not sure she sees it that way," said Vega. "I think she was pissed off that you disciplined her and then she told her boyfriend, and then he and Neil marked up your porch and messed with your car."

"They're in Liberty Pure?" said Cara. "I thought that was a neo-fascist thing. I figured they just vandalized this place at random. I see the name all over town."

"It wasn't random," said Vega. "You were targeted. And it is a neo-fascist thing."

"I talk a lot about fascism in my class, about trends. Comparing *Richard the Third* to certain political movements. But not overtly— we're not supposed to do that."

"Maybe a little of that sunk in with Claire Bishop, too," suggested Vega. "She cast you in the role of the hippie teacher trying to tread on her right to cut class and be a dipshit. I know I don't live here, but you could, if you wanted to, you could try to bring a lawsuit against those punks, since your sheriff isn't so likely to take action."

"I don't think I'm going to do that," said Cara. "I'm not afraid. As I told you, I'm not interested in making anyone like me. But I also have Ethan," she said, lifting her gaze to the ceiling. "I can't have anything come down on him."

Vega thought of Cap and Nell and felt an unfamiliar sting that was difficult to identify—it was like regretting something she'd not yet missed out on.

"You have your son to think about," said Vega.

"My nephew, actually," said Cara. "My sister is in rehab for the eighth or ninth time, so he is living with me until further notice. The responsibility of his safety is almost greater than if he were my own." Her eyes bore into Vega's. "Do you understand?"

"I do."

"If Neil Klimmer wants to pee on my porch, fine," said Cara.

"What about your car?"

Cara had some ice in her now.

"I needed a new one anyway," she said. "Wasn't worth the paint job."

"You have my card," said Vega. "Feel free to call me anytime."

"Okay," said Cara, slightly defrosted.

"If you remember anything about Zeb, or anything you think is relevant, or even not relevant, please . . ." said Vega, without finishing the sentence.

"I doubt I will," she said. "That was quite a few semesters ago."

"Would it be all right if I stopped by again at some point?" asked Vega. "I can call or text first."

"That's fine," said Cara, her voice soft now.

"I'll get out of your way, then," said Vega. "Have a good night, Ms. Simms."

Vega didn't move right away. She followed Cara's gaze down to the tabletop and noticed some uncooked grains of rice scattered across the surface. They looked like little iridescent bullet casings.

"One more question," said Vega. "Do you have a gun in the house?"

"This is Oregon," said Cara, no beats missed. "I have two."

5

BEAR THOMAS WAS SHOVELING SNOW ON THE SIDEWALK OUTSIDE his office when Cap arrived. He wore a bulky tan coat and black gloves, and the scrape of the shovel had a rhythmic sound as Thomas brought it against the pavement, then up, flinging snow toward the curb.

"Hey, Bear?" said Cap as he approached.

Thomas looked up, his face flushed under the bill of a flat cap, and gave a broad smile.

"Mr. Caplan," he said, pulling off a glove and extending his hand. "Pleasure. Can you believe they make the old man do this?" he said, tapping his shovel against the ground.

"You look like you're up to the challenge, if you don't mind me saying," said Cap.

"Seems you're saying I'm in good shape, so I don't mind it one bit."

Thomas laughed and stood up straight, and Cap could see how tall he was, over six feet, and still barrel-chested, like he'd looked in the video clips.

"Are you a few early?" said Thomas, checking his watch. Before Cap could answer, Thomas continued, chuckling: "You all right if I finish this path? Someone slips, they call their lawyer."

"Take your time," said Cap, backing up a step to give Thomas room.

"Much appreciated," said Thomas. "You're up from Pennsylvania, that right?"

"Yeah," said Cap. "North of Philly. But from Brooklyn originally."

"Nice town," said Thomas. "But a heck of a price tag, NYC. You get a lot more up here, quality-of-life speaking."

"You get a lot more anywhere outside of the five boroughs," Cap added.

"That's the truth."

"Not many places that expensive," said Cap. "Maybe New York and the Bay Area."

"Pssh," said Thomas, dumping more snow on the heap. "It's kooky-crazy out there."

"I've heard stories," said Cap. "People bringing suitcases full of cash to open houses."

Cap breathed deeply through his nose and felt tiny icicles start to form in his nostrils. Almost ten degrees colder here than Denville, he thought.

"You used to live out there, if I'm not mistaken," he said, his voice low.

Even though Bear Thomas looked like he could take Cap down in a fight, Cap still wanted to communicate that he was not a threat, so he stood very still and kept his distance.

Thomas paused in his work, removed his flat cap by the bill, and scratched his head, which was mostly bald.

"You a college-ball fan, then?" he said.

"Sure," said Cap, pushing his hands into his pockets. "NFL, too."

Thomas let out a short laugh. "Then you really got the wrong guy."

"Maybe not," said Cap. "Chargers picked you up, memory serves."

Thomas set the flat cap back on his head and grinned. "Didn't make it past training camp," he said, not sounding upset.

"That's not nothing."

"No, I suppose not," said Thomas. He brought the shovel down hard into a plank of ice that had been buried under the powder. "But I haven't played in a long time."

He scooped up the crumbled ice and threw it onto the heap. Then he looked straight at Cap.

"Remind me what kind of house you're looking for again?"

There was always a moment, Cap thought, if you were pretending, when you had either to come clean or to go all-in on the act. Both options had risks and benefits, but Cap knew he wasn't capable of patching together an elaborate lie, if for no other reason than that he was too exhausted to keep all the false details straight.

Also, he trusted his impressions, and his takeaway so far was that Thomas seemed friendly and only somewhat resistant to talking about his past.

"I'm not exactly looking at present," Cap said.

Thomas nodded, like this was a thing he already knew. He tapped the shovel against the ground. Once, then twice.

"What are you looking for, then, exactly?"

Still friendly; a little more resistant. Cap didn't answer, held his breath a second.

"I get it," said Thomas, nodding at Cap. "Not what. Who—that right?"

"Sorry for not being straight with you. I'm not a hundred percent sure why I'm here," Cap said, glancing at the shops across the street. "Actually, that's not completely true, either."

"You seem to be a little truth-averse there, Mr. Caplan," said Thomas. Then he raised his eyebrows and added, "That's the name, right?"

"Yeah, that's my name," said Cap. "Look, I'm a private investigator, and I have this business partner—well, full disclosure, sometimes she's my business partner—and she's been hired to find Zeb Williams. And when I looked you up and saw where you lived, I thought I'd try to meet you and see if you might be in a mood to reminisce."

Thomas rested his palm on top of the shovel's handle and stared at Cap. "To help out your sometime business partner?"

"Correct," said Cap, hearing how shaky it all sounded.

Thomas looked away from Cap, shoveled stray bits of ice from the path with the tip. Cap knew he was losing him and knew he had a chance only if he kept going.

"It's complicated," Cap began.

Thomas shook his head. "No, it's not, Mr. Caplan," he said. "It actually sounds pretty simple."

"Oh yeah?"

Cap was prepared to be told to fuck right off, but also acknowledged the unpredictability of the moment. This was the same world, after all, in which Zeb Williams had run the other way.

"Yeah," said Thomas. "You gave yourself away, why you're really here, and I get it. I've had one of those, too."

Cap squinted at him, confused, said, "A sometime business partner?"

Thomas laughed, and it was the loudest yet, more genuine than when he thought he was going to make a commission on a house, and more joyful than when he realized he wasn't.

"No, you fool," he said, still laughing. "A *she*."

Vega opened her eyes and saw the door to the motel room upside down through the tangle of her hair. She kicked her legs down from the handstand and stood up straight.

She suddenly had another idea about what crinklecut the recruiter might want to hear. She logged on to Reddit and started lurking around. It didn't take her long to find him: the most recent subreddit where he was posting was listed as /freespeechtactical. His most recent comment, three hours earlier, was "Not enough young people are involved. It's not enough to be angry."

Vega posted as a response: "Good students need a good teacher."

She left the laptop on the bed and took a shower. When she emerged from the bathroom a few minutes later, with a towel wrapped around her midsection, she saw her phone on the bedside table light up, and grabbed it.

It was not an upvote from crinklecut. It was a voice mail from Vega's father. They didn't speak much, Vega and her father; they didn't have much to say to each other. He and Vega's mother had divorced when Vega just learned to walk. He was a seesaw alcoholic—would go a month or two sober, and then, the following six months, would drink himself into a hole. Up and down, throughout Vega's childhood.

When Vega was twenty, her mother died from cancer, and Vega's father not only showed up at the funeral sober, but announced he'd stopped drinking for good as soon as he'd heard the news: his ex-wife's dying was the apparent moment of clarity. He apologized to Vega in accordance with the steps of AA, but Vega had a limited appreciation for his wake-up call.

Vega visited him and his second wife on some holidays to say hello, and sometimes he would send her a link to a Web site about

Jesus. A by-product of his quitting booze and marrying a woman he met at church was that he was currently very Jesus-oriented. The last time Vega had been to their house, there had been a life-sized inflatable crucifix in their backyard, like a pool floatie, though they didn't have a pool.

But calling and leaving a message at 7:07 a.m. was unusual for him. Vega thought it was a misdial, but then opened up her "recents" and saw he had left just under a one-minute voice mail. No accident. She tapped the message, listened.

"Alice, there's a thing on the car . . . the car. . . ." He stopped and started, then said to Bitsy, his wife, "I'm leaving her a message right now." Back to Vega: "Someone put graffiti on the car, and it says your name. There's some language on the car. We can't drive it like this." Back to Bitsy: "Is it coming off with the Lysol?" Then, back to Vega: "Are you at home or are you working?" He paused, his breathing sounding labored. "I just hope you call me soon."

The message lingered for a few more moments and then stopped. He had not sounded sad—just confused, tired, old. Vega squeezed the sides of the phone in her hand and then tapped his name, put the phone to her ear. He picked up before the first ring ended.

"Alice?" he said, still out of breath.

"Yeah, Dad, it's me. What's wrong with your car?"

He huffed. "Well, Bitsy came out and saw it first. Someone spray-painted all over it. It says 'bitch' everywhere. And then, on the hood, it says your name."

"Dad, what does it say exactly?" Vega said, struggling to keep her breaths even so her heart rate wouldn't rise.

"It says 'bitch' all over it and that you . . . you're a bitch," he said, stumbling over the words.

"Did Bitsy see anyone do it?"

"What?" he said. "No, she just came out and saw it. Now all the neighbors are outside."

"Okay. Dad?" said Vega, trying to keep him focused. "I want you to hang up, take pictures of the car, and send them to me. Then I want you to ask your neighbors if they saw anyone. Then go to wherever you get your car serviced, and I'll wire you some money to have it cleaned or painted or whatever. So that's five things. Hang up, take pictures, send pictures, talk to neighbors, get your car fixed up. Got it?"

"Yes, Alice, I got it," he said, a slight edge entering his tone. "I don't know what you're getting into."

"I'm good, Dad," said Vega. "I'm sorry about this. I think it has to do with the case I'm working, but I'll take care of it. Won't happen again."

"I pray for you every night, niña," he said. It sounded like a warning.

"You should use that time to check your front window and make sure no one's vandalizing your property," said Vega. "Sorry again, Dad. Do the five things, please."

"Alice—"

She hung up on her father, and then immediately sent a text to the Bastard: "what is the quickest way to capture private e-mail traffic between two parties, assuming gmail-type servers, etc?" She saw the three flashing dots, so waited a minute, until the response came through: "Get me the laptop. I'll see what I can do."

Vega finished drying off and quickly got dressed. She stared at her reflection in the mirror above the dresser, tugged the sleeves of her jacket like a groom preparing for the big day. A groom needs a bride, she thought.

Her phone buzzed with the photos her father sent: front, back, driver's side, passenger side. It was "basic" and "bitch" in red spray paint on the hood, doors, windows, over and over, big letters, small letters. Except on the rear windshield was also her name. Just so they could be sure she would get the message.

She glanced up at herself in the mirror again and said aloud, "Got it."

It didn't taken the Bastard long to find the golf club where Matt Klimmer was a member, and to figure out that Tuesdays and Thursdays were the days when both Matt and Neil Klimmer signed into the club's registry, their tee time set for 9:00 a.m. Today was Tuesday— Vega didn't think much of luck, but still appreciated flipping the ace and wasn't about to squander it.

First, she drove to the Ever Creek Golf Club, about twenty miles south of Ilona, and parked opposite the entrance in the cul-de-sac; she stayed behind a delivery truck and pretended she belonged there.

Around eight-forty-five, she saw Matt and Neil Klimmer pull up in Matt's Range Rover. Matt got out and handed his keys to the valet, chitchatting and laughing. Then Neil got out, staring at his phone, the hood of his sweatshirt pulled over his eyes. Matt walked behind the Range Rover and aimed the key fob at the trunk, which popped and rose a few inches.

Matt shouted Neil's name, then pointed at his feet, like you would call a dog that had just peed on the sheets. Neil curled his shoulders forward and shoved his phone into his pocket, lifted the lid of the trunk, pulled out two sets of golf clubs, slung one over each shoulder, then grabbed a duffel bag and closed the trunk.

Matt said something else to Neil—Vega couldn't hear it; she was too far, and the engine of the delivery truck in front of her was running, but his face was right in his son's face, and he was talking and looked like he was chewing something he didn't want to be chewing. Then he went into the clubhouse, and Neil trudged behind him, carrying all the gear.

Vega took off as soon as they were both inside and drove back to Ilona. She passed the Klimmers' house and parked down the road, then got out and walked to the driveway, up to the front door. She rang the doorbell and waited.

A stout woman, about sixty, wearing jeans and a utility smock, opened the door.

"Hi, I'm looking for Lila Klimmer," said Vega.

Concern crossed the woman's face, and she held up one finger to Vega. She retreated into the house, leaving the door open.

Vega peered inside, saw the high-ceilinged living room, picture windows, and skylights. Then she saw the stout woman coming down a curving staircase, followed by Lila Klimmer. Vega got ready to talk fast.

The stout woman held her arm out toward Vega, presenting her to Lila. Lila came to the doorway.

She was around Vega's height, but big-boned in the way Vega imagined a Scandinavian person would be, with shoulder-length blond hair styled like an anchorwoman's, leggings, and a lightweight gym hoodie. She had a light sheen of sweat on her face.

"Hi, Ms. Klimmer? I'm Alice Vega. I just started with *The South Oregon Gazette,* and I'm hoping I could just have a few minutes of your time?"

Vega spat out the words like she had a timer running.

"Oh, I . . ." said Lila. "I'm in the middle of something."

"I understand, it's just that . . ." Vega paused. "I'm hoping I could interview you?"

Lila touched the ends of her hair on one side, rubbed the strands between her fingers. "What kind of article are you writing?"

"It's about family businesses in southern Oregon."

Lila placed a hand on her hip, relaxed her stance. She laughed gently. "Then it's my husband you really want to speak with. He's not in."

"Actually, I was hoping to get your perspective," said Vega. "Everyone knows that the wives have always been the backbone of the operation. So I want to talk to you—the modern pioneer woman."

Lila stopped playing with her hair and removed her hand from her hip, stood up straight, instantly puffed up. Apparently, she enjoyed thinking of herself as a pioneer.

"Please, come in," Lila said. "You said your name was Alice?"

"That's right."

Lila smiled and led Vega into the kitchen.

A sturdy rectangular wooden table stood in the center of the room, and Lila gestured to the wooden stools surrounding it. Vega sat.

"Would you like anything to drink? Sparkling water?"

"Sure, that would be nice."

Vega scanned the room, took in the white porcelain bowls lining a set of wooden shelves next to the window over the sink. Heard the hum of the stainless-steel fridge. The temperature was pleasantly cool; a light smell of cinnamon hung in the air.

Lila went to the refrigerator and filled a glass with ice from the dispenser. Then she opened the door and removed a bottle of water.

Vega took her phone out of her pocket and set it on the table.

"Okay with you if I record?" she said.

"Oh, sure, of course," said Lila.

Vega tapped the button.

"So you're part of a big Ilona legacy," said Vega. "Starting with your father-in-law, right?"

"Well, yes," said Lila. "Actually, even before that—Matt's family has been in the area over a hundred years, back when it was still the Wild West."

"That's right," said Vega. "And interesting your husband didn't take over the logging business from his dad."

"No," said Lila, like she was a little sorry to break this news. Then she laughed: "I mean, yes, it's interesting, but, no, he found his calling with property, small businesses."

"The diner in town," said Vega, pointing at her.

"Yes, and a lot of the shops. He really has a feeling, an instinct about what to buy when."

Lila recited this in a way that made Vega feel she'd said it a few times before.

"So," said Vega, upbeat. "Logging to real estate to . . ." She flipped her hand and held it up, like she was a waitress holding an imaginary tray. "What's the next generation going to do?"

Lila looked lost.

"Oh, Neil?" she said, with an air of discovery.

"Yes," said Vega, smiling. "Your son—he's twenty?"

"Y-yes."

Small stumble. Adjust the fitness tracker on the wrist. What was it about the age of the son? Vega thought.

"He must go to UO, like his dad?" Vega said. When Lila didn't answer, Vega said, "Don't tell me he broke your heart and went to Oregon State?"

That got a laugh out of Lila. "Oh no. Now, that really would be bad. No, Neil's doing some projects with Matt and figuring it out. It's all fine," she said.

"I'm sure it is," said Vega. "He have any hobbies?"

"Neil?" Lila said, as if she'd forgotten who'd they been discussing.

"Yep, Neil," said Vega. "Any hobbies? Is he a sports guy, or a horse guy, maybe? Just looking for a hint which way he might lean, career-wise."

"He's working from home for now, doing some freelance coding."

"Coding!" exclaimed Vega. "He's a computer guy, then, yeah?"

"Yes, that's right," said Lila, now humble.

"That's where the money is," said Vega. "What kind of coding work does he do?"

"Right now he's doing some work for an insurance group, billing and things like that."

"Well, that sounds boring," said Vega, feigning disappointment. "What's he really want to do? What's his passion?"

"Oh, wow, that's a tough one," said Lila. She seemed to wake up a bit, buoyed by Vega's enthusiasm. "As I said before, he's still figuring it out, but maybe at some point he'll make it down to Silicon Valley?"

Uncertain but hopeful, thought Vega. Good.

"That's so funny you say that. I'm from California," Vega said, placing her hand on her chest. "And I have a friend in the Palo Alto area. I might be able to talk to him, about Neil."

"Do you think so?" said Lila. "That would be incredible."

"It would be my pleasure," said Vega, making sure each new idea coming out of her mouth sounded like an even more delightful discovery than the last. "I really love connecting people," she said, picking her phone up from the table. "Except . . ."

Vega made her mouth a straight line.

"What is it?" said Lila, concerned.

"I've done some programming in another life," Vega said, waving her hand dismissively. "And if I could take a look at what Neil's done, I might be able to give my friend a sense of his skills."

"That would be amazing," said Lila. "Could you . . . could you come back when he's here? He could show you what he can do."

"I bet he could," said Vega. "But why waste time? If I can take a look at his work, I can text my friend right now."

Lila cast her eyes downward, worried. "It's just, I wouldn't know what to show you," she said.

"Not to blow my own horn," said Vega. "But I know my way around a device. If I can see a laptop, I might be able to tinker."

Lila paused, seemed to remember she'd just met Vega: Pull it back.

"Hey, that's okay," said Vega. "I can definitely come back. I mean, I have to go out of town for a few days, but I can swing by next week," she said, tapping her phone, checking her calendar.

"Are you sure? Next week?"

"Pretty sure," said Vega. "If not, I'll text you."

Lila brought her fingers to her lips, thinking it over. Vega couldn't intuit her exact process but knew this: if you made someone think she had a thing, and then she thought she was going to lose it, it didn't matter what the thing was, just that it had once been hers; she had it in her hands and let it slip away.

"Wait," said Lila. "Maybe I can bring his laptop up here. I don't know his password, but, I don't know, just in case."

"Absolutely!" said Vega. "Just in case."

Lila got up from her seat and headed for an open doorway at the opposite end of the room from where they'd entered. Vega grinned like an idiot until Lila was just out of sight, then thought a little about how exactly she would convince Lila to give her the laptop.

Before she got too far, though, she heard the murmur of a car engine, twisted around on the stool, and saw Klimmer's Range Rover pulling into the circular driveway. Matt was behind the wheel, Neil next to him. Matt was talking but looking straight ahead, his mouth opening wide, Vega thought. Raising his voice. Neil slumped against the door and shrugged the seat belt off.

Vega clicked her tongue against her front teeth in disappointment. She watched Neil get out of the car and trudge toward the house, talking to himself, sneering.

He came through the front door and yelled, "Mom! Where's the fucking mallet putter?!"

Then he was muttering; Vega couldn't hear the words, but stayed put and watched him trapped in some kind of shadow jail on the doormat. Neil stepped back and forth and side to side. Matt stayed in the car, looking at his phone.

"Mom!" Neil yelled again, his voice cracking.

"She's downstairs," Vega called to him.

He looked at her, shocked and embarrassed, and hurried into the kitchen, tracking mud on the tile.

"The fuck?!"

His tone was aggressive, but he didn't get too close, stayed standing at the opposite end of the table. And even though it was his house, and Vega was the trespasser, he had the look of someone who'd been caught.

"Who you talking to over there, Neil?" said Vega, nodding to the front door. "Seems like a pretty heated argument."

"Get out of my house."

"Or what?" said Vega, taking a sip of water.

Neil slammed his palm on the table and said, "Or I'll call the sheriff."

"And tell him what?" said Vega. "That your mom invited me in and gave me a sparkling water?"

He didn't have an immediate response and continued to glare. Then Lila appeared through the back doorway, holding a laptop with six or seven cords hanging from the ports.

"Neil," exclaimed Lila, smiling. A pleasant surprise.

"What the fuck are you doing?!" shouted Neil.

He rushed to his mother and yanked the laptop from her hands.

"Neil, no," said Lila, as if there had been a terrible misunderstanding. "This is Alice, she knows someone who might be able to give you a job."

"No, she doesn't," said Neil, super-annoyed. "And you were just gonna give her my fucking laptop! What the fuck, Mom."

"She works for the *Gazette*, Neil," said Lila, like she was talking to a young child.

"Ugh, no, you dumbass!" Neil yelled. "She tricked you. She's a detective."

Lila's lips crimped into a crooked line as she turned to face Vega. "Detective," she said.

"Private investigator," said Vega, standing.

"You spoke to my husband yesterday in the stable," said Lila.

"Yes."

"What do you want?" she said to Vega.

"Get the fuck outta here, now," Neil said, but he didn't make a move for her, just opened the laptop cover and tapped a key. "Mom, what the fuck did you do to this? You're not supposed to touch it."

"I couldn't even turn it on, Neil," said Lila.

Calm and pathetic, thought Vega. Which made Neil angry and pathetic.

Then Vega considered the next few moves: wrest the laptop from Neil, use it to uppercut his jaw; grab the water glass, smash it into Lila's flat face. Then the housekeeper would call the sheriff, and he'd toss Vega into some stuffy holding cell in Sheriff Yosemite Sam's office.

Lila turned to look at Vega once more. "You should leave."

Vega took one more sip of water and stood up to leave; she tapped the "end record" button on her phone.

"I should. Thanks for the water. Refreshing," she said.

She headed for the front door, walked past Neil, and said, "You probably shouldn't keep your dad waiting, right? His golf clubs aren't going to carry themselves."

As Vega opened the door, she heard Neil yelling at Lila, "What the fuck, Mom?!" She headed straight for the Range Rover.

Klimmer looked up at her. His eyes were stony at first, but then he added a smile, baring a row of uneven teeth. He powered down the window.

"Morning, Ms. Vega," he said. "What brings you by?"

"I didn't get a chance to meet your wife yesterday," said Vega. "Seemed impolite."

"Is that the real reason?" he said, keeping the smile.

"Sort of," said Vega, glancing over her shoulder. She could still hear Neil scolding his mother. "My father—he lives in California; his car got vandalized."

"I'm so sorry to hear that," he said, as if it had died in a war.

"It's funny—I think whoever did it might have been asked to do it by someone they met on social media."

"Social media's for idiots," Klimmer said, consulting his reflection in the side mirror.

"I thought it was how this generation networks," said Vega. "That's why Neil spends all his time on it."

Klimmer glanced at her out of the corner of his eye.

Then Neil burst through the front door, still holding the laptop.

"What's up, Neil?" said Vega, cheery.

He walked toward her but stayed near the headlights of his father's car.

"Ms. Vega was just leaving, Neil," said Klimmer.

"Not just the property," said Neil, his jaw gritted, eyes filmy and dark. "You should leave town."

"Neil!" shouted Klimmer. "Get back in the house."

Neil seethed, his knuckles white as he clutched the laptop to his chest. Then he turned and ran back inside.

"Good luck with your case, Ms. Vega," said Klimmer. "I hope everything works out for you."

"I appreciate that. Please say goodbye to Neil and Lily for me."

"Lila," he corrected.

"Right—Lila," Vega said, chuckling. "Glad one of us remembered her name."

She didn't wait to see the shape his face took, just got into her car and buckled up and pulled out of the driveway. Even as she drove onto the road leading off the property, she didn't look back at him, just held her arm out the window and wiggled her fingers in a goodbye wave, in case he was watching.

Vega drove back to the motel and called a fed she knew named Cartwright, leaving him a message.

Then she spent some time reviewing white-nationalist alternative-narrative videos on YouTube. She'd always known they were out there, like the way she knew you could get a flesh-eating virus from a water park, but hadn't had any firsthand knowledge. Each video fed into the next: first about how the Holocaust was staged; then a montage of local news about Black-on-white crime; then—and this piqued Vega's interest—an interview with an earnest guy who looked like someone's chubby unemployed uncle wearing a leather jacket that probably fit him in high school. He had a podcast and a book about how young white males were losing their place in society because of feminists. Also, there was no gender pay gap. Additionally, childbirth wasn't painful. And you'll be glad to hear rape doesn't exist.

What a relief, thought Vega.

She was in the middle of a video called Race and IQ when Cartwright called back.

"Alice Vega, I thought I saw your number come through," he said. Vega recognized the Carolina lilt.

"Special Agent," she said, "I need your help."

"That was the small talk, huh?" he said, not sounding offended.

"Sorry, I'm in the middle of a thing."

"I remember that about you," he said politely. "Tending to be in the middle of things. Shoot."

"I'm on a missing-persons job, but I'm running up some white-nationalist types. You ever see that in your line of work?"

"Not me personally, but I can send you some names and numbers. What's the neighborhood?"

"Southern Oregon."

Vega heard a car engine, which sounded like it was right outside her door. She stood and walked to the window, peered out through the curtain, and saw one of the sheriff's cruisers pulling in next to her rental.

"Shit, yeah," said Cartwright, laughing. "There's about four Black people in the state. "They got names, these types?"

"Liberty Pure."

"Liberty Pure?" Cartwright repeated.

Vega watched Sheriff Fenton get out of the car on the passenger side. Rutledge, the wrinkled deputy, sat in the driver's seat. Vega watched Fenton walk toward her room door.

"That's right."

"I might have something," he said. "Let me talk to a friend and get back to you."

"You want to give me a hint?"

"No, ma'am," he said. "Just want to make sure I got the right bell with the right ring."

"Appreciate it," said Vega. "I have to go now."

Vega hung up, and then came the knock. She opened the door, and there was Fenton. She got a better sense than before of how big he actually was: the top of her head came to his chest.

"Afternoon," he said.

"Hi, Sheriff."

He waited for her to ask the first question, and, when it didn't come, decided to answer it anyway.

"Only so many places a tourist can stay around here," he said, holding his arms out. "I know Marty, at the front desk."

Vega gave him a nod to show that she was listening. Some more seconds passed. Though Fenton didn't seem nervous, he was by no means still—hands adjusting his belt, shoulders rising and settling like he had a cramp in his neck.

"Heard you paid the Klimmers a visit," he said.

"I wasn't aware that could be considered police business."

Fenton smiled. "Attempted theft is, however," he said. "Lila Klimmer said you almost walked off with her son's laptop."

"Another way of saying that is that she almost gave me her son's laptop," said Vega.

Fenton ignored her and continued: "She said you made up some story about who you were."

"That's right. I pretended to be a reporter who dabbles in computer programming. I didn't pretend to be a cop, though," she said, shrugging. "If impersonating anyone in any circumstance is illegal here, you really must have your hands full on Halloween."

The last vestige of congeniality washed away from Fenton's face. He leaned his head to one side and then the other, stretching his neck. How's that cramp?

He took a sharp inhale through his nose and said, "How much longer you think you'll be in town, Ms. Vega?"

"I'm not sure, Sheriff. However long it takes to finish my case."

Now Fenton laughed. "By now, surely, you know Zeb Williams isn't here," he said. "Ilona doesn't have that many hiding spots."

"You're probably right about that," said Vega. "Still, I'd like to stay a few days to be extra sure."

"Suit yourself. I just wanted to stop by. . . ." He leaned toward her an inch or two to get a glimpse of the number on the door. "Room number eight. Let you know you're never really alone in a place like this."

Vega knew he was doing his best to sound ominous, and she felt a little bad for him. She heard her phone buzz behind her and hoped Fenton was almost done intimidating her.

"Oh, I'm not lonely," she said. "Plenty of friends. Marty at the front desk, for example."

Fenton rolled his shoulders one more time and seemed to know he was being teased.

"Take care of yourself, Ms. Vega."

"Take care, Sheriff. Thanks for stopping by."

He went back to the car and got in. Vega shut the door and then peered through an opening in the curtain. She saw him speaking to Rutledge, who started the engine. She waited until he pulled out of the space and then the lot before she left the window.

She checked her phone, expecting a missed call from Cartwright, but instead saw a notification on the screen: "You have a new message from u/crinklecut94."

Vega clicked.

Hi—I think your responses on the america board are thoughtful and you sound like you know what you're talking about. Any chance you want to meet in person? Assuming you are in the southern Oregon area?

Looking forward to speaking.

Vega shut her eyes for a moment and thought a long time about what she would write back to crinklecut before she put her fingers back on the keys. She had to sound eager and young, which wouldn't be hard. But there was another thing—if crinklecut had recruited Neil Klimmer or Derek Fenton, she had to take the chance that either they weren't that close or that Neil wasn't organized enough to tell his mentor about a PI making trouble in town.

She would have to be someone else entirely and make it convincing enough so that crinklecut wouldn't even think to question her.

She tried to recall the tone of the people posting on the subreddits, and decided she had to do her best to sound like she'd lived a normal life but somehow had been terribly wronged.

Cap sat opposite Bear Thomas at his desk in the corner of the Binghamton Realty office. Both of them were drinking coffee out of small paper cups. Thomas's cup looked like a thimble in his hand; his shoulders spanned almost twice the length of his ergonomic chair's headrest.

"Were you friends with him off the field?" asked Cap.

"Sure, we all were," said Thomas. "You ever play sports?"

"Not like you played sports."

"Okay," said Thomas. "There's camaraderie there; everyone's psyched up to make it to Cal, to play at Memorial." He paused, went somewhere else for a second, staring at a point on his desk. "But, yeah, Zeb and I were friends, outside of practice. We went on a couple of double dates."

"When he was with Carmen Fohl? Or Carmen Wirth back then, was it?"

"Yeah, Carmen," he said, remembering.

"Did you keep in touch with her at all?"

Thomas sighed and said, "Nope. I found her a little snobby. Aloof. She and Zeb were a weird match, but Zeb was sort of a weird guy."

"How so?"

Thomas thought about it, said, "When he was talking to you, he was focused on you, would ask you twenty questions in a row about your life, but then, another day, you'd be lucky if you got a nod in your direction."

"So maybe he was aloof, too?" Cap suggested.

"I think he was just . . ." Thomas paused, held his hand up sideways between his eyes and karate-chopped it forward. ". . . real focused."

Cap pictured Zeb running down the field.

"Were you pissed after The Run?"

"Hell, yeah," said Thomas. "We all were. For me, it didn't even matter it was the Big Game. It was *any* game. We worked hard, man. We had a picture of him in the locker room looked like Swiss cheese from all the darts we threw at it."

"Are you still?" asked Cap.

"Pissed? No," said Thomas, laughing again. "I'm an old man. Don't have the energy. Seeing the replay every year on wackiest compilations—after a while, it stopped bothering me."

"And Zeb never contacted you?"

"After The Run? No way," he said, throwing his empty cup into a trash can a few feet away. He grabbed a pencil from his desk and leaned back in his chair. "You know, I haven't thought of this in a long time, but I ran into Carmen, I don't know, a month or two afterward? She hugged me, which was unlike her."

"On account of the aloofness," added Cap.

"That's right," said Thomas, a smile spreading. "But after she hugged me, she said something like 'He's sorry, Bear, he's sorry for all of it.'"

"They were close," offered Cap. "Maybe she felt comfortable speaking for him."

"Maybe," said Thomas, standing the pencil upright on the desk, his index finger on the eraser. "But, now I'm thinking about it, the way she said it was like she knew for sure. Like he'd told her."

Cap thought about that while he watched Thomas balance the

pencil on its sharpened tip. He knew there was no way it would stand when Thomas took his finger off the eraser, but Cap watched it still, hoping to be surprised.

Vega walked through a Laundromat, avocado-green washers on one side, dingy yellow dryers on the other. Most of the machines were off, only a couple clicking and churning. The air smelled like fabric softener; Vega could picture the bedsheets waving on the clothesline on the label.

An old man with thick black-rimmed glasses sat in a raised booth, squinting at his phone. He glanced at Vega and then nodded toward the back of the room.

The guy Vega was looking for sat in the last chair in one of the two rows, white tee shirt, blue jeans, black boots. Ink up and down toned arms. Lean and young, potentially quick on his feet. The only other customer in the place was a Latina woman folding clothes at a table closer to the doors. A toddler slept in a stroller near her feet.

There was a battered magazine on the chair next to the young guy.

"Hi," said Vega, feigning shyness. "Is this seat taken?"

He picked up the magazine and rolled it into a tube, gestured to the seat with his head, which was shaved almost to the skin on the sides and just a little longer on top. He looked to be around thirty.

She sat.

She'd given some thought to the name she'd use, and chose the most innocuous-sounding one she knew, which also happened to be her stepmother's nickname.

"I'm Bitsy," she said. Then quieter, "You're crinklecut?"

"Actually, it's Edward Cooper," he said, shaking her hand. "But, yeah, that's me. Nice to meet you."

When he smiled, his face brightened, the corners of his mouth and eyebrows and lids lifting like they were being pulled up by invisible strings. There was a long gray bruise following the line of his left cheekbone. Vega had had a bruise just like that before; she knew it had once been the better part of a black eye.

"I like all your tattoos," she said, pointing with her chin to his arm. "How many do you have?"

"I don't know, probably thirty little ones," he said, then presented the inside of his forearm to reveal the image of a fist inside a laurel wreath. "And a few larger ones. Big backpiece, too. I can't show you here," he said, and then he laughed, so she did, too. "You have any?"

"Not yet," said Vega. She curled her shoulders in and lifted her feet, balanced on the toes of her boots like a bored sixth-grader. Anything to look younger, smaller. "Hopefully, soon, though."

"What are you thinking about?"

Vega blew air through her lips.

"Something simple, probably?" she said. "Like an '88' in the middle of a rose, so it's kind of hidden, you know?"

"That's a good idea," he said. "The hidden part, I mean."

Cooper tapped the rolled magazine against his palm. "I liked what you had to say online," he said.

"Thanks," said Vega, eager.

"I'm not just saying that," said Cooper, still hitting the magazine into his hand, like a Little Leaguer loosening up his glove. "Lots of people have the right intentions, but there aren't too many who can get specific like you." The edge of the magazine landed in his palm and he squeezed it. "What do you do for work?"

"I, uh," Vega said, looking over her shoulders, "I'm a high-school teacher."

"I knew it," said Cooper, tickled. "I could tell from your posts you weren't playing around. What school?"

Vega winced. "Hey, I'm . . . If it's okay, I'd kind of like to keep things a little private."

Cooper stared at her. His eyes couldn't decide if they were dark gray or brown.

"It's just," Vega said, combing stray hairs behind her ear, "I've never done this before. Met someone IRL who I met online." Then she let out a pathetic laugh. "I've never even been on an Internet date."

Cooper slumped in his seat and chuckled. "That's good," he said. "You're smart. I could be anyone."

Vega stared at her hands in her lap and smiled.

"Tell you what," said Cooper. "Let's get to know each other a little; then you can tell me more about yourself when you're comfortable with it. I got an idea," he said, producing a pen from his back pocket. "I'll give you my cell, and you can text me if you want, if you don't want to send me a message online. Sound good?"

Vega turned to face him and nodded.

He smiled and tore a small corner off the magazine cover, scribbled down the numbers.

"Good," he said, handing her the scrap. "Can I ask how long you've been teaching?"

"A few years," said Vega, shrugging. Then she sighed and said, "It's sort of a frustrating job."

"Yeah?" said Cooper. "How's that?"

"We're not allowed to, like, talk to the kids about our personal views," Vega said in a half-mutter. "But I see them outside of school time to time. Hell, more than time to time—I live in Ilona, for Jesus's sake. You been there, right?"

"Oh yeah, it's a skid-mark town. Size of a skid mark on your underpants."

Vega made a surprised face but then laughed.

"Excuse me," said Cooper, wearing a satisfied grin. "I dropped out of high school, so I might not be the most articulate person you ever met."

"It was an evocative use of description," said Vega.

"Yeah, it was," said Cooper, laughing. "I talk trash about all these towns, but I also kind of love them, you know? You grow up in Ilona?"

"No, California," said Vega. "But it's the same thing—with the small towns, I mean."

"That's the thing," said Cooper, earnest. "It's the same all over the country. Small towns are like these little . . . You know what a terrarium is?"

"Is that like a garden in a glass ball?"

"Yeah. What I'm saying about the towns—they're like little representations of the whole country. All the good and the bad duking it out, just like in the big cities." He glanced at her, head to foot. "Mind if I ask you how old you are?"

She did some quick math. She'd already figured that, the younger he thought she was, the more believable this would be. If he was around thirty, and Neil Klimmer had been recruited in high school or close, she had to push it as far as she could. She knew if she wasn't too tired she could still pass for late twenties, but didn't want to chance it. She'd spent a lot of time in the sun as a kid, after all; she couldn't hide the splinters at the corners of her eyes and cracks around her mouth when she smiled, but she could shave a few years off.

"Thirty-two," she said. Then she looked toward her shoes. "Old, I know."

"Come on," said Cooper. "You don't look older than thirty, for real. And I'm thirty-one, anyways."

"Just that I know that the people who are getting active are on the younger side."

"You know anyone in particular?" said Cooper.

Vega allowed a guarded smile. "I, uh, had some students a few years back, but they're still around town. They do graffiti and kid stuff like that." Then she whispered, "Call themselves Liberty Pure."

"Oh yeah," said Cooper, encouraging. "Ilona LP's like our youth group—it might be kid stuff, but it all adds up."

"I totally agree," said Vega. "I just want to do something more meaningful."

"It sounds like you've put thought into this," said Cooper. "Which I appreciate. I can tell you this, Bitsy—young people are important to what we're doing, there's no doubt about it. The kids online and the kids tagging and the kids making cherry bombs in the basement— that was me, once. It's all meaningful in its way, but the leadership's not up for overseeing every little thing they're up to. My job is to encourage them and be, like, a touchstone, but, whatever they're up to in Ilona, that's all them, which is good. We know they're there when we need them, you understand?"

Vega nodded.

She hadn't planned this. In truth, on a lot of the cases she worked, she didn't actually plan much of anything. Her job was like staggering blindfolded through the woods, holding your arms out to graze the trees with your fingertips before you ran into them.

She crooked her finger at him. Come closer. He leaned in, and she put her lips to his ear, which smelled like shaving cream and had three healed earring holes on the lobe.

"The students are Neil Klimmer and Derek Fenton. Do you know them?"

She pulled her head away from his, and then he sat up straight and laughed in recognition.

"Sure, I know them. They're good kids. Thinking about things. Bitsy, even though you feel like you're not having an impact, maybe you influenced them when they were in your class."

Vega became bright-eyed. "I never thought about it that way," she said.

"You really should. You've already started the work."

All she'd wanted was to scratch around Cooper's brain a little, maybe run some fishing line between him and Neil and Derek, but here was a much bigger opening between the trees than she'd expected. This guy wants a pure white maiden to save, that's what he'll get.

"Is it okay . . ." she said, looking pained, ". . . if you don't mention to them you met me? I'd like to keep this between the two of us."

She couldn't look at Cooper straight on, because she was still playing up the shyness, so she glanced at him from the side and was still able to see that what she'd said was a little provocative to him. He took a few seconds to respond.

"Like I said, we can take this as slow as you want. I don't want to push you."

"It's okay," she said, patting his leg once and then pulling her hand back into her lap. "I have to learn not to be so scared of everything."

"Come on, now," said Cooper. "You're here, aren't you?"

She turned to face him, said, "Yeah, you're right. I'm here." She looked at her watch and shrugged. "I'll let you go. I'm really glad I came today."

"I am, too, Bitsy," said Cooper, looking her in the eyes. "Once you wake up, you can't go back to sleep. You know what I mean?"

Cap felt an unfamiliar lightness in his limbs as he drove through Scranton and then Wilkes-Barre. The Poconos seemed majestic under their snow cover as he looked to the east, and he recognized he was usually not one to admire the physical beauty of Pennsylvania, having lived there for so long, and also having sworn a hometown allegiance to New York (Poconos are nice, but they're no Catskills). He had a desperate urge to share it—his mood, the news, the mountains. He told his Bluetooth to call Nell cell. He'd known he had to come clean with her at some point, tell her that Vega had visited and asked him to work a case, and that he'd declined and now found himself wanting to feel useful, to be challenged, to think.

"Calling Nell cell," said the nice lady. Even she seemed extra helpful today.

Nell's phone rang three times and went to voice mail, and Cap said, "Hey, Bug, I'm almost home. Got a lot to tell you. But it's all good, don't worry. I'm, uh, looking out at the Poconos—remember went we went snow-tubing? You were—what, ten, eleven? I haven't thought of that in a long time. You didn't like it at first, and then we couldn't get you out of that thing."

Cap caught a glimpse of his smile in the rearview. Google-image "wistful," and that is what you will get, he thought.

"Nell cell calling," announced the Bluetooth lady.

"Answer," said Cap, his smile more defined now.

"Dad?" said Nell.

"Hey! I'm almost home—" he began.

"Did you get my texts?" she interrupted.

"Texts?" said Cap, glancing at the dashboard screen. "No, they don't come through on the Bluetooth, for some reason."

"Okay," said Nell, and let out a tense sigh. "Don't look at your phone now, though, okay?"

"What's happening, Nell?"

"I'm fine. Everything is fine," she said, reminding Cap of a flight attendant on a plane steadily losing altitude.

"Nell!" he said, sterner now. "Talk to me."

"No, Dad, it's fine," she said, matching his tone. "Em is on his way. Please, just get here soon."

Cap knew he was way over the limit but didn't care. He frequently lost his temper with Nell for speeding on Denville's streets, and here he was, surging over the paved bumps that sandwiched the middle-school crosswalk. He took his foot off the gas as he turned the corner of his street and just tapped the brake, pulled the wheel hard to the left so the car wouldn't mount the curb, and began to decelerate as he saw the single red flashing light of an undercover car in front of Cap's house.

He pulled into the driveway and saw Nell and his old partner, Em, standing on the lawn, talking, both calm. Nell seemed fine; her face struck Cap as being the worried face of a parent whose kid was sick, but only with a stomach bug, nothing fatal. More weary than scared. Still, Cap could feel heat and liquid in his throat, ready to come up.

He turned off the engine and ran from the car, hugged Nell without saying anything.

"Dad, I'm okay," she said firmly.

Em was speaking as well, but Cap couldn't hear for a minute. He focused on Nell's head parked on his shoulder. She was only about an inch shorter than him now.

"You're okay," he said, pulling away from her.

"Yeah," Nell said. "Like I told you."

Cap got the feeling she was laboring to remain unannoyed by his anxiety, lips pursed, arms folded.

"Hey, buddy," said Em, cutting in.

"Hey," said Cap, accepting a handshake and shoulder tag.

It wasn't until then that Cap really looked. He'd been so fixated on seeing Nell that he hadn't actually processed the content of what she had texted him, about her car being broken into. Now he saw it. He rested his hands on his hips and walked toward the hatchback.

The rear windshield was broken, a jagged-edged gap in the lower right corner, cracks splintering across the glass. The bass drum was still in the trunk, but as Cap got closer to the car, he finally understood the damage.

There was a hole in the drum the size of a grapefruit in diameter, a clean cut.

Cap's hand went to his forehead like he was checking for fever. He attempted to form the first question.

"I'm getting two officers here so they can canvas and capture prints," said Em. "See if anyone saw anything."

"Tell me again what happened," said Cap to Nell.

"I was in my room, listening to music," said Nell, calm. "Then I came downstairs to get water, and I saw it near the door."

"The door?" said Cap. "Inside the house?"

Nell and Em glanced at each other. They had clearly already discussed this. Then Nell held up the six-inch circle of mylar that had been cut from her drum so Cap could see it.

"Mail slot," she said.

Cap came toward her, pointing at the circle.

"Inside the house," he said. "You touched it."

"We'll still dust it," said Em, keeping the peace. "We can maybe separate Nell's prints out."

"I wasn't thinking it was part of a crime scene," Nell said. "It was just this weird object on the floor."

Cap rubbed his chin and said, "Did you see anyone?"

Nell shook her head. "I came outside, saw the car. Didn't see anyone. Texted you, then him," she said, nodding toward Em. "Then you called back."

"We're not going to get any prints," Cap said to no one in particular.

"Still worth a try, man," said Em.

"I mean, he might or might not be wearing gloves, our vandal," said Nell, walking away from them.

"Where are you going?" said Cap.

"Gonna go ask Bosch if he or Mama Bosch saw anything," said Nell, heading toward their neighbors' house.

"You want to wait for my guys?" Em called after her.

"They're sort of skittish around new people," Nell called back.

"She's right," Cap said. "She'll get more out of them than your guys will."

Em nodded and took a step toward Cap but still kept a little distance.

"Cap, I set up a rookie to stake out tonight," he said, pointing across the street. "Right there. Just so you and Nell can sleep."

"Yeah, that won't be happening," he said, dazed, staring at the smashed windshield. "But thanks."

"Anything you need," said Em, following Cap's gaze to the mail slot. "It's not exactly egging your house, you know? Doesn't feel like a prank to me."

"No," said Cap. "It doesn't."

"Can you think of anyone who might want to send a message to you or Nell? Try to scare you, Big Bad Wolf–style?"

Big bad, thought Cap.

"Not off the top of my head, but I know someone who might have an idea," said Cap.

They both stood there and looked at the mail slot some more. Suddenly Cap didn't feel quite so on edge. Once he'd seen Nell and seen what the actual damage was, the fear had come and gone. He knew it would come back, but for now he felt the familiar calm of clinical observation cut with the blunt edge of being pissed off.

Cartwright the fed called Vega as she waited in her car at the foot of Cara Simms's driveway.

"Liberty Pure is a problem," he'd said. "Leave it to you to find them."

"Yeah?" Vega said, intrigued.

"They've been connected to some unpleasant events, nationwide, but they haven't garnered any major attention yet. Some assaults, some property damage, some bomb threats."

"Any actual bombs?"

"I'm getting there," said Cartwright. Vega pictured him in an office with his feet on his desk. "We've heard a word there might be a bigger thing soon. A place of worship, maybe even a monument."

Vega squinted her eyes so Cara's house became blurry.

"You don't know which one, or you can't tell me?"

Cartwright laughed in what Vega thought was a subdued Southern way.

"I can tell you what's relevant to what you're doing. You said these guys were all kids?"

"Far as I could tell."

"Okay, then, we know there's a lot more of them, and they've been around for a while."

"So these guys, in Ilona, Oregon, they're probably not in charge of anything."

"Not likely," said Cartwright. "Truth is, leadership's been sneaky, but there's a strong West Coast element, and right where you're kicking up dirt might be right in the middle of it."

"You don't say," she said, seeing Cara's car turn onto the road leading to her house.

Vega said a quick goodbye and hung up with Cartwright. She waved at Cara as she approached, but Cara did not wave back. The boy, Ethan, was in the passenger seat, and his head was down. Which made Vega think.

Cara stopped the car in front of Vega's, hood to hood, and got out, so Vega did, too. Cara had a look Vega recognized—the brittle mask of desperation and anger that parents wore when something was wrong with their kids.

"What are you doing here?" Cara said, slamming the car door.

"I wanted to check on you," said Vega, then nodded at Ethan. "Is he all right?"

"No, he's not all right," said Cara, her voice unsteady. "He says some boys he didn't recognize, older boys, shot paintballs at him as he was riding his bike from school to a friend's house. His chest . . ."

Vega peered over Cara's shoulder to Ethan, now saw a splatter of red on his shirt, neck, chin.

"Bruised?" asked Vega, knowing the answer.

"Yes, bruised," said Cara, now getting angry. "Some as big as baseballs, for Chrissake. Bright purple . . ." She trailed off, then shook her head and said, "I told you this was the one thing, Ms. Vega, this responsibility. Once you have them, kids, you're restricting your own movements."

"You have to know I didn't tell anyone anything about you. I didn't share any information that you shared with me," said Vega.

"I guess my house is just being watched, then," she said like a taunt. "Or you're being followed."

"That's all possible."

"They'd said what they had to say," Cara hissed in a whisper. "They'd already made their mark with the paint. It was done. It was you, because of you, that this happened."

Vega knew it was the truth.

"I'm sorry. Does he need to go to an Urgent Care?" asked Vega.

"I have an appointment to take him to the pediatrician tomorrow," Cara said, her eyes like little lasers. "I'd like you to leave me and my nephew alone now. Please don't try to contact me again. Do you understand?"

"I understand" was all Vega could say.

Cara glared at her for an extra moment and then got back into her car and continued up the driveway.

Vega felt her phone buzzing, but wanted to leave Cara's road before she picked up. She slid back into her car and drove away from the house, headed in the direction of the motel.

When she glanced at her screen, she saw there was a text from Cap—a photo of a car along with the words "Call me please." Vega stuck a pod into one ear and clicked on Cap's name with her thumb, then "audio." He picked up after a ring.

"Hey," he said, not sounding particularly panicked.

"Hey," said Vega. "Whose car is that?"

"Nell's," said Cap. "She was upstairs when it happened. I wasn't here."

Vega shut her eyes for a moment, hearing Nell's name. She hadn't realized she'd been hoping Nell hadn't been involved until that second.

"Anyone on the property?" said Vega.

"Nope," said Cap. "But our guy didn't just bust the windshield— he cut a hole in one of Nell's drums in the trunk. Then he put the piece he cut, the circle, through the mail slot. In the front door."

Vega gripped the wheel.

"You call Junior?" she said.

"No, Nell called Em," said Cap. "He searched the premises. He's got a couple officers coming by to work the case."

"What about Bosch?"

"Nell's talking to him and his mother now."

"They'll talk to her before any cop," said Vega, getting it.

"Yeah. You know, Vega, we can't be sure this isn't random, right? Maybe just a prank," Cap said, bitterness stacking up in his voice. "Or maybe someone I've rubbed the wrong way working Vera's cases." He paused, gave a curt laugh. "An aggrieved defendant. Or, who knows, maybe there's a human out there who doesn't like Nell."

Vega tried to picture him: his crooked tie, circles under his eyes, pacing.

"The probabilities are low," she said.

"Yes," he said, hissing on the "s." "They are low. They are not a thing, as Nell would say. What is a thing is that the only time I've been in a news cycle in recent memory was the Brandt case. When I worked with you."

Vega stopped at a red and made a loose fist with her right hand.

"I'm sorry about the car. And the drum," she said.

He didn't respond; all she could hear was the static of wind blowing in the background.

"I can wire you money today," she said. "To get it cleaned up."

"I don't need money, Vega," he said. "I need for you not to piss people off who know where my daughter sleeps."

"Caplan, you're angry. I get it—"

"You get *nothing*," he snapped. "You move through your life without a plan, and that's fine, that's great, your intuition has served you very well, but it does not do much for me and my kid—do you hear me, Vega?"

The light turned green, but Vega didn't move—no cars behind hers.

"Are you there?" he said.

"Yeah," she said. "Here."

She could hear him breathing.

"Do you have anything to say?" he said after a few seconds.

"I'm sorry, and I'll pay for everything."

"You already said that," said Cap. "And it's not enough."

Then he hung up on her.

The light had turned red again. Vega tossed the phone onto the passenger seat, put the car into park, and got out. She didn't know what to do with her hands suddenly—they were heavy and tingling, like she'd been sleeping on top of them. She made a fist with her right hand and raised it high, was ready to bring it down on the roof of the car like a gavel, but just lowered it slowly.

Then another car came, and the light turned green, and Vega got back in her car and left, her hands still numb.

Later, after Em and his guys had left—after they'd asked all the questions, and Cap and Nell had provided all the answers; after the rookie had settled into the stakeout position in his cruiser across the street—after all of that, Cap made one of the three dishes he knew how to cook for dinner, the rotisserie-chicken tortellini bake.

Leftover rotisserie chicken with cooked tortellini from the package in a baking pan, with a lot of marinara and shredded cheese melted on top.

Nell hadn't said much since the cops left, alternately texting with friends and working through an assignment for AP physics at the kitchen table.

Cap caught a glimpse of the equations as he set down forks and plates and almost got a headache.

"'What is the velocity of the wheeled catapult after the weight is ejected?'" he read aloud. "Sounds dangerous."

"You really wouldn't believe how dangerous the world of AP physics is," Nell confirmed. "There are always weights being ejected from catapults, balls shooting from cannons, bullets out of guns." She tapped the eraser of her pencil on the paper. "There's a problem that keeps coming up where there are two loads of uneven weight on a pulley, and you have to figure out which side's going to come down first. And it's not necessarily the heaviest one."

"You lost me at the guns," said Cap.

Nell laughed without opening her mouth, just a "hmm."

"Hey, Dad?" she said, as if their conversation were just starting.

"Yes, Bug."

"I listened to your voice mail. You said you had a lot to tell me?"

Cap leaned back against the counter. He had a vague memory of feeling carefree when he left the message, the snowy mountains in the distance forcing him to recognize the beauty of the day. It felt like long ago.

"Yeah, I do," he said, crossing his arms. "I was in Binghamton today, talking to a guy named Bear Thomas."

He told her the whole story, starting with his conversation with Bear and then backing up even further to Vega's visiting him in person. Nell pointed at him with her pencil.

"I can't believe you didn't tell me all this," she said, though she didn't sound angry. "Vega was right here?"

"She was."

"And you went to interview a guy for her case even though you're not working the case?"

Cap scratched the back of his head and said, "That's right."

"Huh," she said.

"What's that supposed to mean?" he said, pulling oven mitts over his hands.

"It means 'huh.'"

"Don't give me that"—waving his mitted hand at her. "It's a loaded 'huh.'"

Nell held her pencil in the middle between two fingers and tip-tapped it against her notebook like a seesaw.

"From an objective observer's perspective, it seems maybe you should have told Vega yes."

Cap held out his hands and said, "Do you see any objective observers in the room?"

"I have the benefit of hearing it for the first time with a fresh ear," said Nell, innocent.

"Fresh ear," Cap mocked, peering through the glass door of the oven.

"Don't deride my fresh ear," said Nell, laughing now. "You have to admit, you should have just taken Vega's case. Even in a long-distance capacity."

"I admit nothing," said Cap, staring at the casserole dish. He sighed and added, "I admit it felt good to talk to Bear Thomas, to be involved in something a little more challenging than the work I do for Vera."

"I accept your admission," said Nell. "That wasn't so hard, was it?"

She set the pencil down and looked at her phone while Cap opened the oven door.

"I've got some new information, too," she said. "I've been texting around. There's a girl who goes to St. Paul's. Sounds like she was harassed by some guys online, and then her car was broken into."

"Yeah?" said Cap, a wave of hot air hitting his face.

"Yeah," said Nell. "Her jacket was in the front seat, and whoever broke in cut a hole in it. Put it in her locker—the hole." Nell shrugged. "Kind of similar to what happened to us, wouldn't you say?"

Cap gripped the ends of the pan with his mitted hands and lifted it out of the oven.

"A lot of jerks out there," he said, placing the pan gently on the range.

"Thinking I might talk to her. The St. Paul's girl," said Nell.

Cap turned around to face Nell, pulled the mitts off his hands, and dropped them on the counter next to the oven.

"How about I tell Em about it instead?" said Cap.

Nell tapped her pencil—tip, then eraser—back and forth on her homework.

"Dad," she said, as if she'd been putting this conversation off but now couldn't avoid it any longer. "I know some of these people. They're my peers."

"Nell," said Cap. "You want me to enumerate the reasons why you should leave this to professionals?"

Nell pressed the eraser of the pencil on the tip of her index finger, counting off.

"One, whoever broke into the car and cut up the drum could be dangerous. I'll argue that's a stretch. If they wanted to hurt us, they wouldn't have put so much energy into trying to scare us. Two," she said, eraser landing on the middle finger. "DPD will be more effective. I tend to disagree. You send cops to interrogate, any kid will shut right up, because they don't want to get in trouble, even if they haven't done anything wrong. Three," she continued, onto the ring finger. "DPD's smarter, more experienced than me."

She gave him a shaming sort of look. If she had been wearing librarian glasses she would have peered at him from over the tops of the frames.

"I'll give you the latter, but not the former. Four, cops have access to information, priors, et cetera. I'll argue that may or may not be helpful in finding our guys."

"How so or how not?" said Cap, placing a hexagonal silicone trivet in the center of the table.

He was unable to keep himself from nosing around Nell's theory.

"My sources say the St. Paul's girl met these guys on subreddits," she said, scrolling on her phone. "You know what those are, Dad?"

"Sure," said Cap.

Nell gave him a skeptical glance, and Cap laughed.

"I don't live in a hole, you know. I have read some news in the last few years," he said, setting the pasta dish on top of the trivet.

"Good, then you know what I'm saying is true," said Nell. "Redditors, Xchanners. They spend a lot—*a lot*," she repeated, for emphasis—"of time making threats online. Probably from their parents' suburban basements."

Cap scooped a heap of pasta onto Nell's plate, then onto his own. "So?" he said.

"So they don't have priors!" she said, frustrated. "They probably never even ran a red. This was probably the riskiest thing they've ever done," she said, waving her hand toward the front of the house.

"Okay," said Cap. "To your first point, which is the most important point: Like I said, I have read some articles. It is exactly this population that tends to cross over into the legal and illegal purchasing of firearms. And it's a pretty slippery slope into domestic terrorism from there."

Cap paused, realized he had a lot more to tell her.

"Vega's been tangling with these types in the case she's on right now," he said. "I'm thinking that's why we're a target. It wouldn't take someone long to find my name linked with Vega's online. Too much of a coincidence."

He watched the information settle.

"I thought she was looking for the football player."

"She was. She is," said Cap. "Also, she's managed to piss off a white-nationalist group that apparently goes beyond the West Coast. We don't really know the capabilities here."

"Why didn't you tell me that part sooner?" she said.

"Hey, need-to-know basis, all right?" he said, avoiding Nell's eyes. "Now you know everything there is to know." He took a bite of food, tried to act like a normal guy having a normal dinner.

"'Kay," she said. "So it's fair to say some of these guys are dangerous, but not all of them, Dad," said Nell, pausing to chew. "I'll argue not most of them. Most of them are just in a permanent cyber-circle-jerk with each other."

Cap swallowed too quickly, the acid from the tomato sauce scalding the back of his throat.

"All right, all right," he said, coughing.

Nell grinned, glad to shock.

"Please, Dad," she said, clasping her hands together in mock prayer. "Please, let me do a little due diligence. It's all I want for graduation."

"I thought you wanted a car with decent pickup for graduation."

"A car with decent pickup and this," she said. "Look, I promise, I'll just do recon and report back to you. Then you can tell Em or not tell Em. Let me just talk to this St. Paul's girl, find out what she knows. Oh, and I have one more reason—I have five."

"What's five?"

"It was my drum they cut," she said, still and serious. "You know what I'm going to say, don't you?"

Cap shrugged.

"This time . . ." Nell began in a low voice.

"Don't you say it," said Cap.

"It's personal."

Cap shook his head at her, and for a moment he thought of confronting her about the left-behind beater. But he let it pass. Instead, he sighed and offered one last feeble argument:

"Finish your homework first, please."

Nell's eyes brightened as she hopped up from her chair and came around the table to kiss him on the head.

"I will, I promise. Best dad ever," she announced.

Cap rolled his eyes with exaggerated effect but was quietly proud and pleased to have a daughter who never stopped asking questions and only stopped moving long enough to kiss her old man on the head.

Vega tried to write a text to Cap after he hung up on her but didn't get very far. She didn't even start typing; there was nothing else she could apologize for, and so what was left? Now she sat on the edge of the bed in her motel room, sorting through e-mails on her laptop, the phone at her side. It was dark outside, and the room was silent—the heater under the window wasn't humming; the fan in the bathroom seemed to have stopped. When she thought about it, she actually couldn't recall hearing any other guests, either in the rooms next to hers or right outside. There were a few other cars that came and went, but no people.

Around six, her phone lit up with a text, and Vega grabbed it. The message was from Rachel the waitress, asking her to call. Vega glided past the disappointment that it was not from Cap and tapped Rachel's name; she picked up right away.

"Hey. So Claire texted me—she needs my help," Rachel said, her voice hushed.

"What kind of help?"

"She hasn't been home in two days. She told my mom she's at Derek's."

"Does she want you to go and get her?" said Vega.

"No," said Rachel, and paused. "She says that Neil and Derek are going to this Burger Village off the interstate near Boynton tonight, and she thinks they're going to, like, vandalize it after it closes, but she says she's freaked out about it, so that makes me think, maybe they're planning to do more than just tag it."

"She didn't tell you anything more specific?"

"No, it was just a text. Just: I'm scared, will you meet me there. Bring anyone who think might be able to help. But not our parents."

"What time?"

"Burger Village closes at eleven, so I think right after that. Eleven-fifteen?"

"Do you think she's telling the truth?" asked Vega.

"What do you mean? About being scared?" said Rachel, then, without waiting for Vega's answer, said, "Yeah, she hasn't asked for my help in . . . I don't know, maybe never?"

"I can be there," said Vega. "You don't have to come if you'd prefer not to."

"No, I want to go," said Rachel. "She asked me to be there—I want to be there. Could we meet there?"

"Sure," said Vega. "We should think about what our ideal outcome is."

"Right," said Rachel, struggling to focus. "I think I just want to, like, wave her down, and she can come with me if she wants to."

"You think Derek will put up a fight about that?" said Vega.

"Probably," said Rachel. "I don't know. . . . Maybe, if you're with me, maybe it will be easier than if we just went over to his house? And we could call the police about the vandalism, maybe? Not Ilona police, obviously."

"You want to give her an out if she wants it," repeated Vega.

"Yeah, that's really it," said Rachel, sounding relieved that Vega understood.

"So what do you think? Ten-forty-five?"

"How about ten-thirty, to be safe," said Vega. "But one condition: if I tell you to leave, you have to leave. No questions, okay?"

She could hear Rachel breathing. Then came the response: "Okay."

When they hung up, Vega pulled the pods from her ears and dropped them on the table. Then she picked up her phone and knocked it against the knuckles of her left hand hard while she thought about things. Something about the thick, solid sound it made helped her think. Also, it was what she'd been missing earlier when she decided against punching the roof of her car: a little bruise always felt nice.

6

VEGA PULLED INTO THE PARKING LOT OF THE BURGER VILLAGE around ten. She parked as far away from the restaurant as she could get, in a corner of the lot bordered by trees, the leaves black in the dark. There were two other cars in the lot, closer to the entrance. Vega watched as another car and three trucks came and went through the drive-thru and then left.

At ten-thirty, she texted Rachel one word: "Here."

There was no response, not even dots. Vega figured she was on the road and didn't want to look at the phone.

At ten-thirty-eight, a white four-door cruised into the lot, where it stopped and started. The driver parked about five spaces from Vega and cut the engine abruptly. Vega doubted the driver would be able to see her, but shrank down in her seat a few inches anyway.

Claire Bishop got out from the driver's side, visibly drunk. Vega recognized her from her pictures online. She was thicker than Rachel, but her clothes were tighter—faded jeans with holes in the knees and a tube top.

She struggled with each task, shutting the driver's-side door and digging for her keys in a small fuzzy backpack. She rocked side to side on her feet, mumbling, though Vega didn't see anyone else in the car.

"Your sister is here," Vega texted to Rachel. "She is alone and fine," she added, seeing no need to include the drunk part. Rachel would see for herself soon enough.

Then Claire stumbled. Later, when Vega thought of these moments, she would remember how Claire hadn't appeared to trip over her feet or a hole in the lot's surface. It was more like her legs buckled one at a time, so that she didn't hit the ground too hard, and she ended up on her hands and knees. She didn't make a move to stand.

One minute passed. Then another. Claire was still on all fours.

Vega took one more look at her phone to see if Rachel had texted. Still blank. Vega got out of the car and walked quickly to Claire, cold wind rushing through the trees. Claire turned her head to looked at her but didn't move from her position.

"Hey, you okay?" said Vega.

"No," said Claire, then muttered something unintelligible.

Vega squatted next to her and could smell something astringent-harsh on her breath. Vodka with notes of nail-polish remover was Vega's best guess.

"You're Claire, right?" said Vega. "Rachel's sister?"

"Yeah," Claire said, not looking at her. "I'm drunk."

"Yeah," said Vega. "I can give you a ride somewhere. Do you think you can stand?"

"No," she said right away. "No way."

"Try to sit back," said Vega, placing one arm around Claire's shoulders. "Then I can help you up."

Claire started to rock backward and said loudly, "Don't drop me, okay?" Vega thought, for just a second: I can't drop you; I'm not even holding you.

Then it was all fast—Claire lying facedown in the lot, and the door of the back seat opening, and two people scrambling out of it.

Vega released Claire and reached for the Springfield. She got her hand on the gun and tried to pull it out from the holster, but that was a few seconds too many—the first guy from the back seat was on her, pinning her arms at the elbows on the ground. He was big, over six foot and strong, and he wore an old-man rubber mask that had a big floppy nose and ears; Vega could smell the latex and see the lips and teeth of the guy through the mouth hole of the mask.

Vega lifted her head off the ground and whacked him in the teeth as hard as she could with her forehead. He grunted, and she felt his grip on her arms loosen just a bit, but that tiny piece of lever-age evaporated, because then another guy materialized out of the air, wearing a sweatshirt and jeans and the same old-man mask, and he brought his boot down hard on Vega's right wrist, and it was like the trunk of a car popping open, the way the fingers of her hand unfurled, past her control.

The first guy was still on top of her, breathing the latex breath, and then the second guy kicked her in the kidney and ribs on the right side of her torso, and then there was another—she could hear running footsteps coming from the woods. The first guy stood and dragged her up with him, holding tight to her forearms, and she jabbed her right knee into his groin, but it didn't land as hard as it was supposed to—he was too tall, and the pain from her ribs made her hunch. Without the ability to steel up her stomach muscles, every punch she could land, elbow block, clinch—everything was weakened.

"Fuck!" the first guy shouted.

His grip on her slackened, and Vega yanked her left arm from him, but then the third guy, the one who'd come from the woods, was behind her, wrenching her arms back, and Vega made a sound without intending to, the pain a white spike through her right hand and wrist clear up to her shoulder. The second guy from the back seat, who was smaller, hit her with a hook to her ribs, and Vega coughed but could still see straight—could see, in fact, muddy brown eyes through the holes of his mask—and even though she knew sugar and adrenaline were surging through her blood to prep her body for whatever damage it was in for, she could still think, and later she would remember thinking, that that first hit to the ribs hadn't felt too confident. But then he took another one, and it was sharper and landed harder, and then another, and she knew if her ribs hadn't cracked before on the right side they had now. Then he hit her twice in the face, the first a jab to the left cheekbone, below the eye. But it was the upper cut to her jaw that did it. Her bottom row of teeth slammed into the top, and then it all began to spin, and she had to shut her eyes.

When she opened them, she was on the ground, on her left side. She reached her left hand up to touch the side of her head where it throbbed, recognized she'd been dropped after the upper cut. Her left eye was swelling shut quickly, so that only a small blurry sliver of light was visible. The lid of her right eye mirrored the left, fluttering reflexively.

She saw the three guys, still wearing the old-man masks, cold air puffing from their mouths, backlit from the LED lot lights. She could also see Claire, standing near the car. The guys were watching Vega. Claire wasn't; she was texting.

"You hear us?" said the second guy, the one who was tentative at first. "Mind your business. Get the fuck out before you have another accident."

She willed her right hand into a fist but it wouldn't go. It felt like a beanbag hanging from her wrist, and still the bolt of pain shot through her forearm.

"Yeah, you're mad clumsy, Basic," said the big guy, the one who'd pinned her.

Vega made a sound in her throat, but no words came out. She let her eyes close; the last thing she saw was Claire, still dull drunk but finally, finally, looking at her.

She was aware of movement: car doors opening and closing and engines starting, the murmur of her assailants' voices. She kept herself still and feigned unconsciousness until all the noise was gone.

Then she opened her right eye, though the left wouldn't follow. She scraped her feet against the ground, seeing if they might support the lower half of her body, but it didn't work.

Her mouth was full of blood; she spat out a long string of it.

She held her breath and propped up her upper body with her left forearm, like she was doing a side plank. The right side of her torso thrummed with pain as she sat up, and she made sounds without meaning to, grunts from the back of her throat punctuating every movement.

She found that her wrist and hand hurt less if she held her right arm tightly in a diagonal to her chest, so she did that. Then she pushed off the ground with her left hand and slowly stood up, her shoulders hunched forward to avoid any extension of her midsection and ribs. Her right side ached every time she breathed. She'd had a cracked rib years before, when she was still in fugitive recovery, after a fight with a stubborn skip who'd swatted at her with a frying pan. This was worse. Either multiple or deeper cracks, or both.

She took small steps to her rental and pulled the fob from her pants pocket with her left hand, unlocked and opened the door. She turned her body so that she faced the lot, her back to the car, held her breath, and bent over a little so she could sit.

She let out three staccato yelps as the muscles between her ribs pressed against each other. She sat in the driver's seat and swung her legs into the well.

She pulled the door shut and looked at her face in the rearview. The left side was ballooned, the eye sealed shut, a tiny gash on her forehead from where she'd head-butted the big guy's teeth. She angled her face up to examine her jaw, which was starting to swell on both sides. More blood had gathered in her throat and mouth. She hadn't realized she was clenching her teeth, so she opened and closed her mouth a couple of times, and then felt a tooth jangling around on the lower row. She touched it with her tongue, and it slid out of the gum easily. Vega pushed the engine button to turn the car on, powered down the window, and spit out the tooth onto the ground along with some more blood.

She examined her teeth in the rearview, stuck her tongue through the hole; the tooth had been a canine. There was not much blood anymore.

It was after eleven-thirty now. Rachel had never shown.

She pulled on her seat belt with her left hand and wrapped the fingers of her right hand as tightly as she could on the wheel without jerking her wrist too far in either direction. Seemed like she could still use her right while turning. Which was all she needed to get back to the motel. Everything else could wait.

At the motel, Vega gathered her things. She didn't have much. One overnight bag, a duffel, a laptop bag. Toothbrush, hand lotion, sunscreen for her face.

It took her ten minutes to pee. Only a few seconds to complete the act, but many minutes to get her pants down and back on with minimal use of her right hand, her abdomen radiating pain as she stood up.

Before she left the room, she rinsed her mouth out with warm water from the bathroom sink and watched the threads of blood circle down the drain.

She took the two key cards for the room from her wallet and placed them on the bedside table, next to the phone. She carried her bags out the door, one at a time, and set them on either side of the door frame. She grabbed a dry-cleaning bag from the closet bar, and the empty ice bucket, and left the room for good.

Standing outside, she took out her phone and tapped the Ryde app, did some quick math in her head. She set the destination as Medford, about 140 miles south of Ilona. "Searching for Rydes," flashed a bar at the bottom of the screen.

While she waited, she took small steps to the end of the hotel walkway, where there were two vending machines and the ice dispenser. She set the bucket on the tray and pressed the chute, watched the ice drop out a few cubes at a time. Vega took the full bucket back to where her bags sat. She held the dry-cleaning bag open with her bad hand and scooped some ice into it with her good one, then twisted the top to make a little bundle, gently set it against her blackening eye, and gasped with relief. The ice couldn't touch the pain, but the cold helped. Vega hadn't realized how hot the skin had been.

"Driver located!" blinked the Ryde app. "Enrique will be here in 40 minutes." According to the Ryde tracker, Enrique's car was currently twenty-five miles away, in Eugene, heading south.

Vega leaned against the door and kept icing her eye, taking a break every few minutes, when the ice began to burn. She scrolled down on her map app, watching the vein of I5 cross into California and thought that, if Enrique was willing to drive for forty minutes and then go another two and half hours to Medford for a middle-of-the-night surge fare, maybe he'd be willing to go a little farther.

"Enrique is here! Look for the white Toyota Corolla."

Vega slid on sunglasses as the car pulled into the parking space next to her rental, a few feet from where she stood. She picked up her laptop bag and slung it over her left shoulder, then grabbed the ice bucket.

Enrique got out of the car and rushed to get her other bags. He was a head taller than Vega, slender, his bare arms not showing a lot of definition, with black hair gelled and spiky on top.

"Hi—Alice?" he said in a hushed voice. It was just after one in the morning.

"Yeah," she said, dropping her bag in the trunk. "Enrique, right?"

He nodded and smiled, didn't seem fazed by Vega's sunglasses. He brought the other two bags to the trunk while Vega opened the door to the back seat on the passenger side. She sat down slowly, her rib cage throbbing. She tried to take a deep breath but couldn't—that was actually when the pain was at its worst, she was discovering—so she breathed shallowly and coughed. She moved her legs inside, using her left arm to help lift them so she wouldn't have to use any of the muscles under her ribs. Then she reached over and pulled the door shut.

She drew the seat belt across her body with her left hand and kept her right arm close to her chest so the belt pinned it tightly, which seemed to help stabilize her wrist and ease the pain.

"It's a good time to drive," said Enrique as he buckled his seat belt. "I-Five will be empty."

He reversed the car out of the space and drove them out of the parking lot. Vega watched his eyes in the rearview, stripes of light from the street traveling down his face. He was not looking at her.

"That's the idea," she said.

Her voice sounded strange to her, like there were cotton balls packed in her cheeks. She removed the sunglasses and brought the bag of ice to her face again. She closed her good eye and slouched in the seat, but somehow that made all the pain worse—she felt everything acutely—the splinters in the ribs; the ache rippling through her jaw; the pulse from the hole in her gum.

"Do you need help?" Enrique said, calm.

She saw him watching her in the mirror but didn't try to hide her face. Eventually, he was going to see her.

"Like a doctor?" he added.

"No, I'm good," she said. "Is there a twenty-four-hour pharmacy around here that you know of, though?"

"Not close, I don't think," Enrique said. "We'd have to go back up to Eugene? Do you want to do that?"

He watched for her reaction, eager to help. Stemming either from kindness or a preference not to have people bleed in his car.

"No, thanks," said Vega. "I can wait until Medford."

Enrique nodded politely as he took the on-ramp for I5. There were only three or four other cars on the road with them. The sky was black with puffs of gray rainclouds. Vega leaned her head against the window, enjoyed the chill of the glass.

"You a student up there in Eugene?" she said.

"Not anymore," said Enrique. "But I went there for a while."

Vega couldn't read him exactly; it was hard not seeing his whole face. If he'd graduated, then that information would have been offered simply, with little to no change of expression, as if he'd been asked if he was right- or left-handed. But if he'd dropped out, there was a good chance he'd give it away in his face—either the shame of the downcast eyes or the defiant lip curl.

"I had two jobs when I went to community college," said Vega. "Never finished, though."

"Me, neither," said Enrique. "I make more money doing this, you know?"

"Sure, you do," said Vega. "Rescuing stranded women in the middle of the night in the middle of nowhere."

Enrique met her eye in the rearview. She could tell he was looking at the bruise, which had begun to turn purple and blue.

"Your man do that to you?" he asked.

"Nope," said Vega right away. "Fell down some stairs."

Even though he looked away from her, Vega knew there was a chance. She unzipped her laptop bag.

"You working tomorrow?" she said.

"Not until the evening," he said. "But I can make my own hours, you know, so maybe I can always start earlier."

"Flexible."

"Yeah."

Vega let that sit a minute. She unzipped a smaller pocket within the laptop bag.

"Flexible's good," said Vega.

She removed a stack of fifties from inside the laptop bag pocket and set them neatly on the seat beside her.

"Enrique," she said.

He glanced back at her, and his eyes found the bills.

"This is three thousand dollars," she said. "You can have it if you drive me to California."

Enrique sat up straighter, looked at her, then the bills again.

"California's big," he said.

"It is," said Vega. "I'm going to the Sacramento Valley. Should take about eight hours from here."

Enrique tapped his fingers on the wheel.

"Someone looking for you?" he said.

"Like who?"

"Like police."

"No," said Vega. "I know we just met. You don't have a whole lot of reason to trust me or not trust me. But that's what the money's for."

"To trust you?"

"No," she said. She laughed a little, and it hurt her ribs. "To not think too much about it."

Enrique swallowed. "You pay for gas and Monster Ultra Black, too?"

"Sure, why not."

"You still want to stop in Medford for a pharmacy?"

"Yeah."

She closed her eyes and imagined holding the jar of Advil between her knees and puncturing the safety seal with her thumb.

Then Enrique said, "When we stop, I'm going to count it, okay?"

She opened her eyes, saw him staring at the money. Ultimately, she was still unsure if he was soft inside or just in it for the payout.

Vega nodded and guessed he was probably a little of both, which was just fine.

She hadn't been asleep.

Still, she went through the motions of someone just waking up as Enrique pulled into her driveway around nine in the morning. She opened her good eye and unbuckled the seat belt, stretched her neck from one side to the other.

The pain, all the pain, had gotten worse. She'd taken ten Advil since Oregon and felt nothing, no difference. The skin on her cheek and eye had swelled like an overripe fruit, the colors blue and purple, her eye crusted shut with blood and tears. During the drive, her jaw had fallen open with a sharp snap every time she'd just reached the crest of sleep. Her ribs had become sensitive to even the slightest inflation of her lungs, so she took only small, quick breaths.

Enrique got out of the car and opened the door for her.

"You need?" he said, offering her his arm.

Vega shook her head.

"Could you take the bags, though?" she said, pushing her chin toward her front door.

Enrique nodded, went to the trunk.

Vega slung the strap of her laptop bag over her shoulder and swung her legs out of the well; gripping the headrest with her right hand as best she could, and holding tight to the top edge of the open door's window with her left, she slowly stood.

She had to hunch, couldn't keep her body upright, felt each little stomach muscle twitch and jerk. Slowly, she took mouse steps toward the two concrete stairs of her front porch. Enrique passed her and took both stairs in one stride.

Vega grabbed the wooden railing and took the steps one at a time, the skin around her ribs screaming. She coughed, and her good eye watered, and she was out of breath when she reached the porch.

"You want me to bring them inside?" said Enrique, looking her up and down.

It was the first time they'd really seen each other face-to-face in the light. He was older than she'd thought, with some gray hair near his ears and laugh lines around his mouth.

She nodded, unable to speak. She pulled her keys from her pocket and unlocked her door. Two deadbolts, then the main lock, then open. Enrique picked up the bags and brought them inside, set them down on the living-room floor. He came back to the porch, and Vega stepped inside, switching places with him.

"You going to a doctor?" he said, squinting at the swollen side of her face.

"Sure," she said. Then she added, as if she'd hitched with him from the mall, "Thanks for the ride."

He nodded and hurried down the steps as if she might change her mind about the thick fold of cash she'd handed him in Medford. Then he pulled out of the driveway and was gone.

Vega shut the door and locked the bolts, lifted the laptop bag off her shoulder, and lowered it to the ground.

Her house was cool and full of indirect light at this time of day. The living room smelled like bleach. The lady who came to clean once a week when Vega was out of town was a big proponent of bleach wipes.

Vega walked into the kitchen, the bleach smell stronger here, the tan floor and counter tiles gleaming. Then she headed through the narrow doorway down the stairs. When she bought the house seven years before, she'd learned it was considered an advantage to have the basement fully finished, the idea being that one could set up an entertainment space, or a home gym, or a rec room for the kids. Vega had done none of these, only kept the washer and dryer there, and four stacks of storage bins in a corner.

Though she hadn't labeled any of the bins, she had an idea where to look. The item she needed was in the middle bin in a tower of three; the apparent challenge would be moving the one on top. She grabbed the handle of the lid on the top bin with her hand and yanked it, the muscles on the right side of her torso screaming. The bin tipped over and fell to the carpeted floor, the lid popped off, and the contents spilled: old phones and chargers.

It was the bin under the bin with the phones that she wanted. She popped the top of the middle bin and looked inside: about twenty prescription-drug containers. There had been a time when Vega always swiped an item or two from a skip's house. She never spent a lot of time thinking about why she was doing it; it was a just a thing she did that felt good. "Everyone's got trophies," said her old boss, Perry, matter-of-fact, when he'd seen her. She'd never used any of the items. The pills and phones had stayed in the bins in her basement since she'd moved in.

The pills were old, all long past their pharmacy-printed expiration dates, but Vega had seen plenty of junkies fishing through old folks' garbage, relying on even a speck of the drug's effectiveness. Vega sifted through the bottles until she found the fifteen-milligram Oxy.

She left the mess on the floor and climbed the stairs to the kitchen, slowly. Pressed the container to her breast with her bad arm, twisted the top off with her good hand. Shook a pill out and swallowed, then leaned her head under the kitchen faucet and drank a stream of cold water.

To the refrigerator, where there were three boxes of energy bars. Vega took a bar from the top box, tore the wrapper open with her teeth, and began to eat it, the processed peanut butter grainy against the roof of her mouth.

Into the bathroom, where she dumped half a bottle of body wash into the tub, then ran the water somewhere between warm and hot. She sat on the edge and slowly took off her pants and underwear, with much effort reached down to one side and then the other to tug off her socks. Then, finally, one shirtsleeve at a time, before pulling the whole thing off with her good hand. Unclasped her bra with her thumb and two fingers and rolled her shoulders forward to shrug it off, onto the floor.

She looked at herself in the full-length mirror on the back of the bathroom door as the glass began to steam. A horseshoe of blue had developed along her jawline, the right half of her face nearly unrecognizable between the swelling and the twilight color scheme. The ribs had begun to bruise as well, rusty brown and red, and she was hunched over as if her head were a tremendous weight pulling the rest of her body down to the ground.

The tub was ready. She stepped in carefully, holding on to the sink counter, then lowered herself in. The water was good. She made some noises, first because of the sting, but then from relief, and then she dipped her head once under the surface to clean her face. She wanted to lie there for an hour, to wait for the water to lose its heat, for her skin to pucker and turn soft and white. But she really didn't want to fall asleep, and she knew, once the Oxy hit, with its silent sandstorm of relief, she wouldn't be able to force her eyelids open.

She flipped the stopper on the drain and pulled herself up to standing, gripping the faucet and the tub's edge. Then stepped out, patted herself somewhat dry, and ran the towel over her hair so it wasn't dripping.

Into her bedroom, to her dresser, middle drawer. She took out a tank top and yoga shorts and put them on. Then she lay on her bed, on top of the gray-striped comforter, and watched the lines that the sun made through the blinds on the honey-toned wood floor.

Her breaths became deeper, longer. The last thing she remembered before dropping off was that her ribs didn't hurt anymore when she inhaled. Good, she thought, uncharacteristically optimistic. One less thing to worry about. Then she was long gone, asleep, with gooey neon dreams, for fourteen hours. Over and out.

She did that for four days. Woke up: sometimes day, sometimes night. Another pill, another protein bar, another bath. Iced the face. Slept with her arm folded over her chest. When it was day, she stared at the patch of the bedroom floor where she used to do her handstand every morning.

She didn't turn on her phone.

When she had enough energy, she propped the laptop on her bed and looked down the column of her e-mail inbox, the tiny letters swimming. She had a hard time focusing on them but was able to make out Rachel Bishop's name on a message with the subject "are you okay please call."

Vega stared at the e-mail—it was one long paragraph, and it gave her a headache to read all of the text smashed together, so she only picked up words and phrases here and there: "Claire stole my phone," "cut my tires up," "She said you won't be coming back," "please call!!! I'm so sorry!!!"

Vega didn't send a reply. Instead, she lay on her side and watched all the clips of *The Abilene Dart* that she could find online. Then she ordered the complete DVD set and ate ramen bowls and fruit smoothies with extra bananas while she watched every episode of the two seasons, over and over. Dart, the character, was the obvious hero of the show, but he also could be a little bit of a rascal.

In one storyline, the Abilene Dart assembles a group of drunks from Stymie's, the local saloon, and Dart tricks the gang of thieves that has overtaken the town by luring them into a gulch. He and the drunks ambush the gang with the bows and arrows Dart gets as a gift from a childhood friend, the Apache chief.

With his last gasp of life, the head thief reaches for his pistol, but Dart is always one step ahead. Then comes the climactic moment of the episode, when he pulls the silver star off his shirt—Vega remembered seeing it in the cigar box in the Airstream like an ancient artifact preserved. On the show, Dart throws it sideways, a whistling sound splitting the air as the star spins, the blades between the points extended, and then the star sinks into the head thief's neck. The head thief releases the pistol and reaches for the star, then slumps and dies.

"No sleep like the sleep under the stars," says Dart.

7

A WEEK LATER, SHE WENT TO SEE HER FATHER.

She'd been to three doctors and a dentist. She now wore a cast on her right forearm that wrapped around her thumb and the lower part of her palm, keeping her wrist straight. The periodontal surgeon at her dentist's office had inserted a screw into her gum in the space of the missing tooth, where it would eventually fuse with her jaw and then be capped with a crown.

There was nothing to be done for her ribs or her face. They would have to heal by themselves.

The pain was the pain. It was shrinking day by day, but bad at night. Vega had stopped the Oxy. Now she overlapped Advil and Tylenol.

Her father lived in a town outside of Fresno, a little less than a two-hour drive for Vega, but one she didn't make often. All the houses on his street were similar: single-level with narrow porches, most of them split into side-by-side duplexes. Only a few had garages; most people, like Vega's father and his wife, parked their cars on the street.

Vega pulled in behind her father's car in front of his house. She got out and sniffed the air like a dog, smelled a faint scent of camp-fire smoke, and walked all the way around her father's car. The graffiti had been painted over, the color a solid berry-blue.

She headed up the three steps to his house, pulled the screen door open, and knocked on the main door. A few seconds later, her father opened it up. He slapped both hands to his mouth when he saw her face.

"Alice, Alice," he said, the repetition perhaps a confirmation that she was actually standing in front of him. "What happened to you? Who did this?"

He placed his hands on Vega's shoulders, and she let him. While he stared at her in amazement, she examined him, saw that he was wearing a chunky wool sweater with a high collar. She had never seen him wear such a thing, but, then again, she didn't see him that often, so didn't exactly keep tabs on his transforming fashion choices. While she was growing up, his appearance was the last thing he paid attention to; he would frequently wear stained shirts from the hamper, since regular Laundromat trips were not a priority. Also, now, unlike when Vega was growing up, he wore a thin gold cross around his neck at all times, even in the shower, even when he slept.

"Just fell down some stairs, Dad. Light blew out, and I tripped."

"Stairs? Where?" he said, as if seeing the stairs would help him understand.

"At my place, down in the basement."

"Does it hurt?" he said, touching his own cheek.

"Sure. But it's fine."

"Your arm, too?" he said, seeing the cast.

"Yeah, the wrist. It'll be off in a month."

Vega did her best to not open her mouth too wide. She didn't want to get into a discussion about the missing tooth.

"Do you need an ice pack? Or Bactine?"

"It's fine, Dad. I went to a doctor. It's all healing the way it's supposed to. Can I come in?"

He still seemed concerned, but Vega was done making him feel better about her injuries.

He invited her inside, and Vega stepped into the living room, which smelled like lemons. The house was railroad-style—living room, kitchen, bedroom all in a row, the small backyard through a side door in the kitchen.

"Did you see the car? It looks nice," he said, asking and answering.

"It does."

"Do you want coffee? I can make some," he said, heading toward the kitchen.

"No, thanks," Vega said, following him.

"I'm fixing the cabinets," he said. "Are your cabinets loud?"

"Loud?"

"When they close," he said.

He opened and closed the door of the cabinet above the sink; it made a little slapping sound.

"No," said Vega.

"We don't like it," he said. "So I got these."

He picked up a sheet of tiny circular adhesive bumpers and showed her.

"Do you think they'll work?" he said.

Vega shrugged one shoulder and said, "Try them."

He nodded and stared at the bumpers like he was steeling himself for a much larger challenge than affixing them.

It was another by-product of his years of drinking, Vega thought. Years of being a barely functional human, not knowing how or not choosing to do laundry, prepare a hot meal, fix a cabinet. He hadn't been able to hold down a job for more than a month or two, and lived in a series of sublets and SROs. Sometimes he'd stayed with family, aunts and uncles and cousins. Vega's mother would only let her see him when he was living with one of them.

So now all of the minutiae that made up the daily life of someone who has a job and maybe a kid or a pet that Vega's father had missed all the years he was drunk—even though by now he'd done most things at least once or twice—it still gave him pause, even pressing a silicone sticker onto cheap particle board. He opened the package and peeled one of the bumpers from the sheet.

"I don't want to damage it," he said of the cabinet door. "We'll move out someday, and I want to get our security deposit back."

"Did you talk to your neighbors?" said Vega.

"Yes, I did," he said. "Well, Bits talked to the lady across the street, because they're friendly, but I talked to the folks on either side of us. None of them saw anything."

He held the cabinet door steady with one hand, as if he were going to drive a nail in, and held the bumper between two fingers of the other hand, hovering around the border.

"What did you ask?" said Vega.

"What do you mean?"

"What questions did you ask the neighbors?" said Vega.

He paused, lowered his arm from the cabinet.

"If they saw anyone spray-paint our car. They didn't."

"Did you ask anything else?" said Vega. "Like what time they got up. What time they went to bed the night before. If they saw or heard anything different from usual. If they had any dogs that barked at any unusual times."

"You said to ask if they saw anything," said her father. "That's what I asked. We don't work for the police. How would we know to ask any of those questions?"

He sounded more defensive than impatient. Now, that was a thing about him that he'd always had, drunk or sober: he always felt comfortable in the role of the offended party. Vega used to think the reason he had clung to religion so fast and hard was that he was impressed to find, finally, a bigger victim than himself.

"Because it's common sense, Dad. If you're trying to get details about something, you ask for details."

He looked at her plaintively. "I did exactly like you told me," he said. "It was our car that was ruined, so I don't see why I'm to blame."

"You said there was no actual damage to the interior or the body or any of the machinery," said Vega. "Your car's not ruined. It's right outside."

He lifted his hand again, holding the bumper close to the corner of the cabinet door, still hovering.

"It was hurtful for Bitsy to see it," he said.

"I'm sorry about that," said Vega. "Someone figured out that you're my father, and that person's trying to get to me through you."

"Who, Alice?" he said, pulling his hand away again. "Who is so angry at you?"

Then she watched it fall into place for him.

"You didn't fall down the stairs," he said, the betrayal deep in his voice.

"No."

"What kind of case is this, where there are punks tracking down your family members?"

Suddenly he seemed flustered. He looked like he was lost on the street.

"Have you talked to your brother?" her father said, realizing the relevance of his questions as he was asking them. "What about his kids?"

"Tommy's fine, Dad," said Vega. "The kids are fine. We have different last names. The people who did that to your car found you online, and you're a Vega. There's nothing to link Tommy to me on social media, so he's safe."

Her father shook his head. "You shouldn't be in this type of work," he said. "It's dangerous for you, and now it's dangerous for me."

Again he held up the bumper between his thumb and forefinger so that it almost touched the cabinet door, but still he refused to stick it anywhere.

"It's actually not dangerous for you. It was dangerous for your car, which is now fine," said Vega, also staring at the bumper, wishing he would just put the thing on the door.

"It was the car last time, but what is it going to be next time?" he said, with an air of resignation.

Vega stretched the fingers of her right hand, tapped her nails on the countertop. She tried to detach from everything her father was doing that was irritating her: his assumption of the role of someone who could offer advice, his abrupt disapproval of Vega's career, his suspicion that the attacks on him and Bitsy and their property might escalate, and, the worst offense of all, the fact that he was probably right about that last one.

"That's why I'm here," Vega said. "Before the next time."

Her father opened and closed his lips, preparing to speak, but didn't. He held the cabinet door firmly with his right hand, as if it would move by itself in the breezeless kitchen, and lifted the bumper closer toward it with his left. The bumper was almost on the wood now, less than an inch away, but still he hesitated.

Vega pinched it from his fingers and stuck it on the cabinet door near the corner. It wasn't perfect, a little closer to the bottom edge than it was to the side. Vega shut the cabinet door roughly, though not quite a slam, and it landed on the frame with a muffled pat.

Vega's father stared at her with a mix of surprise and disbelief.

"Fixed," said Vega. "What are your neighbors' names?"

"That's Gene," said her father, aiming a thumb over his shoulder to indicate the neighbor to the right. Then he pointed in the other direction: "That way's two women—Marisa and I forget the other one's name. Nicki?"

He opened the cabinet door again and peered at the bumper, ran his thumb over it.

"They all work, though. Won't be home."

"What about Bitsy's friend across the street?" said Vega.

"Jocelyn. She's retired and doesn't go out too much. Homebody."

"What's the street number?"

Her father thought, then said, "Twenty-seven."

"I'll be back in a few," said Vega.

She turned and left the kitchen. As she walked through the living room to the front door, she glanced at the long wooden cross hanging above it.

"Bits already talked to her," Vega's father called.

Vega didn't answer, just lifted her hand in a wave to show she'd heard him.

Then she was out the door, down the front steps, directly across to number 27. She pressed her finger against the worn doorbell button, heard a buzzer inside the house.

She waited a couple of minutes but didn't buzz again. Soon she heard slow shuffling footsteps, and then the door opened. It was a woman in her seventies at the doorstep of eighty, with her hair dyed dark and thin brown penciled lines for eyebrows. White powdery makeup barely covered the age spots dotting her forehead and cheeks. She grimaced at the sight of Vega's bruise. Vega did not wait for her to speak, put on a big, warm smile.

"Hi, I'm Alice, Bitsy's stepdaughter. Are you Jocelyn?"

Jocelyn's eyes grew with recognition and she smiled.

"Why, yes, I am. You're Mauricio's girl?"

"That's me," said Vega, extending her hand.

"It's a pleasure to meet you," said Jocelyn, stretching out both of her hands and swallowing Vega's up with damp, cold skin. Then she pointed to Vega's face. "Are you all right? That looks quite painful."

"Looks worse than it is," said Vega. "Just had a run-in with a flight of stairs, that's all."

"My goodness," said Jocelyn. "Please, come in, come in."

"That's okay," said Vega. "I don't want to take up too much of your time. I'm wondering if I can ask you a couple of questions about what happened the other day, with my dad's car."

"Yes, that was terrible. A terrible thing," she said. "This is a nice street. Believe me, I've lived on some not-so-nice streets."

"Me, too," said Vega. "Do you remember what time you got up that morning?"

"I'm always up by five," said Jocelyn, full of pride. "But I was inside."

"When's the first time you came outside?"

"A little before seven, I think," she said. "Bitsy rings my bell and she says, 'They ruined Maury's car.' I didn't understand her at first, and then I saw it." Her face crinkled up with the memory. "Just terrible. We usually don't have to worry about stuff like that."

Vega nodded and tried to appear understanding, but she was getting tired of hearing what a nice neighborhood it was. Nice neighborhoods meant nothing. She'd seen shit in the basements and bathrooms and garages of nice neighborhoods so repulsive that it would make Jocelyn's skinny eyebrows fall right off her forehead.

"Do you remember hearing anything out of the ordinary between five and six-forty-five?" asked Vega.

Jocelyn shook her head. "No, I don't think so. I suppose I could have? But nothing loud or what you'd call memorable."

"Got it," said Vega. "Are you friendly with your neighbors?" She aimed her thumbs to the right and left. "On either side?"

"Oh sure," said Jocelyn. "That's Denny over there," she said, nodding to the left. "And other side's Micah and Gabby. They're trying for a baby," she whispered.

"Great," said Vega.

"I told her won't take her long. There's something in the water," Jocelyn said, wearing a clownish grin.

"Yeah?"

"Well, sure—the gal next to them, she's got three. Just had a baby girl a couple months ago. Cutest thing, but that gal's got her work cut out."

"What's her name?" said Vega.

"Naomi," said Jocelyn. "She's a pretty girl, but you can see how tired she is. Says she gets four hours sleep if she's lucky."

"That's not much," said Vega.

Jocelyn lifted her hand to the side of her mouth, like she was sharing a secret. "Better her than me."

"Which house did you say she was in?" Vega asked.

"Thirty-one," said Jocelyn. "The one with the kiddie car in the front yard. You can't miss it."

"Thanks," said Vega. "And thanks for speaking with me. You've been very helpful."

Jocelyn beamed. "It was so nice to meet you, Alice," she said. "Bitsy and your dad are just so proud of you. They talk about how you've been on TV, and all the good work you do for kids."

She and Jocelyn said goodbye, and then Vega walked to number 31, a white house with brown window frames and paneling. There was a plastic pedal car in the front yard, along with an empty kid's pool and a tricycle. Vega opened the chain-link gate and walked to the front door, pressed the buzzer. There was no answer, and no noise inside. No baby crying or toddler yelling. Either naptime or not home.

She tried knocking, and then crossed the street to her father's house, let herself in. He was not in the living room or the kitchen, where he'd been when she left. The sheet of bumpers remained on the counter. She assumed he was in the bathroom, or maybe the backyard, but then heard murmurs coming from the bedroom.

Vega approached the doorway connecting the kitchen and the bedroom and saw her father on his knees with his elbows resting on the bed, hands clasped. Eyes closed. He either did not hear Vega or pretended not to, but Vega suspected the former, since he wasn't moving at all except for his lips. He was talking, but making only the quietest sounds, all the muscles in his mouth moving rapidly, like he was reciting a poem he knew well.

Vega knew he prayed, so wasn't exactly surprised, but had just never seen him in the act. It was a strange thing, the way he was kneeling like a Precious Moment figurine. It seemed so childish to Vega, but she guessed that was the thing about people who believed in God. You were always the child in that relationship, and you were okay with it. And even though she never gave it any serious thought, maybe that was why the whole thing had never been for her. She didn't have any romantic feelings about childhood. In fact, she much preferred being all grown up, and as for kneeling in front of anyone—she was not okay with it.

.   .   .

Vega parked in the lot outside a place called "Yoga Toes." Years before, she'd gone to some classes there, and it had been called something else. But that was a long time ago—eight or ten years back, Vega figured as she locked her car.

It was morning, but the lights inside the studio were dim, and there were about a dozen women inside moving through Warriors. A sign on the door read: "Class in session. Please wait until class has ended before entering. Namaste."

Vega waited. She peered inside over the rims of her sunglasses at the instructor, a petite Latina with a head of blond curls. The instructor was flexible like a dancer, back-bending into a full bridge, up on her toes.

Vega scanned the other women in the class. Only two or three could match the instructor, including a tall Black woman in the back row. When the class broke out of the bridge, all of them bending their elbows, lowering their backs slowly to the ground, the Black woman tiptoed her feet toward her hands and then raised her right foot, pushed off the closest wall with the ball, and kicked both legs up into a handstand.

She came down quickly, and the instructor smiled and gestured to her. The other women clapped. Vega stared at the Black woman and thought she looked familiar. Her face did, anyway, but Vega remembered her with different hair—short, with a streak of white; now she wore it in long braids clasped in a single ponytail and had lost the streak.

The handstand woman gave a small, shy bow. Then the instructor turned on the lights. The women rolled up their mats and chitchatted. Vega stood outside and watched most of them leave.

She waited until only the instructor and the handstand woman were left. They were talking, stacking foam blocks in a corner.

Vega went inside.

"Hi, how are you today?" the instructor said warmly, in the middle of a laugh.

"I'm good," said Vega, leaving her sunglasses on. "Do you do private lessons here?"

"Hmm," said the instructor, approaching her. "Some of our instructors do, but not in the studio. I can give you some of their cards . . . ?"

"Okay," said Vega, watching the handstand woman, who was

still stacking blocks. "I'm sorry," Vega said to the instructor. "Excuse me?" she called to the handstand woman, who turned her head. "Do you teach private lessons?"

The instructor and the handstand woman looked at each other, not expecting the question.

"I don't teach here anymore," said the handstand woman.

"We lost her as an instructor last year," said the instructor, crossing the room to a small desk in the corner.

"I remember you," said Vega to the handstand woman. "I used to come here when it was Ashanti Yoga, a long time ago."

"That was a long time ago," said the handstand woman, and Vega instantly remembered her accent.

That is, she remembered how it sounded. She could not have identified it, pointed to the country on the map where it came from, though she remembered the exact tone and timbre of the voice.

"You were an apprentice then," said Vega. "You taught with a woman named Kirsten."

"You do have a good memory," she said. "Kirsten moved to L.A. three or four years ago."

"So do you teach private lessons, at people's homes?"

"No, I don't teach anymore at all," she said. "But Laila will have some names for you. Good yoginis."

"Just need a couple of minutes here," Laila called from the desk. Then, to no one in particular: "I want to text Julia to see if she still does privates."

"Julia will be perfect for you," said the handstand woman. "I'm in culinary school now."

Vega took off her sunglasses. She watched the handstand woman's expression turn, but she didn't seem shocked. Just perplexed.

"That doesn't look so good," she said, gesturing toward Vega's face.

"Would you be able to teach me to do a one-armed handstand?" Vega asked.

The woman glanced at Laila, and in a burst Vega remembered her name.

"Ameyo," she said. "Born on Saturday."

Now she seemed surprised.

"How do you possibly remember that?" she said.

"I took a class here on a Saturday," said Vega. "That's how Kirsten introduced you."

"Still," said Ameyo, shrugging a muscular shoulder, "that's a touch creepy." She didn't seem concerned, though. Instead, she was amused, smiling.

"I'm somewhat creepy," said Vega, not at all trying to be cute.

Vega looked over at Laila, who was now talking on her phone quietly. She was encouraged that Ameyo was not continuing to shut her down.

"Do you think you could?" Vega said again. "Teach me to do a one-armed handstand?"

Ameyo shifted her weight to one leg and crossed her arms, sized Vega up. Her eyes landed on Vega's cast.

"That's going to slow you down," she said. "Easiest way to get to a one-armed handstand is from a two-armed."

"Without this," Vega said, lifting the cast, "I'm confident with a two-armed. From the way you went up that wall from the wheel, it looks like you are, too."

"Laila will get you some other girls who can do it as good as me. Maybe better," said Ameyo, though she didn't sound like she believed it.

"You're still talking to me, which means you'd consider it even though I'm clearly injured," said Vega. Then she said, her voice softer: "And I liked *your* handstand."

"There you go, with the creepy again," said Ameyo, but she wasn't showing any signs of panic.

Instead, she was flattered, flirty, her eyes narrow with intrigue and expectation. Vega wasn't sure she had her yet. But Vega knew she had her for at least another minute or two, and she was pretty sure she could get her for another minute after that. Sometimes that was enough.

8

CAP WOKE UP ON THE COUCH WITH A SCREAMING HEADACHE, HIS stomach roiling. The night before, he'd polished off a six-pack for his dinner while Nell was at Jules's place. She had placed an order for a new bass drum, Em's rookie was long gone, and Cap had barely slept, listening for the sound of the mail slot creaking open. Now he put the Sig back in the closet and went for a run, ignoring his discomfort and nausea. When he got home, he forced himself to have two pieces of toast, took a shower, and set about to work for the day in his office, writing up a report for Vera and sending e-mails about the new case they were starting.

He kept himself neatly distracted for most of the day, pausing only to use the bathroom and refill his coffee mug. He did his best not to watch the clock in the upper right corner of his laptop screen, but around 2:00 p.m. he began the countdown to when Nell would get home. When she came through the front door at 3:53, Cap's shoulders sank with relief.

He hurried from his office to the living room, where she sat on the small stool next to the front door, taking off her rain boots.

"Good, you're here," she said. "I have developments."

"I can't wait," said Cap, leaning against the wall. "How've you been?"

"Fine," said Nell, dismissing the small talk. She stood and tugged at the sleeve of his sweatshirt. "Can we go in your office to use the big wall?"

"I guess," said Cap.

The "big wall" in Cap's office was actually just a standard-sized wall, but it was unique in that it was the only wall in the house without a picture or a hook or a light fixture on it. When Cap started his private practice years before, he would sometimes tape index cards to the wall to organize his thoughts, and Nell liked to sit on the love seat and watch him. She was the one who'd given it the nickname.

Cap followed her into his office, and she walked right up to the wall and set her backpack on the floor at her feet.

"I already started jotting things down," she said, pulling out a stack of yellow sticky notes with black writing. "Remember Ruthie Morris?"

"Sure," said Cap. "From junior high. She likes boys, and they like her, right?"

"That's putting it mildly, but yes," said Nell, flipping through her notes. "And, just so you know, I'm not slut-shaming here. No judgment whatsoever."

"Live and let live," said Cap, trying to peer at the notes.

Nell moved them over her shoulder, out of his line of vision. "Let me get organized first," she scolded.

Cap backed off and grinned.

"Okay, so," Nell began, "I talked to Ruthie, since she goes to St. Paul's. She knows the girl whose car got broken into. They're hi-in-the-hallway friends but not close. But she hooked me up with this guy who's tight with the girl with the car, so I stopped by St. Paul's this morning before school and talked to her. Let's just call her 'The Girl.'"

Nell stuck a note on the middle of the board with "the girl" written on it in black ink.

"Does 'The Girl' have a name?" said Cap.

"Yes," said Nell, impatient. "It's Alexis, but this is just to keep things simple right now. Need-to-know, right?" She raised her eyebrows at him.

Cap smiled. "Proceed."

"So her boyfriend," she said, sticking a note on the wall that read "boyfriend" next to the first note. "He's into posting on this subreddit called 'Central Air PA.' It's mainly for Pennsylvania millennials and teens," she said, sticking another note above the other two, "central air." "I looked at it—seems to be a lot of freedom-of-speech, anti-nanny-state stuff."

"Let me guess. Racial slurs and misogynistic content?" said Cap.

"Yes, but not that obvious. You have to go looking for certain posts," said Nell, sticking up another note that read "Central Air/ JQ." "So Alexis, the girl, wanders into this post in Central Air with the header"—Nell tapped the letters—"JQ. Give you one guess what that stands for."

Cap tilted his head and shrugged.

"'Jewish question,'" said Nell.

Cap laughed, mostly out of surprise. Also, he didn't quite know what else to do.

"So the girl told me she doesn't really trust Black people, but Jewish people are white, right, so this offends her." Nell turned her head to look at her father. "I didn't even begin to get into the flaws of her logic. It would have been like arguing with a puppy." Nell turned back to the wall. "So she posts something like 'Hey, that's not cool. I learned about World War II in history class, blah, blah,' and all these guys jump on her, say how Hitler should come back from the dead to rape her. Really a selection of the best and brightest here," Nell rattled off without much emotion, glancing at her notes.

"Jesus, they wrote that?" said Cap.

"Dad, yes," she said impatiently. "You said you read articles."

"I have," he said. "I just wasn't prepared to hear those particular sentiments in your voice."

"Better get used to it," said Nell, examining the notes already on the wall. "So she shuts down her account, and the next day she wakes up and her windshield's broken, and her jacket's all cut up. And . . ."

Nell pulled her phone from her back pocket and brought up a photo. Cap squinted at the screen: a hand holding up a circle of denim between the thumb and index finger like it was a scientific specimen.

"At least they're consistent," he said.

"Helpful for us," said Nell. "So, by this point, the girl and her boyfriend"—she tapped the "boyfriend" note—"they've broken up, and the girl really doesn't think he'd do something like this, but he might know who did, so I found him and talked to him, too."

"All before school?" said Cap.

Nell paused, scratched at her hairline with her thumbnail.

"I might have missed first period," she said.

"Bug," said Cap.

"Dad, don't start. I've cut class, like, five times in my life. Can we focus, please?"

Cap sighed and gestured to the wall for her to continue.

"The now ex-boyfriend says he knows some guys through his older brother," she said, sticking another note above "boyfriend": "brother." "Brother is the one who got Boyfriend into Central Air, and he's, as Boyfriend, his own little brother said, a 'loser douche,' doesn't have a job, dropped out of college, still lives at home, spends a lot of time on these subreddits, and might know someone, so . . ."

Nell paused and smiled at Cap, blinking innocently, like an animated deer.

"You went to talk to him, too?!" said Cap.

"Yeah," said Nell, a little guilty.

"Did you go to school at all today?"

"I made it eventually," said Nell. "I only missed pottery and Russian Lit Survey, and those are both electives anyway."

Cap rubbed his temples. "So you questioned this guy at his house, the brother?"

"I did. I don't think he's talked to a girl who wasn't his mom in a while. Kind of weird."

The pain returned to Cap's stomach. Not the dull ache from too much beer and not enough food, but the acute jabs that had become routine ever since he returned from California. He knew they were related to stress, didn't need a shrink to tell him that, and imagining Nell alone in a basement with a socially stunted shut-in with white-supremacist tendencies was enough to trip the wire.

He hunched over only a little, but Nell noticed immediately.

"Hey, are you okay?"

He nodded. "I can live with questioning witnesses or suspects in a neutral setting like school, a mall, a crime scene," he said. "But you have to promise me not to go to anyone's house again. There are just too many unknown variables."

"Dad, this was fine. I took one look at him and knew I could handle myself if shit got real."

"All I'm saying," said Cap, attempting to keep his tone calm, "is I've been in a lot of situations that appear manageable, and then they quickly become unmanageable."

"Got it. I promise," said Nell, eager to move on. "So he says that he met some of these guys in real life a while back, at, like, a trivia night for casual racists, and one of them bragged about busting a window on his history teacher's car because she was a feminist lesbian, in his words, and deserved it, and I convinced him to tell me the name, which is"—she produced another note for the wall—"Brett Hardecker."

"This guy gets a name?" interjected Cap.

"Yes," said Nell, pointing at him. "You'll see why. These," she continued, sticking up six more notes, "these are the user names of the posters from Central Air who made particularly gross comments to the girl online."

Cap scanned them all: TDNow; IEatDogFood; cuck4cocopuffs; FreeAmerican06; treehouselvr; humbuuug492.

"So all we have to do now is confirm that one of these," she said, tapping the names, "is Brett Hardecker, and I think we have enough evidence to at least have Em question him."

She and Cap stared at the wall for another minute, and then she turned to him.

"Well, what do you think?" she said.

Cap moved his head from side to side, a thing he did when he was weighing things out.

"It's a solid theory," he said, "but circumstantial. If one of these users is Hardecker, we can't just send Em over there. Maybe Hardecker had nothing to do with it. He's clearly not the only one who's on this board and shares these types of opinions."

"So we're not looking to *convict* the guy—I'm just saying this is a good lead," said Nell.

Cap smiled at her. "It's a great lead," he said.

She smiled back, somewhat shyly. "You really think so?"

He nodded.

"Thanks," she said, reviewing the wall.

"Hey, though, how'd you get the brother to tell you all this?"

"Oh," said Nell, shrugging, "I just told him I'd hate to have to make an anonymous call to the police linking him to vandalizing the property of a former cop and personal friend of the police chief."

"You shook him down?" Cap said in disbelief.

"Only a little, really," said Nell. "So we need to figure out who the user names belong to. Any ideas?"

Cap shrugged. "Let's do a little research on Hardecker."

"On it," Nell said, as eager as a first-week recruit.

She took a picture of the wall with her phone and headed for the door.

"Working dinner in an hour," she said over her shoulder, leaving the room before Cap could respond.

He stared at the wall and rested his hands on his hips. "Okay," he said softly to the air, aware that no one in the world could hear him.

Vega sat in her car on the street outside a run-down ranch-style in a town twenty minutes from where her father lived. It was nighttime now, just after ten, and the street was quiet. She had spent the day talking to every one of her father's neighbors.

As Vega had suspected, the young mother had heard something in the middle of the night—people laughing outside her house. Watching from her window while feeding her baby a bottle of formula, she'd seen three young men who appeared drunk to her, shushing and teasing each other. They were in the middle of the street, and she thought about calling the police, but the young men quieted down, and then her baby was done with the formula, and it was time for both of them to return to bed, because she needed to take full advantage of every minute when she could sleep. So she hadn't seen any of them vandalize Vega's father's car.

But before the young mother left the window, she'd heard one of the guys call one of the others by something that sounded like "Nikolai." She remembered it specifically because it was the name of the villain from her favorite movie while she had been in high school.

It turned out there weren't too many Nikolais with California drivers' licenses in a fifty-mile radius surrounding Vega's father's house—only five, to be exact, and only three of those could be considered young, under forty. Out of those three, only one had purchased a laptop a year ago from a Best Buy in Fresno, with a traceable serial number and IP address that made it easy for the Bastard to hack into young Nikolai's network and identify him as a twenty-year-old active participant on certain online boards frequented by racists and woman-haters.

But the Bastard didn't need to remind Vega that the only way he could trace who had instructed Nikolai to trash Vega's father's car was to have the device itself.

According to the lease agreement the Bastard had dug up, Nikolai rented the house with one other guy, Jonathan Purser, who was nineteen years old, worked at Subway, and spent most of his time playing either poker (mostly losing) or first-person shooter games online.

At ten-eighteen, Vega got the text from the Bastard she'd been waiting for: a list of the names of Nikolai and Jonathan's neighbors on either side. She checked her makeup in the rearview. Her cheek and eye were still puffy, but she'd covered the skin with concealer, using tips she'd learned on a YouTube video. Now she thought she looked like she'd possibly been born with an asymmetrical disfigurement, or perhaps a case of Bell's palsy. Either way, the more natural it seemed, the better.

She slung her laptop bag over her shoulder, got out of the car, and walked across the empty street to the house. She walked up the driveway, taking in some quick details of the cars parked there—one Toyota, one Honda. Bumper stickers were "Save Mono Lake," "Ski Tahoe," "Proud Parent of a xxx Honor Student," with the school's name scratched off.

Vega heard music as she got closer, not too loud, hip-hop. Vega knocked three times, hard, with the knuckles of her index and middle fingers. The music got quieter, and soon the door opened, and there was Jonathan Purser. Shoulder-length dark hair, long narrow face.

"Hi, I'm a safety consultant for PG&E, and I need to take a look around your property if you don't mind," Vega said, flashing her investigator license quickly.

She watched Purser's eyes grow large and then small as he tried to examine Vega's ID, but she returned it to her pocket right away. He glanced at her cheek and eye only for a moment. Vega knew she needed to keep talking and not let any time lapse during which he might start asking questions.

"I just came from the Berringers', next door," she continued. "The carbon-monoxide levels are off the charts in their basement, and I need to test yours."

Purser stared at her, dumbfounded.

"Are you"—Vega checked her phone screen—"Nikolai Stevens or Jonathan Purser?"

"Yeah, Jon Purser," he said.

"Is Nikolai Stevens here as well?"

Purser nodded.

"Then you should get him," said Vega, feigning impatience. "You've got a serious potential health hazard here. Excuse me," Vega said, walking inside.

Purser didn't attempt to stop her, just produced a sort of choked, gurgling sound, then called over his shoulder, "Niko!"

Vega came into a mess of a room, a large TV with tangled cords and video-game consoles on one side, beanbag chairs and a stained formerly white couch with sagging cushions on the other. It smelled like a school bathroom.

Nikolai appeared. Vega recognized him right away from his photos online: the oily shaved-sides, long-on-top haircut, the heavy-lidded light-colored eyes. He wore an oversized black tee shirt and baggy jeans. As soon as he saw her, she knew she was safe: he looked at her blankly, confused, a little pissed that a stranger was in his house. He had no idea who she was. For her this confirmed a hunch—that he and his buddies had been taking orders from someone else to spray-paint her name on her father's car.

"She's from PG-knee," said the boy who'd answered the door, sounding a bit desperate.

"Are you Nikolai Stevens?" she asked.

"Yeah? You shutting down power again?" muttered Nikolai.

"Hopefully not," said Vega, removing Bitsy's meat thermometer from the inside pocket of her jacket.

"Then what's this about?"

"Your neighbors next door, the Berringers, have dangerous levels of carbon monoxide in their basement. I'm testing every house on the block, and you're up first." She pressed a button on the thermometer, and it beeped.

"She says we could die in our sleep," whispered Purser.

"I don't smell anything," Nikolai said.

"Carbon monoxide doesn't have a smell," said Vega, walking around the room, holding the meat thermometer in front of her. The cap covered the five-inch stainless-steel needle.

For a few minutes, no one spoke. Nikolai stared at her while Purser glanced back and forth between Vega and Nikolai, nervous. Then Vega sighed, heavy on the drama.

"Good news and bad news," she said.

She didn't follow that up with anything right away, and Purser grew increasingly anxious.

"What's the bad news?" he said, barely holding it together.

"You've got a little CO in the air here," Vega said.

"Shit," said Purser.

"So what do we do?" said Nikolai, unimpressed.

"Well, the good news is, it's not much, so you could probably just open your windows, but I need to check every room." She pressed the button again on the thermometer, and once again it beeped. "I'd like to start in the basement, then kitchen, bathroom, then bedrooms last."

Vega pretended to write a text on her phone and could sense both boys staring at her.

"There a problem?" she said, looking up.

"I just don't like people I don't know in my place," said Nikolai, sulky.

"Hey, trust me, I don't like being in your place. However, if you die in your sleep from carbon-monoxide poisoning, my company will be held liable. And if anyone under your roof dies in his sleep, or, let's say, anyone in the surrounding houses dies, and you happen to squeak by because your lungs are just a little bit more tolerant of CO than theirs, then, when I fill out my report and write that the resident was duly warned of the potential dangers and chose to ignore the warning, you will be held liable. Nikolai Stevens," she said, adding his name for punctuation.

"Dude, let her look around," said Purser.

Nikolai sniffed and scowled at Vega, then finally shrugged. "Basement's through the kitchen."

"Well, thanks," said Vega.

She went to the basement and walked around for a few minutes, stepping around boxes and a dingy washer-dryer unit. When she came back upstairs, she saw Nikolai and Purser sitting on the couch, watching TV.

"Basement's clear," she said.

Then she spent a few minutes in the kitchen, holding the thermometer out in front of her like she was a psychic with a smudge stick. She returned to the living room.

"Kitchen's good," she announced. "Bathroom?"

"Right there," Nikolai nodded toward the hallway from which he'd come. "On the left."

Vega nodded, went into the bathroom, and closed the door behind her. The yellow tile on the floor was streaked with dirt from muddy shoes, or feet that had been outdoors in flip-flops. The shower curtain was stained with a rust-brown line down the middle. Mirrors and fixtures cloudy with mildew and dust. Vega pressed the button on the thermometer, heard it beep.

She opened the bathroom door, and Nikolai stood there. Purser stayed in the living room, the TV blasting a home-reno show.

"All good?" Nikolai said.

"All good," said Vega. "I guess just the bedrooms are left. Then I'll be on my way."

Nikolai squinted his eyes at her, then shrugged in the direction of one of the bedrooms. "That's his," he said, nodding toward Purser in the living room.

Vega gave him a may-I-take-your-order smile and crossed the hall into the bedroom. She shut the door behind her, walked around, and pressed the button on the thermometer three times. Then she emerged; Nikolai hadn't moved.

"There's another bedroom?" she said.

Nikolai nodded. "That's mine," he said, pointing down the hall.

"Great."

She went to the doorway and did a cursory glance of the space, saw the silver laptop ("Quicksilver Metallic" was the color as it was listed at Best Buy) lying on top of a rumpled bed. She turned to close the door behind her, but Nikolai stuck out his hand and grabbed the door's edge, holding it open.

"I need to shut the door," Vega said. "To get an accurate reading."

She watched him think about this, his eyes peering over her head at his room. Think it through quick, genius, she thought as she felt a drop of sweat making its way down the back of her neck. Why would an energy safety consultant steal your shit?

After a minute, Nikolai released the door, and Vega smiled again, polite and impersonal, and closed the door in his face. She walked in a circle in his room, tried to make her footfall heavy in case he was listening right outside. She pressed the buttons on the thermometer once, and then twice, to make it beep. Then she stuck the thermometer in her back pocket and walked to the bed.

The laptop had a square sticker on the lower right-hand corner of the cover—white with a red border and black logo, which Vega recognized from a shoe brand. She pulled her wallet from the inside pocket of her jacket and removed her Costco card, then squatted next to the bed and stuck the card under a corner of the sticker.

She wiggled the card back and forth until the whole sticker was off. It was a little wrinkled, but would be fine. Vega stuck it to the tip of her index finger of her left hand as she shrugged off her laptop bag and opened it up with her right hand. She pulled out an identical laptop to Nikolai's, except that the one she'd brought was brand-new, not scuffed like Nikolai's. She'd made a stop at that same Best Buy in Fresno where Nikolai had purchased his laptop the year before, and, lucky chance, the model was still in stock.

"Hey, what's going on?" Nikolai called.

"I got two different readings," said Vega, setting the new laptop down gently on the bed. "I have to reset the device. Should only be another minute or so."

Vega placed the sticker on the lower right-hand corner of the cover of the new laptop and smoothed it over with her fingertip. Then she took Nikolai's laptop and slid it into her bag. She stood and grabbed the thermometer from her back pocket, pressed the button again.

She opened the door, and Nikolai was still standing there, waiting for her, getting antsy.

"You guys are good," said Vega, tucking the thermometer into the inside pocket of her jacket.

Nikolai stared at her, his expression blank. Vega headed out of the room; Nikolai didn't move, so she walked around him. It was a little awkward.

"We're good?" said Purser, eager.

"Yep, all clear."

"Great," he said, with a burst of an exhale.

Vega glanced to Nikolai as he stepped into his bedroom.

"You shouldn't have any problems," Vega said, her hand on the doorknob. "Anything strange, just give us a call."

Nikolai was in his bedroom now, out of Vega's line of vision. Could be doing anything, she thought. Could be picking up his laptop.

"What number should we call?" said Purser.

Vega opened the door and hustled out.

"Customer Service," she said over her shoulder. "On the Web site."

She heard him say, "Uh, okay," as she hurried across the driveway and then the street to her car.

He's opening the laptop, pressing the power button. Any second he'll see the wrinkled sticker, and the generic screen of an unconfigured device.

She slid into the driver's seat and didn't bother shrugging the laptop bag off her shoulder or fastening the seat belt. Started the engine and pulled away from the curb, sped to thirty, then forty by the end of the block. She took a wide, fast turn around the corner and kept going, ignored the seat-belt chime until she hit a red right before the interstate. She knew Nikolai wouldn't be fast enough on his feet—no one would be—but she stared in the rearview anyway, waiting for the next thing.

Cap sat in his parked car, drumming his thumbs against the wheel. There was a coil in his stomach, tight and glowing hot. The coffee he'd picked up from Dunkin' Donuts sat untouched in the holder behind the stick shift.

He had the fight with Nell from earlier in the day on repeat in his ears.

She had done some online research about their primary suspect, Brett Hardecker, and it had become clear, after reviewing a series of Facebook posts and tweets questioning the validity of affirmative action and railing against the Jewish-run media machine, that it was a good chance Brett was their guy. Em had been tied up the past couple of weeks, busy with a heroin trail between Philly and Cleveland, with Denville as a midpoint. Apparently, he couldn't squeeze in an investigation of a boring old case of vandalism.

When Nell was at Jules's the night before, Cap had driven by

Brett's house in a neighborhood not far from Cap's house and seen a man, too old to be Brett but probably just the right age to be his father, leave at 8:30 p.m. in a black work uniform, the words "Levon Pretzels" printed on the back of his shirt ("A Little Salty, A Little Sweet," Cap recalled the catchphrase).

Nell had been angry enough when she'd found out he'd done recon without her, but then things really got out of hand when he'd told her she couldn't come with him for the close.

"It doesn't make any sense for you to go," he'd said.

"It doesn't make any sense for you to go, either," she'd said, starting to get heated. "You're not a cop anymore, and you work for a lawyer. At least I can go under the impression that I'm a friend of the girl's, and I'm looking out for her well-being."

"Then you'd be entering the situation as an aggressor, and you're not getting any information that way, much less a confession."

"And you're getting a confession as just, like, a . . ." She'd struggled for words. ". . . a concerned townsperson?"

"You're forgetting you promised me you wouldn't go to anyone's house because of the unknown variables."

She'd looked incredulous then, said quickly, "But I'll be with you. I promised I wouldn't go alone."

"I don't recall there being any conditions on the promise," he'd said.

It had come out sounding more self-righteous than he'd intended. Nell's face steeled up.

"Are you fucking kidding me with semantics right now?"

"Watch your mouth," Cap said, his voice steady and firm, pointing at her.

They stared each other down for a minute, and then she just left, grabbed her car keys, not even bothering to pretend she had band practice.

And Cap let her go. There was no forbidding anymore. Not that there ever had been; not like he'd ever needed to. But now the ground had shifted. Now it was on Cap to make her want to stay. Soon it would be him wishing she would call him from college, hoping she would choose to visit for a weekend. It wasn't just that she was his adult child; she was another adult human who could give her time to or guard her time from other adult humans of her choice. It had pretty much been the case since she was twelve or thirteen, but now, every day, the solidity of her self-rule became more and more evident.

There was also the scorching lack of Vega in his life, which might not have made a difference even a couple of months before, when they had not been in contact for so long. But her reappearance, the distance between them when she visited, her honesty, then the piecing together of their rapport—it had made him feel awake without realizing it. And he was angry, but he still missed her. People are never one thing, he thought, rubbing his eyes, exhausted by the thought of it. He was exhausted by feeling everything, and also exhausted by feeling numb for so many months.

But he had to admit, talking to Bear Thomas, doing the research with Nell as his partner, it gave him something. For lack of a more self-help-y word, a goal. Right now the goal was the confession: Yes, it was me, punk-ass douche bag Brett Hardecker, who broke into your baby girl's car and crossed the forbidden threshold of your home. I did it. Take me away and have your police acquaintances charge me with criminal mischief.

Nothing in Cap's experience led him to believe this was how it would go down.

But he knew that, without Dad there, he'd have a better chance of getting to Brett. Even if Mom was home, men were generally more angry; women more sad. Cap remembered this from countless interviews he'd conducted as a cop, all the times men poked their fingers into his chest and women cried while clutching his shirt. Of course, there were always women willing to throw a punch and dig their nails into his cheeks. Cap would just have to see which ramp this pinball would take.

At eight-thirty-two, he watched the front door to the Hardecker house open, and the same man from the night before emerge, wearing his pretzel-factory uniform, get into his car parked in the driveway, and drive away.

Cap scooted down in his seat a couple of inches until the car rounded the corner. Then he sat up and got out.

He crossed the street, thinking how the house was similar to his, two narrow above-ground floors leaning slightly to one side, uneven streets paved over the old coal mines in all of these towns. He stepped up the two concrete steps and pressed his fingertip against the buzzer.

While he waited, he heard a high-pitched moan coming from inside. It sounded to Cap like a throttled accordion, stuck on one long, sharp note.

A woman opened the front door, but the flimsy screen door still stood between her and Cap. She was short and wide, wore thick glasses, and had a pageboy haircut. Cap put her age around sixty.

"Who are you? I'm Mama," she told him.

"Hi, Mama," said Cap. "I'm looking for Brett Hardecker. Is he your boy?"

"He's my grandson," she said.

Mama did not have a whole lot going on in the tooth department, Cap noticed. But he tamped down his prejudgments, because, so far, Mama was easier to talk to than most suspects' relatives.

"Is he at home right now?"

"Yep. Who are you, though?" she said, as if he'd already told her and she'd just forgotten.

"Hi," he said. "I'm a gym teacher at Holy Name High School. I found something of Brett's, just wanted to give it back to him."

Mama seemed taken aback. "Found something? What is it?"

"I can't be sure," said Cap, reaching into his jacket pocket and pulling out an envelope. "But I think it's money."

Cap had printed Brett's name and address on the envelope and stuffed it with ones. It was an old tactic; usually, he and other cops had used it to get invited into houses where they wanted to have a look and didn't want to wait for a warrant. It was like being a vampire, being a cop. All the doorways were cursed. But the trick only worked with certain people: kids, old folks, or those racked with desperation of one kind or another. Which, in Denville, was a significant portion of the population.

"Where'd you get that?" Mama said, her eyes round, like Christmas ornaments, behind the frames of her glasses.

"Found it in the school parking lot," said Cap.

"Brett must have dropped it," said Mama, putting the pieces together.

"That's what I'm thinking," Cap said kindly. "Is Brett at home? I'd like to make sure this gets to him."

"Oh yeah," said Mama, pushing the screen door and holding it open for Cap. "Come on in. What you say your name was?"

"Williams. Kids call me Coach Williams. Or just Coach," Cap said, stepping inside.

The living room was small and dark, tan carpeting on the floor and a brown-and-yellow-striped wallpaper on the walls. There was a cage in the corner with a cat inside, which started screeching when it saw Cap. That was the high-pitched sound he had heard before.

"Is that cat all right?" he asked.

"Yep, she's just in heat," said Mama, walking with some effort to the bottom of a staircase. "Brett!"

The cat paced in the cage and continued to scream. Cap winced.

Mama shuffled over to a threadbare wingback chair in front of a television. The sound was off.

"She just does like that for a week, and then she stops," Mama said, looking toward the cage. "I don't even hear it anymore."

Cap could not conceive how that was possible, but did not want to chance risking the rapport he'd built up with Mama by questioning it.

"Isn't that something?" was all he said.

Mama grinned at him and then bellowed, "Brett! Your teacher's here!"

Cap smiled back at her. He knew it would all come apart soon, so he was prepared to talk fast.

A door opened upstairs, and Brett appeared on the staircase. He was big, definitely overweight, but tall, too, with greasy hair and two or three days of an adult man's beard growth on his cheeks and chin.

"Who're you?" he said, his voice deep.

"He's your teacher!" Mama yelled from the chair.

"He's not my teacher, Mama. I never seen him before."

"Hi, Brett," said Cap. "My name's Max Caplan."

Cap waited only a second while he let the name land. There was a chance Brett didn't even know him by name, had only received an address and orders online.

"Says his name's William?" said Mama, as if she hadn't heard either of them. "He has the money you lost."

"I don't know him," Brett said, coming down a couple of steps.

"He's right, Mama," said Cap. "He doesn't know me personally."

Mama didn't get up from her chair, her expression slowly matching her grandson's.

"But he knows my house, don't you, Brett? Over on Pixley Road?"

There was the drop. Brett couldn't hide his shock, and he ran down the stairs, jumping the last three. He crashed into a small table on the landing, making a diamond-shaped mirror fall to the floor and shatter.

"What in hell's the matter with you?" yelled Mama.

Here we go, thought Cap as he put his body in front of the door.

"Brett, I just want to talk," he said, holding his arms out in front of him.

Brett panted and charged at him, shoved him with both hands, then tore the door open and bolted.

Cap fell backward into a tray table and then to the floor, but scrambled to his feet quickly.

"If you're going to call the police, ask for Emerson," he said, heading out the door.

"Emerson," Cap heard Mama say. Then, reflective: "Who in hell's Emerson?"

Cap took off out the door, saw Brett down the block, still running. Cap ran after him and shrank the distance between them in a minute. Turned out Brett was big but not that fast, and Cap's twenty-mile-a-week habit was paying off.

Soon Cap was right behind him, ten feet, then five.

"Where you gonna go, Brett?" he called.

Brett turned his head, which was enough to slow him down just a little bit more.

Cap jumped, arms open, and landed on Brett's back like a squirrel on a tree. They both went down hard on the sidewalk. Cap's top and bottom teeth knocked against each other as his chin rammed into the back of Brett's head.

Brett didn't move for a few seconds, shocked by the impact. Then he started to wiggle, but not enough to shake Cap off.

"Brett," Cap said, his jaw aching. "I just want to talk."

Brett lifted his head and spat blood.

"Aren't you gonna read me my rights?" said Brett.

Cap rolled off him and sat on the pavement.

"Nah, I don't do that anymore," said Cap. "Cops are on the way. You can keep running, and I can keep chasing you and bringing you down, or you can stay put and reduce your likelihood of injury."

Brett thought about it and started to push up on his hands slowly. "I'm not telling you shit," he said.

"You do you," Cap answered.

He rubbed the hinges of his jaw, which he knew would start hurting any minute now, though they didn't yet. He held his hand out straight in front of him, and it was still. As he heard the sirens, he thought about the other sirens for some reason, the mermaids that pulled the sailors in to their deaths. That's when he realized something had cracked open in his head, and it wasn't a bad thing.

Also, his stomach didn't hurt. Not one little bit.

Cap got home around midnight, and Nell still wasn't there.

Em had shown up, and didn't arrest Brett but convinced him to come to the station for a voluntary interview. Cap waited patiently at Reception while Brett was questioned; then Em came out and said Brett was a puddle of sludge, spilled everything he had to spill, giving up the screen names of the guys who'd set it up (he claimed not to know their real names), said it was his idea to break into the car and pull the stunt with the drum. Swore up and down and sideways he was sorry and would never do it again.

Cap was tired but invigorated. Even though his job at Vera Quinn's was full of almost weekly successes, cases wrapped up in neat little boxes, this was different. Not that Brett Hardecker was the most formidable opponent, but tracking him and breaking him down made Cap feel useful in a way he had not felt in a while.

He was out of his mind to share the news with Nell, to tell her that her research was solid and had led to an actual valid confession. That kind of stuff only happened on TV.

But as soon as he saw that her car was not in the driveway, his buoyancy dissipated. For a change, he wasn't worried—now just sad, and feeling extra alone because there was no one to share the victory of the day with.

He parked and went inside, got a beer from the fridge, and turned on the TV. Then he waited. Twelve turned into one, and two.

Nell didn't exactly have a curfew with him: she'd never needed one. She was generally home by eleven or would stay at a friend's house, and she would text him even if she wasn't communicating anything substantive, just to check in, to make sure he was eating a proper dinner or not falling asleep on the couch.

At two-eighteen, the headlights of Nell's car flashed through the living-room window, and Cap turned the volume of the TV up a few notches in an attempt to make it look like he was in the process of doing something routine, just totally natural to be watching TV and sipping a beer at two in the morning, as if he'd not been watching the clock, waiting.

Nell came through the front door and did not seem surprised to see him. "Hey," he said from the couch.

"Hi," said Nell, quieter and stiffer than usual.

She hung her coat up and walked into the living room, stood by the arm of the couch.

"What are you watching?" she said.

Cap had to look at the screen to answer. "History Channel," he said. *"Alien Search."*

"Uh-huh."

Cap was heartened that she didn't scurry right up the stairs, but figured he'd better keep talking.

"So my question is, why would aliens want to walk among us? We're pretty terrible here, you know?" he said, glancing to see if she would crack.

"You're not really watching this, are you?" said Nell.

"Nope," he said, sighing.

"You've just been sitting here, waiting for me, right?"

"Right."

She nodded, kept her eyes on the TV. "Sorry I ran out," she said. "I felt like you didn't trust that I could handle something I really believe I'm ready for."

"I know, Bug," he said. "I'm sorry, too. You just have to know, my whole life, my whole job for twenty-five years, I've been in situation after situation where there are so many unknown risk factors. And I have screwed more than half of them up."

She took a deep breath; Cap could tell she was impatient with the mini-lecture she'd heard many times before.

"I appreciate that," she said. "But don't you think I should have the chance to screw up my own situations for a change?"

"You're about to go to college," Cap said, his voice on the verge of a laugh. "You will have nothing but chances to screw up your own situations for four years."

"Fair," said Nell, perching on the arm of the couch. She began to pull at a stray thread on the upholstery. "So how'd it go with Hardecker?"

Cap nearly fell off the couch with the anticipation of telling her how it had gone with Hardecker. He told her the whole story, and seeing the smile grow on her face was like watching a firework burst.

"So we got him, right? That means we got him?" she said, disbelieving.

"Well, he has to be charged and arraigned, and then Mama and his dad will probably get him a lawyer and plead it down, but, yeah, it's looking like we got him."

Nell faced forward, the smile still there. "And he gave up his collaborators, too?" she said.

"Yep. The screen name of the one who paid him to do the job, anyway."

"Doesn't Vega have a guy who can help with that?" Nell suggested.

Cap's enthusiasm drained a bit, thinking of Vega. He nodded, kept the smile up.

"When's the last time you talked to Vega, Dad?"

"Um," Cap said, assessing the most reasonable lie, "couple days ago?"

"Right," said Nell. "What'd you talk about?"

"I told her where we were on Hardecker," he said, returning his gaze to the alien caves on the TV screen.

"Yeah? What'd she say?"

"She's still working her case in Oregon," he said. "Chasing leads. Being cryptic. You know, Vega stuff."

"'Kay," said Nell.

She stood up and interlaced her fingers, brought her arms over her head in a stretch. "I'm going to sleep," she said. "Aren't you even going to ask where I've been all this time?"

"I figure you'll tell me when you want to," he said, not believing how casual he was playing it.

"And you're, like, cool with that?"

"Sure."

Nell shrugged, mimicking Cap's nonchalance. She headed toward the stairs, but stopped to lean over the back of the couch and kiss him on the top of his head.

"You're a great dad and a great investigator, Cap," she said kindly. "But you're a terrible liar."

Cap laughed and shook his head. "It runs in the family, Bug—better watch it."

Nell yawned at the foot of the stairs. "So when are you going to sleep, you think?" she said.

"Soon," said Cap. "Don't worry."

"Never do," she said, then hiked up the stairs.

Cap watched the alien documentarians on mute for a few minutes. He figured it was almost midnight on the West Coast and thought about texting Vega, but got stuck on what he would write. "I'm sorry, I shouldn't have blamed you for what happened. And your vaguely sensed plans are better than most people's long-thought-out and best-laid."

He thought about it some more and even went so far as to pick up his phone and tap out a few words, but then he erased them. Then he wrote a few different words and erased those. And then it was almost four in the morning, and he left his phone on the couch and stood up. Made sure all the windows and doors were locked, and stood outside of Nell's bedroom until he could hear the gentle cadence of her deep sleep breathing, and then he went into his room and got into bed, and finally collapsed into sleep as the radiators started to hiss with morning heat, the new boiler wide awake beneath him.

9

EVERY DAY, VEGA GOT UP AROUND SUNRISE AND DID PUSH-UPS WITH her good arm, keeping the bad arm in the cast pinned to her chest. Then she did some squats and lunges, which hurt her ribs but not terribly, so she started adding reps here and there.

Then she would have some peanut butter on a slice of toast and some tea, stare out the window in the middle of the back door in her kitchen, and look at the palm tree there, listen to the birds get drowned out by the tree cutters and lawn mowers in the neighborhood as the morning went on.

Every other day, Ameyo would come. She helped Vega set up for the one-armed handstand with other exercises—Chair Pose, Warriors, Fan. After they met a few times, Vega told her she was ready to try the handstand.

"You don't want to fall on this," said Ameyo, tapping the cast.

"What about against the wall?" Vega said.

"Mm," Ameyo said, pretending to think about it. "I don't think you should. If you fall, you'll have to start over."

Vega knew Ameyo was right. Still, she wanted to find another way.

So she waited until Ameyo left and ordered some gym mats online. The kind that she used as a kid in PE—navy blue, tri-fold, four by eight feet. The next time Ameyo came, Vega showed them to her, and Ameyo laughed gently.

"Those aren't that soft, yeah?" was all she said.

But that day, after Ameyo left, Vega tried.

She unfolded one of the mats and started in a one-armed Down Dog, which was easy enough. Then she walked her legs toward her hand and the wall; the pressure built on the left arm, but Vega felt sturdy. She knew she would have to work the right arm hard after the cast was off to catch up; the left was stronger than it ever had been.

She tightened her core, fought the ache of the ribs, and pressed her back against the wall. Then lifted one leg and kept it bent at the knee, slowly extended it. She began to lift the other leg, left arm starting to shake, and was trying to straighten out the second leg when the pain in her ribs got sharper suddenly, like something was about to snap, and then her left arm buckled at the elbow and she fell, on the mat, on her side.

She let out a cry, and didn't recognize the sound. She had kept her bad arm tucked in tightly enough to her chest so that she didn't land on it, but currently everything above the waist and below the neck ached and pulsed.

She didn't get up right away. Instead, she stayed on the mat for a few minutes and rested her head on the cool vinyl; the smell of the polyethylene reminded her of a freshly zipped body bag.

Ameyo was not upset with her—Vega wasn't sure what the thing would be that would make her upset—but Ameyo did seemed a little dismayed, her smile tempered, her voice quieter than usual. Vega had no desire to lie to her. She was paying her a lot of money. Vega found that if she paid people enough they didn't care if the truth was unpleasant. So Vega had told her what had happened with the fall.

Ameyo didn't say anything right away, just instructed Vega to move through Warriors, and Ameyo stood next to her, doing the poses alongside.

"I wonder why you did it," she said after a few minutes, as if she were thinking aloud to herself.

"What?" said Vega, tucking her hip up and swinging her arm down into a triangle.

"Why you went up the wall like that when you know it's bad for you."

Vega brought her legs together and stood up straight.

"I thought I was ready."

"Hm," said Ameyo, then squatted on the mat, her knees aiming outward. "Come do this."

Vega squatted next to her.

"I think you're smart," Ameyo said, leaning forward and planting her left palm on the mat in front of her so it was centered.

Vega did the same with her left hand.

"You know you're not ready, yeah?" said Ameyo, rising up on her toes, her butt aiming toward the ceiling.

Vega did the same, felt the pressure build in her left arm, lower back, toes.

"But you still do it," said Ameyo, taking in a gusty breath through her nose.

Ameyo leaned forward on her arm, lined up her knees on either side of her elbow. Vega tried to do the same, and her left arm started to shake.

"This is the Crow," said Ameyo, slowly tilting her whole body forward so her feet barely lifted off the ground. "You're supposed to use two arms, but we'll try one."

Vega did what Ameyo did. She felt the tips of her big toes hovering just over the mat. Her left arm continued to shake but seemed sturdy.

"Crow's close to the ground," said Ameyo, speaking with some effort as her chest puffed in and out. Her left arm was at an angle, and her entire body was balanced on top of it, like a beach umbrella stuck in the sand.

Vega tilted her body a little more, trying to do the same.

"You won't be able to hold it for long," said Ameyo. "But if you fall . . ."

Vega started to tip forward but bent her elbow and leaned her body to the left, then crumbled to the mat. Nothing hurt.

"You don't have far to go, yeah?"

Vega watched Ameyo, who was not watching Vega. Ameyo stared at a point on the mat and rocked back until her toes touched the ground. Then she exhaled loudly, released her arm, and sat cross-legged on the mat. She touched her hand to her forehead, as if just to feel the light sweat there, not wipe it away.

.   .   .

Later, Vega stared at the wall where she'd fallen a few days before. She went into the bathroom and looked at her eye, still ringed with blue, the horseshoe bruise along her jaw now gray. She lifted her tank top and examined the bruising on her ribs and abdomen. The skin there was healing quicker than her face and bore a tawny-brown pattern, like an animal. She took a shower, wearing a neoprene rubber glove over the cast on her arm. Washed her hair with her left hand.

When she got out, she timed how long it took to dry off and get dressed, which was only eight minutes, down from thirteen the week before. Then she came back to the living room, where she had her laptop set up on the couch and the rubber tumbling mats on the floor. She stared again at the wall where she'd tried to do the handstand and the mats that broke her fall.

Get in line and wait, she thought. Then get to the front of the line and wait some more.

A week later, Vega sat on the couch and combed through ZIP files sent by the Bastard. He'd found Nikolai's screen name on Reddit, picked through sixty days of posts and messages from his handle and e-mail, and found a fair amount of communication between him and someone with the screen name RepoRiot on the topic of "tagging." RepoRiot's most recent IM to Nikolai had read, "text PayNow info for the job." Vega wrote an e-mail to the Bastard asking him to get into Nikolai's PayNow account and see what kind of payments he'd been receiving lately.

She read some reviews and tech specs for clip-on microphones that she could connect to her phone and wear on the inside pocket of her jacket. She placed an order for one with the description boasting "high pickup sensitivity."

Then she figured it was time to find Cooper.

It didn't take long. He'd written a post a few hours earlier on a sub called /rightstuffforteens. "You should be able to think and say whatever you think and say in this country, period. Mean words aren't hate crimes." His newest post read, "Find a teacher you can trust. They're out there."

Vega leaned her head back and stared at the exposed beams on the ceiling; from her angle, the dark wood against the white paint looked like the rungs of a ladder.

She stood up and went to her bedroom closet, pulled out her laptop bag, unzipped the front pocket, and found what she was looking for: a scrap from a magazine cover with Cooper's phone number.

She returned to the couch, picked up her phone and created a contact, entered the number, and wrote a text: "Hey it's Bitsy. Liked your last post." Added a thumbs-up.

She clicked "send" and waited.

He wrote back in less than a minute: "Hey!!! So good to hear from you. Wondering where you went."

Vega lay down on the couch, wiggled the fingers of her right hand, and felt the tendons stretch deep underneath the cast. She tapped the call button with her thumb.

"Bitsy, that you?" said Cooper, sounding close.

"It's me," said Vega, looking up at the beams again.

"It's so good to hear your voice," he said. "When I didn't hear from you, I thought maybe you got a little shy."

Vega laughed, but it was quiet. "Actually, I had to come back to California. My dad is having some health problems."

"I'm sorry to hear that," said Cooper. "Is he all right?"

"He will be," said Vega. "It's a good thing I'm here, though. I just . . . I wanted to say sorry for disappearing."

"You don't have to apologize," said Cooper. "Gotta take care of your family."

"Yeah."

She closed her eyes, tried to picture him. The tattoos on the arms, white tee shirt, jeans, black boots, just like her.

"Hey, are you sitting on your couch right now?" she asked.

Cooper laughed, sounded surprised, maybe even a little shocked, which is how Vega wanted him to feel.

"No, I'm at work."

"Where do you work?"

"Landscaping. Lawn care at its finest," he said in a commercial-ready voice. "Really, though, it's a lot of debris removal—clearing downed branches and making everything pretty."

"Do you like it?"

"I guess," he said. "I like being outside, so it's a good job for me, especially since deer season's over."

They were both quiet. Vega wondered how long it would take for him to crack. It took the better part of a minute, which was more than most guys could take.

"Like I said, you don't have anything to apologize for."

"That's not the only reason I called. I wanted you to know . . ." She paused, let the tension stack up. "I want to be involved. Really involved. Not like the kids. I want to meet people in the organization."

"That's good news," said Cooper. "Let's talk when you come back to Ilona. You'll let me know when you get here?"

"You'll be the first person I call," she said, tilting her head back farther, trying to make her voice husky.

"Good," he said, sounding out of breath.

"Good," she repeated. "I'll talk to you soon."

"Hope so."

It all came down to seconds—that was Vega's whole business, her whole life, and it was an impossible thing to gauge, but it also happened to be what she was good at. How many were too many, how few were too few. Right now she had to time what she was going to say for the slice of a second before Cooper hung up. She shut her eyes, could see the imprint of the beams in white on the back of her lids. She pictured him holding the phone in his hand, about to tap the red button.

"Cooper," she said.

"Yeah, you still there?" he said. "Bitsy?"

"I haven't been totally truthful with you."

"That's okay," he said. "You want to talk about it?"

"I do," she said, her eyes still closed. "I didn't just want to apologize, or ask to be involved—I mean, I did want to say those things, but it's a lot more selfish, why I called."

Cooper laughed; Vega could tell it was a close-mouthed laugh, a "Hm."

"You really don't seem like a selfish person," he said. "But go ahead, shoot, why'd you call?"

Vega took a small breath, did her best to sound like someone taking a chance.

"I know I only met you once, but I feel like I've known you a very long time," she said quickly. "That's all. Bye."

She opened her eyes and hung up. Rested the phone on her chest, still in her hand. After a minute, a text came through. It was from Cooper, and it was one word: "Same."

10

VEGA MET JEFF WALL OUTSIDE THE RIDING ACADEMY WHERE HE worked, about a two-hour drive north from her place. After the Bastard produced Wall's name from a search for Jack Klimmer's former employees, Wall had not been difficult to find. He'd been a trainer for twenty-five years, prepping horses for competition all over California, but not racetrack. These weren't races with two-buck-bet tickets behind them; they were equestrian contests—hunting and jumping events. Though not as famous as the award-winning riders and their instructors, Wall's name still popped up in plenty of the industry announcements at the end of the blurbs: Horse: Dark Knight or Christopher Robin or King Arthur. Trainer: Jeff Wall.

The main building at the riding academy looked like a rustic country club, painted barn red, with fenced-in tracks behind it. Vega saw kids on horses, riding, jumping steeples. She watched men and women come in and out of the front door with their kids, mostly slender girls with their hair in tight ponytails.

Vega stood in front of her car and held a cup of tea in her bad hand and a cup of coffee in her left. When Jeff Wall came through the front doors, she lifted the coffee cup in his direction.

He nodded and smiled, walked toward her. He was tall and fit, his face tanned and wrinkled, with sparse blond hair on his head and arms.

"Mr. Wall," Vega said, cheery.

"Howdy," he said. "Alice, is it?"

"It is," said Vega. She handed him the coffee. "I took a chance you'd take milk and sugar."

"If it's coffee before noon, I like it," said Wall. He tipped his head to the side to get a look at her cast. "That from a horse?"

"I wish it was that good a story," said Vega. "Just stairs and wet boots."

"I couldn't tell you how many bones I've broken," said Wall. "First was my arm when I was ten years old. Horse was named Cally."

"You never forget your first," said Vega.

She took a chance that Wall would appreciate the provocation. Men opened themselves up to women who could handle some salt.

Wall smiled but set his eyes on the ground. Gentleman, was what that told Vega.

"Should we take a walk?" Wall said, pointing to a field adjacent to the track.

"Sure," said Vega.

They walked alongside the border fence of the track toward the open field. The day was warm, but overcast.

"What's the name of your book again?"

"West Coast Horse Farms: A Retrospective."

"Sounds like my kind of book."

"It's mostly photographs," said Vega. "Like the one I sent to you. I'm interviewing people who have unique insight on the subject."

"I don't know about insight," said Wall. "I got some experience, though."

"Exactly what I'm looking for," said Vega.

"Fire away, then," said Wall.

He led her along a slim dirt trail into the field. Vega could hear the horses' feet thump on the track behind them, the voices of the trainers and instructors shouting commands.

"So how long have you been a trainer at Redwood Riding Academy," she said.

"As long as it's been around," said Wall. He squinted at the sky, said, "So that's sixteen, seventeen years?"

"And you worked farms before that, right? It said on your bio on the Web site you were at one down in Solvang—southern California?"

"That's right. I was training horses for boarding schools. There's a lot of them down south, have riding programs."

"Were you always interested in the education aspect?"

Wall made a sound that was part cough, part laugh.

"No," he said. "I never was. That's the people who pay you, though, give you benefits, so you can make a living."

"Gotcha," said Vega. "Starving's okay when you're young, you know?" She glanced at his left hand, saw a band on his ring finger, added, "Then you get a little older, have to provide for your family."

"That's the truth," he said, nodding.

"So, before Solvang, did you work any other ranches in California?"

"Actually, up in Oregon for a time. That's where I'm from."

"Oh yeah, whereabout?" said Vega.

"Little town you've never heard of," he said with a polite smile.

"Try me."

"Place called Ilona, south of Eugene."

"Ilona," Vega repeated. "Sounds familiar. I've been doing a lot of this research, see, so I've been all over. Wasn't there a guy who kept some horses up there, a logger by the name of Klimmer?"

Wall stopped walking and turned to her.

"Jack," he said, like he was recalling the name from a dream. "Yeah, I worked for Jack when I was a kid, just out of high school. Have you been up there?"

"Yes, last month. Talked to Matt Klimmer. Did you know him, too?"

"The son, right? He was a couple years older than me. I didn't know him too well."

Wall kept walking. Vega allowed him to go ahead a few paces so they were single-file. She sensed he wanted to say more but needed some room.

"Klimmer—Matt Klimmer still keeps a few horses."

"Uh-huh," Wall said.

Vega watched the back of his head. You have something to say, don't you?

"He owns about half the town, businesses and farmland."

Wall was silent, turned his head toward a patch of trees to his left.

"But, between you and me, he was kind of an asshole."

Wall laughed and stopped walking, waited for Vega to catch up.

"I didn't want to say it," he said, warm and conspiratorial.

Vega laughed, covered her mouth in an effort to seem demure. "I mean," she said, "I could see the spoiled brat inside even though he's twenty years older than me."

"You wouldn't be wrong there," said Wall. "I'd hoped he'd grown up after all this time, but people are who they are, I guess." Then he shook his head. "We don't need to dwell on it."

"The thing about it is," Vega said, ignoring Wall's attempt to move on, "I got a feeling he was trying to hide something from me."

Wall looked at her sideways. "Like what?" he said.

"I don't know. I was just asking him about horses. He was acting like a man with a secret."

"Funny you say that," Wall said, quiet. "Between you and me?"

He met her eye then, offering a deal.

"Of course."

"He had a streak, him and his friend." Wall winced, trying to remember. "Can't remember the name now. Big fella. He and Matt Klimmer were always tight."

"Fenton?" Vega said, already knowing the answer.

"Yeah, that's it—Fenton."

"He's the sheriff now," said Vega.

"Sheriff?" said Wall. "As in law enforcement?"

"That's right," said Vega. "Does that surprise you?"

Wall picked up a thick stick and stuck it into the ground, then used it as a staff as he kept walking. "Suppose anyone can change. That was all a long time ago."

"I think," Vega said, "people are more like horses. You can see their personalities when they're young, and then they grow into them."

Wall faced forward as he walked.

"Mr. Wall," said Vega, "if you don't mind me saying, you're acting a little bit like a man with a secret, too."

Wall chuckled. "I don't have any secrets," he said. "Matt Klimmer and I didn't part ways on the best terms, is all. His father, Jack, who hired me, went downhill real quick. One day he was well, and the next day I come to work at five, like always, and Matt meets me at my car and says he had to put his dad in a facility overnight. Let me go on the spot. Wouldn't even let me say goodbye to the horses."

There was an old bruise hidden in what Wall said, but it was nowhere near the surface, just a memory of something that used to hurt.

"Were you close with Jack?"

Wall shrugged. "In a way. But I only worked for him about a year. I was sorry I couldn't say thank you to him in person, but Matt said he was too sick."

"Did you know what happened?"

"Matt didn't say."

Wall stopped walking. Vega stepped a few paces ahead and then realized he was staying put.

"You writing a book about horse ranches, or the Klimmers?" he said.

He didn't seem angry, just a little hurt that he'd been duped.

Vega knew she either had to keep filling out the lie or to drop the act. She picked the latter, took a chance she'd get further with Wall by coming clean.

"Neither," she said. "I'm a private investigator, and I'm looking for Zeb Williams."

Wall rested his hand on the top of the stick and leaned on it, with the bottom digging into the ground.

"I never met him," he said.

"But you knew he was in town?"

"Yeah, but I let him alone," said Wall. "He came there so no one would bother him, I imagine."

Then he shrugged again and kept walking straight ahead, past Vega, as if he were moving toward a specific thing in the distance. Vega caught up.

"You could've just said that, ma'am," Wall said. "I could have told you over e-mail that I never met Zeb Williams."

"I wanted to speak with you in person, so I said what I needed to say," said Vega. "I think Klimmer and Fenton know something about Williams, and I've been looking for people who might have an idea about that. I'm sorry about the act."

Wall raised a hand to block the apology, wouldn't look at her.

"I don't know anything about what Matt Klimmer and Fenton knew about anything."

"You already told me quite a bit. It sounds like Klimmer wanted you out of sight pretty quick the morning he fired you. Like maybe he didn't want you to see something."

"Just the horses," said Wall. "He just wouldn't let me see the horses, wouldn't let me near the stable, because he happened to start renovations on it that morning."

"What kind of renovations?"

"He brought in a whole crew to pour concrete down over the stable floor, right after they took Jack away. Told me it was something Jack had scheduled for a while." Wall shook his head. "Jack never told me about any of that."

Vega thought she might as well show the last of her cards, since she'd come this far.

"Do you know what facility Jack Klimmer was in, after the stroke?" she asked.

"Not sure," said Wall, sighing. "And Matt made it pretty clear he wasn't going to stay in touch." Then he paused. "There was a place on the coast, a luxury type of hospice—I remember Matt saying his dad was going to be near the water, and wasn't that fine. Then he winced at Vega. "So why's this going to help?"

"I'm not sure," said Vega.

Wall glanced sideways at her. "You said you were an investigator—like a detective?"

"That's right."

"Seems to me there's something about the timing, with Jack getting sick and me getting fired. Always thought there might be, but didn't know what it could be. I don't want to tell you your job, but, seeing you're the investigator, you could probably figure that out."

There was a dash of dismissiveness in his tone, but Vega felt he'd earned it.

"If you'll excuse me, I need to get back to work," he said, and took off toward the track. "It's too bad," he called over his shoulder to Vega. "I was looking forward to reading that book."

Vega stood in the field for a minute or two by herself. Then she headed back to her car, buckled up, and checked her phone. There was a text. "Maybe: Nell Caplan," read the ID:

"Hi Alice. This is Nell Caplan. I got your number from my dad's phone. Let me know if you can talk. Hope you are well."

Vega tapped the "info" button and then Nell's number. Nell picked up after one ring.

"Alice, is that you?" she said, her voice wide awake.

Vega fought a smile and said, "It's me. Hi, Nell."

"Hey, how are you?" Nell said, animated.

Vega hadn't spoken to or seen Nell since the Brandt case, almost two years before. She'd been struck by Nell's demeanor, her unforced maturity, effortless kindness. Rare in adults, rarer in teens. Rare in humans of any age.

"I'm fine. Is everything okay?" said Vega.

"Oh yeah. No emergencies or anything. I wanted to call you because I was wondering . . ."

She paused, breathing heavier; it sounded like she was outside, walking. Then she continued: "So has my dad been updating you, about the situation here with Hardecker?"

Vega considered this question. She hadn't talked to Cap since she left Ilona. Since before the Burger Village parking lot.

"I haven't talked to Cap in a while," said Vega. "I had to come back to California for a few weeks."

"Oh," said Nell with genuine concern. "I hope everything's all right."

"Yes, it's fine," said Vega.

"That's good. . . . So you haven't talked to my dad?" she asked, sounding resigned.

"No, I haven't. Is everything all right over there?" said Vega.

"Yeah!" said Nell. Then she continued, assuming a professional tone: "We found the guy who broke into my car and cut up the drum, and Em questioned him and got the screen name of the guy that put him up to it. I remember my dad saying a long time ago that you have a hacker friend?"

"I do."

"Should I send you the name? Maybe your friend can try to find him?"

"Sure."

Vega smiled, thinking of Nell smiling. Vega had never wanted kids, because of the distraction, and because you could lose them. But if she could get a kid like Nell, who just popped out of an Easy-Bake Oven ready-made, she might think about it for a minute. Vega was reminded of what Dart had said about Zeb's being able to read people. You either learned it or were born with it. Vega had a feeling Nell was the latter, and suddenly felt compelled to glean everything she could from her.

"I think I wrote it down in my dad's office—hang on, I just have to run downstairs," said Nell, keeping Vega on the line.

"Anything else you notice?" said Vega.

"As pertains to?"

"Anything," said Vega, watching the grass in the field wave in the breeze. "In your conversations with people, in your research. You didn't meet this Hardecker, right?"

"Right, just my dad did."

Vega thought she could hear a little resentment tucked inside the word "dad."

"I looked around for him on social media—narrowed him down to a handful of user names on this local Reddit board and took a guess."

"Oh yeah?" said Vega. "How'd you do it?"

"Um, so I just found him with his real name on Facebook and Insta, and at some point, he listed *The Turner Diaries* as his favorite book—it's like this white-supremacist fantasy trash about a race war, but it's the Bible to some of these guys—and one of the user names we were looking at was 'TDNow.' "

"Turner Diaries Now."

"Exactly," said Nell. "This guy doesn't quite seem smart enough to separate his online persona from his IRL persona. Here's the name," she said, then reading, "RepoRiot—I hope this helps."

"Thanks, Nell. It helps," said Vega.

"Good . . . I'm glad."

Nell paused again, sounded like she was walking faster, maybe up some stairs.

"Hey," said Nell. "Did you and my dad— Is there a reason you're not talking that I should be aware of?"

Vega thought quickly about how best to answer. She had no reason to lie. "The last time we spoke, we argued. I think he was upset that I put you at risk. You'd have to ask him, though, about how he felt exactly."

"Oh," said Nell. "I didn't know."

She sounded sad, and Vega couldn't stand it.

"Look, your dad—I think he was right. You shouldn't have to pay for what's happening in my case."

"It's okay," said Nell. "I got a good bass drum for a hundred on eBay."

From someone else, the comment could have dripped with bitterness; from Nell, it was just the truth.

"There's another thing, though," said Nell. "If you and my dad haven't really been communicating—did he even tell you about Bear Thomas?"

Vega froze at the sound of the name. Specks of rain began to dot the windshield.

"The Cal holder?"

"Yeah. He lives in upstate New York, and Dad went to see him."

"Huh," said Vega. "When was this, do you think?"

"I'm pretty sure right before the car-drum incident."

"Do you know what they talked about?"

"Not everything," said Nell. "My dad did say that the biggest surprise was that he thinks Zeb Williams contacted his girlfriend"—Nell paused—"I don't know her name?"

"Carmen," said Vega.

"Yeah, Carmen," Nell continued. "My dad said Bear Thomas thought Zeb might have called her after he ran off the field."

Vega let the information sit next to her in the car for a second before responding. "Did Bear know that for certain?"

"That's what I wondered, too," said Nell. "Not for certain for certain. But I think Bear had a hunch they talked."

Vega stared at the windshield, thinking. "That's unexpected."

"I know, right?"

Vega did some math, estimated how long it would take to get to San Francisco from where she was. Four hours, maybe?

"Nell, I have to go. I appreciate your work, though. You don't have to do anything else. I got it."

"Of course, yeah," said Nell. "If I find something, or remember something, I can let you know, right?"

"That would be great," said Vega. "Thanks."

After they hung up, Vega stared at the phone screen. She thought about the text she was about to send and rewrote it a couple of times in her head before deciding that direct, as usual, was best.

She made it in just under three hours. The skies were still overcast and drizzling with rain as she crossed the Bay Bridge into the city.

She remembered the way to the big yellow house without GPS, parked across the street, and rushed up the steps to ring the bell.

Unlike last time, Anton Fohl himself came to answer the door, in a rush, not Samuel the assistant. He looked a little more disheveled than before, if not his clothes (still pressed, still tucked), then his expression and posture, eyes pinched with weariness, shoulders curled forward.

He fumbled with the lock on the front door and then opened it, took in Vega's appearance, and seemed taken aback.

"Ms. Vega," he said. "Are you all right? Your eye."

"It's fine," said Vega. Then she lifted her cast and said, in an effort to avoid any further discussion on the topic, "This is also fine."

"What happened?" he said, standing aside for her to come into the entry hall.

"I was in an accident," she said. "I'm fine."

"Good," he said, not bothering to dwell on the details. Then he grew stern: "Did you happen to hear any of my voice mails?"

"Not really," said Vega. "Didn't read your texts, either."

He sighed, pouty.

"I read yours," he said, producing the phone from his pocket and reading from the screen: "'I need to meet your wife. I'll be there at three.'" He shook the phone at her and said, "I can respect your non-traditional work ethic, but I am still your employer."

Vega squinted at him. The laid-back, open-floor-plan guy was gone. Now he was just Old Money.

"You indicated before it wouldn't be a problem," he said, then lowered his voice. "Not involving my wife."

"We have a little bit of a different recall of that conversation, but that's okay," said Vega, continuing before he could interrupt. "Leaving your wife out of it didn't matter before. Now some new information has surfaced, and I need to ask your wife about it."

"Mind telling me what that information is? Seeing I am your client?" he said, crossing his arms.

Vega took a peek into the future, imagined telling Fohl about Bear Thomas's hunch, and him trying to be cool about it. She'd had a lot of time wasted in her work from men trying to be cool.

"I can tell both of you at the same time," said Vega. "Or you can fire me, and I take the information with me."

He stewed about it for a moment and then said, "That won't be necessary."

He took off in the opposite direction from the room where he and Vega had met for the first time, through a white swinging door into a long restaurant-style kitchen with stainless-steel kitchen equipment. There was another swinging door at the back of the room, which he pushed and held open with two fingers for Vega.

She followed Fohl into a sunroom that was similar in layout to the entry hall but narrower, one wall all glass, with greenery on the other side. Fohl kept up his healthy pace toward the glass; Vega realized he was heading for a door in the corner and assumed they were heading into a garden.

As they approached the door, though, she saw they weren't going outside at all, that there was actually a greenhouse on the other side of the glass wall that spanned the width of the house.

"I've told her everything, FYI," he said, standing in front of the door.

"Okay."

"There are no more secrets between her and me."

He seemed pretty eager to tell Vega what a communicative marriage he had, all of a sudden.

"That's just great news," said Vega. "Can I meet Mrs. Fohl now?"

"Of course," he said, barely moving his lips.

Fohl opened the door, and a wave of warm steam piped out.

Vega followed him inside. The ceilings were about twelve feet high; tall plants and stubby succulents lined the borders of the room. The humidity was gummy in Vega's throat and nose. Sweat instantly sprouted on her forehead and neck, moisture gathering in the sleeve of her cast.

"Car?" Fohl called, sounding tentative.

"Here," said a voice.

Fohl led Vega down a small walkway, and then Vega could see her, sitting on a footstool in a corner, surrounded by vines twisted around wooden dowels stuck into neat squares of soil.

She glanced at Vega.

"Hello," she said.

She was petite and fair and blonde, with nearly transparent eyebrows and lashes, the delicate bones of her face arranged like a doll's—a gift-box bow of a mouth, rounded cheeks, and a small nose pinched up at the end. She didn't look to be in her fifties, but Vega saw none of the usual evidence of plastic surgery—not the too-tight forehead or tugged eyelids. She wore yellow garden gloves and was scraping a small spade along the inner curve of a flowerpot that held a slick-leafed plant.

"I would shake, but . . ." she said, holding up her gloved hand.

"It's okay," said Vega, holding up her arm in the cast. "Alice Vega."

The faintest shadow of a smile appeared on Carmen's lips. "Yes," she said softly, and then, "That's fine, Anton," to her husband, without looking up, continuing to move the spade around the pot.

"All right," Fohl said, wiping his forehead with his shirt sleeve. "Should I have Minna bring you a water?"

"I have some," said Carmen, nodding toward a refillable bottle at her side, still staring at her husband.

"Okay," said Fohl. "I'll give you some time."

He actually reminded Vega of Samuel the assistant, except that he didn't bother to ask Vega if anyone should bring her a water. Then he left, and the women were alone.

"Were you in an accident?" said Carmen.

"Yes."

"Anything internal?"

"No."

"That's good," said Carmen. "Still, the surface injuries make you tired at the end of the day, just from carrying your body around."

Carmen placed the pot on one of the squares of soil. She picked up another pot, this one square, like a small crate, filled with purple flowers.

"Do you have any personal experience of that?" asked Vega.

"I was in a car accident when I was thirteen," she said, turning the pot in her hands, examining the flowers. "My grandfather was driving. He fell asleep."

She didn't offer anything else, and Vega didn't ask.

Carmen rubbed a petal of one of the flowers between two fingers and sighed. "You wanted to speak," she said.

"Yes," said Vega. "I have some new information, and I'd like to ask you about it."

Carmen lifted the pot over her head and scratched at something on the bottom with her thumb.

"I'd have thought you'd come sooner," she said with some tenderness.

Vega wasn't convinced that Carmen wasn't talking to the plant.

"I didn't see a need for it," said Vega. "Before now."

Carmen set the plant back down and said, "My father hired a private detective in the eighties, right after Zeb left, but he, the detective, didn't get very far. How far have you gotten?"

She picked up a green spray bottle and began spritzing a white liquid onto the leaves of the first plant she'd been tending.

"I spent some time in Ilona, the town in Oregon where that picture was taken. I talked to some people he knew there. But I had to come back to California prematurely to take care of some things, so I paused the case."

Carmen's light eyebrows moved around; they looked like loose feathers from a pillow.

"I don't know if Anton was aware of that," she said. "That you paused the case."

Vega couldn't quite assess if she was being scolded or not.

"No, probably not," said Vega. "But I don't think he cared either way."

"And why would you say that?" asked Carmen, her inquiry soft but holding a tiny toothy bite.

"I just spent about seven minutes with him face-to-face while he walked me through the house. Not once did he ask about my progress," said Vega. "Leads me to believe expedience isn't his priority."

"I see," said Carmen, angling her head down, shielding a grin. "There was a specific reason the first detective didn't get far. To be fair, it wasn't his fault."

Now she stood, and Vega realized Carmen was taller than her by at least three or four inches, her arms and legs long, matching the vines behind her. She also wore a gardener's waist apron with shears of various sizes tucked into the pockets.

"I didn't give him anything to go on," she said.

Then she passed Vega and went down the walkway, stopping to examine a spiky bush covered with pink-and-red buds. Vega followed her and stared at the bush. She thought the leaves and the buds had the look of a plastic Christmas arrangement—pretty, but unbelievable.

"Sounds like a waste of your money," said Vega.

"A waste of my father's money," said Carmen, pulling a small pair of scissors from her apron pocket.

She began to snip wrinkled leaves off the bush and hold them in one fist.

"I never wanted a detective in the first place," she said, slicing off a stray twig.

"You didn't want to find Zeb?" said Vega.

"I didn't say that," said Carmen evenly. "I didn't have the easiest time at Cal. Everyone knew who my family was. They'd call me Patty Hearst as a joke."

She didn't seem upset as she described her youth, but spoke of it with the same tone she'd used when she told Vega about her car accident: a sad, strange thing that had happened to her and could not be changed.

"A plane would pass, heading for the Oakland airport, and people would point to me and say, 'Your ride's here.' Things like that."

"But not Zeb," said Vega.

"No, not Zeb," said Carmen. "We met in a class, and he had no idea who I was or who my family was, and even when I told him, he couldn't care less."

She leaned close to the buds and took a breath through her mouth.

"We didn't have a lot in common," she said, confessionally. "We probably would not have gotten married. My father only accepted him because he was on the football team. In the end, he probably would have thrown a fit if Zeb had actually proposed."

"Then why'd he pay for a detective to find him?" said Vega.

"Because my father couldn't stand the PR," she said, clipping another leaf. "After Zeb ran off, it spread pretty quickly I was his girl-friend. My father saw it as some kind of slight to the family name, so he hired the detective. I suppose he wanted an apology—for Zeb to beg forgiveness of me and the institution of college football."

She stuck the small scissors back into the pocket of her apron and pulled out a larger pair, ran her hand along the surface of the bush, grabbed a branch, and tugged.

"Loose," she said, yanking the branch free.

"You didn't care about him coming back," said Vega.

"I cared," she said, the softness back in her voice now. "I was . . . embarrassed. If someone wanted to run away from you, why would you stop him?"

Vega began to feel the heat of the room radiating off her skin. She stared at the branch in Carmen's hand—a spiny, brittle thing.

"When the detective brought back that photo, the one Anton gave you, I took one look and . . ."

She paused and let the branch drop into a bucket on the ground. The fall was surprisingly graceful.

"Zeb never looked at me like that."

"Were you angry?" asked Vega.

Carmen interlaced her fingers, pushing the gloves down more firmly on her hands. She squinted, thinking about it.

"I don't think so?" she said, unsure of the memory. "I just wanted it to be over with, the reporters, kids on campus having a new way to tease me. I loved Zeb when we were together, but it would have meant nothing if a detective sent by my father dragged him back to me."

She began pulling other stray branches from the bush. Tug, yank, snap, drop. Vega watched Carmen's hands move swiftly, as if she knew exactly where the dead branches would be.

"You were resigned to him never coming back?" Vega asked.

"Yes. Almost immediately." She looked up now, at the steamed glass roof. "I watched him run off the field that day, watched my father's mouth drop, and the first thing, my first response: I laughed. It was just so funny. So absurd.

"That was a difficult thing to explain to people, so I stopped talk-ing about it."

"So, maybe," Vega began, "you might hold back certain information if you wanted all the attention to stop."

Carmen held up a twig that had broken off a larger branch. She stared at it.

Vega continued: "If you'd found some kind of peace with the whole situation, and were okay with Zeb not coming back, maybe you thought it would be best to stay quiet, maybe not tell some guy who worked for your father everything you knew."

Carmen tossed the twig into the bucket, kept pulling out branches. "Now we come to your new information," she said, a slow, small smile spreading. "You know he called me, don't you?"

"Not for certain," said Vega. "But I had a hunch."

Carmen continued to smile; Vega couldn't tell if she was impressed or offended.

"How did you come by this hunch?"

"It was Bear Thomas's hunch originally. He surmised that you and Zeb spoke at some point after The Run."

"Bear Thomas," Carmen repeated, staring at a red bulb. Then she focused on Vega again. "It's the truth. Zeb called from Oregon. What's the town called?"

"Ilona."

"That's right," said Carmen. "I remember it sounded like 'Alone-a.'"

"When did he call you?"

"He'd been gone a couple of months. I remember one of the girls in my sorority calling my name—we only had a couple of phones in the house in those days, and when I picked up the receiver and I heard him breathe, before he said anything, I knew it was him.

"There was no privacy in that house, so I pulled the phone as far as the cord would go, and I went into a closet and sat on the floor, and he asked how I was, and then I asked him how he was, and we, both of us, we weren't saying much to each other. It was strange."

Carmen picked up the bucket of branches and walked past Vega to another plant, this one tall, set against the glass wall, its giant teardrop-shaped leaves fanning out from the slender stalk.

"What did he say?" said Vega.

Carmen set down the bucket and squatted, ran her fingers along the bark at the base of the plant.

"He said he was sorry," Carmen said. "For leaving me in the middle of all of it. He didn't mean to hurt me."

"Did you believe him?"

"Yes," Carmen said right away. "He always told the truth. He would prefer to stay quiet instead of lie."

She took a large pair of shears from the pocket of her apron and trimmed brown crust off of a leaf.

"Did you ask him why he did it?" said Vega.

"No."

"Why not?"

"Because I didn't care," said Carmen, getting exasperated, looking up at Vega. "I didn't care about any of that. I asked him if he was coming back. *That's* what I cared about."

Vega paused to give them both a rest; she didn't want to upset Carmen and stop the flow of information. Then: "What did he say?"

"He said he didn't know," said Carmen, turning back to the leaf. "And I knew that meant no."

"And you never told your father's detective that?"

"No. I've never told anyone that he called." She sighed. "I haven't thought about running into Bear in a long time. I hadn't seen him since the day of the game. He always seemed to me a decent guy, and I don't remember what I was thinking exactly, but I think I just wanted to share it with someone who knew Zeb and wouldn't be angry. If I'd wanted to commiserate, I could've walked into any dive bar on Telegraph."

Carmen snapped the leaf off the stalk and dropped it into the bucket. Then she stood and began peeling off her gloves.

"My husband hired you without me knowing. He thought, if I could finally have some closure with Zeb, maybe it would make me happy and save our marriage, I guess?" she said with a blithe air. "Frankly, I'm not sure."

"But he didn't know about the phone call," said Vega.

"No, he didn't," Carmen said. "Anyway, I looked you up online. You seem to have a high success rate of finding people."

She stopped talking then, just folded her gloves and placed them inside the pocket of the apron.

"Ms. Fohl, there's a thing I'm not understanding," said Vega. "From what you say, you've long abandoned the idea that Zeb Williams will resurface, and you figured out that I already knew about the phone call. So you agreed to meet me in person just to tell me the case is closed?"

Vega was calm, but was getting tired. Her body ached from the long drive, and the sweat dripping off her earlobes, eyelashes, steeping her bra and underwear, was starting to irritate her.

"Yes, but . . ." said Carmen, still looking at the gloves in her apron. Then her eyes found Vega's. "But do you have a chance of finding him? The detective my father hired didn't get very far."

"Do I work for you now?" Vega asked, genuinely interested in the answer. "Your husband hired me, so, legally, I can only share my progress with him. But if I work for both of you now, then I can also share what I know with you. So . . ."

Carmen looked away again, the concern visible on her brow. Vega noticed how the sweat merely coated the surface of Carmen's skin, as if she were a selkie on a bank, as if it belonged there. Vega thought perhaps it was because Carmen spent more time in the controlled tropical temperature of the greenhouse than she did anywhere else.

"Yes, I think so," Carmen said. "I think you work for me now. Both of us, I mean."

"Okay," said Vega. "I'll tell you and your husband everything, but could I get a glass of water first?"

An hour later, Vega sat with Fohl and Carmen in the room where she'd first met Fohl. Vega sat on the couch facing the mirror, and Fohl and Carmen sat on the couch opposite her, a cushion apart from each other.

"Do you think this Klimmer knows where Zeb went?" Fohl said.

"I don't know," said Vega. "Like I said, Klimmer's son and his friends had been harassing my family long-distance, so I had to come back here and take care of that. Klimmer might not have all the answers, but one day, right before Zeb took off from Ilona, they had a fight that was significant enough for an old man who was just a bystander to remember, so, to me, that's a thread to follow."

"Do you think Klimmer and—who's the sheriff—Fenton?" Carmen said.

Vega nodded.

Carmen continued, notes of panic lacing her voice: "Could they have threatened Zeb?"

"It's possible," Vega said. "I'll have to follow up when I go back."

"When do you think that might be?" said Fohl.

"Couple weeks. I'd like to get this off first," she said, lifting her cast.

"What if Klimmer and Fenton have nothing to do with it?" said Fohl.

"Then I'll keep asking around. But usually people who have nothing to hide tell you everything, especially if it has to do with a celebrity. Klimmer and Fenton were both pretty cagey with me."

Carmen had removed her gardening apron and changed into a patterned blouse and wide-cuffed jeans that seemed to swallow her body up.

"What do you think they're hiding?" she said.

Vega glanced at her reflection in the tilted mirror on the wall: the blue ring around her eye, the cast.

"Klimmer's and Fenton's sons are into some nasty stuff online. I'm not sure of the scope of it yet."

"They're much too young to have anything to do with Zeb," said Fohl.

"Klimmer and Fenton used to be into nasty stuff, too," said Vega. "True, there may not be a direct connection, but there's a pattern of violence and cover-ups by local enforcement, and a mess of lies, big and small. Somewhere in there is an explanation for why my family is getting harassed. And somewhere in there might be a trace of where Zeb went. Or where he is now."

Fohl and Carmen considered this in their ways: Fohl clasping his hands in a ball, nodding to an inaudible beat while he repeated Vega's arguments to himself, Carmen appearing to shrink even farther inside her clothes, her face seeming even paler than it had been before, nearly translucent.

"They don't necessarily cross," said Vega, making an "x" with her arms. Then she uncrossed them and held them parallel in front of her. "But they may very well line up side by side."

"How long will it take? To wrap up?" said Fohl.

"I need about two or three weeks for all of my injuries to heal well enough so that I'm able to work," said Vega. "After I get back to Ilona, I'll need a week to recalibrate. Then I'll give you a firm estimate, and you decide if you'd like me to continue."

Carmen now turned her face away from both her husband and Vega, staring at a potted plant near the window.

"I haven't been doing consistent work since I left Oregon, but I've kept track of my time and can prorate those charges. Also, you shouldn't have to pay for the recovery time for my accident, so I can prorate these next couple of weeks as well," Vega rattled off, not giving it a second thought.

Fohl smiled broadly, looking like someone had just given him a free margarita on the street.

"No," said Carmen, her face still turned away. "No," she said again, more firmly, facing Vega.

Fohl stared at his wife and then turned to Vega as if she might be able to decode the substance of what was happening.

"Car?" he said.

"We'll pay for your time. All of your time," said Carmen, her voice louder now.

Vega almost opened her mouth to argue. It was typically her policy to err on the side of charity toward the client, but then she heard her old boss, Perry, in her ear: Take the money, kid. Don't refuse a generous impulse.

"If that's what you'd like," Vega said.

"It is," said Carmen. "I don't believe you should have to suffer financial loss because you're injured. Also, you're doing work online and gathering research that way, so I can't imagine much time is being wasted."

Fohl no longer looked like a giddy slots-winner; the smile was long gone. He reached his hand out to touch his wife's knee and said again, "Car?"

"This is a good idea," said Carmen definitively, and stood up from the couch. "Ms. Vega, I would like to walk you out, if that's all right."

"Sure."

Vega stood, and then so did Fohl, looking like he was in shock. Vega shook Fohl's hand and left him in the room with the couches.

Carmen was fast, drifting across the floor of the entry hall. Vega sped up, and then they were both at the front door, which Carmen unlocked. She stepped outside with a great deal of purpose.

"Which one's yours?" said Carmen, standing on the sidewalk.

"Across the street."

Carmen turned around to look at the house then, and Vega did, too. Fohl was at the window, watching them. Carmen waved her hand limply, and Fohl waved back. Then Carmen headed toward Vega's car, and Vega followed her.

"I wanted to tell you before you left," Carmen said. "I didn't think I cared what happened to Zeb, but when I thought of that phone call . . . I do," she said, her lips alternately quivering and pursing. "I don't need to have him here with me. That time is . . ." She paused and shook her head. "It's gone, I know that. It was in the ice age. But the idea that he might be hurt or have been hurt—I would just like to know. Not that I could have saved him, but if there's anything to be done now, I could do that."

"I'm not sure what that would be," said Vega.

Now Carmen's gaze turned cool. Confident. "I have money, Ms. Vega. So much that the number almost becomes meaningless when I see how my investments accumulate each year. I'm in the position to fix a thing if it needs to be fixed. Let's leave it there."

Vega unlocked her door and said she would be in touch. She got into the driver's seat, and Carmen still stood next to the car. Vega turned on the engine and powered down the window. Carmen leaned her head down.

"Your injuries," said Carmen. "That happened in Ilona?"

Vega buckled her belt, looked at her blue eye in the rearview.

"There are certain risks in my line of work. I know about them" was all she said.

"Yes, I'm sure you do," said Carmen. "All the more reason you should be compensated."

"It's appreciated," said Vega. "How often would you like updates on progress?"

"I don't know. What's normal for this type of case?"

"Once a week. Then more as needed, if things develop quickly."

"That sounds fine," said Carmen, standing up straight and backing away from the car so Vega could pull out. "Thank you for coming, Ms. Vega."

Vega nodded, took her sunglasses from the cup holder, and put them on.

Carmen stood in the middle of the street, suddenly seeming distressed.

"What is it?" said Vega.

Carmen shook her head, came back to the car window, and leaned down so they were face-to-face.

"There's something that's never made sense, that I never really thought about until now, about when Zeb called me. Something I thought I heard in the background when we were talking," she said.

"What's that?" said Vega.

Carmen squinted as if to see the memory more clearly.

"The sound was familiar to me only because I used to hear it all the time as a girl, at my grandfather's ranch," she said. "But it just didn't register."

She paused again.

"What?" said Vega.

"Just before he hung up, like a drum in the background, a pattern of like . . ."

Carmen slapped her palms against her thighs lightly. One-two-three, one-two-three, rapid succession. She didn't have to say it.

Vega knew, so she said it instead: "Horses."

11

CAP GOT HOME FROM WORK AROUND SIX AND WAS SURPRISED TO see Nell's car in the driveway. He had a moment of panic, trying to remember if she was supposed to be at his place or Jules's.

"Thursday, it's Thursday," he said aloud as he parked his car behind Nell's.

She was definitely supposed to be at Jules's, and Nell was not one to forget schedules. So, Cap figured, something had to be wrong, either with Nell or with Jules. He hurried up the front steps and through the door.

"Nell!" he called, not seeing her in the living room or kitchen.

There was no answer. He ran upstairs to her room and opened the door.

She sat at her desk with her giant headphones on. When she saw him, she took them off and hung them around her neck.

"Hey, Dad," she said, cheery.

"Hey," he said, out of breath. "Everything okay?"

"Yeah. What's wrong with you?"

"It's not my night," he said. "Aren't you supposed to be at your mom's?"

"Oh yeah, right," she said, stretching her arms above her head. "I told her I wanted to hang out here tonight, and I'll spend an extra night at her place next week, if you're cool with it."

"Cool with it," Cap repeated.

"Great," said Nell.

She removed her headphones from her neck and placed them on her desk.

"Because I think we need to have a talk."

Cap's initial panic had subsided but was now replaced with dull concern. He felt instantly guilty.

"I think I probably need a beer for this," said Cap.

"I think you probably will," said Nell.

He turned and went downstairs, Nell behind him. They went to the kitchen, where he got a beer from the fridge and threw Nell a bottle of water.

"I talked to Vega yesterday," said Nell.

"Pardon?"

"Alice Vega. I talked to her. Yesterday."

Cap had heard her the first time. He was just challenged by imagining the specifics of the scenario wherein Vega and Nell would have had a conversation without him.

"She called you?"

"No," said Nell. "I called her."

"You called her."

"Yes."

His instinct was to ask why, but the cop training kicked in, and he refrained. The why would become clear. Facts first.

"What did she say?" he asked.

"She said you two haven't talked in a few weeks."

Cap walked to the kitchen table and stood behind the chair that Vega had sat in when she came to see him. It seemed very long ago to him now.

"Is that true?" said Nell.

"Everyone lies sometimes," said Cap. "Even Vega."

"Okay, but she has no reason to lie to *me*, and if she's not lying, then . . ." Nell didn't finish her thought, waited for Cap to do the honors.

"I'm lying."

Nell stared at him and allowed a slow blink.

"You're lying," she said softly.

He took a slurpy sip of beer off the top of the can. Nell held the bottle of water in her hand like a crowbar she was about to use for punitive purposes, tapping the cap against her palm.

Cap shrugged and sighed. "I lied to you," he said. "I never told Vega that I met Bear Thomas or that we got Hardecker."

"Why?" said Nell, incredulous. "I thought we were all working together. It doesn't matter now—I told her everything. But why would you hold that back from her? And why lie to me about it?"

"Bug, there are some things that I can't always be a hundred percent transparent with you about," he said.

"Oh, come on."

Something switched in Cap, seeing Nell's dismissal.

"You're not always a hundred percent transparent with me, though, right?"

Nell stopped tapping the water bottle on her hand. She looked down—not necessarily ashamed of anything, just thinking.

"It's okay, Bug, you're an adult. I mean, you've been an adult for a long time, but now it's official, and it's okay. You're allowed to keep things from me. And I'm an adult, too. I'm allowed to keep things from you, especially if they might be harmful."

"But this was our thing that we were working on together, as two adults," she said. "Three adults, including Vega."

"I wasn't trying to exclude you from anything," said Cap. "I got pissed at Vega when"—he searched for the words—"her shit spilled over into our lives. Our house."

"I see your point," Nell said, like a litigator. "What exactly do you think I'm not telling you?"

"I don't know," Cap lied. "Maybe places you're going or people you're meeting when you're out with your friends."

"Was there a particular moment when you thought these things?" said Nell.

"No," he said, pushing the bluff.

Nell unscrewed the cap from the bottle and took a sip.

"If I told you exactly where I've been every minute . . . Wait," she said, holding up a finger. "Let me rephrase that. If I told you exactly where you *imagine* I've been every minute, you would have told me the truth about this? Because I don't believe that."

"Okay," Cap said, feeling beaten. "Okay, got it."

Nell grinned, vindicated.

"So did she have anything?" Cap said. "Your new partner, Vega?"

"We didn't get into it. She said she had to go back to California for a while, didn't say why."

"California?" said Cap, like he'd never heard of it. "She's not in Oregon anymore?"

"Not when I talked to her. I asked her if everything was all right, and she said yeah. But she'd say that no matter what, huh?"

"Yes, she would."

"Dad, you should call her," said Nell. "I'm sure she has more intel about the case that she didn't want to share with me. And . . ."

She paused. Cap could tell she wasn't trying to draw out her thoughts to be dramatic, though he found himself unable to wait for the rest of it to crystallize.

"What?"

"Her voice was different," said Nell.

"Different how?"

"I don't know," she said, shaking her head at the murkiness of the memory. "She didn't, like, have a lisp or anything, but something sounded different in her speech. Like she had something in her mouth."

"Like gum?" Cap said, though he'd never seen Vega chew gum.

"I don't know," Nell said again. "Kind of like when I got that tooth pulled and had to keep the cotton right there," she said, pointing to her jaw. "Remember when I was thirteen? Kind of like that."

Cap stared at the top of the beer can and thought about what was likely and not likely. If the given was that Nell's drummer ears were virtually perfect—she could often correct the rest of her high-school marching band when they were a fraction of a second off the beat—and she had heard something wrong with Vega's voice, then what was not likely was: Vega was chewing gum, sucking on a mint, or eating a Skittle. Far more likely was: Vega's mouth was swollen, or something was wrong with her teeth. Possibly from necessary dental work, or possibly, probably, most likely, from a fight.

Not many days after, Vega woke up early, even for her. It was just after four-thirty, still looking like the middle of the night outside. All stars and no birds.

The night before, she'd thought about Cooper, and Neil Klimmer, and Zeb Williams. All three of them, and where their tracks crossed and uncrossed. Then Cartwright the fed had called.

"If you could find anything for us, like a name, we might make some real headway with the Pure on the West Coast."

"You're making a deal with me, Special Agent?"

"Look, Vega," he said. "I'm not offering you a Scooby Snack in exchange for intel. I can send someone tomorrow from the field office in Portland, and if you want me to, I'll do it. You want to get them arrested for vandalism, animal cruelty, sure—get them prosecuted. Watch it move through the system, and then they're back and they're more pissed off and they're dicking around the same little old ladies they were before.

"We won't make a thing stick unless we can track some leadership. You cut off the head, the limbs are gonna die."

"I thought it didn't work like that," said Vega. "Won't the limbs keep regenerating? Like sea stars?"

"I was gonna say the Swamp Thing, but same difference," said Cartwright. "Sure, 'course they'll come back, but there'll be a lag, and that's as good as anything. It's a sleeper-cell pattern: there'll be a new generation, and another one, but what we can do is swat them while we can. It would help to get some names."

"I'll see what I can do," she said. "If I'm successful, would your guys in the field office be able to help me with another thing?"

"Like what kinda thing?"

They'd talked for a little while longer, and then Vega had finally gone to sleep.

Now she sat up on her elbows as if she'd heard something. She got out of bed, felt the soreness in her gum from her brand-new crown, the shadow of an ache in her ribs. But the pain didn't stop her anymore, didn't make it hard to breathe or move, didn't cloud her thinking.

She went from room to room, pausing and glancing in at each doorway, until she ended up in the living room. She turned on a small lamp in the corner and looked at the blue gym mats against the wall. Maybe this was the thing that had woken her up. An alarm clock inside her. Ready.

She went to the mat and bent forward, touched her toes and then the floor, felt the stretch in the back of her legs and lower back, then placed her left hand flat on the mat so that it was lined up with her head. She pushed into Downward Dog and walked her feet toward her hand and the wall. She breathed, and then she kicked up her right leg, bent at the knee, foot on the wall. She waited until she felt steady, her ribs only filing minor complaints instead of screaming obscenities.

She kicked up the left leg and lined it up with the right, her body an upside-down "L." Abdomen tight and solid, left arm straining but not buckling. She straightened one leg, then the other, her ankles just barely touching the wall.

Her ribs were a little angrier now, but she breathed and pushed the air into her lungs. Her left shoulder and arm were burning, sending threads of heat into her neck, but she could tolerate it. More important, she knew she wasn't going to fall. Slowly, she brought her feet away from the wall, only about a half-inch, so she wouldn't lose her balance, but now no part of her was touching the wall. Her left arm was supporting her whole body, plus her cast.

Vega stayed up for only a minute or two, and then was able to kick her legs back down without crashing to the side. She stood up straight, feeling the hum and shake in her left arm. She rubbed the muscles in her neck and figured it was close to five now.

She estimated she could take a shower, get dressed, pack a bag, and be on the road by six. She might even have time to stop for gas.

12

IT WAS DARK BY THE TIME VEGA GOT TO PORTLAND. SHE CHECKED into a motel near the airport and reread the e-mail the Bastard had written to her a couple of weeks before about the senior-care facility where Jack Klimmer had likely been living. "Good news/bad news" was the subject of the Bastard's e-mail.

> Only one hospice/nursing home on southern Oregon coast in the 1980s—called Shady Days.
> Bad news: No patient records of any kind, no scans, no names. Maybe originals in a storage facility somewhere but don't hold your nose waiting.
> Good news: Looks like a nurse sued Shady Days Senior Care after she was fired, and they settled out of court. Not a big facility so not a big staff, not a lot of turnover. Here's the extra good: she was laid off in spring of '85, smack in your target. Complaint filed by her attorneys attached.

Vega opened the attachment and read the whole thing. She didn't have a great handle on lawyer-speak but was smart enough to pick up the gist. Especially the part about the last patient the nurse had treated.

The nurse was still alive and worked in a hospital in Portland, so that was the first Oregon stop Vega had to make. She was transparent in the e-mail expressing her reason for wanting to meet, and the nurse, named Linda Vincent, agreed to see her.

Vega met her in a courtyard outside the main entrance. Vega recognized Linda from the social media links the Bastard had sent as she pushed through the revolving doors. Linda was petite and round, with strawberry-blond hair in a pixie cut. She had a youthful look, even though she was in her sixties.

"Linda?" she said, extending her hand. "Alice Vega."

"Hello," said Linda, shaking her hands vigorously in the air. "Sorry, I just put on hand sanitizer."

Vega retracted her hand and nodded. "Can I get you a cup of coffee?" she said, nodding to a food truck at the curb.

"Oh, I'd love some tea."

They walked to the curb, and Vega ordered two teas. While the man in the truck prepared the drinks, Linda began to talk.

"No one's asked me about Shady Days in a long time," she said. "There was a local paper interested in the story a few years after, and I told McElhinny—he was the exec director—I was gonna talk. I signed a confidentiality agreement initially, but the statute on that was way up."

Vega paid for the drinks and handed Linda one of the cups.

"Sorry," said Vega. "Would you mind backing up a little bit? What happened right before you were fired?"

"Let's go sit," said Linda, and headed toward a stone bench against the wall of the building.

Vega followed her, and they sat.

Linda took the lid off her tea and wound the string of the tea bag around her finger, bobbed it up and down. "I was twenty-nine, working at Shady Days two years," she said. "That's all I wanted to do at that point, was work with the elderly. And I was used to a certain routine with patients—they got admitted, doctors did the intake, then they got settled in their quarters, and we nurses would make the rounds and administer care."

"It seemed, when I read the complaint, that there were levels of care—like, certain patients needed more than others," said Vega.

"That's right, standard stuff," said Linda. "I usually worked with the more infirm folks. They called it Level Three. Level One were the people who needed the least amount of care, Level Two were the intermediate, and then Level Three were the patients who needed diapers and help feeding and drinking and dressing. I was young and strong, so I could do that stuff—help patients sit up and turn them over."

"Then there was Patient X," said Vega.

"Yes," said Linda crisply, taking a sip of her tea. She clicked her teeth. "Holy moly, that's hot." She shook her head as if she'd taken a shot of tequila, then continued: "Patient X comes in, wheeled in a wheelchair, and he gets put in a room on my rounds, but I know he doesn't belong here."

"How could you tell?"

"His chart said 'stroke,'" said Linda. "That was not his main problem."

"What was his main problem?"

Linda huffed out some air, impatient. "Guy had a lesion on his head, and bruising all over," she said, drawing a circle in the air above her head. "From a fall, it looked like."

"Did he say that he'd fallen?"

"He wasn't so coherent. But he'd have these moments when he could get the words out, and he told me someone beat him up. I asked him who, but he never answered."

"So what did you do?"

Linda sniffed out a laugh. "Like it says in the complaint, first I went to the attending doctor, Dr. Delorio, and I told him I didn't think this guy was in the right place: He might be concussed and he needs a different kind of physical rehab than we can offer. It's possible the guy had a stroke because of the head trauma, but the head trauma wasn't even listed in the chart.

"And Delorio, me and him were friendly, but he said, Roy McElhinny, the exec director, wanted this patient in this room on this ward specifically. And Delorio, he didn't say, 'I agree with you, Linda,' but I could tell he did. He wasn't blind.

"So I went to McElhinny. He was a stuffed shirt, but I never had any beef with him: did his job, knew everyone's names and what they did. I told him this patient had a head injury—whoever did the head-to-toe botched the placement. Shouldn't be in Level Three. Shouldn't even be in Level One—my professional opinion, he should've still been in a hospital."

Vega took the lid off her cup and let the steam cloud her face. "Because the wound seemed fresh?"

"Absolutely," said Linda. "I did some time in a domestic-violence clinic—I know abuse when I see it."

"What did McElhinny say?"

Linda leaned closer to Vega and narrowed her eyes. "That patient placement wasn't my responsibility and I should butt out." She sat back against the wall and widened her eyes again. "He didn't say 'butt out'—I don't think I ever heard him say the word 'butt'— but he told me to mind my own business, more or less."

"What did you say?"

Linda slurped the surface of her tea. "I said, 'Excuse me, Mr. McElhinny, sir, it's exactly my responsibility, because I have to know how to treat my patient—we need to run labs and an MRI. And, also, doesn't this patient's family care that he's been misplaced?'"

Linda paused, stared and squinted into the distance, straight ahead.

"That's when he fired you," said Vega.

Linda laughed and sneered. "Not right then and there. The next day, he calls me in and says he has to lay people off, no reason, no nothing. I was so shocked, see, I didn't put it all together, and then I go home and talk to my husband about it. Then I see the connection. My husband says maybe McElhinny didn't like a woman talking back to him, but there was plenty of women worked there who did just that, myself included."

She shook her head, added, "No, it was that patient. He didn't want me to make trouble about that particular patient."

"So you sued?" said Vega.

"Sure did," said Linda with some pride. "Look, me being honest with you, I cared about that patient the way I care about all the patients, meaning enough to do my job well, but also not too much, so I can sleep at night.

"I never did a thing wrong at that job, and having a layoff on my résumé—that wasn't going to happen. I sued him and Shady Days to protect myself."

"I get it," said Vega, resting her elbows on her knees. "The law was on your side, looks like. McElhinny settled."

"Yes, he did," said Linda, nodding. "I don't expect to get money just for looking pretty, see, but I felt like he owed it to me."

"You ever find out what happened to the patient?" said Vega.

"No," said Linda, a little bit regretful. "I had to stay away after the suit. I like to think it all worked out for him, but, honestly, I don't know."

Vega pulled out her phone and brought up a picture of Jack Klimmer that the Bastard had found from a news story about the effect of the 1981 windstorms on the logging industry.

"This him?" she said.

Linda took the phone from Vega and brought it closer to her face.

"That is absolutely him," Linda said, smiling. Then her smile shrank, and she said, "He was a healthy man there."

"He was," said Vega.

Vega suspected Linda felt guilty and thought about saying something, maybe try to make her feel better, but then she decided against it. What would it help to hear that from a stranger, or really from anyone? Vega knew from experience that if she felt the weight of guilt for a thing she had or hadn't done a long time ago, it was just her and her bathroom mirror at night, and nothing in between.

It was dark by the time Vega drove past the I-PUD. She kept her lights low and slowed down as she approached the trailers. Then she pulled over and killed the lights, waited, and watched. All the trailers had little lights over the doors or windows. Some were on, and some were off. Vega squinted into the distance, where she knew Dart's trailer was parked, but couldn't even make out the shape.

Around ten, the door to the Stargazer, the tiny trailer, opened, and the tattooed man who'd given her directions to Dart's place emerged. He looked the same, except he was now wearing a shirt. He dumped water from the same yellow bucket he'd emptied when Vega had met him the first time. Then he went back inside.

Vega got out of her car and took a small black backpack from the passenger's seat. She walked carefully onto the dirt, but when she discovered it was wet and soft and soundless from rain, she sped up and went to the door of the Stargazer. She knocked a few times.

The door opened right away, and the tattooed man was there, a cloud of floral incense seeping out of the trailer. He looked confused but not angry.

"Hi, you remember me?" Vega said, not waiting for him to figure it out. "I was here about seven weeks ago, and you gave me directions to Dart's trailer."

"That's right," the tattooed man said, as if he'd been on the verge of placing her.

Vega opened the backpack and showed him its contents.

"Could I come in for a few minutes?" she said.

He stared inside the bag and held the door open for Vega. Vega held on to the handle next to the door and pulled herself up and into the trailer.

She quickly took in the room: like Dart's but smaller, a flat bedroll in one corner, a hot plate and a small sink in the other. There was not a lot of clutter—a folding chair, a couple of suitcases, a small round table, a television. It was a nice surprise.

"There's seventy-five hundred dollars in here," said Vega, tugging on the handle. "I would like to rent your trailer for three weeks. If this sounds good to you, I'll give you an hour to get your things together, and you can make some arrangements. Then you'll give me the key, and I'll give you this," she said, holding up the backpack. "No questions on either side."

The tattooed man continued to stare, alternating between the backpack and Vega's face.

"So?" she said.

He touched his head, combed his fingers through his split ends.

"You're just gonna give me that cash," he said.

"Yes," said Vega. "In exchange for your trailer."

"For three weeks," he said, starting to grasp the details.

"For three weeks."

The tattooed man looked around. "And I leave now," he said.

"I'll give you an hour."

"To get my things together."

"Yes," said Vega. "Can you do that?"

"Yeah, I got friends," he said.

"Good," said Vega. "So?"

He exhaled and coughed, pointed to the sink. "Water pumps in but leaks. You gotta keep the bucket under there and dump it." Then he walked over to a chunky plastic box, about two by two feet. "That's the commode. Holds about five gallons. We dump it near the Port-O's at the construction site off Creighton." He paused, then added, "Not legal or anything."

"I don't have a problem with that," said Vega. "So?"

The tattooed man nodded, first just a little bob, but then he seemed to gain some momentum with it.

"An hour?" Vega said.

"Shit, I don't need an hour," he said, sniffing hard. "Gimme five minutes."

"Sure," said Vega. "You okay if I stay right here, or do you need privacy?"

"I don't need privacy," he said, shaking his hair out of his forehead. He seemed entirely at ease with the situation. "Lemme just get my toiletry."

The tattooed man went to the small sink and collected a toothbrush, toothpaste, a travel-sized bottle of Scope. He grabbed one of the suitcases and opened it, stuffed the items inside.

Vega zipped up the backpack and watched him pull clothing from cabinets and drawers and pack them into the suitcase. It took less than ten minutes for him to finish.

He picked up a black rain-boot next to the door, turned it upside down, and shook a key onto his palm. He handed the key to Vega.

"You can test it if you want," he said.

"That's okay," said Vega.

It's not that she trusted him. She just wasn't worried about locking the door.

Vega handed him the backpack. He took it from her and unzipped it, surveyed the money again.

"Your neighbors," said Vega. "I'll tell them I'm your cousin, and you're out of town."

"Yeah," he said, obviously having not thought of it before. "You won't have to worry about them, much. Josie, in the camper right across, she needs help with her trash and compost now and again. Seyla and Brock, they're in the light-blue trailer, they work logging and fishing on and off, so sometimes they're here, sometimes they're not. I feed their cat when they need me to, water the plants inside. Angelo's in the camper, he chews gummies all day. And Dart, you met him. He's just nuts, don't ask me for shit."

"One more thing," said Vega.

"What's that?"

"I need you not to stay in Ilona, and not to tell anyone outside of this camp about me. To everyone in the camp, I'm your cousin, Bitsy. Sound good?"

"Bitsy," he said.

"Right. You got a relation who can get sick?"

He didn't understand for a second; then it landed right on him.

"Yeah, I got an uncle. He lives near Portland."

"That's where you are then. Cousin . . . ?"

Vega let it hang. Then he got it.

"Jason," he said.

"Cousin Jason," Vega said. Then she pointed to herself and said, like she was introducing herself to an alien, "Cousin Bitsy."

"Cousin Bitsy," said Jason, and he started to laugh. He slung the backpack over his shoulder and picked up the suitcase. "See you in three weeks," he said.

"No, you won't," said Vega. "I'll leave the key in the boot under the crate with the CD player. I'll be gone by then."

"If you say so, Cousin," he said, tickled by the lie. "Thanks for the cash."

Vega didn't say he was welcome. Instead, she held the door open for him so he could jump the eighteen inches to the ground with his bags.

"Remember," she said. "No one in Ilona knows I'm here."

"Come on, Cuz," said Jason, laughing. "You think I'm gonna stay in this shit town now I got a dime?"

The next morning, Vega woke up when it was still dark, rain pattering on the windows of the Stargazer. She got into her one-armed handstand; while upside down, she spotted an orange swath of fabric under the sink.

She came down from the handstand and approached the sink, pulled the fabric out. It was stiff in her hand, like it had been coated and dried with papier-mâché; she figured Jason had stuffed it there to catch the excess water from leaky pipes. She unrolled and flattened it on the floor. It was a sleeveless tee shirt with an image of a tree and a raccoon on the front. "Pine Preservation," it read underneath the tree. Vega picked up the shirt and shook it out once, then again, and then pulled it on over her tank top. It sat on her torso like a shell.

She waited until the sun was up and out and the rain cleared a little, then grabbed her phone and stepped outside. She walked away from the trailers, toward the road. She put on her sunglasses, smiled big, and took a selfie, stretching her arm as far as she could, getting trees and sky in the background.

She sent the picture to the Bastard with a note: "Instructions to follow."

When she got back to the camp, she saw an older woman wearing a green bathrobe and flip-flops, leaning out of the door of the trailer directly across from the Stargazer.

"Hi," said Vega, big and friendly. "You must be Josie."

"Fuck, yeah," said Josie, unaggressive. "Who're you, now?"

"I'm Jason's cousin, Bitsy," said Vega. "He had to go see our uncle outside Portland, so I'm watching his place."

"Not much to watch," said Josie.

Vega laughed as if she'd never heard a joke so clever. "He said you were funny."

Josie cracked a smile. "What's your name again?"

"Bitsy," said Vega. Then she held up her fingers to indicate a little bit. "Short for 'Elizabeth.'"

"Josie," said Josie. "Short for 'Josie.'"

"Very nice to meet you," said Vega, trying her best to put a squeak in her voice.

"Yeah, okay," said Josie. "Nice to meet you, Little Bit."

Vega grinned and waved once more before she headed up the stairs into the Stargazer. She was relieved when she got inside, and spent a couple of minutes rubbing her cheeks, the muscles sore from all the smiling.

That night, Vega met Cooper in front of the Laundromat. She saw him before he saw her: still a few inches over six feet, still fit, broad shoulders whittling down into a tapered waist. He held his phone in one hand and scrolled with his thumb, up and down.

Nervous, Vega thought.

"Hey," she called as she got closer.

Cooper looked up and waved with his whole arm above his head, like she was on a boat approaching the shore. He smiled, chest puffing up with a big intake of breath. Vega noticed that his upper lip was split on the left side; it looked like a thick, fresh paper cut, the skin around the corner of his mouth red and raw.

"Hey, Bitsy," he said. Then he saw her cast and stopped smiling. "What happened to you?"

"Not important," she said, then made a big show of swallowing. "I was in a parking lot back home, and some kids took my bag. I tried to grab it back, and then one of them pushed me, and I landed on my hand wrong."

Cooper rubbed his cheek, made a fist, and knocked it against his thigh.

"That is fucking egregious and appalling," he said. "You, of all people, you're trying to teach kids, and then . . ." He stopped mid-sentence, too appalled to continue.

Vega nodded, forcing the corners of her mouth down. "I think maybe it was my fault," she said. "Maybe they knew I didn't like them."

"They were Black, right?"

She nodded.

"They do whatever they want," said Cooper. "That garbage you hear on the news about white cops killing unarmed Black kids, that's, like, the rarity."

"I try not to watch that kind of news," Vega said.

That made Cooper laugh. "There's my girl," he said.

Vega laughed, too, then looked at the ground and said, "It really doesn't hurt anymore. I don't want you to worry about it."

"That's not gonna happen," said Cooper. "I'm glad it doesn't hurt, but I'm gonna worry about it and get angry about it."

Vega allowed a timid smile and pointed to his mouth. "What happened to your lip?"

"Now, that's really nothing," he said, and laughed, self-deprecatingly. "Bitsy, something you should know about me—I get in a lot of fights. Sometimes I say what people don't want to hear, and shit just goes down."

"It's, uh, bleeding," said Vega.

"Yeah?" said Cooper, touching his lip with his finger and examining it. "Shit, I'm sorry, that's gross." He patted the pockets of his jeans, pulled out a tissue folded into a tidy square, and daubed the cut.

"I'm not skittish around blood," said Vega.

"I could guess that about you," said Cooper. "I think your whole trick is, you're tougher than you look."

She shrugged and said, "You haven't said anything about my idea."

"You sure you want to do this tonight?" he said. "It's late."

"I'm ready," Vega said, presenting her cast. "I get angry about things, too."

He stared at her, and Vega felt it in her stomach. She was Bitsy the Nazi-curious teacher, and she was not. At this moment, the clash of the two felt like a welcome takeover.

Then Cooper's phone chimed. Vega peered at the screen but tried not to be obvious about it. She couldn't make out any individual words within the white text block.

"All right, Bitsy," he said, his voice low and rough. "Want to go for a drive?"

Vega told Cooper that she was prone to motion sickness if she wasn't driving, so she had to take her own car. She followed him about a hundred miles east, toward the center of the state.

She kept the window open, and the rain blew in. The tops of the trees on either side of the interstate bowed toward the center, and Vega could smell and almost taste them, pungent and briny in the back of her throat.

She followed Cooper's car to an exit just outside of Bend, then down some paved streets that became narrow roads. The left blinker on Cooper's car began to flash and continued for about a quarter-mile, giving her ample notice.

They were on an even thinner road now, the woods tight on either side. Soon the road opened into a driveway leading to a three-story house with natural cedar siding and tall windows on every level.

Vega parked behind Cooper and tapped the record button on her phone, clipped the small mic to the inside pocket of her jacket.

She watched Cooper get out of his car and stretch his arms above his head, then do a little back twist. He came to her window and leaned down.

"You ready?" he whispered.

She got out of the car, and they approached the house together. A few lights were on, some of the windows bright and some dark— made it look like a mid-December Advent calendar.

Cooper knocked on the front door, and they waited.

The man who opened the door was in his sixties, fit, his eyes small or squinting—Vega couldn't tell which. The skin on his face had a texture to it, lightly scarred with crevices and bumps, as if it had been scraped against a cheese grater. Vega thought it more likely that he'd been burned.

His eyes moved quickly from Cooper to Vega.

"Evening," he said to both of them. Then he shook Cooper's hand. He extended his hand even farther to Vega and said, "Joe Lanahan."

Vega shook it. "I'm Bitsy."

"Bitsy," said Joe, as if he were identifying the flip side of a flash card with certainty.

"Short for 'Elizabeth,'" said Vega, pushing the sheepish.

"How's your arm, there?" said Lanahan. Then he shot a glance to Cooper.

"Healing up nice," said Vega. "Should be off in two, three weeks."

"That's good news," said Lanahan. "Whyn't you both come on in, instead of standing out there like you're selling Bibles?"

Cooper laughed with enthusiasm at the joke. Vega smiled, tried not to make a lot of eye contact.

Once they were inside, Lanahan shut the door behind them. The ground floor was a living room and a kitchen with a counter as separation; otherwise, it was open, large arched windows along one wall.

Lanahan offered them drinks, and Cooper said no, thanks, so Vega said no, thanks.

"Come on, now, Bitsy, don't be shy here. You thirsty, say so," said Lanahan.

"I guess I wouldn't mind a water?" she said.

"There you go," said Lanahan, a note of pride in his voice. "Cooper, you sure?"

Cooper gave a quick shrug that made him seem younger, goofier. "Water's good," he said.

"All right, waters, on the house," said Lanahan.

His voice bounced, but he didn't smile, and his eyes remained static.

"Have a seat, and I'll be right with you."

Vega followed Cooper into the living room, where there was a couch with a suede cow print, and two tan leather seats on either side. Cooper sat on one end of the couch, and Vega sat on the other, right on the edge of the cushion.

Lanahan joined them, holding a circular tray with a gold rim. He placed the tray on the wooden chest in front of the couch. On the tray were two tall glasses of water and a small plate of cheese squares and Triscuits.

"Go ahead, have some food," he said, sitting in one of the tan chairs. "I got more, too—just figured you might not want to eat too much too late." He glanced at his watch. "Almost midnight now."

"Thank you," Vega muttered.

She reached forward and took a cracker.

"So," said Lanahan. "Here you are. I've known Cooper a long time. He tells me I need to meet someone, I trust him."

Vega bit into the cracker. She hadn't had a Triscuit in a long time. A thing she didn't remember about them was that they were messy. An avalanche of crumbs fell from her mouth onto her lap. It was a good fit for Bitsy, though, so she went with it.

"I'm so sorry," she said, holding her hand over her lap as if she were trying to protect the crumbs.

Cooper jumped from his seat and took a napkin from the tray, then passed it to Vega. She nodded gratefully.

Lanahan watched, still not smiling, but also, as far as Vega could tell, not upset.

"I'm a teacher?" said Vega, brushing the crumbs off her lap into the napkin.

"I saw your profile on the Cascade High School web site," said Lanahan. "Freshman English."

Vega knew the Bastard would never let her down but was still relieved to know he'd sneaked his way into the high school's faculty Web site to post her fake profile along with a photo. Vega had instructed him to take it down at 6:00 a.m., taking the chance that no one from the school would be doing site maintenance overnight. He'd also created fake LinkedIn and Facebook pages for her.

"Yeah, that's me," said Vega, then pretended to be embarrassed. "Not a great picture, though. I don't know what I was thinking with the orange shirt."

Lanahan smiled politely.

"Neil Klimmer and Derek Fenton were in my class a few years back. When they still, you know, had acne," she said, laughing at her own joke. When she saw Lanahan wasn't amused, she kept up with the small talk: "Cooper knows those kids; I thought maybe you might, too."

Lanahan glanced sideways at Cooper and cleared his throat. "He's told me about them."

"Oh, good," said Vega, almost panting with relief. "Anyway, like I was saying, I think I have some good ideas about how to get your message out."

"What message would that be?" said Lanahan.

"Um . . ." said Vega, genuinely unsure of what he wanted to hear.

Lanahan leaned forward and rested his forearms on his knees. "You have to understand something, Bitsy. We are fighting an uphill battle here, but I think you already know that. We don't have an endless supply of chances, so we have to make them all count." He paused, stared at her with intent. Then he said, slowly, "Now, I'm going to ask you to be specific with your answer when I ask you: what message would that be?"

Vega swallowed the last of the cracker, balled the napkin in her fist.

"The message is simple," she said, allowing her voice to become steadier, more assured. "Save the white race. Save the world."

She held Lanahan's gaze, saw Cooper out of the corner of her eye sit up straighter. She could suddenly hear all of them breathing.

"That's the word," said Lanahan, pointing at her. "How are you going to help us do that?"

"I have a lot of access to a lot of kids. A lot of them, especially the girls, trust me. You walk through Cascade—any high school, really— and you throw a dart, you're going to hit an angry teenage boy. But

that thing you always heard, about girls maturing faster than boys—
it's true. Teenage boys tend to be sloppy and undisciplined. They
make dumb mistakes. If you get the girls at the right time—right at
that moment when they know they're going to be pinned as either
a slut or a virgin, when they realize how much the world is priming
them to fail—and you can harness *that*? It'll crush any boy and his
fucking limp-dick excuse for anger."

Lanahan stared at her. Cooper rubbed his palms on his jeans and
looked back and forth between the two of them.

She continued: "Cooper told me you and he can't possibly keep
tabs on all the Liberty Pure boys making trouble, right?"

Cooper nodded first, then Lanahan.

"I could eventually do that for you. But, for now, my goal is to
organize the girls. And if I organize the girls, I can also organize the
moms."

They were all silent for a moment. Vega heard the refrigerator
motor whirring in the kitchen.

Then Lanahan let out an audible breath and said, "I got one
question for you, Bitsy."

"What's that?"

"Where the hell you been?" he said gravely.

It was like air had been released from the room. Cooper laughed,
and Vega smiled.

"Everything you just said—I've been telling my wife for years. I
think women are inordinately important to this fight. Always have
been. Online is one thing, but if you can talk to people, to kids, face-
to-face, that's how you get them to listen. We've just never had someone like you willing and talented enough to take it on. But there's risk
involved in what we're doing here. Risk to you, you understand?"

"I know what I believe is controversial," said Bitsy. "I know how
and when to keep my mouth shut."

"I believe you," said Lanahan. "You have to know going in, if you
get fired, if you get arrested, you tell anyone my name or Cooper's
name, or divulge any information about the Pure and what we're
doing, we're going to deny we know you."

"So, even if I don't spell out you're the West Coast leadership, I'm
on my own?" Vega said.

Lanahan didn't answer. The refrigerator had stopped humming, but there was another sound—a series of clicks, too fast and uneven for the second hand on a clock. Vega couldn't place it but used it to calibrate how long it took for Lanahan to respond. Twenty-seven clicks.

Finally, he said, "Correct."

Vega shrugged. "That's really no different than how I live my life any other day. On my own, I mean."

She glanced at Cooper. His eyes had changed color again; now they were green and mossy, like something growing on a forest floor.

"There you are," said Lanahan. Then he clasped his hands together. "Now, I don't mean to be rude, but it is late, and tomorrow's another workday. I'm sure you have an early morning ahead of you, too."

As they all stood and headed to the front door, Vega heard the clicking sound more clearly. Lanahan rushed past her and slammed his fist against the wall in the kitchen near the door. The sound stopped.

"Got a whole little mouse family," he said, smiling. "Mama, Papa, bunch of kids. Just moved in. My guy's coming tomorrow."

Vega laughed, and then so did Lanahan and Cooper. Then they all said goodbye, and Vega and Cooper walked to their cars.

"Thanks again for everything," she said earnestly as she turned around to face him.

"Thank me?" said Cooper. "What you said in there—I never heard anything like that."

"It's just the truth," said Vega.

She couldn't see much of his face in the darkened driveway. He took a step toward her, and for a second she thought he would try to hug her, but instead he stuck out his hand for a shake. She put her hand in his, and he gripped her and didn't let go. He tugged her toward him, so close she could feel his damp breath on her face. She could still only make out the vaguest outlines of his face, like a pencil sketch.

"Anyone call you Elizabeth?" he said, pressing his palm even tighter on hers, sucking up any air between the two.

"Certain people, but they need my permission," she said. "You can."

The Bitsy she'd set up would have giggled, but Vega wanted to evolve to match Cooper. You think this is intense? Just wait.

In the dark, his smile looked like a wound.

"After you called, I couldn't stop thinking about you. I tried, but I couldn't. Still can't," he said.

"Don't try," said Vega.

He pulled her closer.

Then she kissed him. He tasted like blood and sweat and something alive and young. The takeover was still in effect. So here we go.

Back inside the Stargazer, with the flimsy door locked, Vega sent two big audio files to Cartwright the fed and fell asleep holding her gun next to her head on the pillow, like a husband.

13

CAP ATTEMPTED TO WORK IN HIS OFFICE BUT WASN'T GETTING FAR. He'd turned the thermostat way down, because the boiler seemed to be overcorrecting for its predecessor, and now it was too cold, but he couldn't find the energy to walk down to the basement and adjust it again.

He looked at his phone, made sure nothing new had come through in the last thirty seconds. Nothing had. He opened his texts and scrolled to find his last communication with Vega, which had been the picture of Nell's car with the busted window. Then he scrolled up a little farther to where he'd written, "Don't get yourself into trouble, V."

And her response: "Too late."

Cap tapped her name, then "audio." He stood up and began to pace, listening to the dull buzz. After two rings, she picked up.

"Caplan," she said, like she was expecting him.

"Vega," he said, standing still. "Can you talk?"

"Yeah."

She sounded a little out of breath, and there was also static fuzz in the background. Cap figured she was driving.

"Is everything . . ." he started, then stopped. "Are you okay, Vega? Nell said you had to go back to California."

He felt lighter instantly. Why pretend? he thought. There would always be time to argue.

"Yeah, I was there for a few weeks," she said. "I just got back to Oregon."

There was a pause. Vega wasn't jumping to fill in the blanks for him, and he hadn't talked to her in so long he felt disoriented by the silence.

"Where are you staying?" he blurted out.

"In a Stargazer," said Vega. "It's in a trailer park. I rented it."

"Like a sublet?"

"Sure," said Vega. Then she added, "Everything okay with you?"

Cap couldn't discern whether or not her voice sounded strange. "Yeah," he said, letting out a breath.

"I'm glad you called."

Cap looked around, as if someone was listening in. "Me, too," he said.

"I have this idea," she said. "I think you might get it."

"Wait, let me say what I called to say," said Cap. "I know you're okay, but did you get a tooth knocked out or anything like that?"

Vega didn't answer right away, and Cap's chest thumped because he knew he was right.

"Vega, did you get in a fight in Oregon, and that's why you went back to California? Besides what happened to your dad's car?"

He wasn't sure if he could hear her breathing or just the shushing background noise from being on the speakerphone.

"Hang up, okay?" said Vega.

"Uh, no," Cap said.

Vega sighed, irritated. "Just for a second. I'm parking, and I'll call with video."

Cap hung up and waited a minute. He ran his hand through his hair, as if that would make him look less tired, but he knew there wasn't much to be done in that area that wouldn't take a lot of time and perhaps strategic cosmetics or shadows. Then "Alice Vega" blinked on his phone with the camera icon flashing. He tapped the screen. Connecting . . . connecting.

She was in the driver's seat of her car. Seeing her face was like cold water first thing.

She pulled down her bottom lip, showing her teeth like a horse, and tapped a canine. "This one's new. It did get knocked out."

Cap felt like he'd swallowed a couple of dice. "You got in a fight," he said.

"No," said Vega. "I got beat up."

The dice multiplied, so Cap now had the supplies for an Atlantic City craps table in his throat. "Who?" was all he managed to say.

"Three guys in a parking lot," said Vega. "Pretty sure they were the baby Nazis from town."

"You couldn't see them?"

"They had masks. One at a time, I might have had a round. Jumped by all three—I got this," she said, pointing again to her tooth. "Black eye, three fractured ribs, which are healed up now for the most part. And . . ."

She stopped speaking and moved the phone farther back on the dashboard, so she could have both hands free. Then she moved her right arm in front of the screen and pulled up her sleeve, revealing a cast on her forearm and wrist, wrapping around the thumb and palm of her hand.

"Fractured wrist," she said. "That's almost healed, too, but I had to come back up here before I could get the cast off."

Cap brought his hand to his mouth. He'd been with Vega when she'd been thrown around in the past—a rusty nail from a plank of wood above her eyebrow, a knife wound in her abdomen. He knew better than to worry, and for the most part he didn't, because he'd been next to her at those moments, usually suffering equivalent or more severe damage. But this felt like the deep end with his hands tied, because she'd been alone.

"I'm sorry," he said, quiet.

"Line of work," was all she said. "Can I tell you my idea?"

"Okay," he said, running his socked foot along the bottom of his desk. "Shoot."

"Guy named Matt Klimmer here owns some land which was once his father's ranch. I talked to another guy, name of Wall, who used to work for the father back in '84, '85. Wall said Klimmer told him the dad had a stroke and he'd had to put him in a facility overnight. Then he fires Wall and shuts the ranch down and gets a concrete floor poured in the stable. Immediately. And all that takes place right after . . ."

Vega paused. Cap had a feeling he was supposed to say something.

"After what?" he said.

"Right after the last time Zeb Williams is seen, by a witness, in the town of Ilona, which is the last time he is seen aside of fanatics' wishful thinking."

"So," Cap said, "you think Klimmer put his father away for life because he saw something?"

"That is what I think," said Vega, her eyes cast above the screen, at something through the windshield, Cap thought. "And another piece—I think maybe Matt Klimmer had a thing for Cara Simms."

"What makes you say that?" said Cap.

"Zeb and Klimmer had an argument, and no one knows what it was about."

Cap blew air out of the side of his mouth.

"When you talked to Cara, she didn't mention that, though—Klimmer having feelings?"

"Maybe she didn't know," said Vega. Then she paused, still looking out the window, and said, "You know Nell called me."

"Yes, I learned this after the fact," he said, trying not to smile too much.

Now he found himself pleased by the image of the two of them having a conversation—not stressed, like before.

Then Vega said, "Caplan, we're settled up, okay?"

"What do you mean?"

"I appreciate you talking to Bear Thomas," she said, looking at him again. "And talking the case out with you helps, but I think there's something you were right about."

Cap sat up in his chair, forcing it to coast back a few inches on its wheels. He was playing up the surprised reaction to make Vega laugh, but at the same time, he was genuinely surprised.

She didn't laugh. She shook her head.

"This is a thing I mean, and I'm not going to say it again," she said. "You were right not to take this job with me. It was a shit move of me to ask you."

"Vega—" he began, but she cut him off.

"Just shut up a minute, and let me finish this."

Cap's fingers were numb from squeezing the phone. The way she'd said "finish" had a dark inevitability around it.

"I will not ask you anymore," she said.

"Vega, you can ask me for anything, anytime."

"You're missing the point," she said. "I'm not done asking you because I don't want to bother you, although it's true, I don't. I'm done asking you because I don't want you here."

Cap felt a dot of pain on the very top of his head, like someone was just marking the spot where he was about to drill down with a skinny steel bit.

"Okay," he said, unsure of what else to say.

"Okay," said Vega. "You don't have to check on me, either."

Cap laughed and tried to make it lighthearted.

"Considering all your many injuries, maybe I do," he said.

She shrugged, looked above the phone again, distracted or even bored.

"Maybe someone will at some point," she said. "It just won't be you. Bye, Cap."

Then she hung up on him. Cap could no longer feel any of his fingers; a hundred micro-drill bits were boring into his scalp now. He stared at the dark screen for a minute and then called her back. She didn't pick up, so he tried again. Then a few more times.

Eventually, he gave up and wrote her a text, tapped "send," and held the phone to his brow like he was trying to read the fortune trapped inside.

Vega kept her thumb on the screen, right where she'd tapped the red "end" button. Then she made a sound like a bark in her throat with her mouth closed.

She listened to the light rain pattering on the glass, let her breath deepen, heart rate slow down. She closed her eyes. She heard the phone buzzing with calls coming through and ignored it.

After a few minutes, she opened her eyes and picked her phone up from the seat. Cap had called half a dozen times and sent a text, which read: "About Klimmer's feelings for Cara—the girl always knows."

Vega met Cara Simms at a Taco Joint off the interstate. Vega sat at a table in the corner. A bean burrito sat in a basket in front of her, untouched. She watched Cara come through the front door and search the room. Vega lifted her hand in a wave.

Cara came to the table.

"You're back," she said. "Your arm—what happened?"

"An accident," said Vega. "You want any food?"

Cara glanced toward the counter and shook her head.

"I don't eat this stuff," she said, without judgment. She sat across from Vega. "Who did that to you?"

"Not important," said Vega.

"That makes me think it's important," said Cara, stern.

"I couldn't see their faces," said Vega, squinting one eye. "But I'm pretty sure it was Neil Klimmer, Derek Fenton, and a friend."

Cara clenched her jaw. "That's why you left town," she said.

"There were a few reasons."

"I told you it would happen," said Cara, suddenly impatient. "Why did you come back? What do you hope to accomplish here, by yourself?"

"Not by myself," she said, flicking a fingertip in Cara's direction. "You're here, too."

Cara scratched at her hairline with one finger, waiting for the next thing.

"I have a question for you about Matt Klimmer," said Vega.

"What?" said Cara, panic passing in her eyes.

"Were you ever involved with him romantically?"

"What?"

"Did you and Matt Klimmer ever date, even as kids?"

"What does this have to do with anything?"

"I'm trying to gauge here," said Vega, "how angry he might be at someone who you were dating. What exactly he'd be capable of."

Cara looked to a poster on the wall advertising a two-for-one breakfast deal.

Vega continued: "Dart saw Klimmer and Zeb arguing in the middle of the street. When he first told me about it, I thought maybe Zeb was telling him to back off buying you out. But I don't think a real-estate deal would have made Klimmer that excited, especially because, from what I know, he had plenty of money from his dad. That kind of thing didn't seem to make him nervous. Or angry."

Cara looked back to Vega.

"But maybe something else would. Like, if he felt rejected in some other way. That stung."

Cara reached across the table and picked up the cutlery kit that had come with Vega's meal. She tore the plastic in half from the top and removed the napkin, rubbed her nose.

"I slept with him once," she said. "About a year before Zeb came. He'd been after me since high school, and I never . . . I was never interested."

"Why not?" said Vega.

"I knew who he was," Cara said, tapping the table with her finger. "Spoiled and cold."

"Tied frog's legs in knots," added Vega.

"Yes," said Cara, somewhat defensive.

"Some women like that in a guy."

"Not me. And I found him repulsive, physically," she said plainly. "Remember when I told you before it was a fair deal? It wasn't. Matt way underbid me, but I was desperate. I needed more than what he was offering, and he knew it."

She picked up a napkin and balled it in her fist.

"I don't even remember him making the proposition. Or me agreeing. It was just . . . agreed."

She paused, waiting for Vega's reaction. When she saw Vega was remaining quiet, she continued.

"I slept with him." Cara shook her head with the weight of the memory. "So that he'd give me just a little more money for the property."

"And?"

"And what?" said Cara, irritated.

"Did he give you more money?"

"Yes, he did," Cara said, angry now that Vega had made her say it. "Not much, but I needed it."

"What about after?" asked Vega.

"What do you mean?"

"Did Matt call you after? Show up at your house?"

"He came by the shop a lot, as I was moving out," said Cara. "At that point, I just ignored him. Like before." Cara brought her hands to the opposite arms, like she was cold. "Do you think that I . . . that Matt really did something to Zeb?"

Vega leaned back in her seat. "I think Matt had a lot of resources and an imbalanced sort of temper. And if he had, say, convinced himself that someday you and he would be together, and then, suddenly, a handsome stranger came into town and upended all his plans, he might have been inclined to act irrationally."

Cara stared at the table and shut her eyes, her forehead creasing up.

"I never thought that I could have so much to do with it," she said. Then her eyes opened. "People have seen Zeb since. The 2s, they still post pictures."

"Like Elvis and Bigfoot," said Vega. "All blurry, nothing confirmed. And it's been a long time now. Without DNA or dental, we have nothing."

Cara nodded, anxious.

"What now?"

"You should go home," said Vega. "Plan's the same—don't tell anyone you've seen me. I have to work out a couple more things."

"Okay," said Cara. She looked like she was thinking about a skinned knee.

"You sure?" said Vega.

Cara shook free of her thought, but not completely. "I haven't seen you," she confirmed.

Cara looked in her lap. She was so intent on it, Vega thought she'd dropped something there.

"You have anything else you want to talk about?" said Vega.

Cara shut her eyes hard and squeezed her lips together. She reminded Vega of a kid holding her breath because it was the only recourse she had to get what she wanted. Then her eyes and mouth burst open, and she looked at Vega like she was ready to have a confrontation.

"I want you to guess," she said. "You know everything, anyway. I have another thing I haven't told you. I want to see if you can guess."

With most people, a game like this would have rubbed her in all the wrong ways, but with Cara, she thought there might be a greater purpose to it, so she decided to play along.

"Okay," she said. "How many guesses do I get?"

The tension dropped from Cara's face a little. "I'll give you two."

"Will you tell me what it is if I don't guess correctly?"

"Don't worry about that," said Cara. "Just guess. The only clue you have is, it's something I didn't tell you before."

Vega raised her index finger.

"I have a question relating to the clue."

"You're like my students," said Cara, only somewhat amused. "The ones who're trying to move their B-pluses to A-minuses. The grade grubbers."

"You're only giving me one clue," said Vega, ignoring the comparison. "I should at least get a question."

"Fine, you get a question."

"This thing you haven't told me—is it because you didn't think it was relevant, or you forgot, or . . ." Vega watched Cara's face, which she kept pretty still until Vega paused. ". . . it was too painful to bring up?" said Vega.

Cara blinked and looked away. So what could be painful? Vega thought. A pregnancy? No, this wasn't that big.

"A fight," said Vega. "Did you have a fight with Zeb?"

"Yeah, we did," said Cara, sad now that the game was done and all she was left with was the unpleasant memory.

"Is that why he left?" said Vega.

Cara rolled one shoulder forward in a shrug.

"I didn't know it was going to be for good," she said. "We had a fight, and then he took his stuff and left. I thought he'd be back in the morning, but he wasn't."

Vega stared at her, trying to straighten out the timeline in her head.

"That was the last time you saw him?" she asked.

"That was it."

"What was the fight about?" said Vega.

Cara sighed. "It started with him asking me about Matt, what was my relationship with Matt, which makes sense now, since Dart saw them arguing. And I remember just thinking: Who the hell is this guy, coming in here, with his heiress girlfriend back in Berkeley? He's trying to give me trouble for jerking Matt's chain? It was hypocritical male bullshit," she said, getting angrier. "I never questioned him, never asked him for a damn thing. All of a sudden, he's pissed that I had a life before he got here."

"So he left," said Vega.

"I told him to leave," said Cara, regaining a degree of self-possession. She shut her eyes again, and rubbed the heel of her hand on her forehead. "I really didn't think that would be the last time I saw him."

"Do you remember where he was going?" said Vega.

Cara glared at Vega. "I told you, he never told me where he was planning to go next."

"No, I mean that night," said Vega, quick to clear it up. "After you kicked him out, did he say where he was going to sleep that night?"

Cara paused. Some teenagers came in through the front door, boisterous and goofy. Cara glanced over her shoulder in their direction. Then she turned back to Vega.

"It must have been the barn," she said, as if this made perfect sense.

"The barn in the field that used to be Old Man Fenton's but Klimmer owns now?" said Vega. "Where Dart and Zeb used to shoot fruit?"

"Yeah. I guess I never thought about it. I was so pissed off at him."

"What makes you sure that Zeb was going to sleep in the barn that night? Did he tell you that?"

"That's just it—I don't think he said those words," said Cara. "The last thing he said to me, after I told him to leave, was 'Good, I'd rather wake up covered in bat shit than sleep here.'"

"Bat shit?"

"Yeah. I never realized," she said, then registered Vega's expectant expression. "That old barn in that field—full of bats. We'd talked about how the only way Ivan could stand to sleep there was because he was so blind he couldn't see them all up there in the rafters."

She cast her eyes up to the ceiling, as if the bats were right there, and laughed.

"It sounds a lot crueler than it was."

Then her eyes wandered to the loud kids, guffawing between their orders.

"You know what the funny thing is?" she asked Vega.

"What?"

"I'm a high-school teacher, and I really don't like kids," she said. "I don't like the happy ones or the sad ones."

"You like your nephew," Vega countered.

"I do," said Cara, without offering any other explanation. She grabbed her dirty napkin and stood, looked at the kids again, and added, "It's my problem. Not their fault I was born angry."

Later, in the trailer, Vega looked at the last text from Rachel that had come through when she was in California: "I know you have no reason to trust me either but for some reason I trust you so I think you should trust me too because we have to."

Vega hadn't thought about that too much when she'd first read it. She was still not a thousand percent convinced Rachel had not assisted in setting her up, but appreciated Rachel's emotional honesty. It matched the initial impression Vega had taken away from their discussion in Vega's car, with the rain pounding the roof. She'd also believed Rachel when she said she'd observe the customers in the diner.

"Let me know if you can talk," Vega texted.

A minute passed; then Vega's phone buzzed, with Rachel's name blinking.

"Hello."

"Oh my God, is that you?" Rachel said, hushed.

"It's me."

"Are you okay? I'm so sorry about what happened. I tried to call you. Where are you?"

"I had to go back to California," said Vega.

"Oh," said Rachel. "Are you okay, though? Claire told me. I mean, she told me some of it, but not all of it. She said they broke your arm. Did they break your arm?"

"They fractured my wrist. It's fine."

"I just didn't think they would do that," she said. Then she laughed. "That's not true. Of course, *they* would do that. They're a bunch of effing animals. I didn't think Claire would do that. I know that's dumb. She's so in with them now." Rachel paused. "Did you, uh, go to the police?"

"No," said Vega, scrolling through an e-mail the Bastard had just sent.

"Right, what good would it do," said Rachel, with a mix of relief and frustration. "I mean, it's like a total irony here. The sheriff's the last place you would go—"

"Rachel," Vega interrupted. "I have to ask you something. I'd like you to answer it honestly."

"Okay," said Rachel, up to the challenge.

"Did you have any knowledge that Claire was trying to set us up that night?"

"No," Rachel said, drawing it out so it was almost two syllables. It reminded Vega of the way little kids talked: "No-wah." Rachel continued: "She met me at home and acted all scared. I tried to convince her to stay with me right then and not go to Burger Village, but she said she had to show up or it would be too suspicious. She said she had to borrow my phone, and when I left the house to meet you, she'd slashed my tires. Then I had to wait for my dad to get off his shift at midnight to use his car, but it was too late."

She was crying now, Vega could tell.

"I told her about you in the first place because I was saying, This woman can help us, but I was so dumb about it, because that's how they got you there—me."

"Rachel," said Vega, thinking of the thing she could say to capture her attention, "fuck guilt, okay? I'd like you to focus. Have you talked to your sister?"

Rachel gulped and said, "Not since that night. I know she's become this other person, you know, but I want to help her, because I'm an idiot. It's like I thought she was like Sir Thomas More but she's really like Henry the Eighth, you know, from *A Man for All Seasons*?"

"Right," said Vega.

"Have you read it? Or seen the movie?"

"Sure," said Vega.

She had not read it or seen the movie.

"I thought she had some principles or something, but I don't think she does," said Rachel, her words cut by sniffs. "She's just like one of these guys now that shitpost on Reddit, like a robot. They don't care about anyone or anything, and they think that's really original. It's like you think you're the first people in the history of the world to not give a fuck? You think that makes you special?"

She paused to catch her breath, but Vega could hear her crying.

"Shoot, I can't believe talking about them made me swear," she said, her voice choppy. "I'm trying not to swear in general. My dad says I'm too smart for it, and he's such a good person—he makes me want to be smarter."

Vega winced. Rachel's admonition stung something undefinable inside her, lemon juice on a cut she didn't know she had.

Rachel sighed, continued: "I still love my sister, you know; the love just like comes out of me! I worry about *her*, and it should be the other way around. You probably think I'm the biggest effing loser."

"I don't," Vega said. "I think you always tell the truth, which is a rare thing. Are you still working at the diner?"

"I was there today," said Rachel, congested. "Matt came in for a while."

"Was he there to settle up the register?"

"I don't think so," she said. "Sometimes he just stops by on the way to see his girlfriend."

"Matt Klimmer has a girlfriend?"

"Yeah, I thought you knew," said Rachel. Then she laughed, but stopped it short. "Sorry, you seem to know everything, I thought you knew about Abby, too."

"Abby," repeated Vega. "Does his wife know?"

"I don't know about that," said Rachel. "It's not the biggest secret, though."

"Anything else you notice at the diner?"

"Not really," she said. "Wait, I wrote some stuff down. Hold on."

Vega waited, read through the Bastard's e-mail again, and let it digest. After a couple of minutes, Rachel returned.

"So this was a while ago—like, right around when you left? Maybe before. There's this girl, Kelsey, she also waits at the diner. We went to high school together, too, but I was, like, never really great friends with her. Her brother, Conor, is seventeen or eighteen or something, and he came to see her to get her car keys, and they had a fight, and I was listening to them but pretending not to listen, you know?

"He had two friends with him, and they had guns."

"What kind of guns?" said Vega.

"Um, long ones. I don't really know about guns. My dad has a handgun, but these were more like rifles. But kind of weird-looking."

"Were the barrels long?" said Vega, typing a search term into Google.

"Yeah."

"With a piece on the top, looks like a canteen?"

"I think so."

"I'm going to send you a picture; you tell me if that's what you remember seeing these boys carrying."

Vega copied a photo from the Shopping tab and texted it to Rachel.

"Yeah, they looked just like that!" said Rachel, sounding pleased. "How'd you know?"

"They're paintball guns," said Vega. "Do you know Kelsey's address?"

Rachel knew more or less where Kelsey lived, with her parents and her brother, Conor. Vega wrote it down and thanked her, felt bad about lying that she was still in California but only for a second. Rachel wasn't crying anymore when they said goodbye.

Vega went to the front windshield. She saw some stars above the cushion of the treetops. Through the rectangle of the glass, it was like she was watching the view on television. It was nice, the light blurry through the smudges.

It was almost midnight, and Vega knew she should probably try to get some sleep, at least go through the motions. Without realizing it, Rachel had given her a clean place to start. Vega touched her new tooth with her tongue. It didn't feel sensitive or nervy anymore. Now it was like it had always been there.

Cap was having some trouble focusing. He'd just gotten off the phone with Em, and had let Nell listen in. Brett Hardecker had confessed to the crime of breaking into Nell's car and claimed he acted alone. His family had offered to pay for the damage if the DA agreed to drop the criminal charges and keep everyone out of court. Em said it was up to Cap. In his words, the DA could not give a dozen shits if a prosecution on teenage criminal mischief moved forward. And the last fly on the sticky strip was that Brett was still under eighteen.

Now Cap was helping Nell with the bass drum again, while they danced around an argument.

"You think we should drop it," she said, having already decided that's what he thought.

Cap shrugged as he lifted the drum.

"He's a kid, Bug. Kids do dumb stuff."

"And don't you think they should be persuaded against that?" she said. "Especially since this dumb stuff is racially motivated? And by the way, if he was some Black kid in Philly, they'd swallow the key."

"I don't disagree with you," said Cap. "Hear me out: We scared the piss out of him. It is possible he's learned his lesson. The ultimate goal here, the best possible criminal-justice outcome, is that people change for the better."

Nell picked up the snare and shook her head. She opened the front door.

"That's a nice story, Dad," she said. "It's just a whole bunch of bullshit, but it's a nice story."

"Come on," said Cap, carrying the drum to Nell's car.

She opened the trunk.

"You can still stalk him online if you want," said Cap.

"Please don't patronize me."

"I'm not patronizing you," said Cap. "You can follow this kid all you want. If he gets into trouble, we tell Em to shine a light on it."

Cap heaved the drum into the car. He didn't see the beater anywhere but didn't say anything. Nell slid the snare in, then shut the lid.

"So, if he goes online an hour after the county cuts him loose, starts flexing about how he got the laugh on the Jews of Denville, we bring him back in."

"I'll call Em myself," said Cap.

He could see she was thinking about it. She'd taken to wearing a black leather bomber jacket that was once Jules's. It was cropped on Nell, since she was taller than her mother, and Cap thought it made her look like a real grown-up. Like a woman in her twenties that he would see at the supermarket or in an airport somewhere. It made him proud and scared.

"I have to go," she said, stern. "But this discussion isn't over."

Cap held his hands out, said, "I wouldn't assume it was."

Nell's face softened. "Don't wait up, Dad. I mean it."

"I won't," he said. Then he said, "The Jews of Denville. That sounds like a PBS thing. From the people who brought you *Downton Abbey*."

Nell rolled her eyes but also laughed for real. "Dad, dorky," was all she said, and then she got in the car.

She started the engine, and the music was ambient thumps and hums. Cap slapped the roof twice, like he was on the factory floor, approving the vehicle for operation. Then he stepped back, out of the way.

"Love you," she said over the music.

"Love you!" Cap called, but he wasn't sure she could hear him.

She drove away, and Cap went inside. He locked the door behind him and went upstairs to change, still in his work clothes.

When he passed Nell's bedroom, he saw that her desk chair had fallen backward. He went into her room and picked it up, pushed it toward the desk.

This time, the beater was sitting there in plain sight next to some textbooks, mocking him with its presence. He picked it up and squeezed it.

"Nope, nope, nope," he said, and left the room, went back down the stairs.

He walked to the front door and took his phone from his pants pocket, thought he should give her some time to realize she forgot it and come back. So he did. He didn't go back upstairs to change. He sat on the couch and tossed the beater onto the cushion next to him. Then he turned on the TV and moved between sports and news networks; his eyes were gliding over the tickers, but he wasn't absorbing any of the numbers—the scores, the odds, the national debt, and unemployment.

Cap looked at the clock on the cable box. It had been a half-hour since Nell had left. She hadn't come back.

The rate with which he bounced between the two sides of Overprotective Black Hawk Dad and Rational Chill Dad was accelerating, and it was becoming too hard to fake being the latter. He couldn't pretend anymore with Nell, maybe not with anyone, that he wasn't worried when he was. What was the point? What was the reward?

Whatever it was, it was not enough.

He took his phone from his pocket and scrolled through the

contacts, found Gwen, Nell's friend Carrie's mom. Might as well get the evidence bagged first.

He wrote Gwen a text: "Hi Gwen, it's Max Caplan. Wondering if Nell is at your place rehearsing with Carrie and Nick tonight."

He sat for a few minutes, continuing to flip channels, and settled on hockey. He played a little game with himself, pretending not to be looking at his phone screen, but he was actually looking at his phone screen.

Then a text came back from Gwen: "Hi Max! Nell and Nick aren't here tonight. Everything okay?"

Cap stood up, reading the words a few times. Everything okay?

"Yep. Thanks," he wrote back.

He thought about texting Jules but then nixed the idea quickly. Not that he was primarily concerned that Jules might think he was a less responsible person than she already did, but it was a factor. Also, why worry two people.

The acid in Cap's stomach started to curl again; he felt the pain high on his torso, right under his ribs. He pressed his palm into the ache and bent over a few inches at the waist.

He tapped Nell's number and thought, Fuck it. Directly to voice mail. Cap hung up before the recording ended.

A moment later she called, and Cap answered.

"You okay?" she said, sounding out of breath.

"Yeah, Bug, I'm good," he said, forcing his voice steady. "How's rehearsal going?"

"Fine," said Nell.

Cap couldn't be sure, but he thought she sounded a little cagey.

"So the drums are okay—everything's working?" he asked.

"Yeah?" she said, now confused. "Dad, are you sure you're okay?"

Cap wiped his forehead with the back of his wrist and looked at the skin—damp.

There was no point and no reward in pretending not to worry, he thought again.

"You left the beater for the bass here," he said. "And I texted Gwen."

He leaned against the wall and listened to Nell sigh.

"Why didn't you lead with that, Dad? Why do you have to catch me in it? So the DA can plead me out?"

"I was trying to give you every benefit of every doubt—" he began.

"I'm coming home now, okay?" she said, sounding annoyed.

Then she hung up on him.

"Okay," he said to the phone.

He went upstairs, noticed the stomach pain subside as he changed into jeans and his Eagles shirt. Then he walked back downstairs and to the fridge in the kitchen, drank a beer quickly, and stared at the food containers on the shelves. He knew he should try to eat something, the way he knew when he was outside he was supposed to be cold, but for a while there had been a separation between his mind and his body, and it seemed even more profound now.

So he drank another beer.

Soon the lights from Nell's car flashed through the living-room window, and he hurried to the couch and sat down, attempting to look like he'd been there the whole time, committed to watching the hockey game.

She came through the front door and stood there.

Cap twisted his body around on the couch and said, "Hey."

"I'm still pissed off at you," said Nell.

"I'm sorry, what?"

"That's right," said Nell, not moving from the rug just inside the door. "You've been suspicious of me for a long time and tried to play it off like you were cool with it, and I didn't really believe you were, but, still, I didn't think you would text Gwen, first of all," she said, thrusting out her index finger while she counted, followed by her middle finger, "and go nosing around my room for evidence."

"I picked up your chair," Cap said, standing up. "I wasn't nosing anywhere. I saw the beater, right there on your desk."

"So what? Maybe Carrie has an extra. Why did you have to text Gwen?" she asked, sounding hurt.

"I was worried," said Cap, walking around the couch so he was closer to her. "I am worried. About you, about me. About our locks working. I would say all of it keeps me up at night, but it's all the time. I am always waiting for the other thing."

Nell relaxed her stance a little, let her head nod to the side. She rubbed the rug with the toe of one of her shoes.

"*Does* Carrie have an extra?" he said.

"No," said Nell, only slightly defeated. "Do you want to go for a ride and see where I've been going a lot of these nights?"

"Now?"

"Yeah, now."

Cap looked at the clock. It was too late for a school night, and too late for a guy his age to be on the streets. Suddenly he felt underdressed.

"Can I go like this?"

Nell was confused.

"What—you mean, your clothes? Yeah, of course. Where exactly do you think we're going?"

"I try to maintain zero expectations," he said, taking his jacket from the hook.

Nell drove to a road in the Black Creek neighborhood and ignored a traffic safety barricade with a big orange sign in the middle reading "Roundabout Closed Ahead." She snaked the hatchback between a construction cone and the sidewalk, and Cap bit both of his lips so he wouldn't say anything. He didn't want to chance Nell's changing her mind and turning the car around.

Cap noticed at least a dozen cars parked on the short street leading up to the roundabout, most of them with headlights on. There were about twenty or thirty kids, Nell's age or a little older, none he recognized. They were sitting on the hoods and leaning against the doors, smoking cigarettes and vape pipes.

Nell parked behind another car, cut the engine, and kept the lights on.

"That's going to kill your battery," said Cap, still trying to discern what was happening outside.

"It'll only be about an hour."

Nell got out of the car and leaned her head in.

"You losing your nerve, or what?"

"I'm not losing anything," said Cap.

He got out of the car, rested his elbow on the roof, and looked at all the kids. His first thought was that this was some kind of political event, but they all looked too casual. Then he thought it must be a party, but they were drinking coffee and energy drinks, not beer. And he smelled standard-issue cigarette smoke in the air, not weed.

Nell walked around the front of the car to join him. "What do you think?" she said.

"Looks like a nice group of youngsters," said Cap. "Wholesome. Law-abiding, except for driving and parking their vehicles on a prohibited road."

"You don't know what this is?" said Nell.

Cap looked around again and shook his head.

Nell turned her head, tried to see how he saw it.

"Okay," she said, turning back to him. "Back in October, I think, I was at school and I forgot a book in the car, so I went out to get it, and I saw these guys in this old Corolla doing hairpin turns in the parking lot. They were going fast for a lot—like twenty, twenty-five, maybe—and at first I was I was, like, Are these assholes blind? there're spaces everywhere. Then I just watched them for a minute."

Cap gazed over her shoulder while she spoke, and then he started to notice things: the entrance to the roundabout was clear, with no cars blocking it; directly in front of the entrance, along the side of the road, were a Corolla, a Ford Focus, and a sleek old Mustang with a modest tunnel ram attached to the hood. He saw two guys standing in the center of the roundabout, one of them looking into the flip screen of a digital camcorder.

Nell continued: "The driver, he had so much control over the car, you know. He would start the course and make his way through the lot so fast and silent, no skidding, and then he'd do it again. Then I look at his friend in shotgun, and he's got his phone, either filming it all or timing him.

"I waited until they stopped, and I went to talk to them. They don't go to DW, they're twenty-one—they just like the DW lot because it's a good course."

"They're car guys," said Cap, definitive and somewhat relieved. "I knew car guys in school."

"Yeah," said Nell, encouraged. "I got to know them and their friends, and I started coming here a couple nights a week and driving their cars—we do drifting and powersliding—do you know what those are?"

"Drifting?" said Cap. "Like drag racing?"

"Sort of," said Nell. "It's about the length of the drift and how quickly you can come out of it. You hold in the clutch as you get into the turn, and then release at the last second, so the back wheels lock up and you drift. You can also use the emergency brake. Some of these guys can do it with an automatic, too, but I'm not ready for that yet, so I just use their cars for the clutch."

Cap stared at her, finally grasping what she'd been telling him.

"You're racing cars, now?"

Nell sighed and seemed annoyed.

"No, Dad, it's not NASCAR. It's drifting—I mean, it's not a hundred percent safe but it's not that dangerous, per se."

"Per se," Cap repeated, in a state of shock.

"It's not death-wish stuff; these guys are just into cars and filming the races and talking about techniques. And it turns out I'm really good at it," she said.

Cap looked past her again to the cars and the kids. He rubbed his hand over his mouth and chin.

"You're good at everything," he said.

"Well, not true, but thanks."

"Nell," said Cap, sensing a headache starting in his temples. "I know this now—you can't ask me to hide it from your mother."

"Don't worry about it," said Nell. "She already knows."

"She *knows*?"

"I told her a couple of months ago. She came to watch one night. All the guys gave me shit for a while, because she's such a MILF, et cetera."

"Jules knows?" Cap said, pointing at the roundabout. "You told her—you brought her here—and not me?"

"Dad, don't make it weird," said Nell. "We discussed telling you and decided to hold off, since you've seemed a little fragile."

"Fragile?" Cap said, as if he'd never heard the word.

"Yes, Dad. Fragile. And paranoid and anxious and all that. You never should have stopped seeing that therapist, you know?"

It was so much information at once, Cap was having a hard time taking it all in. His first instinct was to defend himself. "You and I just infiltrated a white-nationalist cell," he said. "That's not a job for the fragile."

"Okay, but I wouldn't exactly call Hardecker a 'white-nationalist cell,'" she said. She glanced over her shoulder. "You can watch me and the other guys drive, and then I'll introduce you to the guy I met in the parking lot that day. Slouch. I think you'll really enjoy it."

"Slouch?" said Cap, squinting at the small crowd gathering near the roundabout entrance. "You think you're grown up because you have friends with nicknames describing their shitty posture, huh?"

Nell raised her eyebrows. "Actually, he stands up very straight all the time."

Cap crossed his arms and said, "You think you're grown up because you have friends with ironic nicknames?"

Nell smiled just a bit.

"Dad," she said, and she took a small step closer to him, "I know it's hard to believe, but this"—she waved her hand in the direction of the roundabout—"for me, this was the bridge back to the land of the living.

"Drumming helps, therapy helps, you and Mom help, of course, and my friends, but when I'm really being honest about things that make me feel like I'm alive and safe and actually, like, happy? This is really up there."

Cap looked at her face. When she was little, she always looked happiest when she was busy: building shoebox beds for her dolls, drawing a comic book, arranging a scavenger hunt in the backyard. There was a trace of that happiness now in her eyes, but there was also a giddiness he hadn't seen since a Christmas Eve a long time ago.

"Maybe Vega's your bridge," she said. Then she tapped her head with her index finger. "Something to think about, Caplan."

Cap watched her turn and go to her friends, slap hands, and bump fists. Then they dispersed, and Nell went to the Mustang and held the keys up so Cap could see, swinging them around on her finger. Then she got into the car, started up the engine, and pulled up to the entrance of the roundabout.

All of the kids seemed to take their places, most standing at the sides, in the scrubby grass that grew through the cracks in the pavement. One guy, tall and long-limbed, stood in front of Nell's car, holding a phone, talking to her through the windshield. The filmmaker in the center got on one knee and aimed the camera at the Mustang.

Everything grew quiet for a moment, and then the crowd started clapping and whistling. Nell revved the engine, and the crowd got even louder.

Cap hit himself lightly on the head with his palm. It was always the same message. Every time: Trust the girl.

The tall guy moved to the side of the road and out of Nell's way. He held his phone in one hand and stared at the screen, lifted his other hand up like his arm was an automatic parking barrier. Then he brought his arm down in a chop, and Nell was gone. Not even dust behind her.

14

EARLY THE NEXT MORNING, VEGA WENT TO DART'S TRAILER AND knocked on the door three times. She heard him moving inside, could see the base of the Airstream shake with his footsteps. Soon she could hear him breathing on the other side of the door.

"Dart," she said. "It's me, Alice Vega. I'm the one looking for Zeb Williams."

"I seen you from the window," he said. "Where you come from?"

"I'm staying in that Stargazer. Rented it from Jason. You remember me?"

Dart took a moment with the information.

"Jason the musician?"

"Yeah, guess so. You want to open the door, though?"

Vega heard the door unlatch and stood back while it swung open. Dart held an old revolver at his side. Vega didn't know a whole lot about vintage handguns but figured this had to be some kind of Smith & Wesson special they'd issued to cops in the seventies. Vega examined his face. The last time she'd seen Dart, she'd been watching him on her laptop screen in an episode of his show filmed almost sixty years earlier. He'd been Hollywood-pretty, light eyes sparkling through the monochrome, his smile kind but with a touch of mischief. White hat, silver star.

"You remember me?" she said again.

His eyes were cloudy now with weariness.

"Yeah, you're looking for Zeb. From California."

"That's right. Can I come in?"

He nodded, held the door open for her. "Yeah, okay. I got coffee, but it's instant. Comes in a pouch. You drink that?"

"No, thanks, I'm good," she said, stepping into the trailer.

Dart went to the standing cabinet in the corner and opened the doors, placed the revolver inside on a handgun hanger near the top of the door frame. Vega could also see two rifles standing upright inside.

"Did I wake you up?" said Vega.

"Nah," said Dart. "I don't sleep much."

"Me, neither."

"What happened to your arm, there?" he said, shuffling toward the counter with the hot plate.

"Wrist fracture," said Vega. "Matt Klimmer's son and his friends did it."

"They took a swing at you?" he said.

"They took a few."

"At a woman? You?" he said, shocked.

"Me."

"Sons a bitches," he uttered. "They'll just do anything to anyone."

"Yeah, they will."

"You didn't go to the sheriff here, I know that much," said Dart.

"No, I didn't," said Vega. "I went back to California for a while. Did some research. I'm hoping you can help me with something, Dart."

"What's that?"

"Do you have any kind of an explosive device here?" said Vega.

Dart didn't seem as surprised as Vega thought he might be. He blew air through his lips, and they flapped.

"Used to have a black-powder/titanium mix, but that was years ago. The Worm Child got rid of it when he cleaned my place out."

Dart plugged the hot plate into the wall and set a kettle on top of it.

"What are you looking to explode?"

"Matt Klimmer's stable."

"Okay, then," said Dart, scooping coffee grounds into a cup. "Is there an objective to this activity?"

"There is," said Vega. "It's a long story, and I can't get into it now. But I will. Tomorrow."

The kettle began to whistle. It started choppy and low, and then started to scream. Dart moved it to the counter. He touched his face, scratched the hair on his chin.

"Klimmer's got a propane tank," he said. "Used to be behind the stable. You shoot a round or two into that, you'll get some nice fireworks. It might attract a police presence."

"That's fine," said Vega. "Might you want to come with me?"

"To Klimmer's?" said Dart. "I got nothing to say to him."

"You don't have to," said Vega. "I just need you to talk to the horses."

The sun was out the next day.

Vega drove to the house where Rachel's fellow waitress, Kelsey Sullivan, lived with her parents and little brother and parked across the street, keeping the engine running. She watched the front door as a man in his fifties with a gut and a beard came out, got into a copper-colored station wagon of a certain age, and drove off at seven-thirty-five. She knew she wouldn't have to wait much longer. The first bell at Cascade High was due to ring at five after eight.

Around ten to eight, the door opened again, and out came Conor Sullivan. He wore a baseball cap and jeans and an orange puffer jacket. He got into a burnt-red sedan and drove off, too fast, out of the driveway.

Vega waited a minute, then followed him. She knew he would have to pick one of two routes to the high school and figured he would pick the shorter, since he only had fifteen minutes. When she examined the map on her phone before leaving the trailer, she'd seen there was a stoplight on the corner of River Road and Fourth Street. She estimated Conor was about a minute ahead of her, and knew the red light would last at least a minute, so leaned on the gas as she turned from Third Street onto Fourth Street and saw Conor's car just stopping at the red on the corner.

She slowed down to twenty, counted to ten in her head, slowed to ten and then five, and then gave the gas a little punch and hit his car, heard the scrape of fender on fender. Not a big ding, but enough for him to feel it.

She saw his head bounce forward in his seat and then jerk around to look at her angrily. Vega smiled and shrugged. Silly me.

He got out of the car. As he approached, she saw he was freckled with irritated red patches on his face. He grimaced at her, then leaned over to inspect the damage. Vega checked her rearview. No one coming yet.

"What the hell," he said, tipping his hat back on his head.

"Sorry about that," she said out the window. "You want to pull over?"

"No," he said, somewhat shocked, which swiftly turned to anger. "How did you not see me right here?"

Vega unbuckled her seat belt, opened the door, stepped out, and looked back. A car was coming; Vega waved the driver around.

"Yeah, I don't know. My mind just wandered, I guess," she said.

"What?" said Conor. Then he took out a phone from his back pocket. "I gotta call my dad."

He began to text instead of call, which was good.

Vega shut her door and walked up to where their fenders met, right next to where he stood. She leaned down to get a closer look.

"Oh yeah, I see that now," she said, staring at the dimple her fender had made in his.

"I need to get your information, I guess," said Conor, sounding like he almost felt bad about it.

"Yeah, I'll give it to you," said Vega, still bent at the waist. "Jeez, I just really thought I had more space—that ever happen to you?"

Conor glanced up from the phone, his cheeks flushed. He shrugged and said something unintelligible in response.

"The way it dips in the middle, maybe they could pull it out with a plunger," she said. "You ever see them do that on TV?"

She stood up straight.

"Have you?"

He squeezed his phone in his hand.

"I don't know," he said, losing patience. "I have to text my dad, okay? Could you just get your information, please?"

"Hmm," she said, squinting down at the dent. "I think I actually might have more damage than you. And, you know, you did stop pretty suddenly."

Now his head popped up, his whole body at attention.

"Bullshit," he said, breathless.

"See for yourself."

Conor leaned down. When his face was about six inches from the fender, Vega placed her left hand on top of her right and brought both hands down hard so the cast on her palm hit the back of Conor's neck. Conor's forehead slammed into the fender, and his body tensed up as if to prepare for a fight but a few seconds too late to carry it through. He slid onto the ground on his side and tried to push up with one arm, but couldn't do it through the daze.

Vega knelt and slapped his cheek with her casted hand. He brought his hands up in an uncoordinated block or attack; Vega wasn't sure which he was attempting, but it was a straight fail on both counts. She jammed her elbow into his cheek, and the skin split under his eye. He yelled and brought his hands up, trying to cover his face.

"Keep your hands to yourself or I will break them," she said. "And don't say anything. All you have to do is nod if you understand."

He nodded, his fingers twitching.

"Your name is Conor Sullivan, right?" she said.

He nodded.

"You like paintball, Conor?"

He didn't move; his hand covered his eye, with blood dripping down in a thick stream.

Vega slapped his free cheek. "Don't make me ask you shit twice. Do you like paintball?"

He nodded quickly.

Vega could hear another car approaching.

"Don't move," she said.

She stood up, saw a woman in a Jeep slowing down. Vega smiled and waved her on.

"Do you need me to call anyone?" the woman said out her window.

"No, thanks, we're good," Vega called, cheery.

"Help!" yelled Conor, his voice caught in a gurgle.

The woman's expression turned sour and frightened as she tried to peer between the cars to get a better look at Conor. Then she gaped at Vega and sped off.

Vega shook her head at him, then went to her trunk. She pulled out one of the cans of blue paint she'd bought from Peller Hardware so many weeks before. She shook it up and down. Click-click, click-click, click-click.

Conor was trying to stand, pulling himself up by grabbing the fenders like Rocky on the ropes. Vega gave him a gentle kick to the chest, and he lost his grip. He grabbed at her boot, but she shook him off. She stood over him and bent down so they were face-to-face.

"That lady's going to call a cop, so I'll make this quick," she said, uncapping the spray paint. "Who told you to shoot paintballs at an eleven-year-old boy seven weeks ago?"

Conor stared at the nozzle of the spray-paint can as if it were a tiny eyeball.

"Fuck off," he muttered.

"Yeah, I know him," said Vega, taking aim. "Close your eyes and mouth, Conor."

Duane Smith was Derek Fenton's roommate. After a few minutes online, Vega figured out that Smith worked as an apprentice at a tattoo studio in a town called Amera, the next town over. She scrolled through Facebook and Instagram accounts looking for pictures of him. It was difficult to tell his height from the photos on the screen, but she could see his build—wiry and lean, strong arms, enough to pin someone from behind.

Then she came across something on the shop's Web site. Buried in a slide show of American Traditional hearts and pinup girls was a photo of a neck tattoo—two thick lightning bolts, side by side. Vega recognized them, remembered reading about them—runic symbols, worn by white nationalists and supremacists, originating from Himmler's SS. Especially popular in prison.

Vega didn't have any tattoos. She clicked on "Make an appointment for a consultation here" and thought, First time for everything.

Red Rose Specialty Tattoos was in a town that seemed even smaller than Ilona, the main drag barely two blocks long.

Vega went through the front door, caught the smell of hospital soap and cigarette smoke. Posters of tattoo designs lined the walls: anchors, ladies, arrows, hearts, knives, bubble drops of blood.

Vega stepped up to the counter and rang the bell, saw a leather chair with a backrest and a leg rest. Also a sink, and a couple of tray tables topped with tattoo needles and small cups. She started to flip through a binder full of drawings of ships and tombstones and sailors.

A short, stocky guy came from another room, wearing a black muscle shirt and black jeans. Vega recognized him from the shop's Web site as Kuffy. He was the one who had gone back and forth with Vega over e-mail and told her to come in at noon.

"Hi. Kuffy, right?" Vega said, putting on the shy.

"That's right," he said, his voice gravelly but surprisingly high-pitched. "Betsy?"

"Bitsy, actually," said Vega. She pinched her index and thumb together to indicate the size. "Like the spider up the spout?"

"Oh yeah," said Kuffy. "Cute."

All of his exposed skin was inked except his face. Vega ran her eyes over the tattoos, but they all blended together; it was difficult to pick out any design over another.

"Do you think you might be able to help me? Like I said in my e-mail?" said Vega.

"You mean with the price?"

"Yeah. You know how sometimes you can get a cheaper haircut with a beauty-school student? You said you might have someone like that, maybe take a little off the price?"

"I got a great guy for you," said Kuffy. "He'll be here in fifteen, twenty. He's been tattooing almost a year—we can take off about thirty percent for you."

"Oh, wow, do you think so?" said Vega, moon-eyed.

"No problem," said Kuffy, magnanimous. "What kind of piece are you looking to get?"

"Not sure yet," said Vega, looking at the images on the wall. "I was kind of hoping you guys could help me decide."

"We can do that," he said. "Full service. You see anything in the book or the walls that grabs you?"

"To be honest, not really," said Vega with a note of apology. She pressed her stomach into the counter and leaned forward, said quietly, "You guys do, like, any white-pride stuff?"

Kuffy got a broad grin on. He reached below the counter and pulled out another binder, this one much thicker than the one left out for display.

"Have a look. You'd have to go to Idaho to get a better selection, guarantee."

"Who's got time for that," said Vega, opening the binder.

There they were. Swastikas, Confederate flags, Celtic cross, dice, bowlcuts.

"You do all of these?" said Vega. "They're really cool."

"Most of 'em, yeah," said Kuffy. "But, here, my boy Duane did these."

He flipped to the back of the binder to a page with blocky calligraphy.

"He's real good at text, if you wanted to get any words."

One word caught her eye. She tapped it.

"Could I get this one?" she said.

Kuffy turned the binder around so he could get a better look. He smiled, revealing crooked teeth. "You could, but that's, like, a club Duane's in. I don't know, they might have some kinda initiation."

"It's just a word, though," said Vega, innocent. "And it's what our country's all about, right?" she added, like she was running for Miss White America.

"Hey, honey, totally," said Kuffy. "Your heart's in the right place, I can tell. But that word, in that style, that's like a trademark of his. He'll be here any minute—you can work something out with him."

"He sounds talented."

"Oh yeah. Him and his friends are really doing things in the world."

"I bet they are."

She saw his gaze shift to somewhere above her head and knew Duane was coming. She backed away from the counter, stood up straight, rolled her shoulders back.

She heard the front door open.

"Here's the man of the hour now. Duane, this is your new client, Bitsy. She's a smart gal."

Vega didn't turn around yet. She looked at Kuffy, her eyes hard.

"Everything okay?" he said to her.

"Hey, Bitsy, is it?" said Smith, still behind her, she estimated about a foot away.

All at once, she thought. Best to do it all at once.

She reached into the inside pocket of her jacket, pulled out the uncapped can of spray paint.

Confusion spread in Kuffy's eyes, but he was still smiling. Then Vega turned around quickly and was face-to-face with Smith. She grabbed his hand as if she were going to shake and gripped hard, pressed her cast against his palm, and dug her nails in a little.

"What—" said Smith, the recognition beginning to hit.

He started to yank his arm away, and Vega sprayed a bright-blue stripe across his eyes. Smith screamed, and both hands flew to his face.

Vega turned as Kuffy flipped up the flap door in the counter and ran at her. She swung her right arm in the cast at his face.

Kuffy gripped the cast with both hands, and Vega brought her left arm forward and sprayed paint in the direction of his eyes, but he jerked his head back, the paint streaming into his nose and open mouth.

He released her cast—it was instinct, Vega knew. Your face or head gets hurt, your hands try to protect it even if that's the moment when you need them the most.

Vega jumped toward Kuffy, the fumes clouding her nose, and threw an uppercut to his chin. Kuffy fell back into the counter and then onto the floor, scraping his tongue with the fingernails of one hand, his other hand covering his face like a catcher's mask.

Now Vega turned to Duane, who'd fallen to the floor and was yelling, fiercely rubbing his eyes. She kicked him hard in the ribs, and he curled his body around the pain, a stream of vomit spilling from the corner of his mouth.

Vega squatted, shaking the paint can up and down.

"You remember me, right, Duane?" she said.

He didn't respond, gurgling spit, his eyes still shut, the lids puffy.

"You held my arms back in a parking lot? Nod," said Vega. Then she hit his forehead with the heel of her casted hand, knocking the back of his head on the floor.

Smith nodded.

"You see why that wasn't a great idea?"

Smith nodded again.

"So, if we could all get in a time machine and go back in time a little to that night, do you think you might have done a different thing?"

His eyes opened the slightest bit, the whites webbed with red, tears leaking out the sides. She held the paint can over his face.

"You think?" she said.

He bared his teeth, like he was about to fight, then gave one quick nod.

"You have a little talent, Duane. That Nazi font in the binder up there—it's not my thing, but there could be a path to a career for you. Your friends, on the other hand, they might be dragging a guy like you down. Don't you think?"

Duane nodded again, slower this time. He turned his head toward the ground and spit up a little more vomit.

Vega kept the paint can hovering over his face, and then pulled her phone out of her other pocket, tapped "record" on the video.

"What are their names, Duane? The guys who talked you into it."

Duane's eyes lolled toward Kuffy, who was hacking and spitting blue puke onto the floor. Duane looked back to Vega; his skin was pasty around the blue stripe; he knew he was out of time and options, and gave her the names.

Next was the house where Derek Fenton and Duane lived. Vega left Duane crawling around on the floor of the tattoo shop, but she had yet to locate Derek. She knew he was part of a crew reinforcing wooden utility poles for an energy company, but didn't know where exactly he was working today. She also remembered Rachel saying Claire had dropped out of school and had no job, so there was a good chance she would be home.

Vega parked at the curb in front of the blue ranch-style. A seasoned white four-door was in the driveway. Vega recognized it in a second: it was the car Claire had driven to the Burger Village parking lot that night.

Vega got out of her car. It was still sunny, but the wind was picking up, long clouds moving fast in the sky. Vega put on her sunglasses and gave the fungo a light swing in the air. It made a sigh of a sound; though it didn't have a lot of bulk to it at all, it was made of aluminum, which would be helpful. Nearly impossible to break in half.

Vega approached the car and remembered looking at it from the ground with blurry eyes. It seemed smaller now, and in worse condition, the sunlight exposing all the rusted corners. Vega peered inside—the seats were ripped here and there, cardboard boxes littered the back seat. One of the boxes was open, full of empty food-storage containers.

Vega stood a couple of feet from the car's hood and practiced her swing. She was hitting from the left, since that was the stronger side these days. The doors and side windows could wait.

She wrapped her right fingers around the bat's handle, her left hand over the right, and then raised the bat above her head like she was about to knight the windshield. Staring at the small dream-catcher dangling from the rearview mirror, she brought the bat down on the glass, right in the center.

It sounded solid, like a sandbag being kicked, and the windshield cracked in the middle. The center splintered in front of Vega's eyes in five different directions: two long, three short. Just one more tap, she thought.

She lifted the bat and smashed it again on the glass, right above the epicenter of the web, and the windshield collapsed.

Most of the glass showered down onto the dashboard and seats, and Vega shut her eyes behind the sunglasses as she felt the sprinkle of pebbles spraying up. The dreamcatcher twirled in the wind.

Vega backed up and swung at the driver's-side window—once, then twice, the glass shattering inward. She whacked the driver's-side door until the center caved in like a funnel.

The front door of the house opened, and Claire came running out, barefoot, wearing jeans and a football jersey that looked like it was made for a young boy.

"What the fuck?!?" she screamed, running toward Vega.

Vega ignored her and smashed the bat into the rear windshield twice.

Claire stopped, backed up at the sound, and screamed again when the glass broke.

"Are you crazy, bitch?! What the fuck are you doing?!"

Claire began to advance again, and Vega pointed the bat in her direction.

"Stop," said Vega.

Claire stopped walking, didn't stop talking. "Get the fuck out of here!" she yelled.

"You remember me?" said Vega, removing her sunglasses. "Huh, Claire?"

Claire stumbled backward, her lips twitching around.

"I got a gun inside," she said, her voice a strained rasp.

"Yeah? Is it mine? I need it."

"No, it's mine," said Claire, all screwed up with pride. "Registered in my name."

"Well, you best get it, girl," said Vega. "You're gonna need all the help you can get."

Claire continued to back up toward the house. "You normie bitch," she said to Vega, shaking her head. "You're dead."

Vega held the sunglasses in front of her mouth and breathed hot air on the lenses, fogging them up. She held them up so Claire could see.

"Nope. Alive."

She put the sunglasses back on her face and went to work on the passenger side.

"I'm calling Derek right now, and he'll be here in five minutes!" Claire screamed.

Vega stopped hitting the car and came at Claire, pointing the bat at her like it was a sword. Claire stumbled up the stairs backward and fell on her ass in the open doorway.

"Is he nearby?" said Vega.

"He's just off Thirty-eight, near the churches. He's gonna kill you this time!"

Vega smiled and said, "Hurry up, then, go and get your phone!"

Claire seemed upset and confused by Vega's directive but followed it anyway, scurrying inside. Vega followed her through the front door.

"You get out of here!" yelled Claire. "This is against the law!"

"You should probably call the sheriff, then, too," said Vega, briefly taking in the thirdhand furniture and the smell of stale beer and fried onions.

Claire grabbed her phone from a counter in the kitchen, and Vega sped up her stride, watching Claire's eyes grow wider as Vega approached. Claire backed up into a pair of cabinets, and Vega kept moving closer to her, with the bat at her side.

"Give me the phone, Claire. Give me the phone, Claire," she said. Then she got close, her face about six inches from Claire's, and Claire froze in her spot. Vega slowed it down to make sure she'd get the message: "Give me the phone, Claire."

Vega stretched out her neck so she was close enough to smell the grease on Claire's skin. Claire shut her eyes, and then Vega kissed the tip of her nose.

Claire shook her head like a bee was in her hair and dropped the phone; Vega caught it in midair and ran back outside.

She tossed the phone up above her head, swung with the bat, and hit it.

The case broke in two, and the phone itself went flying up and across the driveway, landing in the street with a crack. Then Vega went back to work on the car, knocking the side mirror right off, so it dangled.

Claire stood in the doorway and watched. She'd been stunned silent for a few nice minutes but now started screaming again—about how Vega was dead and a bitch and a dead bitch. Vega kept ignoring her. Though she knew she had to get to Highway 38 to find Derek Fenton, she would have liked to stay and pound the car into scrap. It was a far more enjoyable thing than she had expected it to be.

Oswald Utility Specialists had two vans in a line by the side of the road outside of Ilona. Vega spotted the logo on the van doors: a lightbulb with a sun in the middle. There were three guys in hard hats and tool belts—two standing by the base of a utility pole, one about twenty feet up, connected by a waist harness. None of them were Derek Fenton.

Vega parked behind the second van and sent a short message to the Bastard along with an address: "Can you scramble the Wi-Fi for 1 hour here plz." Then she reached into the back seat for the paint can and the fungo.

She got out of the car and walked quickly to the guy closest to the road. He had a reddish mustache and was maybe thirty.

"Hey," she said.

He looked at her eyes and then her hands, spray-paint can in one, small metal bat in the other. A lot flashed over his face—alarm, confusion, hostility.

Vega stopped walking and held her arms at her sides, weapons pointed down. Even if Mustache still had concerns, at least his fight-flight instinct might be quelled if Vega didn't pose an immediate threat.

"I'm looking for Derek Fenton," she said. "I have to speak with him."

Mustache opened his mouth.

"I understand he doesn't pull his weight," she said. "If you wanted to, you could carry on with whatever you're doing here. I'll only be a minute."

Mustache thought about it.

"His dad's the sheriff, sweetheart," said Mustache, almost kindly.

"You're either in my way here or you're out of it," she said. Then she tossed the paint can up and it spun in the air. She caught it, her eyes not breaking her gaze. "I'm going to do what I'm going to do whether you're around or not. Now, *I* know he's useless. I'm pretty sure you know he's useless. Why don't you look at it like letting me do you a favor and taking him off your hands for a couple of days?"

When Mustache glanced toward the vans, Vega knew Derek must be inside one of them, even though she hadn't seen him.

"He's asleep in the front seat," Mustache said.

"Thanks," said Vega. She started to turn around, but then said, "You wouldn't happen to have a spare key to the vehicle, would you?"

"Should be unlocked," said Mustache.

Then they separated, and Mustache jogged over to the second guy on the ground and said a few words to him, nodding in Vega's direction. The second guy bent over an industrial portable toolbox, pulled out a handheld hammer drill, and turned it on. The whirring was pretty loud, but then both men walked to the pole, and the second guy began to drill into the concrete base. The sound was spectacular now, reminding Vega of the dentist's office. She touched her new tooth with her tongue, then approached the van.

It became clear why she hadn't seen Derek at first. He was lying down in the front seat, head leaning on the door near the wheel, big boots up on the passenger-side window. Eyes closed, mouth open, asleep.

Vega went to the driver's-side door and stood next to the side mirror. She leaned the bat against the front tire and yanked the door open.

Derek's eyes shot open as his shoulders and head tipped out of the van. He scrambled to hold on to the top of the seat and the steering wheel so he wouldn't fall, but Vega grabbed the neck of his shirt and heaved him out before he could get a grip on anything. He hit the ground, landing on his upper back, his shoulders hunched forward and head curled up. Probably all that football training, thought Vega—he knows how to avoid concussions.

Vega grabbed the fungo and swung it hard, like a golf club, right into Derek's ribs on his left. Derek grabbed his side and yelled.

Vega leaned over and sprayed the blue paint into his eyes, and Derek twisted and bucked and slapped at his face.

"Where's my gun, fuckface?" said Vega, calm.

Derek reached out a hand to grab her, but he had his eyes sealed shut, so Vega took a swing at his fingers.

He screamed, and Vega turned around to check in with Mustache and the second guy, still drilling, not looking.

"My gun," said Vega. "Where is it?"

"F-fuck—" Derek began, clutching his broken fingers.

Vega stood with her boot pressed against his right ankle and held the tip of the bat to his knee.

"Open your eyes," she said.

He opened one.

"I'm going to smash both of your patellas. Which are your kneecaps. You won't be able to walk, and it can take a year to heal. So, unless you want your girlfriend helping you on and off the toilet— tell me where my gun is."

"Fuck you, you fucking—"

Vega kept her foot firm on his ankle and dropped the paint can. Then she lifted the bat with both hands tightly gripped around the handle and brought it down fast on his right knee. She heard the cracks, imagined the bone shattering like glitter into the blood stream.

Now he screamed, only once, a sharp, short sound, and Vega

squatted down, grabbed his hair, and pulled it, as if this might make him open his eyes.

"My gun," she said.

"Gable," he uttered. "S-sold it to Kent Gable."

"The antiques guy?" said Vega.

"Pawn shop in the back," said Derek, his tongue sweeping his lips.

"Really?" said Vega. "Huh."

Derek didn't look so great. Spit kept frothing out of his mouth, and mucus started pouring from his nose. Vega peeled one of his eyes open, saw the pupil like a black button. This was shock.

Vega pulled her phone from her inside pocket and opened up the "voice record" app, tapped "record."

"What's your name?" said Vega.

He didn't answer right away, so Vega set the bat down on the ground and poked him in the chest with her finger, keeping his eye open with her other hand.

"Your name."

"Derek Fenton," he mumbled.

"Derek Fenton," she repeated. "My name is Alice Vega. Did you assault me in a parking lot seven weeks ago? Yes or no is good."

The eye twitched, the lid attempting to close, the pupil moving back and forth, shrinking a little bit.

"Yes," he said.

"Prove it," said Vega. "If someone watches the CCTV footage, what will they see you do?"

"I . . . I held you down . . ." he started.

"Right, and what did I do?"

"You head-butted me in the teeth."

"And then what did you do, right before I kneed you in the penis?" said Vega.

"I pulled you up to stand. . . ."

"Why?"

He blinked and then focused both his wobbly eyes right on her.

"So the other guys could take shots at you."

Vega smiled at him, ruffled his hair, and said, like he was a newly potty-trained toddler, "Yeah, you did."

.   .   .

Vega picked Dart up and then drove to the Klimmer house. She braked abruptly and parked in the circular driveway, behind the black Camry. She saw a compact there, too, but no Range Rover. Neil, no Matt, she thought. Dart, sitting beside her, was wearing jeans that looked like they may have fit him ten pounds ago but now hung around his waist, held up by a thick leather belt, the buckle sagging in the middle like the centerpiece of a birthday banner. He also had the revolver tucked inside his right pants pocket in a nylon sleeve.

"I remember this place," he said.

"You know where the stable is, right?" said Vega. "Right back there? You see it?"

Dart peered out the window. "I see it," he said. "Same place it was before."

"You know what to do?"

"Get the horses out. Wait by the door."

"That's it," said Vega. "But wait until I get in the house, okay? I don't want anyone to see you back there."

"Yeah," said Dart.

"You got that Smith?"

Dart patted his pocket.

"See you soon," said Vega.

She got out of the car, took some running strides to the door, and rang the doorbell a bunch of times with her thumb.

The stout woman opened the door and looked at Vega's face, and then the bat.

"Lila," said Vega.

The woman backed up, then turned and ran up the stairs.

Vega walked into the living room, took in the tasteful furnishings. Rustic country, a catalogue might call it. She examined the stone figure of a cowboy riding a bucking horse on top of the mantel, next to framed pictures of the Klimmers.

Lila came rushing down the stairs, but stopped halfway down the flight and stared at Vega with frightened recognition.

"You . . ." she said.

"Me," said Vega, approaching the staircase.

Lila shook her head, confused. "What do you want? Why are you here?"

"A few things," said Vega, standing at the bottom of the stairs. "A few reasons."

"My housekeeper's calling the sheriff right now," said Lila, gripping the railing, doing her best to be brave.

"Yeah, he's busy today," said Vega. She lifted up her arm in the cast so Lila could get a good look. "Your son and his friends did this."

"Neil?" said Lila. "No, that's a mistake."

"Lila, I'm not going to be here very long. I just want you to ask your husband about the stable. Ask him why he had it filled in with concrete so quickly. Ask him what's under there, Lila."

Lila gripped the railing with her other hand now, her body folding at the waist.

"What . . . what are you saying?" she said, sitting down on a step.

Vega sighed. Poor Lila wasn't taking it in.

"Also ask him what really happened to his dad, okay?"

Lila shook her head and didn't answer.

"Neil in his room?" said Vega.

"No," said Lila, pulling herself up. "Don't touch my son."

"Downstairs," said Vega. "Got it."

Vega flashed on when she'd left the house before, remembered that Lila had left through a doorway off the kitchen to get Neil's laptop. As Vega turned in that direction, Lila stumbled down the stairs.

"Don't you touch him!" Lila yelled.

Vega swung the bat hard into the spindles at the bottom of the staircase. The one closest to her cracked almost in half, the wood splitting. Lila jumped back.

Vega pointed the bat at her.

"Don't be a dumb mom. Be a smart mom."

Lila scrambled up the stairs, and Vega ran out of the living room and through the kitchen. She found an open door next to the bathroom and went down the carpeted stairs to the basement.

She heard Neil's voice, without any sense of urgency: "What's going on up there, Mom? Feli break something?"

The basement was furnished—part sports bar, part boy's room—with liquor signs on the walls, a light fixture made of antlers, a bed, and a dresser.

Neil sat with his back to Vega, at a desk in front of a desktop with two large monitors. On one screen was a first-person shooter game,

Twitter feed on the other. He had headphones around his neck and sipped an energy drink. He kept punching "enter" on his keyboard with his middle finger and groaned, annoyed.

"What's—" he said, turning his head.

Then he saw Vega, and his mouth dropped open. He jumped up, and the chair slid back on its wheels.

Vega held the bat with both hands and put one foot in front of the other. Neil was not a huge guy, but he'd known how to hit her in the parking lot. Vega touched her new tooth with her tongue.

"Hey, Neil," Vega said. "Wi-Fi's down, huh?"

He froze.

"Better find a landline," she said.

His eyes went to the stairs. About ten feet from both of them.

He made a run for it, and Vega swung, cracking the bat against his elbow. He screamed and fell backward into the desk, knocking over one of the monitors.

Vega walked slowly to Neil, as he perched on his desk, his injured elbow grabbed in his opposite hand. He breathed heavily through his teeth and watched her approach.

"You like tech, huh?" said Vega. "You can make a lot of friends that way."

Neil didn't say anything; his eyes kept searching the room for something that might help him.

"Keyboard's wireless, right?" said Vega. "Go ahead, pick it up."

Neil's breathing accelerated. He glanced at the keyboard.

"Come on," said Vega, taking another step. "Go."

She came at him now with the bat over her left shoulder, and Neil clumsily grabbed the keyboard. He pushed off the desk and bent forward; he was close to her now, and Vega tightened up the muscles in her stomach as Neil swung the keyboard at her abdomen.

He didn't have a lot of momentum without the use of his right arm, so the hit didn't land too hard. Even so, Vega felt her spine and head and whole nervous system light up like the board after Pac-Man gobbles the power pellets.

She punched him in the jaw, and he fell back again, this time onto the ground. Vega dropped the bat and pulled a charging cube plug out of a power strip on the desk, stuck it between her teeth like a hobo's cigar.

He halfheartedly grabbed her ankle, and Vega let him, then kicked him hard in the ribs with her other foot and squatted down. He was curled up now, with multiple pain targets, which was what you wanted in a fight.

Vega grabbed his hair and pulled the paint can from her inside pocket.

"Hold still, now."

She sprayed an "x" over his face, including his eyes, and tucked the can back into her pocket. Neil coughed and screamed, slapped at his nose and eyes.

Vega saw his thick tongue, pink with a white film on the surface, as he yelled, and she pinched his nose and spit the plug into her hand before shoving it into his mouth. She sat on his stomach.

"Swallow," she said. "Swallow, Neil."

Neil's eyes popped open as he grabbed Vega's arm. Vega squeezed his cheeks with one hand, nails digging into the skin, slivers of blood starting to spread.

"I'm not leaving until you swallow this, so get the fuck to it."

He tried to open his mouth but his lips just flapped and wiggled in Vega's hand; then he pushed his chin forward, possibly trying to accommodate her request and swallow the plug, but Vega knew that it wouldn't go down easily, that it would probably stop at the top of his esophagus.

Vega pulled her hand off his face and hit him fast, with the side of her casted fist, across the bridge of his nose. He coughed and yelled, pushed the plug out with his tongue.

Vega reached up to the desk and grabbed the energy drink. She moved up a few inches so she straddled his chest, and shoved the plug back into his mouth.

"Swallow," she said again, pouring the energy drink into his mouth to lubricate the process.

The drink was orange, and he coughed most of it up, like a little carbonated volcano erupting from his lips.

"Can you not even do this right, Neil?" said Vega.

Then came the stumbling footsteps of Lila down the basement stairs.

"Let him go!"

Vega sighed and stood up, dropping the empty can on Neil's face as he sputtered and moaned.

"My husband is just down the road, at the Tack and Saddle," said Lila. "It's not even ten minutes away."

She advanced swiftly to the bottom of the stairs but then stopped short, realizing she was possibly not ready for a physical confrontation.

Vega gazed down at Neil, looking disappointed. Then she stepped around him and headed for the stairs, picking up the bat along the way.

Lila pressed herself against the wall, out of Vega's path.

"You know he's a Nazi, right?" said Vega.

"Get out of my house," said Lila, trying to be brave, chest expanding and shrinking like there was a balloon under her breastplate.

Vega took one more look at Neil on the floor and then ran up the stairs, two at a time.

She jogged through the kitchen, out the front door, and toward her car; only then did she look back at the Camry and the compact, which she assumed were Lila's and Neil's cars, and stopped. She took out the paint can and shook it up.

On the windshield of Neil's compact, she sprayed "NAZI." On the windshield of Lila's sedan: "NAZI MOM."

Then she put her business card under one of the wipers on each, got in her own car, and drove over the gravel and the partition between the field and the driveway toward the stable. She saw the horses, counted three.

As she accelerated over the dirt and pulled up in front of the stable, she saw Dart taking his time coming through the door, carrying a tin washtub.

"They ran when I hit the basin," he said, a charmed expression on his face. "Not too feisty, though."

"Come on!" called Vega.

She pulled up closer to him, and he dropped the basin and got in. Vega turned the car out of the dirt and onto the grass. She drove behind the stable and saw the propane tank.

It was about four feet tall, and almost as wide.

"What're you waiting for, girlie?" said Dart, reaching for his revolver.

"Hang on," said Vega. "That's a big tank, Dart."

He squinted. "I thought you needed a big noise."

"I don't think it'll blow just the stable."

"Could blow your car up, too," he said, not sounding entirely opposed to the idea.

"And maybe some people," said Vega. "That may or may not include us."

She heard a faint siren and holstered her gun. Then she peeled out of the field and ran over a line of shrubs, the three horses standing calmly in the field, watching her go.

Vega left Dart in the car on the street. As she came through the door of the antiques shop, with the fungo at her side, she heard the little bell jingle above her head. She made her way to the counter in the back, where Kent leaned on the glass, turning the pages of a magazine.

"Hey," he said, friendly. Then he pointed at her and snapped his fingers. "Remind me of your name."

"Vega."

"That's right. I'm—"

"Kent Gable."

"You got it. Everything okay with the fungo?" he said, his eyes wandering to the bat. Then he grinned and said, "No refunds, I'm afraid."

Vega set the bat down on the glass case. "I don't need the bat anymore. I'd like to trade it."

Kent wrinkled up his eyebrows. "Not in the habit of doing exchanges," he said.

"You have my gun," said Vega.

Kent did his best to seem surprised. "I don't think so," he said. "The only gun I have is a vintage cap gun—a toy. If you're interested?"

"My gun's a Springfield nine-millimeter. Derek Fenton brought it in. He said this place is a cover for a pawn shop."

Kent paused and took a small step away from the counter.

"You're friends with Derek Fenton?"

"Not really," said Vega. "He took that gun from me without my permission."

Vega tapped the bat, and it rolled on the counter toward Kent.

"The bat for my gun, which is registered in my name."

Kent placed a finger on either end of the bat and picked it up, examined the aluminum.

"Looks a little scratched up," he said, scrutinizing her over the rims of his glasses.

"It's gently used," said Vega. "But what's great about it is, it doesn't have a serial number that any law-enforcement agency could use to track its owner. So, even if it came into your possession through an unusual circumstance, you couldn't get fined for it. Unlike a stolen gun. Where I'm from, grand-theft firearm felony is about"—she squinted, pretending to think about it—"ten K or a couple years in state prison. Not sure what it is up here."

Vega leaned her forearms on the counter.

"You can either take your bat back, which will not put you in prison if you get caught selling it, or take your chances with my gun. Which will put you in prison as soon as someone runs the number. Up to you, Kent."

Kent was calm and genuinely seemed to consider his options for a few seconds. Then he pulled the stepladder off the wall and unfolded it, just like he'd done when Vega had come in a few weeks before. Holding the bat in one hand, he climbed the steps of the ladder and placed it on the shelf; the wooden wall mounts were shaped like open pillories, just waiting for the heads.

Vega parked on the road, and she and Dart made their way to the trailers. Josie stood in her green bathrobe, watering the plants on the ground around her door.

"Afternoon," she said to Vega. Then she narrowed her eyes at Dart.

"She don't care for me," said Dart at full volume. "And I don't care for her."

Vega ignored him and said, "Howdy. Nice day, huh?"

"Pretty nice," said Josie.

Vega and Dart walked past the Stargazer, toward the Airstream. Dart started up the steps and pulled a key from a chain around his neck, so small it looked like it would fit a child's diary.

"I'm gonna have a snack," he said, unlocking the door.

"Okay," said Vega. "I don't think anyone saw you back there. At Klimmer's."

Dart coughed and turned his head to the side in the doorway.

"Don't much care if they did," he said. Then he added, "I enjoyed that. You think we can take another drive tomorrow?"

"Sure," said Vega.

He smiled at her, and Vega remembered it was the same smile (charming, devilish) from the last scene from the last episode of his show—after the horse trader's widow gives him a young colt as a thank-you for saving her life.

"You ever think about why you do things?" he asked.

"Not really," said Vega. "I know why I do things."

"Yeah, I used to think I did, too," he said, still smiling at her. He nodded, said, "Afternoon, whoever you are."

Then he shut the door.

15

IT GOT DARK, AND THEY STILL HADN'T COME FOR HER. VEGA SAT IN the Stargazer, sending e-mails, thinking. She stayed awake, and the time in the corner of her laptop screen kept jumping: eleven, twelve, one, two.

She stretched out on the bedroll and shut her eyes for a minute, the Springfield in her right hand. Then she heard them: men's voices. There were flashlight beams, too, crisscrossing outside, shining through the grimy brown window.

She got up, crouching to steer clear of the light, and stood next to the window, her back to the wall. She pulled back the shade an inch and saw them.

Just figures, no faces. Three of them. Whispering but not, their breath visible like smoke. One of them was tall. She could tell by his bulk it was Sheriff Fenton. She tightened her grip on the gun. Talk fast; shoot faster.

Then Vega heard the group move past the Stargazer. She went to the front window, still hunched over, watched them head for Dart's trailer.

Now they were out of her line of sight. She went to the door of the trailer and opened it, nice and slow. She stepped into her boots and down into the mud.

She walked around the Stargazer and let her eyes adjust. The moon was slim and provided little light, but she could see the yellow streams from the flashlights dancing on the Airstream's side. She stayed close to the wall and craned her head around, watching.

Fenton rapped his knuckles on Dart's door.

"Wake up," he said, over and over. "Wake up, wake up."

It took Dart some minutes. Then the door opened, and Fenton shined the flashlight in Dart's face. Dart covered his eyes with his arm and groaned, still half asleep.

Vega walked around the Stargazer, sticking to the wall.

"Where's Alice Vega?" said Fenton.

"Huh?" said Dart.

He seemed genuinely confused; he really did go back and forth, Vega thought, between the two: the roguish cowboy from TV, and the tired old man from real life.

Fenton's buddies each grabbed an arm and began to pull Dart out of the trailer. He made sounds—no words, just calls of alarm.

Vega felt her heart jump around and the very top of her head burn. She held the gun in her right hand, supporting it with her left, and walked forward, swift and silent.

"Where is she?" said Fenton, his voice low and urgent.

"I'm here," Vega said.

Fenton turned in her direction and lifted his gun at the same time. The other two dropped Dart, and he stumbled backward into the Airstream but didn't fall. Then they pointed their guns at Vega, too. That made three guns on her.

She stood still, aiming her shot at Fenton's head.

"You had a full day, Ms. Vega," he said, aiming his shot at her head.

"I like to keep busy."

"Huh," said Fenton. "You want to tell me what's to stop me from putting a bullet through you and the old man right now?"

"Sure," said Vega. "You got a pen? You might want to write this down."

"I have a pretty good memory," said Fenton, keeping the beat. "Try me."

"You're all liars," said Dart.

The thug closest to Dart swung an elbow back into his chest. Dart crumpled again, but still didn't fall to the ground. He coughed, a deep, dry hack that sounded like it had been buried in his lungs a long time.

The burn on the top of Vega's head spread to the back of her neck. She took two short, huffy breaths through her nose.

"Tell them not to do that," said Vega. "Or I'm done talking."

Fenton laughed. "Well, if you're done talking, then we go back to the first arrangement, with you and the old man getting killed right now. And, seeing it's the middle of the night, we can take our time with it, too."

"You do that, you won't have a chance to stop what's about to happen."

"Now, exactly what in the fuck does that mean?" said Fenton, the laugh still in his voice.

"Remember my friend who's a fed?" said Vega. "He's interested in your town, after all."

Fenton was quiet. Vega couldn't make out the expression on his face, but could see his shoulders hunch up a little. Then he turned toward his guys.

"Don't touch him," he said. Then, to Vega: "Talk."

"I have an audio recording of Duane Smith confessing that he, along with your son and Neil Klimmer, assaulted me in a parking lot seven weeks ago.

"I also have PayNow records showing that Neil Klimmer paid people in California and Pennsylvania to vandalize property, which will raise his criminal charges from conspiracy to coercion, bumping up the jail time to years instead of months.

"Then I have some circumstantial evidence that Zeb Williams's body is buried underneath Matt Klimmer's horse stable. Do you want to hear about that, too?"

Now Fenton's shoulders were almost level with his ears, his gun still pointed at her.

"*I* sure would," said Dart, bent over from the hit, his voice hoarse.

The thugs shifted around, too, suddenly uneasy.

"You send all that to your friend the fed?" said Fenton.

"Only some," said Vega. "And he's a steady guy. Not going to jump until I say there's good reason to."

Fenton thought about all of it for a few seconds.

"What do you want?" he said.

"I want to talk alone, me and you," said Vega. "I want to go somewhere else without any firearms pointed at me. I won't point mine anywhere, either, but I want it in my holster while we talk. And I want you and your friends to leave Dart out of it."

Vega wasn't sure if Fenton was going to come back with a junior-high "Why should I?" but thought she'd cut him off before he had the chance. "Alternatively, the fed gets everything—it's set to send from an outside server at five a.m. In about three hours."

"That might happen anyway," said Fenton. "And what's to stop me from finding a way"—he lingered on the thought and then finished it—"to persuade you to cancel the order for the outside server?"

"I guess we'll just have to trust each other for a little while," said Vega. "And hope it works out for the best."

Fenton waved to his guys to lower their weapons, and they did. She saw his shoulders relax, and his arm start to lower as if it were mechanized. Even though she couldn't see his face, Vega knew his expression probably poorly veiled his elaborate fantasies of torturing her. Vega began to lower her arm, too, and thought, Knock yourself out, boss.

A half-hour later, they were sitting at opposite ends of a folding table on the ground floor of the sheriff's station. It was just the two of them in the building. Vega's gun rested in her shoulder holster, and Fenton's sat on his hip.

"When you say 'circumstantial,'" said Fenton, "what does that mean exactly?"

"I have some pieces of information specifically relating to Matt Klimmer's stable. I talked to a nurse at the senior-living facility where Jack Klimmer was admitted right around the time Zeb Williams left town without a word. She said that Jack Klimmer had suffered a head trauma before being admitted, not a stroke."

Fenton sat back in his chair and folded his arms.

"So what?" he said. "One nurse's opinion about something that happened in the eighties—what's that prove?"

"On its own, maybe nothing. But I also talked to Jeff Wall. You ever meet him?"

Fenton shrugged. "Name's familiar. Who's he?"

"A ranch hand at the Klimmers' until Matt fired him one day, out of the blue. Wouldn't let him say goodbye to Jack, wouldn't let him say goodbye to the horses in the stable. Wall said Matt had the stable renovated the morning he left, poured concrete in over the old dirt floor."

"Coincidence," said Fenton, but again, Vega got the feeling he was hearing it all for the first time.

"Sure. The last day Zeb Williams was seen in Ilona, he was arguing with Matt Klimmer in the middle of the street in front of Cara Simms's coffee shop. You and Matt go back a ways, so you probably know how he felt about Cara Simms."

"That was a long time ago," said Fenton. "Matt and Lila been married more than —"

"Thirty years?" said Vega. "Since Zeb Williams disappeared and Matt Klimmer knew he still didn't stand a chance with Cara Simms."

Fenton rubbed his upper lip, like he was brushing a mustache he once had.

"So you think . . ." he began.

"So I think," Vega picked up, "Matt Klimmer was so angry that he killed Zeb. I'm willing to allow for the possibility that it was an accident. I think Jack Klimmer found out or was there to see it. I think Matt buried Zeb's body underneath the stable and beat up his father, made up some story, and paid off the right people at the nursing home to keep Jack there and shut him up. And Jack was either scared or disoriented enough to stay put."

Fenton's hand had migrated to his mouth. His eyes bulged for a moment, though Vega could tell he was still trying to play it cool as he refolded his arms.

"This is crazy," he muttered.

Vega shrugged. "Not really," she said. "Each person is capable of a certain spectrum of things. When you figure out what each spectrum contains, you just have to turn the dial up. Everyone is capable of killing someone; only a certain person with a certain spectrum conceals a body and quarantines the only potential witness, who happens to be his father."

Fenton pointed at her and said, "How would you know what kind of a spectrum Matt Klimmer has? You just got here. I've known him my whole life."

"Yeah, you go way back," said Vega. "I know he's enjoyed a cushy sort of life while you've had to get your hands dirty. Your dad used to have farmland, too, right? Until Matt bought it."

"That was a good deal for my dad," said Fenton. "He needed that money to retire."

"Are you telling me you never wished it was the other way around, that you could just buy up properties like in the Monopoly game? Line up all those little cards?"

"I've been in law enforcement since I was twenty-four," he said, his voice loud but starting to crack.

"Public service," said Vega. "Noble. How about before that, when you were both in high school, and you wrote his papers for English class? Seems strange that he's the one who went straight to UO, while you got stuck going to community college."

"I made it to UO," said Fenton. "Just got my A.A. first."

"Nothing wrong with that," said Vega. "You know Matt Klimmer better than anyone, though. You seem to think it's a stretch that he could do what I suspect him of doing."

"Hell, yes, I think it's a stretch," said Fenton. He moved around in his chair, turned his body sideways, and pointed his whole hand toward Vega, like a karate chop. "What you've presented is barely circumstantial. You got anything else except third-party observations? If that's all it takes to get your fed friend excited, then I would imagine there'd be some kinda appeals process if he took any action."

"He's not excited by it," said Vega. "He asked me to get Joe Lanahan, West Coast head of Liberty Pure, so I did. I got him on audio."

"Lanahan doesn't mean anything to me," said Fenton, petulant.

"No, but Lanahan knows your son and Neil Klimmer, by name at least, knows they're good little Purists, right? If my friend gets Lanahan in a room and has something bigger on him, who knows what Lanahan might say to get out of it?"

Vega watched that land. Fenton scooted backward, the legs of the chair screeching on the floor.

"My boy and Neil—they're just kids fucking around."

"Harassing children and poisoning animals. That's some fucking around."

Fenton made a face like he'd tasted just-turned milk.

"There's no evidence of that."

"Right, but the evidence I do have, the confession plus victim account plus CCTV footage, the assault your boys took part in—of me."

Now the whirlpool began to spin in front of him. His eyes took on a glaze while he thought about it.

"And if there's a way to prove that your son had a hand in paying people in other states to commit any kind of crime, that'll bump up his charges, too."

Fenton came back to attention.

"Derek didn't do any of that," he said with a mix of confidence and pity. "Kid barely makes enough to pay his rent. He's not in the union yet."

"Hope you're sure," said Vega. "Hope Neil Klimmer doesn't decide to share the love when he's interrogated. Seems to be a little bit of a pattern that the Klimmers make the messes, and the Fentons clean them up."

The sheriff sneered but stared at the wall, away from Vega, which told her it was possible he hated the situation more than he hated her, though just for the moment.

"You got what you wanted. We're talking," he said, thumping his chest with his palm and blithely gesturing to her. "What do you want now?" he said, still not meeting her eye.

"Two things," said Vega. Then she hit the table's edge with her fist in the cast, and the table bounced. "Look at me, you fucking lapdog."

Fenton looked at her, shocked.

"Two things," she said again. "First, I want you to open up Klimmer's stable. Take out the concrete floor. I want to be there when you do it. If he's got nothing to hide, fine, you put it back."

"Who's gonna pay for that?" whined Fenton.

"That's a you problem," said Vega. "But it gets done tomorrow." Now she shrugged. "Doesn't matter."

"I can't just show up at his place at eight in the morning with a wrecking ball."

"Sure, you can," said Vega. "Use your son and his crew. I don't care."

Fenton looked like he was about to say something else but stopped. He rested his arms on the table stiffly. Then he said, "What's the second thing?"

"Leave Cara Simms alone. Communicate that to your son and any other alt-right incel bowlcut skinhead conspiracy survivalist paranoid psychos in the area. Okay?"

The sheriff jerked his head up and down in a choppy nod.

"You do those two things," said Vega, "and the only information my friend gets is about Lanahan, and you'll have to take your chances with what he chooses to say or not say about your son. But my friend won't hear anything about the attack in the parking lot."

"Anything else?" said Fenton.

"Nope, I think that's it," said Vega, standing. "I'd get started. If you're going to tear up Klimmer's stable later today, you should probably make some calls."

"All right, now, look," said Fenton, like he was trying to talk her down a few quarters at a garage sale. "Let me have a conversation with Matt first. To explain to him what's happening."

"You do you," said Vega, "he'll try to talk you out of it. He'll say there's nothing under there."

"There'd be a good chance of him being correct," said Fenton, landing hard on the last syllable. "Concrete floor can be better for the horses in the end, though I don't suppose you'd know that."

Vega wasn't certain what he was getting at now. She was pretty certain, though, that his goal was not to flex about his horse expertise.

"I don't know anything about it, actually," she said. "But what I do know is that, if you don't do as I've told you, my friend gets everything on both of your sons."

Vega headed for the door, then turned back to say, "Text my cell when you know the timing. Are we good?"

Fenton looked tired. He had been such a tough guy before, back when he tried to intimidate Vega the day they met in his office. Now he could barely sit up straight; his face was a puffy mess, the skin around his eyes bloating with exhaustion.

"We're good," he said.

Vega smiled before walking out.

"Then get some sleep, Sheriff. You look like hell."

Vega opened her eyes a little after six. She rolled off the mat onto her stomach, pushed up to a plank, then did a Downward Dog. Bounced on the balls of her feet once, twice, and kicked up her legs on the third bounce and folded her right arm across her chest like a Miss America sash.

Her left arm got hot almost immediately, the fingers of her left hand stretched so wide on the floor it felt like the skin would split.

The balance was a challenge, especially when she closed her eyes. The black space of her eyelids disoriented her, made her feel like she was falling even when she wasn't. The air was heavy passing through her nose, pushing out with a buzz, and coming back in with a hum.

As soon as her feet went up and the blood ran toward her head, the thoughts usually skittered and flowed from one thing to another. Not this morning. It was one thought, one thing: Cap, Cap, Cap, like a dripping faucet.

Vega's left arm started to shake. She kicked her legs down and bent her arm, knocked the fist of her cast against her forehead a couple of times.

Then she checked her phone. There was a text from Cartwright the fed at six-twenty-one: "Portland shop picked up Lanahan this morning. Thx." It was now six-thirty-five.

Nothing from Fenton.

Vega got dressed and went outside, walked over to Dart's trailer. She peered in the windows but couldn't see much through the blinds. She pressed her ear to the glass and couldn't hear anything. She stood at the door and thought about knocking, then didn't. Even if there was a small chance she would wake him, she didn't want to take it.

She got in her car and drove to the Klimmers', figured she'd stay across the street from the house and watch and wait. It was almost seven-thirty when she turned onto the Klimmers' road; the house was just coming into view when she heard the siren. Vega recognized the cadence: not police.

Vega pulled over, and the ambulance sped past. She watched it turn right into the Klimmers' driveway and followed it, accelerating.

It was like a curtain drawing back on a stage, foot by foot, as she pulled up. First the newly arrived ambulance, then the first sheriff patrol car, then the second. Then two paramedics wheeling a collapsible gurney. Then the deputy, Rutledge, wearing jeans and a denim jacket with a wool collar—Vega recognized the silhouette from outside Dart's trailer a few hours before. Two other cops, in tan uniforms. Lila Klimmer's Camry with "NAZI MOM" on the hood. Neil's compact with "NAZI." No Range Rover.

And then Lila and Neil themselves, standing in their own driveway but looking lost. Lila wore a robe and sandals, her face streaked with red. Neil stood slumped next to her, leaning on an invisible wall. He saw Vega first and pointed a feeble finger in her direction.

Vega parked behind the patrol car closest to the road, got out, and approached Rutledge, who turned and blocked her, hands out.

"You can't come in here," he said.

"Where's the sheriff?" said Vega under her breath. "He and I had a deal. That's what we talked about when we left the camp last night. You remember?"

Rutledge looked away, unable to admit he'd been there, which, to Vega's mind, was the admission.

"Where is he?" said Vega again. "Where's Klimmer?"

"What's she doing here?" shouted Lila. She turned to Rutledge: "She tried to kill Neil! She did this to the cars. It's because of her that all of this happened!"

She lurched forward like she was going to make a run at Vega, and then Neil pulled her back by the arm.

"What's 'all of this,' Rutledge?" said Vega. "Talk."

He shook his head. He had dark specks on his chin and upper lip where he hadn't shaved. His eyes watered.

"Sheriff's gone."

Vega glanced at Lila.

"He's dead," said Neil.

He didn't seem happy, but he had a strange enthusiasm. It reminded Vega of the way a child would want to be the first to share bad news.

Lila began to sob, pressing the cuffs of her sleeves to her eyes.

"He did it himself," said Rutledge.

Then the paramedics emerged from the front door, one pushing and the other pulling the body in a bag on top of the gurney, a nylon belt strapped across the midpoint.

"Bullshit," said Vega.

"You weren't there," said Neil. "We were there."

"You don't know anything about this!" shouted Lila.

Vega tried to block out her screeching and said to Rutledge, "Did you see the body? Did you take pictures?"

He started to shake his head.

"My dad saw the whole thing," Neil said, somewhat proud.

"Matt laid him out flat and covered him up. To give him some dignity," said Rutledge.

"Is the weapon bagged, at least?" said Vega.

Rutledge nodded.

"It was in Jay's hand," said Neil.

Vega took off across the driveway toward Neil and yelled, "Do you need me to put a fucking extension cord down your throat?"

He backed up into a shrub and fell on the dirt. Lila got between him and Vega and held her hands out like a traffic guard.

"Get away from my son," she said, her skin glossy with sweat and snot.

Vega didn't move, just brought her hands to her sides. She looked at Lila's giant, blurry eyes.

"What happened here?" Vega asked in a near whisper.

Lila shook her head, stricken. The question had disarmed her.

"I don't know," she said. "Jay came over early, said he had to talk to Matt about something urgent, so they went into Matt's office. . . . I was making coffee, and I heard the shot."

"Where's Matt now?" said Vega.

"He was upset," said Lila. "Jay was his best friend." Then she dissolved into tears again.

Vega returned to Rutledge. "Is he still here?" she said, and then, when Rutledge didn't respond right away, she said quickly, "Is Klimmer still here?"

"He took off," said Neil, climbing out of the shrub. "He wanted to be alone."

"You have any idea where he went?" said Vega, looking around. "Any of you?"

Neil shook his head, and Lila still croaked and cried.

Rutledge looked at his hands, which he held out like he'd been grasping something and it had disappeared.

"Did you question him at all? Press him on any details?" said Vega.

"No, I . . ." said Rutledge. "I didn't know . . ."

Vega could see he was not all there; his eyes were taking on a cloudiness.

"I have to leave. Right now, go inside and take some pictures of the scene, okay?" said Vega, keeping her voice low. "Rutledge, you hear me?"

He nodded, a slight movement at first, but then he became more dedicated to the task. He stopped suddenly, however, and asked Vega, "Where are you going?"

"I'm going to get Klimmer," she said.

Rutledge didn't speak, just gave another quick nod and rubbed his bottom lip and chin.

Vega crossed the street to her car and turned her head to take one last look as paramedics slammed and locked the ambulance doors.

Vega found Dart outside the Airstream. He was pacing back and forth, staring at the ground, as if he'd dropped something. He held a carton of blueberries and was eating them one by one.

"There she is," he said when he saw Vega. "The gal who sends pears to heaven."

He didn't smile when he said it, which Vega took to have a meaning, which was that he was less than pleased with her.

"Are you okay?" she said. "Did they hurt you at all?"

"Sheriff's boys?" he said, as if there'd been so many guys who'd pushed him around recently. "Nah. Kinda surprised they didn't arrest me. Maybe he'll come back to finish up the job, though."

"Fenton's not coming back anywhere," said Vega. "He's dead."

Dart looked at her with some skepticism. "He was just here, though," he said. "Can't be dead."

It was always the same, thought Vega. People can't believe it when someone they know dies. It's like they can't fathom that, between the moment they last saw that person and the moment they find out, the person could have been dying, while they've been living their regular lives. Sleeping, drinking chocolate milk, eating blueberries.

"He is," said Vega. "I think Matt Klimmer killed him, but he's telling everyone it's a suicide."

"Suicide?" said Dart, as if the word offended him. "Little Klimmer said that?"

"Yeah."

"That ain't right," said Dart. "Sheriff was a bastard, but that ain't right."

"I agree," said Vega. "I'm going to find Klimmer, though. I think you should come with me."

"You want me to help you find him?" said Dart.

He seemed surprised by the possibility, but also flattered.

"No, I work better by myself," she said. "I'd like to take you somewhere you can be safe."

"I got a lot of firepower in there, I'll have you know," said Dart. He sniffed and stared into the trees.

"Bring all the guns you want," said Vega. "I can take you to the safe house for a while, until I find Klimmer."

Dart slowly headed toward the door of the Airstream. "Is it close?"

"Yeah."

"How long you think it'll take you to find him?"

"Not long," said Vega. "He knows I know everything, and he'll be looking for me. If he ends up here, it won't be good if you're here and I'm not."

Dart thought about it, picked up another blueberry, and popped it into his mouth.

"Just need a few minutes," he said, and headed up the steps to the door.

He went inside and shut the door behind him. Vega looked around at the trees, squinting at the trunks, making sure she wasn't mistaking the movement of low leaf canopies in the breeze for humans trying to camouflage themselves. All she could hear was the drip-drop of water off the leaves onto the mud.

Dart emerged, looking pleased with himself. Vega recognized the cigar box.

"Here," he said, handing it to her.

She opened the box, and there it was: the silver star from his show. She heard the echo of his voice in her head from their first conversation: "Still works, too."

"Turn it over," said Dart.

She flipped the star over in her hands. There was the button; it looked like the knob on a hand-buzzer toy.

"Go ahead," he said. "Press it."

She pressed it. Out fanned the five triangular blades with a snap, in between the star's points. She tapped a blade with her fingertip: not as sharp as she would have liked.

"Can you sharpen these for me?" she asked.

"Well, sure," said Dart. "I'm not given you a second string here."

She tried for a few seconds to remember her favorite line from the show, but she'd been too fuzzy with the painkillers; she couldn't grasp the words now. Something about sleeping under the stars. But because she couldn't recall the line exactly, she didn't want to ruin it. It was enough to hold the thing in her hand and imagine what it could do.

Cara emerged onto her porch as soon as she saw Vega and Dart pulling up in the driveway. Vega got out of the car and jogged up the porch stairs.

"Is that who I think it is?" said Cara.

"It's Dart."

"Wow," said Cara. She sighed and smiled, but also looked worried. "Why are you here?"

"Can he stay here for a few hours?" said Vega.

"Why? What's going on?" said Cara, taken aback, keeping her voice low.

"Sheriff Fenton's dead," said Vega. "Pretty sure Matt Klimmer killed him."

"What?"

"I think Klimmer shot him and tried to pass it off as a suicide." Cara's hand rose to her mouth.

"Now Klimmer's missing," said Vega, turning around to wave Dart inside. "I'm going to find him, but I don't want Dart at his trailer in case Klimmer comes looking for me there."

"What makes you think he won't look for you here?" said Cara.

"It's just not where he'll go first," said Vega.

"But he could," said Cara. "Ethan's upstairs."

Vega stared at the doorway behind Cara. "If I'm thinking like him," she said, "I'd be either hiding or hunting. If I'm hunting, I'd be going to the most likely location of the target, which is not here."

"You're pretty good at thinking like a killer," said Cara.

"Yeah," said Vega. "I appreciate there's still a risk for you." She glanced over her shoulder, saw Dart opening the trunk. "I didn't want to leave him at the most likely location, that's all."

Cara watched Dart over Vega's shoulder, her face softening.

"Sweet and crazy," she said. Then she looked at Vega. "Okay, for now."

Dart was carrying two long canvas duffel bags at his sides.

"How long's he planning to stay?" said Cara. "What's in the bags?"

"His guns."

Cara opened her mouth to say another thing, but stopped when she saw Dart at the foot of the porch stairs, looking up at her.

"Howdy, young lady," he said. "Been some time."

"It has," she said, and then she smiled. "How are you, Dart?"

"I'm old," he said. "You look the exact same, though."

"Like hell I do."

"Come on, now," said Dart. "You look just like Ali McGraw. People still tell you that?"

"No one knows who that is anymore, Dart."

They stared at each other for a moment, and Vega stood there watching them. She thought maybe they were remembering each other the way they used to be back in the day, or they were thinking about their own younger selves. They began to chat again, about the rainfall, their health, Ethan, and the Worm Child.

Vega half listened to them as she texted Rachel: "Hey do you know Klimmer's girlfriend's last name?"

Abby Hatch ran a metaphysical-supplies shop called "Curiosities." "Crystals, candles, and essential oils available," read the Web site text. Vega quickly found out that Abby rented the space from Klimmer, who owned stores on either side as well. The Bastard also sent through Abby's home address; Vega figured she would try there first: the shop appeared to have irregular business hours and was already closed for the day.

The house was downtown, not far from the diner. It was small, one floor, with a pointed roof like a cottage in a fairy tale. There was a narrow porch hung with wind chimes and stained-glass panels. Vega parked on the street; she didn't see Klimmer's Range Rover anywhere.

She stepped onto the porch and knocked on the window of the front door. No one answered, so Vega knocked with the cast on the back of her hand to make more noise. The glass rattled in the door, almost sounded like it could crack if Vega applied just a little more pressure.

Abby Hatch appeared behind the glass and then opened the door right away. She looked to be about Vega's age, but really the first thing Vega noticed was that she looked like a young Cara Simms. Dark eyes and long, straight dark hair. Except Abby wore a long Gypsy skirt with a patchwork design and a frilly crop top, like she was going to a pirate costume party, and Vega couldn't imagine Cara wearing anything like that.

"Hi, do I know you?" she said to Vega.

"Abigail Hatch?" said Vega. She didn't wait for the confirmation, just kept talking: "Your landlord, Klimmer? Killed a person this morning. If you know anything about where he might be hiding out, you should tell me."

Abby retreated half a step back into her house, her hand on the door frame.

"Are you with the police?" she said.

"No," said Vega. "But the next person who comes looking for him will be. And you'll have to make the decision then if it's worth the break on rent to cover up for him."

Now Abby stepped forward in a surge of confrontation.

"I don't get a break on rent," she said.

"All the things you just heard for the first time, the rent's what you focus on?"

Vega leaned in, too, close enough to smell the lavender in Abby's face cream.

"Your landlord is a liar and a killer. I need to find him before he decides anyone else is expendable. Could be you, could be me. If you know where he is, or have any ideas, you should tell me now."

"I don't believe you," Abby said, her voice faltering, stepping back inside.

"Sure, you do," said Vega, sensing the unease in Abby's tone.

"Maybe you know exactly what I'm talking about, because you've seen something, or he said something, and it didn't land quite right with you." Vega took another step forward, so that she was now in the doorway. She leaned on the frame with her casted arm. "But you just ignored it, because it was easier."

"Get out," Abby said weakly. "Get off my property."

"What was it?" said Vega. "He got a little rough one time, and it stopped being fun?"

Abby shut the door briskly, but Vega saw her standing right on the other side, not moving. Still listening.

"And you just kept it to yourself, 'cause that's what girls do. Don't I know it, Abby Hatch." Vega pounded the door with her fist in the cast and watched Abby jump. "You want to wait for him to lose it for real with you?" she said, her voice rising. "You know I'm telling you the future, right? Don't even need tea leaves."

Vega turned around, made it look like she was taking off.

"Wait," said Abby, opening the door. "Could you wait?"

Vega stood at the bottom of the porch steps. Abby retreated inside, and a black-and-white cat appeared in the doorway and stared.

Vega stamped her foot forward in a sucker-jump. The cat bolted inside.

Abby returned, holding an overstuffed black plastic bag. She walked to the edge of the porch, held the bag out by the handles, and offered it to Vega.

"He was here a couple of hours ago," said Abby. "Wearing these."

Vega took the bag and glanced inside. She couldn't see much; the clothes were dark, but there was a sheen to them, and she quickly placed the smell—blood.

"He keeps some clothes here," Abby continued. "He came over and changed and told me to hide those."

"But you're giving them to me," said Vega.

Abby made a humming noise through her teeth as if words were forming but trapped and bouncing around inside her mouth.

Finally, she said, "He was really nice when I first met him."

"Sure," said Vega. "Earlier—he didn't tell you where he was headed?"

Abby shook her head. Vega believed her.

"Thanks for your time, Ms. Hatch."

Vega had again turned to leave when Abby called out to her. "There's something else."

"What's that?"

"He also kept a gun here. And he took it with him."

16

"I'LL BET HE DID," VEGA SAID TO HERSELF ALOUD IN THE CAR.

She headed for the trailers. There were only a few places Klimmer would go with a gun, she figured, and the most likely was to find her. The sun was out, but barely, the downy coverage of rainclouds amassing overhead; it was getting on to five o'clock.

Her phone, sitting in the cup holder, buzzed and sang with a ringtone. Vega glanced at it, saw Cara's name flash across the screen. Vega pulled the phone out of the hole and tapped the speaker.

"Someone just took a shot at the house," said Cara.

"When?"

"Just now, a few minutes ago," said Cara, impatient.

"Anyone hurt?"

"No," she said. "Do you think I'd be this calm if someone was hurt?"

Vega actually did think Cara would be that calm, but didn't say it.

"Where's Ethan?" Vega asked.

"He's in the kitchen," said Cara. "It's as far as you can get from my bedroom without going outside."

"Did you see who fired the shot?" Vega asked.

"No," said Cara, taking short breaths. "It came from the woods on the south side of the house. Hit the windowsill in my bedroom upstairs. Blew half of it right off."

"You see anyone walking around your property since I dropped Dart off?"

"No, what do you think?" said Cara, her voice rising. "You gonna come back here or just keep asking me questions?"

"You call the police?"

"Voice mail kept picking up and transferring me to the sheriff in Ola, but then I hung up after being on hold for a while. Ola's a good forty-five minutes away, anyway." She gasped. "Goddamnit, why'd you have to bring him here?"

Vega felt heat on the back of her neck, climbing up to her scalp like a flame.

"It's not Dart's fault," she said.

"Yeah, no shit, it's not Dart's fault," Cara hissed. Then she laughed and said, "Honey, I don't know you or even like you enough to put my nephew's head on the line for you."

"I understand," said Vega, calm. It was easier to take Cara's aggression head-on than to know it was being aimed at Dart. "You got your gun?"

"In my hand," said Cara. "Dart's got one of his, too. Looks like it should be in a museum."

"I'll be right there. The back door off the kitchen—are there any steps?"

"What?" snapped Cara.

"Steps. I won't take a chance coming through the front door unless you want me to park on your porch."

Cara took a few seconds to think about it.

"No steps in the back," she said. "You can park in the grass—I'll open the door when I see you coming."

Vega took the roads at about forty until she got to Cara's street. She peeled off the driveway and onto the lawn, then around to the back of the house, where she saw the door fly open.

Vega pulled up right next to the door and saw Cara there, holding it open, a slender Ruger in her hand. Vega was familiar with the gun—it was easy to hide and easy to hold. She turned off the engine and opened the car door, almost flush with the back door of the house, and then a shot cut the air, sounded like it was sailing above her.

Cara dropped to a squat and yelled: "Get in here!"

Vega hunched over and ran the two paces from the car into the house, kicking the car door closed as she went. Cara swung the back door shut and sat against the wall.

Ethan, who'd been standing in the kitchen doorway, ran to his aunt and sat with her, burying his head in her blouse.

Dart stood in front of the refrigerator, holding a shotgun about two feet long with engraved plates on the sides of the barrel.

Vega leveled her breath. "Any other shots between the first and that one just now?" she asked the room.

Dart shook his head.

"No," said Cara. "We're not safe here."

"Yeah, you might be right," said Vega, pulling out her phone and pressing a button.

"Might be?"

Vega put the phone to her ear as it started to ring. "Probably," she amended.

Rutledge answered the phone.

"It's Vega. I'm at Cara Simms's place, and one or more people are ambushing her house. Two shots fired."

"Anyone hurt?" Rutledge yelled.

There was background noise—a familiar static, but Vega couldn't place it.

"Not yet, but that seems to be the goal."

"Everyone should vacate the premises until we have time to check it out, but no one can come out there now," said Rutledge, sounding frantic.

"What's going on?"

"There's a fire—right in the office. FD from Ola had to come over. It's not out yet—they think maybe an explosive device."

He paused to cough. Vega looked at Dart, Cara, Ethan, all of them watching her intently. Suddenly she understood everything.

"All right. Please send someone as soon as you can," she said to Rutledge, then hung up.

"Who was that?" said Cara.

"No one's coming. There's a fire at the sheriff's office."

"No one's coming?" said Cara, gawking at her. She reached for her phone on the table. "I got some friends—I can tell them to arm up and come over."

"Think about that," said Vega. "That shot was a few feet above my car. Didn't miss by much."

She watched Cara soak that up.

"What the hell are we supposed to do?" Cara said, looking sick.

"I got the living-room windows," Dart offered, lifting his rifle.

"Don't go near any windows just yet," said Vega, trying to think. She looked at Cara. "Where's your room—where the shot hit?"

"Upstairs," said Cara. "End of the hall on your right. They hit the sill below the window on the right."

Vega left them in the kitchen and ran up the stairs, followed Cara's directions.

The room was cluttered but clean. A desk, a dresser, a vanity, each surface covered with office supplies, neat stacks of paper, small bottles, and cosmetics, everything in its own spot. Two windows on the far wall.

Vega went around the bed and stood with her back against the wall, next to the window on the right. She leaned over just a bit to see the view: the field ended abruptly where the woods began, maybe a couple hundred feet from where Vega's car was parked at the back door. Vega thought about the layout of the house and determined that the kitchen was directly underneath her. She left the room, headed back down the stairs.

Ethan and Dart sat at the table, sharing a bowl of Goldfish crackers. Ethan's hands shook so hard he kept dropping the little fish in his lap. Cara was leaning back against the wall, holding her gun at her side.

"What direction is this?" said Vega, pointing toward the back door.

Cara considered it and said, "South. Front of the house faces north."

"So shooter's in that part of the woods," Vega said, pointing toward it.

"Yeah, that makes sense."

Vega regarded the males at the table. Dart was listening to her, his hand wrapped around the barrel as if the rifle were a staff. Ethan had quit trying with the crackers and was now swiping on his phone.

"Ethan, who are you texting?" demanded Cara.

"Jake."

"Stop it," said Cara. "Don't text anyone right now." She glanced at Vega. "We don't want to have Jake talking to his parents and coming over here, getting themselves hurt."

Ethan set the phone down, dispirited.

"Can you show me the view from the living room?" Vega said, rolling her eyes to the side. Let's talk.

"Sure," said Cara, picking up the hint. "Eeth, you can play Roblox if you want."

Ethan nodded as if it were only for Cara's benefit: not a lot of energy.

"What's that?" said Dart to the boy, pointing at the phone.

"Roblox?" said Ethan.

"Roadblocks—what is that?"

"It's a game."

"Ethan, show him the Wild West one," said Cara. "He'll get a kick out of it."

Ethan nodded, happier. He leaned over and showed the screen to Dart. Dart squinted. Vega was about 80 percent sure that all he could see were floating blotches, but he made a decent performance of it for the boy.

Vega and Cara left the room and paused at the bottom of the stairs.

"I've thought about the options," said Vega. "I think I should go into the woods through your back field and try to find them."

"You don't how many people are out there," Cara said, pointing outside. "And it's getting dark—you won't even be able to see them."

"They won't be able to see me, either."

"What if they kill you, huh? And then come for us?"

"They don't know want you," said Vega. "They want me. They may not even want to kill me, but they want to scare me, make me beg for my life, that kind of stuff. You three aren't the targets. But if you get in the way, I don't think they'll wrestle with their choices too much."

"You know who they are?" said Cara.

"I have an idea," said Vega, standing up again. "I think they set that fire at the sheriff's to tie up the resources.

"Whatever happens, I'll distract them for a while and run out the clock until Rutledge can get here. We're talking twenty, thirty minutes. After that, the police aren't here, I'm not here, you call everyone you know. Or, better yet, get in my car and go," said Vega, handing her the key fob. "It's still a chance, but smaller than trying to get to your car."

"How in hell are you planning to get to those woods without them seeing you?" Cara asked.

"Back door, under my car, crawl through the grass."

Cara stared at her. "You're smart, but you don't always have the best ideas," she said, with a notable degree of kindness.

Vega didn't smile but said, "You are not the first person to say so."

"Nice night for a walk," said Dart, flashing a smile.

He'd been listening from the kitchen doorway, still holding the shotgun, his hand resting on the stock, muzzle on the floor, like it was a cane in a tap routine.

When Cara saw Vega considering it, she said, "Well? Tell him it's a shitty idea already." Then Cara addressed Dart, losing her patience: "This isn't a show, Dart. That's a real bullet that hit," she said, nodding upstairs. Then she pointed behind her, toward the woods, and added—quieter, so Ethan wouldn't hear—"Those aren't extras out there trying to kill us."

Dart seemed only a little daunted by the comments. He blinked innocently and looked to Vega.

"She's right, but I could still use your help," said Vega. Then she said to Cara, "You got any fruit about to turn?"

A half-hour later, it was darker, a light rain hitting the windows. Ethan peered out between the curtains on the living-room window through binoculars. Cara carried a bowl with half a cantaloupe and five apples.

"Which room is right above the porch?" asked Vega.

"It's mine," said Ethan.

Cara nodded, confirming.

"The fruit will be flying, clay-pigeon-style, right there in the driveway," Vega explained to Dart.

"Where am I shooting from?" said Dart.

"Right here," said Vega, facing the front door. "Door will be open. Porch lights on. We'll cut the lights on the south side of the house," she said to Cara. "Your bedroom, above the back door—whatever light sources face that direction that you can turn off, turn them off."

"Yeah," said Cara, starting to understand.

"North side of the house—the north half of the living room, this hallway, porch light, Ethan's room—lights on, all of them. You toss the fruit from Ethan's window. Underhand, aim for the roof of your car."

"Can I take a shot?" said Ethan.

"No," said Cara, stern.

"Look here," said Dart to Vega. "I haven't hit a moving target in a while."

"You don't have to hit them," said Vega. "Just try. And when there's no more fruit, keep loading rounds and shooting. How many you got?"

"I got a box of twenty."

"Fire them all."

"He doesn't have to hit the fruit?" asked Ethan.

"No," Cara answered, looking at Vega. "It's just for the distraction."

"That's right," said Vega. "Lights, noise, maybe exploding fruit. We don't know exactly what they'll be able to see or hear, but we want to pull their attention here," she said, pointing to the porch. "For a few minutes."

Cara produced a small flashlight from the back pocket of her jeans, handed it to Vega.

"Batteries are new," she said. "Supposed to have a five-mile beam, but I've never measured."

"Thanks."

Vega took one last look at them. Dart hoisted his rifle onto his shoulder, his finger looped through the trigger guard, a glint of liveliness in his eyes.

Ethan leaned against Cara, his head against her chest, her hand patting his hair. Cara still held her gun and watched Vega, but didn't seem lit up with panic and anger like she had earlier. Vega actually recognized her expression; she had seen people look at her this way before. A little pity, but acknowledgment of agency. Also known as: It's your funeral.

Vega caught sight of herself in a small round mirror next to the front door. She wasn't sure if it was the lighting or what, but she thought she looked a lot like a ghost, her skin pale against the black clothes. She opened her mouth and touched her new tooth with her tongue. Not a ghost.

· · ·

Vega opened the back door a few inches, squatted in the dark, and waited.

Then came the blistering sound of Dart's first shot.

She opened the back door a few inches more, got on all fours, and then flattened her body as she slid underneath her car. The grass was wet, soaking her clothes; her head rested alongside the muffler.

She heard the rain; she heard the water dripping from the car's undercarriage onto the grass and onto her; she heard her own breath.

Then she heard the second shot.

She took off in an army crawl, only her hands and feet touching the ground, her body in a plank. The grass slowed her down, the wet blades like sand as she grabbed handfuls, her feet sinking at every step.

Third shot.

Vega bent her knees so she could get some speed. Now only her fingertips were touching the ground, her legs in a squat, almost running. She was halfway to the trees, rain in her eyes.

Fourth shot.

As she reached the trees, she pulled the Springfield from its holster and crawled, three-legged-dog-style the last few feet. Finally, she stood and rushed into the woods.

There was more visibility than she would have guessed; the trees were not as dense as they seemed from far away. She waited until she heard the next shot before moving closer to where she thought the shooter might be, with a direct line of sight to the porch, where Dart was blowing the fruit away.

Another shot.

Vega walked quickly, her boots sloshing around in the mud. As the bullet's echo faded, she stood with her back against a tree and tried to listen for any sound of movement, but the rain swallowed everything. The trees drooped and barely shook their branches when the wind blew, like they were breathing with wet, heavy lungs.

Another shot.

She stepped from trunk to trunk until she could see the light from the porch, thought she could even smell the shotshell powder from Dart's gun for a second.

She was a few yards back from the woods' edge, her eyes scanning the trees, the ground, looking for anything: a cloud of breath, a flash of color from a sneaker, a pale face floating in the darkness.

She moved in the direction of where the trees met the field, both hands on the grip of the Springfield. The rain had drenched her clothes, soaked through to her underwear and bra. It dripped off her nose and chin and into her eyes, so she kept blinking.

Then something hit her in the head; the trees in front of her shook. She stumbled a couple of steps and fell to her knees, trying to hold on to the Springfield, but her cast was slick, and the pistol dropped to the ground.

Another shot came from Dart at the house.

Vega saw double, then triple, her vision gone kaleidoscopic from the rain and the bump that pulsed and pounded on the back of her head. She saw her gun a few inches away and reached for it with both hands. Her fingertips grazed the nose of the Springfield when an arm slid quickly around her neck, choking her.

Then she was lifted up to standing, the gun still in the mud.

Another arm snaked around her chest, right below her breasts, and now she was almost entirely off the ground, the tips of her boots scraping against wet leaves. She sniffed small breaths through her nose and hooked her fingers into the guy's forearm, tried to peel it off her. She blinked more rain away and saw all the tattoos on the arm around her waist, especially the fist in the middle.

"Alice Vega—that's you, right?" said Cooper into her ear.

Vega tried to get a straw's worth of air, anything, but she knew she was going to pass out soon.

She removed her right hand from Cooper's choking arm and scratched at the arm around her torso.

"You have no idea what I'm going to do to you," he said, his voice cracking. "I'm gonna make sure you don't pull this catfish shit with anyone else, you understand?"

Vega's shirt had hiked up, leaving her belly exposed, and she reached behind her belt buckle to where she'd tucked Dart's silver star.

"Goddamnit," he cried, sounding hurt. "You did this to yourself, you know? All of this, what's going to happen—what I'm gonna do to your face and your body. It's going to end with me killing you, because you have backed me into that corner, Bitsy." He screamed, a desperate sound. Then he continued: "Alice, whatever the fuck. You had Lanahan put away, and it's my fault, because I believed you. Because I listened to my dick."

It was going dark for Vega. She heard another shot from Dart, but it was muffled, like he was firing through a pillow. She swiped her thumb over the back of the silver star and felt the small button, pressed it. Cooper twitched and loosened his grip at the sound, confused, and Vega swung her arm down and backward, slamming the blades of the star into his thigh. He grunted and dropped her so her feet could touch the ground, his arms still around her. Vega gulped some air and saw July Fourth sparklers spraying in the corners of her eyes.

She gripped the star tightly in her hand, the cast blocking the blades from her palm, then swung her hand up behind her head and felt it land in Cooper's face.

Now he screamed and let go of her. Vega landed on her knees in the mud, inhaling audibly, her throat burning. She grabbed the Springfield and stood, vision fuzzy, head throbbing.

His face was dented like an old Halloween pumpkin, the star planted between the bridge of his nose and the corner of his eye. Cooper batted at the star and then grabbed it with both hands, yanked it out, dropped it. Blood gushed in a sheet over his left cheek; his expression was blank.

It was the natural thing to do. Foreign object inside a body—the body wants it out. But Vega knew it wasn't always the best idea, especially with something sharp.

Cooper wiped the blood off his face, but more kept coming. He stumbled backward, turning his head one way and then the other. Looking for something. Then Vega saw it—a deer-hunting rifle with a scope, leaning against a tree.

"Cooper!" Vega tried to shout, but her throat was too raw. It came out a hoarse whisper.

She advanced toward him, kept the Springfield pointed at his torso. Her head still pounded, basketballs off the backboard of her skull, but her vision had come back to normal—only one of everything.

Cooper stood still, his balance wobbly. He pointed at Vega.

"You don't stop being a bitch, do you?"

"Nope," said Vega, her voice scratchy but audible.

The blood continued to rush down his face, but he no longer attempted to wipe it away. It spilled over his lips, and then his chin.

"You were real, you know, even though you're supposed to be a liar, I think you were real with me."

"I lied to you, Cooper," said Vega. "All I did was lie."

He coughed out a laugh, blood spraying from his mouth.

"Nah," he said, shaking his head. "You felt a thing so deep down you maybe forgot who was Bitsy and who was . . . Alice for a minute." He held his hand to his head, like he had a migraine coming on. "You gotta kill that part of yourself if you want to pretend it's not there."

Then she shot him twice in the chest, and he fell backward, landed flat on the ground with his head at the base of the tree, knocking the rifle over. He didn't reach for it. He didn't move at all.

Vega's breath was dust in her throat. She approached Cooper and squatted and shined the flashlight on his face. Blood poured sideways out of the gash down over his eye, the rain washing it into the mud. Both of his eyes were open, even the one that was punctured. He was dead.

Vega grabbed the rifle by the barrel and stood up. She holstered the Springfield and shined the flashlight on the ground where he'd choked her, saw the flash of silver. She picked up Dart's star, brushed off the blood and the mud, pressed the button twice to retract the blades, and tucked it behind her belt buckle.

She could still see the lights of Cara's house and hear the blast and echo of Dart's shots, but they seemed far away, and for a second she thought maybe she'd never make it back.

All the lights were on at Cara's place when the cops and two sets of paramedics got there. The house glowed in the middle of the field.

The paramedics scooped up Cooper from the woods, put him in a bag, and rolled him in a gurney across the grass from the field to the house.

Sheriff Packwood from Ola took Vega's statement while his deputies interviewed Cara and Dart on the porch.

Vega was only half listening to Packwood. He seemed to move

slowly anyway, so it wasn't difficult to follow him. He was in his fifties, with a cowl of flesh underneath his chin and a chronic wet cough.

Vega looked up at the clouds, the color of dark smoke. No stars. The rain had calmed to a drizzle, and the air was humid.

Sheriff Packwood perched on the rear fender of his cruiser, taking notes with a ballpoint pen and a steno pad, pausing to dab the tip of the pen on his tongue.

"After you stabbed him with the star, he let go of his hold on you," said Packwood, reviewing his notes.

"Yes," said Vega, standing in front of him.

"And you fell to the ground?"

"Yes."

Packwood puffed out his cheeks with air as he looked at his notes and coughed. "Then you picked up your weapon—"

"No," Vega said.

Packwood glanced up at her.

"He pulled the star out of his face. Then I picked up my weapon."

"Then he took a run at you," said Packwood, pointing the pen at her.

"Yes."

"And that's when you fired the shots."

"The first shot," corrected Vega. "It only set him back a second, and then he kept coming."

"And you fired the second shot."

"Yes," she said, without pausing.

Packwood stared at his notes, blew out some air, coughed again. It became clear he didn't have any more questions, so Vega thought she'd ask hers. "They put the fire out at the sheriff's place?"

Packwood glanced up at her, confused. Then he caught up.

"FD got it out, but took them a minute," he said. "Explosive from a cherry-bomb firework and all-purpose antibacterial cleaning fluid. Old building. I got a guy there to monitor, because those things are tricky—you think they're out, but all it takes is one teensy spark on those old wires in the walls and there she goes again.

"You think that he"—Packwood turned his head in the direction of the ambulance, then consulted his notes and—"Edward Cooper—he was responsible for that device."

"I do."

"What makes you say that?"

"He used to make explosives out of fireworks," said Vega. "When he was a kid."

Packwood returned his gaze to his notes with a pleased expression. A one-man show made his job easy.

After a couple of minutes, Vega said, "Am I free to go, Sheriff?"

"Yeah, Jesus, I'm sorry," he said. Then he yawned, which made him cough again. "I'll write all this up tomorrow. The county DA might have a question or two for you, but this all seems straightforward to me. I got your phone number, right?"

It took him another couple of minutes to make sure he had her number; then he told her he didn't have any more questions. They said thank you to each other, and Vega stepped around the mangled cantaloupe in the driveway and stood at the bottom of the porch steps while Packwood's deputy finished up with Cara and Dart.

Cara took the deputy inside to show him the where the first bullet had hit the windowsill, leaving Vega and Dart alone.

"Cantaloupe was a good shot," said Vega.

Dart waved her away. "Fair, at best," he said. "That and one lousy apple."

"Thanks for your help, Dart."

Dart looked away from her, either embarrassed or dismissive of her gratitude, or both. Then he smiled, his eyes heavy.

"Cara's a good woman," he said. "And the boy is smart. If I'd met a woman like her a long time ago, who knows." He rubbed his chin and turned his head to stare at the woods. "I was an ass when I was young."

Cara and the deputy came out of the house, and the deputy pulled Dart aside to ask some more questions. Vega nodded at Cara.

"Where's Ethan?"

"He's getting his toothbrush," said Cara. "We'll stay at the motel for a couple nights. I'll cover a room for Dart." Cara tugged her sweater tightly around her. "What about you?"

Vega shrugged, said, "I'll go back to the trailer for now."

"Be careful," said Cara, sounding annoyed.

"I will."

Cara rolled her eyes. "No, you won't."

. . .

It was midnight by the time Vega got to the trailers.

She parked and got out, pulled her Springfield as she approached the Stargazer. The lights above the doors of the four trailers in the square surrounding the fire pit were on but dim.

Vega walked the perimeter of the Stargazer. She pulled Cara's flashlight from her pocket, clicked it on, stuck it in her mouth, and shined it into the woods. Then over to Dart's Airstream, then back to the Stargazer. She opened the door, flipped the lights inside, looked around. The place was so small, there was nowhere to hide.

She closed and locked the door behind her, kept the gun in her hand.

She examined her face in the grimy-edged mirror the size of a postcard over the Doll Dreamhouse–sized sink. She saw that Cooper's blood had landed in a mist in her hair and on her face, all mixed up with the rain and mud. She saw the skin-burn ring around her neck. Her throat was still charred inside; she hummed and put two fingers to her neck to feel the tremor. Then her eyes began to water, and she hacked dry coughs for a minute.

When she stopped coughing, and stopped looking at herself in the mirror, she stood there in her wet, bloody, mud-covered clothes, holding her gun, for some period of time.

Finally, she set the Springfield down on the bedroll, undressed, and took a shower. She got out and dried off, put on a tank top and yoga shorts, brushed her teeth as if she were getting ready for bed.

She turned off the lights and lay down on the bedroll, placing the Springfield on the ground next to her hip. She listened to the rain, because there was nothing else to listen to. It took on different rhythms as the hours passed. Fast, light, steady showers; heavy sheets that shook the Stargazer; and then, eventually, sporadic drops that landed with plinks on the windows, sounding a little bit like a slow heartbeat, Vega thought as she finally went down. Not hers, but someone's.

17

CAP LANDED IN PORTLAND AROUND ELEVEN AT NIGHT, AFTER TAK-
ing an evening flight out of Newark.

For a couple of days since Nell's drift race, he'd waited, thought about things, wrote Vega fifty-seven texts and deleted them all, considered calling her and practiced what he would say, in the mirror, and in the car, and to the boiler. Nell had been at Jules's and would send a text now and then like a concerned guidance counselor: "Have you given any thought to what we talked about the other night??"

"Yes, Dr.," he wrote back, leaving out the part about confessing his feelings to the boiler.

Then he'd been shaving and cut himself, near his ear, along the jaw. He'd wiped the blood away—there hadn't been much—and he'd found himself looking at the ridge on his busted ear, then the circular scar on his forehead, and thought about how familiar they were to him now, just regular parts of his body. Sure, if he had to choose between being voluntarily maimed and not, he'd likely choose not, and wasn't that normal? But wasn't it also normal to choose to be with someone even if there was a degree of risk? Granted, for most people in relationships, the risk was more along the lines of "I might get my feelings hurt if this person doesn't call me back," not "Many people want to kill this person, and if I hang out with her, they may want to kill me as well." Looking at the dot of blood near his ear, he just didn't think he cared anymore.

He'd told Vera he needed to take some vacation days for a family matter, without elaborating, and had booked a flight for that night.

Now he rented a car and checked into a hotel near the airport. Just get some sleep, wake up early, and text her, he thought as he lay in the hotel bed, sinking into the memory foam. Between the rain on the window, the hum of the heating unit in the corner of the room, and the faint recollection of a thing on TV when someone went into a hotel room and shined a black light everywhere, revealing a seemingly disproportionate amount of fluids and stains, he couldn't sleep.

He kicked the covers off and got out of bed. He took a shower and got dressed and checked out of the hotel, stopped at a twenty-four-hour drive-thru for a large coffee with extra cream and sugar, and then headed for the interstate.

He was tired but awake, the jet lag weighty in his extremities and behind his eyes. He drank the coffee in hearty sips and did his best to shove off the exhaustion.

He thought again about texting Vega. It was almost four in the morning now, and he knew she'd be awake soon, if she wasn't already. But he didn't reach for his phone, just kept driving. All he had to do was see her. He was doing his best not to overthink things.

It was challenging for him.

He drove through Eugene and kept heading south, toward the border, where the GPS told him to go. The sun wasn't rising yet, but the sky was beginning to grow lighter, gray with the rain clouds.

He followed the directions to Ilona from the interstate, and then drove to the center of town and parked in front of a diner. He got out of the car and stretched his arms up, started to walk.

He could just show up, find the trailers where she'd said she was staying. It was such a small town—he could ask the first person he saw, whenever such a person showed up. Cap knew he could text her at any time, but he wasn't ready yet. He just needed to walk and smell some of the air, which was lovely. Campfire smoke and sap and flowers. He coughed, his throat scratchy. He wondered if Oregon would be a place he'd be allergic to.

The street was unpaved, with two concrete strips on either side in front of the businesses. Hardware, antiques, liquor. Cap hadn't seen any people yet, and that was a little weird. He'd been through plenty of small towns in Pennsylvania—from a census perspective, he resided in one of them—and even this early in the morning there were always some stragglers. Old folks, dog walkers. Ilona felt downright ghostly. Twilight Zone time.

Then he saw an unusual thing, the reason for his sudden onset of allergies. It was an old brick building, all of the ground-floor windows and the front door blown out, the edges of the door frame blackened with ash. The smell of smoke hung in the air, and Cap knew that, the longer he stood there, the more he would smell like a cashed-out charcoal barbecue. Smoke from a house fire sank its fingernails in and didn't let go. Easier to get rid of the clothes and get a haircut.

There was a young cop wearing a tan uniform sitting in the front seat of a sheriff cruiser, holding his phone about four inches away from his face and texting with his thumbs. He didn't seem to notice Cap at all until Cap knocked on his window.

The cop jumped in his seat, then powered the window down.

"Hi there," said Cap.

"You need help with something?" said the cop.

"Just directions," said Cap. "Is there a trailer park around here?"

"Yeah," said the cop. "Past the I-PUD, on the left."

"Thanks," said Cap. "What's an I-PUD, again?"

"Public Utility."

"Right," said Cap. Then he nodded toward the building. "Looks like some fire."

"Ground floor's trashed," said the cop, yawning. "Offices upstairs are okay. Nobody hurt."

"That's good to hear," said Cap. "Is it a bank?"

The cop looked at him, a little amused, a little annoyed.

"Sheriff station."

"No kidding," said Cap. "You get the guy who did it?"

"Think so," said the cop.

"Glad to hear it," said Cap, polite. "Thanks for your help."

The cop nodded and powered his window up.

Cap took one last look at the building and then went back to his car. The sun was definitely sneaking up now, the sky much lighter than before. Before he opened the car door, he looked around and saw the tall trees against the gray sky and said aloud, "Beautiful."

Vega awoke with a jump and sat straight up, grabbing the Springfield.

She aimed the gun at the door and didn't move for a minute,

then glanced around the room, which was just as she'd left it when she'd gone to sleep. She lowered the gun only a couple of inches, kept the muscles in her arms active as she stood.

She crossed to the front window and peered outside. The sun was coming up. There were some birds peeping and cheeping, too, but they weren't what had woken her up. Her dreams had been choppy and devoid of sound; she was almost sure there'd been a noise.

She slid her feet into her boots and stood behind the door, then opened it a sliver. Then a little more, and then all the way.

The camp was quiet, no sign of the neighbors. Josie still had the TV on in the trailer across from her, but Vega couldn't be sure if she was awake or asleep in there. Vega had yet to see the couple or the guy in the two other trailers Jason had described.

Vega stepped out of the Stargazer and left the door open. She heard water drizzling out of the trees onto the ground, left over from the rain. She walked around the Stargazer, pausing every couple of feet to fix her eyes in the woods and look for movement. Then she walked around the other trailers in the square, stepping soft, and then over to Dart's place.

She walked around the Airstream once and peered inside one of the curved winged windows on the rear of the trailer. She saw Dart's bed, the mini-fridge, the filing cabinet where he kept all of his pictures and the silver star when it wasn't on loan.

Vega returned to the Stargazer and sat on the crate by the door. She thought about Dart's saying he used to think he knew why he did things.

Then she tried to send a message to Rutledge, asking if Klimmer had turned up yet, but her phone was slow. The home button didn't sense her thumb, and then compensated suddenly, so that the screen bounced from the home screen to the "touch ID" prompt to arbitrary-app-opening. Vega shook the device and watched drops sprinkle from it. Water damage. She turned it off, tucked it into her shorts against the small of her back.

What was Klimmer waiting for? She tried to think like him, go through his motions; she figured he must know his time was up. She knew she was smarter than him, but if it were her, if she'd made the shoddy mistakes he had, if she got trapped in the room Klimmer had locked himself into, she'd find the window with a crack in it.

She glanced at the space under the Stargazer, about a foot. If she was underneath, she could take the first shot if someone tracked her here—knees, shins, feet.

She crawled backward under the trailer, then let her body drop onto the mud. She propped herself up on her elbows and aimed the Springfield straight ahead.

It was hard to keep steady aim; the mud was too deep and wet, and Vega kept adjusting her arms, scrabbling forward every few minutes with her feet. It was like she was sinking. At some point, she decided to lie there with her arms and legs outstretched, cheek on the ground. And wait.

Cap drove down empty roads, still feeling the smoke in his sinuses. He came to the building with a sign out front reading "Ilona Public Utility Department."

"I-PUD," he said.

He took a left, and didn't see trailers or vehicles of any kind at first, so drove about a quarter-mile and then saw a cluster of parked cars in a clearing near the road.

He parked and got out. The sky was overcast now, still cloudy but bright white. As he passed the cars in the clearing, he noticed that one of them had California plates.

He walked toward the trailers, four in a square, and he thought about what he'd say to Vega when he saw her: "I'm here about the ad for a partner"? Then he got embarrassed for even thinking about making such a dumb joke. Vega didn't have any use for cute.

He heard Nell's voice telling him just to say how he felt, that women really do like that, but Cap wasn't sure: "Look, Vega, I know you don't want me here, but I needed to see you and be in front of you, and if you tell me to leave, I'll leave. Also, I've been having stomach pains like there's one of those claw machines in my abdomen, but instead of grabbing toys, it's scratching at my stomach lining. I think if I help you work this case they'll go away and maybe I'll sleep for eight hours again. And I am worried about you. Because that's what people do—they worry about each other." Worth a shot, right?

The glare from the sky made Cap's eyes water; he wished he'd brought sunglasses. It reminded him of driving in a winter storm, with the sun reflecting off the snow, off the sky, off the hood and mirrors. "Snow-blind" was the phrase.

Vega had called the trailer by a specific name, a brand name. It wasn't Snowblinder, was it? It had to be one of the four that made up the square, not the rusted bullet of an Airstream twenty yards behind the main camp, he figured.

As he got closer he sped up—he knew exactly what he'd say, after she opened the door and was surprised and maybe pissed or maybe happy to see him.

He walked to a burnt brown trash can in the middle of the camp and glanced at the four trailers. Then his eye stuck to the name of the small one like a fly on a strip. Stargazer. She should be in there, he thought. It's almost six. She's probably already done the handstand and everything.

He tried not to smile.

He came to the door and had raised his fist to knock when he saw something in the lower periphery of his eyesight. He didn't quite jump, but took a big step back, thinking: Raccoon, snake? What did they have out here? Then he saw it was the hand of someone lying down underneath the Stargazer. Cap put his hand on his gun in its holster but then froze, because then he saw another hand, in a cast stretching out in the dirt, holding a Springfield pistol.

Vega crawled on her belly out from under the Stargazer and stood up. She wasn't wearing a lot of clothes, the entire front of her was covered in mud, and she smelled a little like shit.

"Caplan?" she said, her voice hoarse.

"Hell of a welcome wagon, Vega," he said, laughing. He was so relieved and glad to see her, he forgot about his monologue for a second, but then he remembered: "Look, I know you said—"

She went right to him and hooked her left arm around his neck to pull him in tight, her right arm still at her side holding the gun. Cap stopped talking and wrapped his arms around her waist, squeezing her. He could hear her breathing through her mouth—a raspy hiss. She pressed her cheek against his chin and neck, and he could feel the mud from her face wet on his skin.

Then she kissed him, the fingers of her non-gun-holding hand tangled up in his hair. She pulled away, pressed her forehead to his.

"You're here," she said.

"I'm here."

"What I said before about it won't be you who checks on me—I didn't mean it. I meant it right then, but I don't mean it."

She whispered it all quickly in one breath, and he could barely hear her. Her skin was ice cold, and her shoulders shuddered. He wondered how long she'd been hiding in the mud.

"It's okay," he said. "It's all right."

They stayed there for a couple of minutes, and then the door to the trailer opposite the Stargazer opened up, and an older lady in a green bathrobe leaned her head out.

"What the fuck, you fuckers?" she said.

"Morning," Cap said to her.

Vega unhooked her arm from Cap's neck and took a small step back.

"Let's go in," she said.

"Okay."

"Bitsy, what happened to you?" said the woman.

"Tripped and fell," said Vega.

"You're what they call accident-prone," said the woman, then went back inside and pulled her door shut.

"Bitsy?" said Cap.

Vega shrugged and opened the door to the Stargazer, held it open for Cap.

He stepped inside and looked around.

"This is . . . just awful, Vega. Why not a hotel? Don't you have the Best Western points?"

"Long story," she said, setting the Springfield down on the edge of the sink.

"Hey, do you have allergies? You sound scratchy."

She lifted her head and scraped the mud off her neck, so he could see the red skin-burn.

"What happened to you?" he said, a bit urgent.

"I'll tell you later," she said, connecting her phone to a cable plugged into a socket above the sink.

"Tell me now," he said. "Did someone try to choke you?"

Vega nodded and slid her boots off her feet.

"Who? Who did that? Was it those kids again? Or that guy— what's his name, Klimmer?" Cap said, getting excited.

She shook her head. Then she pulled off her tank top and tossed it to a corner. Her being half naked shut Cap up for a minute. She grabbed a towel and brushed the bulk of the mud off her arms and legs. Cap sat on a folding chair, watched her as she got dressed.

She told him about Klimmer and Fenton, Lanahan, and then what had happened at Cara's place and the woods. She got to the point when she'd stabbed Cooper in the eye with the star. "He dropped me."

"Could you breathe? Could you see?" said Cap, concerned, as if he didn't know the ending.

"Not really," said Vega. "I felt around for the Springfield. And all this blood was pouring down from his eye, I could see that. . . ."

She had been ready to tell Cap the whole thing. But now, with him sitting a few feet away, her skin still humming from his hands, on her fingers the salty smell of his hair, like he'd just been dunked in the Pacific, she couldn't imagine its all going away again. She touched the new tooth with her tongue. Alive. Not a ghost.

"He just pulled the star out of his face and came at me, so I fired. Twice."

Cap's eyes narrowed, and then widened again. He gave the smallest nod.

"He died," said Cap.

"He did."

"Good," he said. "He would've killed you if he could have."

"Yeah," she said, but there was something unconvinced in her voice.

"Vega," said Cap, "he was a white-nationalist soldier. They're all crazy. Ready for the race war and all that shit. And I bet a buck something speedy will turn up in his toxics, for him to come at you with an injury like that. If you were the sort of person who slept, I'd tell you not to lose sleep over it," he said, and he smiled at her.

"I won't. Also, I kissed him," she said, sliding her shoulder holster over her arms.

"Uh, sorry?"

"I kissed him. I was pretending to be Bitsy." Vega registered Cap's shock and became impatient. "Don't be weird about it."

"I'm not weird," Cap said. "I'm just going to find a way to bring up every day how you once kissed a Nazi."

He crossed the few feet that separated them and touched the burn on her neck with two fingers.

"Hurt?"

"No."

"Liar."

She took his hand and pressed her lips against his palm. Not kissing, just parking them there. Cap lost his breath for a second.

"We're not exactly ready for Klimmer if he shows up right now," he said. "You think he ran?"

"I don't know. I thought he'd be coming for me here, but if he is, he's taking his time."

"What do you want to do?"

"I want to park across the street from his place and wait for him. He's got to turn up there at some point."

"Then let's go," Cap said. "But give me a minute—you got a bathroom in this place?"

Vega pointed him to the door and picked up her phone. Rachel had sent a text—the time stamp indicated the night before, but it was just coming through now, and it was only a collection of letters: "t' ni me ne."

Vega tried to text her the word "test," but only the "s" worked. She hit "send" to see if it would go through. The blue bar crawled across the top of the screen but didn't make it all the way.

Vega decided to try the audio and dialed Packwood. She was relieved to hear a ring, and then his voice.

"Everything all right with you there?" he said, gruff. Vega pictured him still in bed.

"Yeah. Sheriff, did you dispatch any of your men to watch the Klimmer house? In case Matt Klimmer comes back?"

Packwood coughed for a few seconds.

"Yes, well, I had my deputy coordinate with Deputy Rutledge so we could have someone out there twenty-four."

"Who's there now?"

"Deputy Rutledge. My other guy was at the sheriff office watching the fire and had to go home for a break. He's not going to get there till noon, and Rutledge says he didn't expect to sleep anyway," said Packwood. "Not a problem I have, personally."

Vega said thanks and hung up. Then she dialed Rutledge, who didn't pick up.

Cap came out of the bathroom, shaking water off his hands.

"How do you sit on that toilet in there?" he said. "It's the size of a Frisbee." Then he saw her face. "What is it?"

"Rutledge, Fenton's deputy, is watching the Klimmer house now." Vega shook her phone back and forth, added, "I left him a voice mail, but I can't text—my phone's not right. Can I use yours?"

Cap handed her his phone, and Vega started to type in Rutledge's number, glancing at her screen and then Cap's.

Then Vega's phone lit up. It was a text from Rutledge. She showed it to Cap.

"What's 'i m r re'?" he said, reading the from the screen.

Vega felt a surge of heat at the base of her neck and said, "It's Klimmer."

In the car, Vega called Packwood on speaker.

"You say your phone is on the fritz?" he said, sounding more awake now.

"It is, but I think the text says, 'Klimmer's here,' and Rutledge isn't picking up. Even if it's just a possibility—"

"Worth checking out, I agree," said Packwood. "I'll be there soon as I can. Call me when you're there. We'll reassess."

They hung up, and Cap took Vega's phone and scrolled around.

"We don't know anything for sure," said Cap. "Your phone *is* on the fritz. That text could say anything."

"Could you keep calling Rutledge, though?" said Vega.

Cap dialed Rutledge again. Again it went to voice mail.

Vega gripped the wheel and stared at the road ahead but also beyond it, into the clouds.

"I messed this up," she said. "I've been thinking Klimmer's pissed at me because I threatened Fenton that I'd bring Derek and Neil Klimmer to the feds."

Cap cracked his neck to one side.

"Because they assaulted you in a parking lot," he said, continuing the story.

"And then their connection to the Liberty Pure thing would

come out, too. When I met Klimmer, he said Neil was a smart kid but got bored at school. Matt said Neil spent all his time on social media, but admitted to me he actually thought social media was for idiots. He thinks his son's stupid, and he thinks Lila—the wife—she coddles Neil, always has. She genuinely thinks her kid's a genius, that he hadn't found his way yet, or some kind of bullshit."

Vega coughed; her throat was still raw, but she couldn't stop talking, not nearly as fast as she was thinking.

"When I shoved the plug down his throat—"

"Wait, what?"

Vega shook her head, impatient. "I shoved a charging cube plug into his mouth and made him swallow it."

Cap's mouth opened a little bit.

"I wasn't going to do it for real; it came right up," she said. "Lila said she called Matt at the Tack and Saddle, which isn't even ten minutes from their place, and he didn't show up. I was there at least ten more minutes."

"You were there ten more minutes after you shoved a plug down the kid's throat?" said Cap, incredulous. "What was there left to do?"

"I was planning to fire a bullet into the propane tank outside the stable," she said, "but I didn't do it. Neither here nor there." She sliced her hand through the air in front of her face. "I'm saying he doesn't like his kid and probably doesn't like his wife, either. And if he doesn't blame me for painting Fenton into a corner, then he backed up his fate timeline and—"

"He blames Neil for being dumb enough to join a white-nationalist gang and doing dumb shit online and, more important, assaulting you," said Cap. "And for setting it all in motion."

"If Neil hadn't, Matt would've gotten away with killing Zeb all those years back and putting his father away," she said with an air of quiet realization.

"If only he'd gotten the girl he really wanted and not a consolation prize," said Cap, who was beginning to understand what Vega saw in the clouds.

Vega parked about fifty feet from the Klimmers' driveway. Right away, she saw the white sheriff cruiser. Also Lila's sedan, Neil's compact, and, right behind the cruiser, the Range Rover.

"Klimmer's car's here," said Vega, pulling her Springfield from the holster.

"So's the deputy's," said Cap, leaving his Sig where it was.

Their feet hit the gravel, and they followed the curve of the driveway toward the cars.

"Doesn't look like he's in there, though," said Cap, squinting at the cruiser.

Vega knew before she knew. It was like the air around her had been siphoned away. She raised the Springfield in front of her and stepped lightly, the gravel crunching underneath her feet as she approached the cruiser.

"He's in there," she said. "He's just dead."

"Jesus," said Cap, breathless.

Soon they were next to the cruiser and could see everything: blood sprayed on the seats and the passenger-side windows; Rutledge's body slumped onto the passenger side, his feet still in the well of the driver's seat, his phone between the gas and the brake. He didn't have much of a face anymore, three quarters of it red pulp, the teeth looking like they'd been sprinkled on his gums at the last minute.

"Window's down," said Vega.

"He lowered it to talk to Klimmer," said Cap. "Right after he texted you."

Vega looked up at the second- and third-floor windows of the house. She didn't see anyone.

"We should go in," she said.

"We should call Packwood," said Cap, squatting next to the car.

Vega already had her phone in her left hand, and tapped Packwood's name with her thumb while she kept her gun steady in her right hand. She squatted next to Cap, their backs flat against the driver's-side door. Packwood picked up after one ring.

"Sheriff, I'm at the Klimmer residence, and Deputy Rutledge is dead," she whispered. She didn't wait for his reaction, kept talking: "Matt Klimmer's car is here. I believe he's still on the property. Is your deputy on site at the sheriff's office downtown?"

"N-no," said Packwood, stumbling. "No, he went home, ma'am. Back to Ola."

"How close are you?"

"I'm a half-hour out if I put the lights on."

"There's a couple of lateral deputies in Ilona—can you contact them and tell them to come here armed and with any kind of Kevlar they might have?"

"Well, surely, but you should get outta there for your own safety."

"I believe Klimmer's wife and son are inside as well, Sheriff. Their cars are here."

The sheriff exhaled, sounding beaten, and said, "Good God."

"As soon as you can, Sheriff," said Vega, and she hung up.

"How long are we looking at?" said Cap.

"He's a half-hour away," said Vega. "There are at least two lateral deputies in town, but I don't know where they are. Could be ten minutes, fifteen. They could be sleeping. Long night."

"So it's just us," said Cap.

"Yeah."

Vega thought about Rutledge's body behind her in the car, the scattered teeth. She turned to look at Cap. "We should go inside."

"One of us should be out here, by his car, in case he runs."

"We don't have to do that," said Vega.

She lifted her shirt and pulled out Dart's star from her belt.

"The hell is that?" said Cap.

"Watch the windows up top, okay?"

"Yep," Cap said, aiming the Sig at the second floor.

Vega stood and ran back to the Range Rover, pressed the button on the back of the star, and jammed two of the points into the front driver's-side tire. The blades made small slits but went all the way through. Then she went to the rear tires, then the front passenger side.

She returned to Cap and crouched next to him.

"He could take his wife or kid's car," said Cap, eyes still on the windows.

"It'll take them a while to deflate—he won't know they're going flat until he's on the road."

Cap nodded, said, "Front door's open a little."

"Let's go in and split up," said Vega. "Assuming living room and kitchen's clear, I'll go downstairs, where Neil's room is, in the basement. You go up—I've never been, but probably bedrooms, right?"

"Works," said Cap, a drop of sweat running down his upper lip. "Are we going to try to persuade him to come with us?"

"I haven't thought that far," said Vega. "I just think we should get inside."

Cap nodded. "I'll watch the windows. You watch the door."

They stood up and hurried across the gravel to the front door. Cap pushed the door open noiselessly, aimed the Sig toward the kitchen, pivoted, and then aimed up the stairs.

Vega pointed the Springfield into the living room. No one. The house looked the same as it had the last time Vega was there. The spindle on the railing was still cracked from Vega's fungo bat.

She glanced at Cap and nodded upstairs. He nodded back at her and took the carpeted steps.

Vega walked on the balls of her feet into the kitchen. There was no one there. A plate with some crumbs rested on the wooden table where Lila had given Vega a sparkling water. The only sound was the sloshy rattle of the dishwasher, which seemed to get louder as Vega stood there, making her think of something about to detonate.

She left the kitchen and headed for the door that led to the basement. It was open; a light was on downstairs, but there was no sound. Vega held the Springfield with both hands and took the first step.

Cap got to the top of the staircase and saw a room straight ahead with the door open. He checked his right and left, and then went inside.

It looked like a study: a dark wooden desk along with some bookcases and a big leather chair. Bronze tchotchkes everywhere—clocks, paperweights, a few framed pictures. Cap left the room.

A door was open at the very end of the hallway. He could see white carpeting and what looked like an upholstered bench, like the sort that would go at the foot of a bed. He approached slowly, passing another door, which was ajar.

He pushed this door open; it seemed to be a guest room, with everything blue and brown, generic photos of ranches on the walls, a window looking out onto a field and a red wooden shed—the stable, Cap figured. Nobody in this one, either.

Cap left the guest room and made his way toward the open door at the end of the hall. He pointed the Sig straight ahead, like he was expecting a shooting-range target to flip down from the door frame. His feet landed with soft pats on the carpeting, the only sound.

He walked the last few feet quickly and got close to the doorway, through which he could see the bench and the bottom half of a bed, its sheets rumpled. Also a ceiling fan turning circles.

He went into the room, understood everything all at once, and lowered his gun.

The first thing Vega saw as she descended the stairs was Neil's desk, looking the same as it did when she'd been there last, except that the computer screens were black. Vega paused on the steps, in the middle of the flight, her back against the wall, and then took one stair at a time.

The light was on, and the rest of the room came into view bit by bit: the beer signs, posters on the walls of bands Vega had never heard of, a wooden dresser, its surface cluttered with action figures. Then there was Neil's bed, tucked into the corner, a clump of blankets on top in the rough shape of a curled-up body.

Vega walked toward the bed, keeping the Springfield aimed at the clump. She heard a quiet hum that sounded like it was coming from inside the walls, maybe from the dishwasher directly upstairs, or the heat turning on.

Quickly she grabbed the top blanket and yanked it off the bed.

Cap took it all in.

He knew he shouldn't dwell there, but he needed a minute. Through the eyes, turned upside down, then right side up, he remembered learning in a college biology class. Iris acts like the shutter of a camera. Click, click, click.

Lila Klimmer was dead. She had been shot in the forehead, close up, from what Cap could tell. Other than the hole in her head, she appeared calm, her eyes open and alert, her head resting on a pillow, faceup. Her arms were splayed at her sides, as if she had fallen asleep sunbathing. Her silk camisole didn't have a wrinkle.

The pillow was saturated with blood and brains. There was also a peacock-shaped red spray on the wall and the tufted headboard.

"Sitting up," said Cap to himself.

His specialty had never been forensics or pathology, but he'd seen enough crime scenes to piece a story together when he needed to. He suspected Lila had been sleeping, then sat up, probably happy to see her husband after he'd been gone a few days. Then, when he was about a foot away, he fired the shot, and she flopped back down.

Cap went to the adjoining bathroom, white tiles and marble and light teak vanity and cupboards. No one there.

He took another look at Lila and left.

Back through the carpeted hallway, down the stairs, past the front door, which they'd left open a crack, then through the kitchen, noticing a plate with crumbs on a table so big it looked like it should be in a Crate & Barrel window display.

Cap went through the narrow hallway at the rear of the kitchen. On his left was a door to the backyard, the field with the stable beyond it. On his right was an open door to a flight of stairs leading down.

He drew the Sig again and started down the stairs. Then Vega appeared at the bottom, pointing her Springfield up at him.

"Jesus," he said.

"Sorry," said Vega, lowering the gun. She leaned her head to the side, regarding his face. "You look bad. What did you find?"

"The missus," said Cap. "Dead."

Vega peered upward, as if the floors and ceilings were transparent and she could see all the way up to the body.

"Do you know when?"

"Hour, maybe," said Cap. "He take out Neil, too?"

"No."

She stepped out of the way so she was no longer blocking the landing at the bottom of the stairs, and Cap came all the way down. She pointed at a bed covered with only a fitted sheet and a pillow; on the floor were a pile of sheets and blankets.

"Not here," said Vega. "Not hiding in the closet."

Cap patted his forehead with his sleeve.

"Gotta be here somewhere," he said, lowering his voice.

Vega nodded, then tilted her head toward the stairs.

"Let's go."

She led the way, and Cap followed, keeping the Sig pointed at the ground. They came to the top of the stairs and paused by the back door.

"You see the plate in the kitchen, with the crumbs?" said Cap.

"Yeah."

"You figure Klimmer had a piece of toast before he iced his wife?"

"I don't know. Maybe it's Neil's," Vega offered, but even as she said it, she didn't believe it: Neil couldn't possibly be an early riser.

"Vega," said Cap, staring out the textured window of the back door. Then he pointed.

She squinted, but it was difficult to make anything out except basic shapes through the rippled glass. There was the stable, but in the doorway, an object, something big and brown and round.

Cap opened the back door, and they were able to see what they were looking at.

The door to the stable was open, and on the ground, in the doorway, was a horse—the back of the horse, on its side, its tail falling limply to the ground.

"There another entrance to that stable?" said Cap.

"Think so, on the other side, looked like a split sliding door, but it was closed when I was in there."

"You see a lock?"

Vega stared at the horse, wondered if it was the one Klimmer had been brushing when they spoke.

"I don't know. I wasn't looking at it."

"We'll find out soon," he said. "You want to go in the front, I'll go around?"

Vega nodded.

"Fast, right?" said Cap. "Catch him off-guard?"

"He's already off-guard," said Vega. "He didn't plan this all that far in advance."

"Right, but now he's really got nothing to lose," said Cap. "Ready?"

Vega nodded. "Go."

They moved swiftly through the grass, side by side until they were about twenty feet from the stable door. Cap glanced at Vega and jogged to the left, toward the side with the propane tank. The stable was dark inside, and Vega couldn't focus on anything past the horse on the ground. If Klimmer was waiting and watching, he'd see Vega before she saw him.

But as she approached the door, as she heard the flies buzzing over the horse's carcass so loud they might have been in her ears, a thing became clear—Klimmer had no plan to escape through the crack in the window. At this point, maybe he didn't even want one.

Vega stood next to the open door, her back against the stable wall, and thought she heard a voice coming from inside—just a murmur or a whisper, quiet against the deafening noise from the flies. She could see all of the horse now, its legs bowing away from the main cavity. Vega didn't think this was the horse Klimmer had been brushing that day. She remembered that that one had had a diamond of white between its eyes; the dead horse's head was all brown, and instead of a white patch there was a bullet hole. There was also a rag tied around its eyes, like a blindfold.

Vega squatted, then got onto her belly and crawled behind the horse so her face was pressed right above the tail. It still smelled like a live animal, like hay and manure. Vega tilted her head up about an inch to see into the stable.

The first thing she noticed was the other horse, dead on the floor. Unlike people, they actually seemed like bigger creatures dead than they did alive, like some kind of dense, immoveable objects, rocks that water would have to flow around instead of over.

Then there was Neil, sitting on the floor, alive, with his head in his hands, wearing sweatpants and a tee shirt, leaning against the stall door; the horse with the white diamond was also alive, in the stall.

There was Matt Klimmer, too, holding his gun, speaking in low tones. He wasn't pointing the gun at Neil, but gesturing with it as he spoke, waving it in small corkscrews.

Vega tightened her grip on the Springfield and leaned her head against the horse. She wasn't confident she could hit Klimmer; there was no way for her to shoot straight without being fully exposed, which meant she would have to pop up over the horse and fire without aiming. Then Klimmer would have some seconds. He'd be disoriented, and he might not even fire at Vega, but Neil was right there, and if Klimmer was gearing up to kill his son anyway, an ambush might speed up the process.

Which meant there was one way.

Vega stuck the Springfield over the horse's body first, then her head. Klimmer didn't see her yet.

Then she quickly came to one knee and called, loud enough for Cap to hear on the other side of the sliding door, "Don't move."

Klimmer pointed the gun in Vega's direction but didn't shoot. Neil twitched and lifted his head.

"What are you doing here?" said Klimmer.

He seemed annoyed, like Vega had just interrupted him in the middle of a massage.

"Looking for you," said Vega.

"This is between me and my son," said Klimmer.

Vega was about ten yards from where Klimmer stood. She could see he was sweating, pale, unshaven. But he did have a strange calm about him: shoulders relaxed, extending the gun in a casual way toward Vega, as if it were part of his arm and he was indicating, There she is, over there.

"Sorry to interrupt," Vega said.

Klimmer sighed, not in the mood for jokes.

"Look, would you just leave?" he said, exasperated. "I told you, this is between me and Neil."

At the sound of his name, Neil froze. His face was tear-streaked and red; his eyes were wide. He stared at Vega.

"See? We're talking about adult things now," said Klimmer, pronouncing "adult" with the emphasis on the "a" instead of the "dult." "We don't need you here to referee."

Vega was about to tell him that Packwood was on his way but then didn't: Need to slow it down, not speed it up, she thought.

"Right, Neil?" said Klimmer, kicking his son's bare foot.

Neil cringed and nodded quickly.

"Saw what you did to your wife," said Vega. "That's fucked up, Klimmer."

Klimmer sneered, the corner of his mouth puckering. Neil stuck his head between his knees and let out a sob.

"You make Neil watch?" said Vega. "That's . . ." she said, lingering on the word, ". . . *super*-fucked up."

"No, I didn't make him watch," Klimmer said, like it was a silly idea. "He was in the basement, playing with himself, as he has done every morning of his life since he was twelve."

"Klimmer," Vega whispered loudly, "*it's fucked up that you know that.*"

Klimmer began to stammer: "All right, all right, fuck you, you bitch. You don't know me. You want me to shoot him, I'll shoot him," he said, aiming the gun at Neil's head.

"Fenton, too," Vega said, holding the Springfield steady. "It's almost like you want to get rid of everyone who's close to you. All because Zeb Williams got your girl a long time ago, and you had to kill him. It's like that was the middle of the black hole, and everything got sucked in after it, your whole life."

Now he was angry. He pursed his lips.

"You're wrong," he said.

"Want to tell me about it?" said Vega.

"The whole mess with Zeb was just the excuse," said Klimmer. "All of this"—gesturing blithely to the horses and then Neil—"this is just what I always wanted to do."

"Kill your wife?" Neil choked out. "That's what you wanted to do?"

Klimmer looked at him with a sour expression. "Your mother was a fine person," he said. "Not the smartest, not the kindest, but she was fine. Her one mistake was letting you grow into what you've become."

"What?!" said Neil, his voice full of snot. "Someone who's actually doing something positive in the world? Someone who's important and believes in something and not just . . . mindlessly buying shit!?"

Vega took aim at Klimmer's shoulder. No matter where she got him in the arm, or even if she ended up missing, he'd likely drop the gun and would be too shocked to do anything else.

"No, Neil," said Klimmer, put-upon. He let out a full breath. "A loser."

Klimmer extended his arm just a little, but Vega knew it was coming and squeezed the trigger.

Then everyone moved, all at once: Klimmer fired, but too late—Vega's bullet hit his arm, and the gun jumped from his hand as he screamed and stumbled back. The horse with the white diamond whinnied and kicked, rammed its body against the closed stall door, which split in the middle.

The door on the other side of the stable slid open, and there was Cap, backlit from the sun. He pointed the Sig at Klimmer, who hadn't fallen but was taking off his jacket with one hand.

Neil had flopped onto to the ground and rolled onto his stomach, covering his ears and screaming, still alive.

Klimmer dropped his jacket. He wore a white shirt, and the blood was spreading on his sleeve, near his shoulder. He began to unbutton his shirt, and Vega knew that he wasn't thinking straight, that he thought the problem was with his clothes spontaneously leaking blood.

Klimmer looked to Vega, then back at Cap, his face white.

"Who the fuck are you, now?" he said.

Cap nodded at Vega and said, "I'm her goddamn boyfriend. Now, stay. Right. There."

The only sound was the horse, still snorting and huffing.

Klimmer turned back to Vega, his shirt half off, breathing through his mouth. Then there were two more shots, one in Klimmer's stomach and one in his neck, and he fell backward to the ground, landing on his side.

The horse screamed and burst through the stall door, thrashing and kicking. It ran for the sliding door, and Cap jumped out of the way as the horse took off into the field.

Neil Klimmer held the revolver and kept pulling the trigger, the cylinder clicking on the empty chambers.

Vega stood and ran to Neil. He sat on the ground with his legs spread out like a frog and pointed the gun at Vega when she got close.

"It's tapped, Neil," she said. "You can put it down now."

Slowly Neil lowered the gun.

Cap came forward from the doorway and knelt next to Klimmer, pressed his fingers against Klimmer's neck.

Vega, not waiting for the signal from Cap, said to Neil, "He's dead."

Neil lowered the gun to his lap and blinked hard a few times.

"Neil, I want you to listen to me. Are you listening?"

Neil lolled his head in Vega's direction.

"I want to tell you this before Sheriff Packwood gets here. You have a chance to change your life, okay?" she said, her voice soft. "It would be great if you could do that. But if you don't, and I hear about it, I will come back here and I will get that charger plug inside of you one way or another, you understand me?" Her voice was even softer now, the way women talked to their stomachs when they were pregnant. "I do not give a fuck that you're an orphan or whatever."

Cap knew he shouldn't laugh but he had to work to tamp down the urge nonetheless. He was high from the adrenaline; his lungs felt like they'd grown and could suddenly accommodate twice as much oxygen; his stomach was settled to the extent that he didn't even notice it was there.

But, also, it elated him, Vega delivering the warning, in her sweetest, most sincere, and somewhat erotic voice, that she would torture this kid if he ever tried to cross her again.

18

IT FELT LIKE A LONG TIME BUT ONLY TOOK A FEW DAYS. ABOUT A week after Cap arrived, he and Vega stood outside the Klimmer horse stable with half a dozen federal agents, Sheriff Packwood from Ola, a representative from the county's forensic-pathology office, and a demolition crew.

They all wore earplugs, except the workmen, who had noise-canceling headphones. The workmen started with the roof—they pried it off the top of the stable with crowbars—and then knocked down the walls with sledgehammers. They brushed away the hay with a stiff-bristled broom, and went to work on the concrete floor.

Vega and Cap were glad to have the earplugs. Two guys with jackhammers drilled into opposite corners of the concrete square for a few minutes, and then pulled the chunks of the slab out of the way, continued, and repeated. After about a half-hour, they were done, and then they started to dig.

Dirt came up in heaps along the edges of the hole where the slab had been. The lead fed from Portland was a woman named Shaw—Black, petite, with short hair in pin curls and pink fingernails. She waved Vega forward. Vega inched closer to the site, Cap behind her a few feet.

The men didn't have to dig far, only about a foot beneath the surface. Vega peered into the hole and saw the ribs first, lined up like a row of farmer's sickles.

Shaw gave a signal to the foreman, who told the men to stop. Then Shaw's agents began to dust and photograph the hole and its contents, because, even if a killing had happened so long ago that there was no longer any evidence to collect, this was still a crime scene.

The agents dusted bone by bone. Soon Vega could see everything—the legs, the arms, the whole rib cage, the spine, and then the skull. The bones were brown, but other than that appeared intact to Vega, like they should be hanging in a high-school science lab.

"Shit," Cap whispered behind her.

She turned to look at him and saw disbelief in his face. She acknowledged to herself that she didn't feel those things, and she wasn't sure and wasn't too interested why not. But she could see Cap was affected, and it was painful for him. His lower back had been bothering him after sleeping for a week with Vega on the flimsy bed-roll in the Stargazer; in the mornings, he would grimace and talk about how old he was, but this was not the same. Was he horrified that this was what happened to Zeb Williams? Was he thinking about how all he or anyone else amounted to was just a pile of bones? Vega didn't know.

"It's okay," she said, trying to bring him back.

He looked at her, and his eyes softened up, jaw loosened. That was the face she knew from the past few late nights and early mornings, as they lay on their sides, facing each other, the Stargazer murky, like they were underwater.

"You were right, V," he said. "I can't believe it. You were right."

Vega took no pleasure in the moment. She turned around to face forward and nodded at Shaw, who nodded back, letting her know she could come closer.

Vega walked to the edge. The agents all wore gloves and face masks. Three were in the hole, dusting and digging around the skeleton, planning not to move the bones anywhere just yet, but to carve out the earth around them.

One of the agents scraped around the fingers of the skeleton's right hand, the long phalanges and metacarpals of the fingers, the jumble of carpal bones in the palm—Vega knew all the names now, since her wrist had been broken. She'd seen pictures and X-rays and diagrams. Seeing them without the skin and the muscle and the tissue, Vega thought no wonder they were so easy to break and smash into nothing—they looked like dirty ceramic bits that Kent, the antiques/stolen-goods trader, would stash in a box in the corner of his shop.

Then she saw something shiny. Just a glint, because it had been buried, too, and it was caked in dirt, just like the bones. Vega squatted to get a better look, then called to Shaw.

"Can I see that—whatever that thing is?"

Shaw joined Vega and leaned over the edge. She was chewing a piece of gum between the molars in the back of her mouth as she gazed into the hole where Vega was looking.

Shaw pulled a pair of black latex gloves from her breast suit pocket and snapped one onto her right hand. She handed Vega the other one.

"Martin, will you pass that, please?" said Shaw, pointing. "You don't have to clean it."

The agent dusting the hand scooped up the object, leaving clumps of dirt on it. He stood and brought it to Shaw.

Vega stood up and slid the glove onto her left hand. Shaw handed her the object with the cushion of damp dirt underneath it.

Vega shook some of the dirt off and saw what it was: a ball, about an inch and a half in diameter, connected to a base the width of a thick straw, only about an inch long. Although it looked like gold, Vega was almost certain it was brass. A green inchworm scooted across the top of the ball.

"That's not him," she said.

"What's that?" said Shaw.

"What?" said Cap, stepping forward to stand next to Vega.

"That's not Zeb Williams," she said. She turned to Cap. "It's a guy named Ivan."

"Okay," said Cap. "Who's Ivan?"

"He was a guy passing through—he couldn't see well, so he used a cane," Vega said, explaining also to Shaw. "I think this is the top of it. I saw it in a picture."

Shaw kept her face straight. She chewed her gum silently and didn't speak right away. Then: "My guys are still going to check the dentals, all the same to you."

"Yeah," said Vega.

"We're going to have to keep that, too," said Shaw, pointing at the cane topper.

Vega stared at it, turned it around in her hand. Then she handed it back to Shaw.

"We're going to take all this up," said Shaw, waving her hand over a portion of the field. "Maybe twenty by twenty. Just in case."

"I don't think he's here," said Vega.

"Just to be thorough, all the same to you," said Shaw, pointing at the skeleton. "You're still interested in the results?"

Vega nodded. "Yes, please."

"You'll get them next week," said Shaw. Then she walked away, around the hole, to get a look from the other side.

"We have to wait for the teeth," said Cap. "It could still be him."

"I don't think so."

Vega stared at the bones and rubbed her gloved fingers together, let the rest of the dirt fall from her hand.

Later, in the Stargazer, Cap was on his back, and Vega lay next to him, on her side, her head resting on top of his shoulder, her nose right under his ear. It was dark and cloudy outside, but the sky had some clear patches, letting the light from the half-moon stream through the front windshield.

Vega was nowhere near asleep; she figured it had to be only about eleven, but Cap was yawning in between questions.

"So Klimmer still did it, right?" he said.

"Yeah," said Vega, feeling her breath bounce off Cap's skin back onto her face. "He was actually telling the truth when he denied killing Zeb."

"That tracks. Right killer," said Cap, then, continuing through a yawn, "wrong victim."

Cap leaned his head against Vega's, and he took a big inhalation that sounded almost like a snore.

"Caplan," she said, sitting up a little.

"Yes," Cap said, forcing his eyes open.

"I know you're tired, but please don't go to sleep right now."

"That's where you're wrong," he said. "I'm wide awake."

"Then ask me more questions."

"All right," said Cap, putting a hand behind his neck. "What's the motive for Klimmer killing the old man, Ivan?"

"Wrong place, wrong time," said Vega. "Ivan slept in this old barn, and Klimmer ends up there one night—I don't know why he goes. Klimmer doesn't mind killing people, I don't think."

Vega sank back down on the bedroll and pressed her lips against Cap's shoulder for a second.

"Zeb and Cara had a fight that night, and Zeb said he was going to sleep in the barn with Ivan. So the three of them end up in the barn: Zeb, Klimmer, Ivan. Klimmer kills Ivan. Maybe he's a wild shot and it's dark, and he thinks he's aiming at Zeb when he's really aiming at Ivan."

Vega ran her eyes back and forth and over Cap's profile. It was too dark to see any details on his face.

"Where does Zeb go?" she said. "Why does he go?"

Then Cap made a sound like he was sniffing through clogged nasal passages, and Vega knew it was a snore.

She scooted up an inch or two, so her mouth was close to his ear. It was his bad ear, the one missing the top ridge, shot off a couple of years before during the case of the sisters from Black Creek, the first case Vega and Cap had worked together. She knew he had a little sensitivity there, but she couldn't resist running her finger along the top, where it was flat but uneven in the place where most ears were curved and smooth like the top of a question mark.

"Caplan," she said.

Again he sniff-snored.

"I killed Cooper in the woods," she said. "I told Packwood that he was coming at me, but he wasn't. His gun was there, but he didn't reach for it. And I shot him anyway. And I didn't mind it, either.

"He knew something about me. I didn't think he did, but he knew I pretend to be someone else so I can do the things I really want to do. And he was right. Not the saving-the-white-race shit, but I wanted to kiss him in Lanahan's driveway that night, and I wanted to kill him in the woods. Because, if you cut me down the middle, Caplan, I'm both of those things."

Cap snored again. Vega pressed her face into his neck, between his ear and his shoulder, and stayed there, wide awake for a long time.

19

SUMMER WAS VEGA'S FAVORITE TIME OF YEAR. SHE KEPT ALL OF HER windows open, wouldn't close them even when there were rainstorms, and the water would douse the floor through the screens. She watched the temperature tick up on her weather app day by day through June, into July—sun after sun after sun, Monday, Tuesday, Wednesday, eighty-seven degrees, eighty-nine, ninety.

In the middle of July, she was between cases. She had been busy since March, when she'd left Oregon and told her clients, the Fohls, that she had not been successful in locating Zeb Williams. They had offered to retain her for another month, but she declined—there was a fourteen-year-old girl who had run away from home in Los Angeles, and the parents had sent Vega an e-mail asking for her help. It wasn't for the same kind of money that the Fohls were paying, but Vega was done with cold cases and missing grown-ass men.

She and Cap texted every day and talked a few times a week. The conversations weren't long—she would have her AirPods in her ears and would go running or do squats or push-ups, and he might be running, too, or he'd be watching sports with the sound off and would tell her what was happening in the game. Sometimes he told her stories about Nell and her racing, and how he really wouldn't know what to do with himself when she went to college. She told him about her cases while she was working on them, but otherwise Cap would usually do most of the talking. That was the way Vega liked it.

On a Sunday morning, Vega was lying on a towel in her backyard when a text from her father came through on her phone. She hadn't seen him since February and hadn't thought about how it had been that long until she saw his name on the screen.

It was a photo of him next to a red four-door, and he was giving the thumbs-up. He looked overjoyed and sweaty.

"Look at this! We finally got A New Car" was the text.

Vega found herself smiling and texted back, "Very nice. July 4th sale?"

After five minutes of flashing dots, the response came back, "Yes!"

Vega set the phone down and leaned back on her elbows. She lifted her sunglasses onto the top of her head, looked up at the sun, and closed her eyes. She didn't have much vanity in her, but one look she did not care for was bright-white eyelids surrounded by a sunned face.

She kept picturing her father's new car, and then decided she was done sitting in the sun. She stood up and went inside to her refrigerator, where she'd pinned the card for a woodworker to the door with a magnet. When she returned from Oregon for the last time, she'd found that a post on her porch railing had split, and ignored it. Then, when she came back from the job in L.A., a handyman's card had been tucked into the pith. She'd never called the guy, but saved the card just the same.

She dialed and got his voice mail.

"I'll get back to you within an hour of you leaving your message, or twenty-five percent off your first job," said the recording.

Vega left a message describing the job and what she was willing to pay for him to make himself available (twice his hourly, plus parts), and figured that, after she took a shower and got something to eat, she could be at her father's place in about three hours, which would, she hoped, give the carpenter time to get there, too. She didn't have a big job in mind, and she was not unhandy, but it would save time to have a professional do it once, and right.

She undressed, dropped her clothes in a corner of the bathroom, and ran the water hot. As she looked at her face in the mirror for a few seconds, she realized she had a ballpoint-pen slash above her left eyebrow, slanting down toward her nose, as if she were a villain in a Saturday-morning cartoon. She rubbed it off with her fingers and wondered how long it had been there.

· · ·

That afternoon, Vega pulled up behind her father's new car and saw the carpenter right away. He leaned against a pickup truck across the street and waved at Vega.

She got out of the car and waved back.

"Hi—Luke?"

"That's it," he said, approaching her. "Alice Vega?"

Vega nodded and they shook hands. Luke had a reddish-gray beard; the skin of his face was tan and weathered like wood; and he wore circle-rimmed glasses that magnified his eyes so they looked liquid. He held a backpack by the handle and unzipped it.

"I think this is what you're looking for," he said, holding up a silver-plated hinge, about an inch and a half long. "This is a thirty-five-millimeter, which is pretty standard. I got some alternates, too."

"Great," said Vega. "If I can ask you to wait here for one second, I'll be right back."

"Sure thing," said Luke, smiling, his lips disappearing into his beard.

Vega went up the porch steps to her father's unit and pressed the button. There was no answer right away, so she pressed it a few more times.

Bitsy opened the door. She had rust-brown hair down to her shoulders, and bangs, and she wore a white dress that didn't have a lot of shape to it, reminding Vega of an artist's smock. Silver cross around her neck. It took her a second to recognize Vega through the fog of not expecting her. Then her face opened up like she was staring at a celebrity.

"Alice!" she shouted.

She hugged Vega, and Vega hugged her back only a little, patting Bitsy on the chubby flesh of her back repeatedly, hoping that would end the hug quicker.

"What are you doing here? We didn't know you were coming," said Bitsy. Without waiting for a response, she called over her shoulder, "Mauricio!"

Vega's father didn't answer right away, and then Bitsy called, even louder, "Babe! Alice is here!" She said to Vega, "We saw you on the news—that skeleton they found on the ranch in Oregon. Just terrible, what people do."

Vega had met Bitsy enough times to know that she expected no response to this kind of statement. It was just supposed to sit in the air, and Vega was supposed to agree quietly and reflect on the terrible nature of things.

She didn't have long—her father came rushing to the door and clapped both hands over his heart when he saw her.

"Alice, you're here," he said, and then embraced her.

Vega allowed the hug to last a few seconds longer than the one with Bitsy, but then pulled away.

Her father held up his index finger.

"I prayed for this," he said to both women. "This morning, I prayed. And here you are."

"That's something," said Vega. Then she turned around and waved to Luke. "This is Luke. He's a handyman." As Luke approached, Vega said to him, "Can you show them the hinge?"

Luke stood at the bottom of the porch stairs and held the hinge out in his hand. Bitsy smiled politely at it, while Mauricio squinted.

"What's that, now?" said Mauricio.

"It's what's called a slow-close or soft-close hinge," said Luke. "When I install it on your cabinet doors, you won't hear any noise when you shut them."

"Is that right?" said Mauricio, reaching out his hand for Luke to pass him the hinge. "I didn't know this was a thing that existed."

"Depending on how many cabinets, it'll only take me an hour, two max," said Luke.

"How much does all this cost?" said Bitsy.

"No, Bitsy," said Vega. "I've already paid Luke."

"We can't let you do that," said Bitsy, somewhat sad.

"Yeah, you can," said Vega. "When's your birthday?"

"January," said Bitsy.

"Late birthday present, then."

"This is a great idea," Mauricio said, shaking the hinge at Vega.

Bitsy led Luke inside, to the kitchen, and Mauricio pointed to the curb.

"Did you see the car?"

"I did," said Vega. "It's nice."

"Why don't you come in?" said Mauricio. "We just went shopping. We have diet soda."

"In a few, okay, Dad?" said Vega. "I have to make a call."

Vega left the porch and went back to her car. She pulled her phone out, tapped Cap's name, and leaned against the driver's-side door.

He picked up after a couple of rings, and Vega let her head fall to one side when she heard his voice, unaware that she'd been straining her neck. She told him where she was and how she'd arranged for the hinges.

"That's so nice, V," he said. "It's a little unexpected."

"Because I'm not nice," said Vega, no offense in her tone.

"No, you're nice, but you just have different ways of expressing it. Like, you prefer to save people from the jaws of death, as opposed to gifting them with home improvements. I bet it made your dad real happy."

"I think so," said Vega. "I heard something I didn't want to hear, though."

"What's that?"

"Bitsy called my dad 'Babe.' It was weird."

Cap laughed. "Could have been worse. 'Babe' is preferable to anything suggestive. Once, my mom told me she thought my dad's scrotum was shrinking. This is still something I think about almost every day."

Vega leaned her head back and laughed a little.

"Hey, was that a laugh? Did I get one?" said Cap.

"A little," said Vega. "What'd you do today?"

"Pretty busy. Valley Diss for some liquids, went for a run, fell asleep on the couch for a few minutes. Getting ready to go grocery shopping. Nell's back here tomorrow, and she'll get pissed off if there's no food around," said Cap. Then he paused. "Vega, go spend time with your dad and Bitsy. You haven't seen them in a long time."

Vega sighed. "Yeah, I will," she said. "I can't handle the Jesus talk for extended periods of time."

"What's the thing that bothers you so much about it?" said Cap, running a faucet in the background. "Besides the fact that you don't believe in it."

Vega thought about it. "I think it dulls them," she said.

"But they like it, right?" said Cap. "It gives them some pleasure and some peace?"

"Yeah."

"Then let 'em have it," said Cap. "My parents, they're not Ortho-dox or anything, but they pay attention, especially my mom. She does all the stuff because it makes her think of her parents. Gives her peace, you know. And a distraction from the rapidly shrinking scrotum."

Vega laughed again, louder this time.

"Call me later, V," he said, the sound of the "V" disappearing into what Vega sensed was Cap's smile.

"No, you call *me*," she said.

"It's like that, huh?" he said. "Gimme one reason why I should call you and you shouldn't call me."

Vega rubbed a smudge of dirt on the roof of her car and said, "Because you're my goddamn boyfriend."

Then she hung up, and rested her chin on the roof for a second, and thought of him laughing in disbelief. Her phone buzzed, and she glanced at the screen.

It was a text from Cap: "Laugh out loud!"

Vega tucked the phone into her pocket and went back to her father's house.

Luke was done in about an hour. He demonstrated the cabinet doors for Vega, her father, and Bitsy. Opening and closing, the hinge glid-ing and shutting silently.

"Look at that," said Mauricio.

"It's one of those little things you never realize," said Bitsy, beaming.

They thanked Luke, who took his bag and tools and left. Vega found herself gazing at the cabinets as if they radiated light, along-side her father and Bitsy.

"How about some food?" said Bitsy, all of a sudden.

"Do you want food?" Mauricio said to Vega.

"No, thanks, I have to get back to my place."

"Next time," said Bitsy, and she patted Vega on the elbow, and Vega allowed it.

Bitsy stayed in the kitchen, taking photos and videos of the cabi-nets to send to her friends, while Mauricio walked Vega to the door.

"We hope you'll come back soon," he said.

"I'll try," said Vega.

"I still pray for you, Alice, every morning and every night."

Vega paused before opening the front door and turned to him.

"For what?" she said.

His focus shifted to the wall behind her, as he tried to sort through the nuance of her question.

"For what?" he repeated.

"What do you pray for me, in particular?"

"Oh," he said, relieved. "That you're safe, that you'll find another career that's not so dangerous, that you'll meet a good man."

"I guess that's okay," said Vega. "You shouldn't worry about me, Dad. I'm pretty resourceful."

"Yes, yes, yes," he said, conciliatory. "Maybe one day you'll wake up and decide to . . . be a banker or a farmer."

Then he hugged her and held on, and Vega let him, but it went on for so long her mind wandered, and she began wondering again how she got the pen mark on her face earlier.

He pulled away and said goodbye, his eyes glassy, and Vega said goodbye and left.

As she came down the front steps, she saw Luke across the street, wiping off a dipstick with a rag. He waved, jogged over to her.

"I'm sorry to ask this—my tank's empty. I'm guessing my gauge just up and went last week some time—it's been saying fifty percent for a while. Any way you could give me a lift to a service station? I'd take a Ryde, but it says the wait's forty minutes."

He said it all quickly, removed his San Francisco Giants base-ball hat, scratched his head, and finger-brushed his hair, which was almost all gray. Vega took a quick intake of him: Nervous, not dangerous. Older than she'd thought at first, which made him less likely to commit a crime. Regardless, the Springfield was tucked into the holster at her side, and it had been a few months since she'd gotten the cast off her right arm; she'd had plenty of time to build up the muscle again.

"Sure."

They got into Vega's car, and she headed to the nearest gas station. Luke made chitchat about the truck.

"It's a '91, so the clock's ticking on it anyway," he said.

"Looks pretty good for '91," said Vega. "You buy it new back then?"

"No, about ten years ago," he said, rubbing the center of his right palm with left thumb. "I move around a lot."

"I saw you have a Seattle area code."

"I lived up there for a long time. Also a little bit in Idaho. From northern California originally, though."

Vega nodded, glanced in the rearview, thought about the pen mark.

"San Francisco," he said. He paused and then added, "North Beach."

At a red light, Vega glanced at his hands. They were wrinkled and tan, like his face, the fingers thick. Then she looked at his face and saw he was looking at her. He smiled, but his eyes were heavy.

"You ever make a decision in a second when you're young, and then you have to live with it forever?"

Vega stared at him, her brain doing its own little Photoshop: no facial hair, no wrinkles, paler, younger, nose a little more pronounced, and not crooked like it was now. But same body—lean, fit, compact.

When the light turned green, Vega pulled over.

She turned to him and said, "How young is young?"

He gave a tired shrug and said, "Before forty, I guess."

"Then, yes," she answered.

He nodded and looked ahead at the car parked in front of them.

"I saw you on the news, you know," he said. "I was glad someone finally found Ivan."

If it had been another time, with another person, Vega would have let him talk it out, but she was aware that this particular set of circumstances might evaporate at any moment, and she needed to know some things.

"What happened that night?" she asked.

Her passenger removed his glasses and pinched the bridge of his nose. Then he began to talk.

"I was at the barn with Ivan, and I couldn't sleep, so I went to the stable, because there was a phone there, and I wanted to call Carmen and just say I was sorry. Matt Klimmer was riding a horse. He saw me leave and followed me on foot.

"Klimmer called out to me right when I got back to the barn. He wanted to fight. Told me to stay away from Cara. I told him he had no shot—Cara thought he was a ten-ton loser. Then he pushed me."

He paused, moved his mouth like he was chewing.

"I was in some good shape back then, and Klimmer wasn't a ninety-eight-pounder, but when he pushed me, I didn't even feel it."

He paused again. Vega knew, though, it wasn't because he was wondering how he should continue; she got the feeling he'd thought about that night so much the narrative could spill out of him at any time like the roll in a player piano.

"You pushed him back," said Vega.

"I pushed him back," he said, sliding his glasses back onto his face. "He fell hard, too, right on his ass. Then I went inside the barn.

"Ivan was in his sleeping bag on the floor, but we must've woken him up with our carrying on. I remember he sat up and said, 'That you, kid?' And I was about to answer him when I hear Klimmer open the door, so I turn, and he's holding a gun on me, and I get so angry at him, like who is this tick under my skin, so I go toward him, because I don't think he's got the talent to actually shoot, and I just grab his hand and slap his face and try to pull the gun away from him, and he takes the shot, but he misses me. I'm right there, but he misses me."

He opened his mouth to speak but said nothing. He rubbed his eye underneath his glasses with one finger.

"Ivan started making these sounds, like a gargling kind of sound, and I ran over to him on the ground. He was sitting up and choking, and I had him by the shoulders."

He held out his arms toward the dashboard to demonstrate.

"My hands were all wet, and Klimmer shined a flashlight on us just as Ivan was going. He kept opening his mouth, like this."

He opened and closed his mouth a few times like a newly caught fish.

"He was trying to get air. Klimmer got him in the neck, and the blood was coming out like a waterfall. And then he was frozen with his mouth open, and that was it."

He put his hand over his mouth and stroked his beard.

"Then Klimmer said his best friend was the deputy and he was going to get rid of the gun and tell everyone I did it. And he was going to call all the papers and say he knew where I was and that I was a killer. And wouldn't . . . Cara be crushed, he said."

He stumbled over her name.

"I just took off. I ran," he said. Then he turned to face Vega and said, "That's what I do."

"No one thinks you did it," said Vega. "We think Klimmer's father saw him trying to dispose of the body, so Klimmer attacked him, too, and said he had a stroke."

Vega's passenger nodded.

"And then he killed his friend the sheriff, and his own wife, too," he added.

"That's right," said Vega. "When you left your card for me—how did you know I would ever call you?"

Now her passenger smiled, the skin at the corners of his eyes creasing.

"I was in southern Washington, near Walla Walla, when I saw the news about the bones. I saw what town you were from online, and I got in my car and drove there in a straight shot. I thought I could race you coming back from Ilona, so I . . ." he began, but then looked down, embarrassed. "I snapped your railing in the middle of the night with some bolt cutters," he said, wincing.

"No kidding," said Vega.

"I was taking a chance you wouldn't get it fixed as soon as you came back, and then, after you'd been back a few days, I would leave my card. But you went away again almost immediately after."

"I had another job."

"I left it for you anyway, and just hoped you'd call. I rented a place in the Kern River Valley, picked up work."

"You moved here, on the chance that I'd call you?" said Vega.

He shrugged and said, "I move all the time."

Vega let that sit a second and then said, "What makes you think I won't call the papers now? Post your business card on Instagram? Call the clients who hired me in the first place?"

He looked over at her and smiled. "I just don't think you'd do it," he said. "I read about you online. You have a thing that points you in the right direction, whether you like it or not."

"You don't know that," she said, but it was a mild rebuke.

"No, I don't," he said. Then he exhaled, closed his eyes. "All my life, I've been looking for someone to tell this to. When I saw you on TV, I knew it was you."

His brow crinkled, and it looked like he was in pain, but only a little bit, like his finger got pricked by a sewing needle.

"I'm not really into guilt," said Vega. "You shouldn't be, either."

He opened his eyes, the crinkle releasing.

"I also wanted to thank you," he said. "For finding Ivan, finally. I know he didn't have any family or anything, but at least they're not just some anonymous bones now."

Vega shrugged, unsure of what to do with the gratitude.

"Hey, can I ask you something?" she said.

"Shoot."

"Why'd you do the thing? Not the thing you just told me about. The football thing. Wrong Way Williams?"

"I wish I had a better story for you about that," he said. "It'd be a surprise to a lot of folks, but I actually don't think about that day at all anymore."

His face brightened up.

"My granny who raised me from when I was nine had died a few months before. I was on the field, and before the snap, I just started thinking about death—my death, and how it's coming. I'm thinking about all the kids I grew up with and their deaths. I'm hearing all the people in the stands and I start thinking about their deaths. Bear's holding the ball, and I'm thinking about *his* death. The cheerleaders, the band, Carmen up there somewhere—all of them—I'm thinking about all the death.

"Then, when I get the ball, I just didn't plan it, it was a clear thing to me. Just run. That's all I could do was run," he said.

"So you were running away from death?" Vega said, a little skeptical.

"That's making it real literal," he said, scratching under his chin. "It was more like: Let's get this started. Get on with it. Go."

"Go," repeated Vega.

"Just go," he said. "See, I wish it was a better story."

"It's okay," she said. "I've heard worse."

Vega drove her passenger back to his truck, which was not out of gas, as it turned out. He got out of the car and shut the door and leaned down to talk to Vega through the open window.

"Take care," he said. "Let me know if you want me to fix that rail-ing. For free, okay?"

"Think you'll be in California for a while?"

"I don't know," he said, sighing. "It's a nice place, like it's always been, just kind of weird."

"You know," said Vega, sliding her sunglasses onto her face, "Ilona's a nice town, too. They used to have a little white-nationalist problem, but looks like it's been taken care of. Cara Simms still lives there, in the exact same house. Never married. Just FYI."

Vega's passenger took off his glasses and rubbed one of the lenses with his shirt flap. He glanced at Vega and said, "Hm." Then it seemed like he was going to say something else, but he coughed instead.

"Thanks again for the slow-close," said Vega.

He put his glasses back on and nodded.

"Glad I could help," he said. Then he held up a hand and said, "Take care."

"You, too."

Vega powered up the window and had started to face forward when she heard him knocking on the glass. She lowered the window.

"I just realized something," he said, his voice light, his lips now visible in a smile through his beard. If Vega didn't know him, she might have thought he was excited.

"What's that?"

He held up two fingers. A peace sign if it had come from anyone else.

"It's not just a 2," he said. Then he flipped his hand around, still holding up the two fingers but now the back of his hand was facing out instead of the palm. "It's also a 'V.'"

Vega laughed. It was louder than she'd intended—she didn't know it had been creeping around in her chest.

Then he waved at her again and jogged to his truck, got in, and drove away, honking the horn once at her and waving again as he pulled out.

Vega turned off the engine and sat in her car outside her father's place for another hour or so. She didn't tell her father she was still there, and neither he nor Bitsy came outside. Vega thought about them in their kitchen, taking turns opening and closing the cabinets, filming each other, and sending the videos to their church friends.

She thought about Cap in the grocery store, picking out food that would make Nell happy.

She also thought about a picture she knew would never come through on her phone, but she could see it anyway—Dart and Zeb and Ethan standing in a row, holding their guns, shooting fruit off crates in front of the barn.

She thought about Cara Simms, grading papers at her kitchen table, expecting the guys any minute.

Vega started her car and finally drove away from her father's place. She leaned hard on the gas, trying to make it home as soon as she could. She wanted to call Cap before it got too late and tell him everything that had happened.

Acknowledgments

I'm not going to lie to you: this was tough.

Even though it's an asshole thing to say how hard it was to find artistic focus during a pandemic, it is nothing but a true story. The following people and books not only made it easier but possible:

Ron Fimrite's book *Golden Bears* was a great resource and gave me an idea about what it felt like to play at Memorial Stadium.

Christian Picciolini wrote a fearless memoir called *White American Youth* about his experience in the white supremacist movement and how he was able to break free. It was enormously helpful in grasping the psychology of the kids who get involved and their recruiters.

Andrew Marantz's *Antisocial: Online Extremists, Techno-Utopians, and the Hijacking of the American Conversation* should be required reading for anyone who seeks to understand the outcome of the 2016 election and what has come after. It also sheds light on why so many young white dudes are having a big old pity party for themselves these days.

While Ron Fimrite provided insight on the field, Michael Ferreboeuf clued me in to what it was like to be in the stands at Memorial in the eighties (bota bag optional!), along with helpful UC Berkeley geography and football facts.

I went to Dr. Samantha Shapiro to get a cavity filled and ended up asking her all sorts of questions about dead teeth and crowns and what happens if you were to get a tooth knocked out in a fight, and she was super-helpful and did not look at me askance one bit! (Also, hands like velvet.)

My editor, Rob Bloom, was just so supportive throughout this whole shitty time. Unflappable and generous and happy to take my calls and respond to my slightly unhinged emails any time of day or night. Also very patient in explaining football to me. On top of all that, his creative input and instincts remain stellar.

Victoria Pearson and her team of copyediting bandits saved my ass on this one. I mean, they always do, but this one especially when I couldn't figure out Adobe Acrobat and half of my first-pass changes didn't make it to second, and they made it possible for me to fix it the way I want it. (Stet the EXTREME GRATITUDE.)

Mark Falkin is a great agent and a great guy. I have no idea how he has time to do everything he does and know all the people he knows and still text back and forth with me about cocktail recipes. Always my fiercest advocate and also fun to talk to.

My mother, Sandra Luna, listens to me talk about myself and overthink every decision I've ever made pretty much every time I talk to her, and she continues to do so with a heart and mind so open I can't believe I will ever be as good a mother and friend to my daughter as my mom is to me, but she makes me want to try.

My glass is typically not even half empty; it's actually totally empty except for some gross silt at the bottom, but my brother, Zach Luna, has endless refills of optimism and encouragement, and it has kept me going on many days.

Beautiful, brilliant force of nature that is Florie—I promise someday you can read all my books, but in the meantime please know I am the luckiest mom just because I get to listen to all the thoughts inside your head that you choose to share with me.

And JP—I love you, and thank you for making everything good.

Louisa Luna is the author of the Alice Vega novels *The Janes* and *Two Girls Down*, as well as *Brave New Girl* and *Crooked*. She was born and raised in San Francisco and lives in Brooklyn, New York, with her husband and daughter.

A NOTE ON THE TYPE

This book was set in Minion, a typeface produced by the Adobe Corporation specifically for the Macintosh personal computer and released in 1990. Designed by Robert Slimbach, Minion combines the classic characteristics of old-style faces with the full complement of weights required for modern typesetting.

Typeset by Scribe,
Philadelphia, Pennsylvania

Printed and bound by Berryville Graphics,
Berryville, Virginia